"Shiveringly gothic. . . . eyes is almost as satisfying as seeing Jasper Blunt p nearly the first page. . . . For best effect, save this one for a windy night when trees scrape against the windowpanes."

—*The New York Times Book Review*

"No one writes Victorian romance like Mimi Matthews, and her Belles of London series just keeps getting better! No-nonsense Lady Anne has renounced marriage and devoted herself to two things— her band of equestrienne friends and her widowed mother still locked in deepest crepe-veiled mourning. But a dashing former suitor blasts back into Anne's shuttered world, bringing passion and change in his wake, and Anne must decide if she will embrace life or remain safe in her chrysalis. *The Lily of Ludgate Hill* made me smile from beginning to end." —*New York Times* bestselling author Kate Quinn

"Mimi Matthews never disappoints, with richly drawn characters and couples whose individual shortcomings become strengths when paired together. In this 'Beauty and the Beast' retelling, we get to root for two underdogs who get to rewrite their own stories."

—#1 *New York Times* bestselling author Jodi Picoult

"Mimi is truly a national treasure. All of her books are filled with such delicious chemistry and heart, and her writing is superb. This one is another winner. Highly recommend."

—#1 *New York Times* bestselling author Isabel Ibañez

"Mimi Matthews has become one of my favorite authors. She never disappoints." —*New York Times* bestselling author Mary Balogh

"This story unfolds like a rose blooming, growing more and more beautiful as each delicate layer is revealed. A tender, luminous romance. I loved it more and more with every chapter!"

—*USA Today* bestselling author Caroline Linden

"Absolutely enthralling: an endearing, novel-reading heroine who's in dire danger; a swoonworthy war hero with a scandalous past; and secrets, lots of secrets. Mimi Matthews's *The Belle of Belgrave Square* is a thrilling, emotion-packed read from start to finish. I loved it!"

—*USA Today* bestselling author Syrie James

"The best book I've read in a long time: gorgeously written, thoughtfully considered, swoonily romantic, and unafraid to examine issues of class, race, and gender." —National bestselling author Olivia Dade

"A moving love story and a vivid re-creation of Victorian life, *The Siren of Sussex* by Mimi Matthews is a treat of a book for the historical romance lover." —Award-winning author Anna Campbell

RULES
for
RUIN

Mimi Matthews

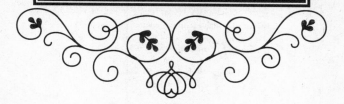

BERKLEY ROMANCE | NEW YORK

BERKLEY ROMANCE
Published by Berkley
An imprint of Penguin Random House LLC
1745 Broadway, New York, NY 10019
penguinrandomhouse.com

Book design by Kristin del Rosario
Interior art: Victorian silhouette © dariodraws/Shutterstock

Library of Congress Cataloging-in-Publication Data

Names: Matthews, Mimi, author.
Title: Rules for ruin / Mimi Matthews.
Description: First edition. | New York : Berkley Romance, 2025. |
Series: The Crinoline Academy
Identifiers: LCCN 2024024495 | ISBN 9780593639290 (trade paperback) |
ISBN 9780593639306 (ebook)
Subjects: LCGFT: Thrillers (Fiction) | Romance fiction. | Novels.
Classification: LCC PS3613.A8493 R85 2025 | DDC 813/.6—dc23/eng/20240531
LC record available at https://lccn.loc.gov/2024024495

First Edition: May 2025

Printed in the United States of America
1st Printing

The authorized representative in the EU for product safety and compliance is
Penguin Random House Ireland, Morrison Chambers, 32 Nassau Street,
Dublin D02 ỲH68, Ireland, https://eu-contact.penguin.ie.

For Daisy Mae

They tell us, again, in a bustling street

Our Crinolines hurt their poor legs or feet.

Not badly, I trust,—'twere the doctor to pay,

My recipe is, keep out of our way.

—Leichter Hock, *Crinoline in Its Bissextile Phases*, 1864

Rules for Ruin

PROLOGUE

April 1864

Euphemia Flite stood outside the iron gates that formed the fortress-like entrance to the bleak stone manor house beyond. The institution's name was wrought in heavy black filigree letters in the arch above: MISS CORVUS'S BENEVOLENT ACADEMY FOR THE BETTERMENT OF YOUNG LADIES.

Spring storm clouds drifted overhead, darkening an already gray sky. They lent an ominous air to the sprawling estate's barren gardens and high weathered granite walls. To the public, it was nothing more than a charity school—the dignified remains of a once grand property outside of London, where ragged orphans and street urchins were taught the skills necessary for honest employment.

Effie had been one of those urchins. The first one. To her, the Academy hadn't been a school. It had been a prison. Her stomach trembled on an uncharacteristic quiver of anxiety to see it again.

It had been more than five years since she'd last passed through its gates. Then, she'd been leaving—a headstrong girl of eighteen, cast out by the Academy's proprietress, Artemisia Corvus, herself. But it hadn't been an absolute expulsion. It had only ever been an exile. Effie had understood then, as surely as she'd understood anything, that one day, whether she liked it or not, Miss Corvus would summon her back.

A week ago in Paris, that day had finally arrived.

Setting her shoulders against the chill, Effie waited for someone to let her in. She'd come straight from the railway station. She was still in her black silk traveling dress, a veiled bonnet perched atop her stylishly arranged ebony hair, and a heavy carpetbag clutched in her gloved hands. Her small black poodle, Franc, was comfortably ensconced within.

Sensing her uneasiness, he poked his beribboned head out of the bag's opening. He looked at her briefly, as if to reassure himself she had the situation in hand, before turning to peer through the gates. His lip twitched in a preemptive snarl.

Effie gave him an absent scratch to soothe him.

Miss Corvus employed no gentleman porter. During Effie's time as a student, the gates had been manned by the junior teachers. Several minutes passed before a door at the side of the house opened and one of them finally emerged. The young woman advanced slowly down the pebbled drive, a heavy shawl drawn around her narrow shoulders, and a large ring of keys in her hand. A pronounced limp marred her gait.

It was Penelope Trewlove. Nell, as she was called by her intimates. There was no mistaking that glossy flaxen hair and beguiling heart-shaped face.

Catching sight of Effie, Nell's angelic countenance was transformed by a roguishly dimpled smile. "I confess, I didn't truly believe you'd come," she said as she drew closer. "Not even when we received your wire from Calais."

Effie smiled in return. It was genuine, not artifice. A rarity with her. So much of her conduct these past several years had been studied instead of spontaneous.

But this was Nell, not an adversary. A version of Nell remarkably unaltered by the passage of time.

Granted, she may have grown taller, and her cheeks were slightly less plump, but her eyes had retained their mischievous sparkle, and her figure was still something to be envied. Above all, she was familiar. Far more emblematic of home than the cold, unwelcoming structure that loomed behind her.

"Nell," Effie said warmly. "I'd hoped yours would be the first face I saw."

"Never mind *my* face." Nell's gaze swept over Effie in glowing approval as she came to a halt on the opposite side of the gates. "How well you look! Lovelier even than when you left us. That's Paris's doing, I'll wager." Her smile broadened, revealing a glimpse of her crooked front tooth. "And this must be the famous Franc!"

Franc stared back at Nell through the bars. He offered none of his usual grumbles. He seemed to sense she was an ally rather than a foe.

"Franc," Effie said, introducing him as formally as if he were a gentleman acquaintance. "This is Miss Trewlove."

"How do you do, Franc?" Nell's dimples appeared again. "Oh, what a little dear he is. And what a continental air he has about him! I feel as though he's judging the unfashionableness of my gown." Her attention fell to the barren ground at Effie's booted feet. "But where are all the rest of your things? Have you not brought any trunks with you from Paris?"

"I left them at Waltham Station. I shall send for them directly after I speak with Miss Corvus." Effie paused. "Providing you let me in."

Nell gave an eloquent grimace. "Yes, yes. Of course. I'm sorry I kept you waiting. Especially in this weather. It's bound to rain any moment." She shuffled through the key ring, selecting a large black iron key. "I trust you haven't been standing here long?"

"The hackney cab set me down not ten minutes ago."

"Ten minutes? Upon my word. I'm surprised you didn't pick the lock."

Effie's smile dimmed. "Is that what the Academy's students have been reduced to in my absence? Parlor tricks?"

Nell slid the heavy iron key into the lock, opening the tall gates with a grating scrape of metal on metal. "What you call parlor tricks, I call useful skills."

Effie didn't doubt it. Nell had always believed in Miss Corvus's questionable aims. It was one of the primary reasons Nell had agreed to stay on as a junior teacher. Indeed, on coming of age, Nell and Effie had both been given that option—a five-year contract, after which they could either remain at the Academy permanently or depart, with a small stipend, to seek their fortunes.

Miss Corvus liked to keep her special girls close. And, as the first and second members of the inaugural class of the charity school, Effie and Nell had been the most special of all.

The gates swung open with a creaking groan. Effie walked through them to embrace her old schoolmate. "Some skills are more useful than others," she said.

Nell hugged her tight in return. "Had you no cause to pick any locks while you were companion to Madame Dalhousie?"

"Not a one, thank heaven." Effie's duties had been confined to accompanying the eccentric widowed madame to art and literary salons, lavish balls, stately dinners, and other social events of both the respectable and unrespectable variety. Such was the life of a lady's companion, even one lucky enough to live in the City of Light.

"Pity," Nell said. "You'll be out of practice for what lies ahead."

Effie drew back, brows notched in a frown. She searched Nell's face. "It's like that, is it?"

"Naturally." Nell released her. "You must have realized it when you received my sampler." She moved to lock the gates behind them, visibly proud of herself. "Clever, was it not?"

The sewing sampler had arrived at Madame Dalhousie's apartment in Paris last week. A masterpiece of advanced embroidery, it had been composed of delicate colored threads stitched into a rectangle of coarse cloth, depicting a stone house and gardens, a jumbled alphabet, and a flock of birds circling above. Four ravens, to be precise, one of which had a white-tipped wing. The latter was the unofficial symbol of the Academy, and a necessary component of any secret message. Taken altogether, it had been a simple enough code. Effie had used it to spell out the unmistakable command: **FLY HOME**.

"Ridiculous, more like." Effie's tone held no malice. Among all the residents of the Academy, Nell was the only one whom Effie counted as a friend. They had corresponded semi-regularly during Effie's exile.

Together, they returned up the pebbled path to the house. Nell's leg hitched with every step. Effie felt the motion as much as saw it. The guilt she nurtured over her part in the childhood accident that caused Nell's injury sprang anew. It never really left her, that guilt, despite the fact that Nell had long professed to hold no resentment over the past.

"You might simply have written a letter to me," Effie said, "rather than making a riddle of it."

"How dull that would have been." Nell linked her arm through Effie's. "It was far more amusing to practice my stitchery."

Their full skirts pushed against each other as they walked. It was impossible for them not to, given the respective size of their wire crinolines. Miss Corvus wasn't a lady to entertain the whims of fashion, but she had made an exception for the controversial, and seemingly impractical, cage-like undergarment. All of her teachers donned them, and most of the older orphans, too. Both Effie and Nell wore theirs like armor.

No one could easily get close to a girl wearing a wire crinoline, not without thoroughly disarranging her. Its sheer circumference provided a modicum of protection. But its daunting size had another purpose. A crinoline made even the smallest female an intimidating creature. She took up space for herself—*demanded* space—in a world where ladies were too often diminished and ignored.

"People never trouble to examine samplers too closely, I find," Nell continued. "And when they do, they're only searching for the flaws, never the meaning. It makes them an ideal vehicle for sending secret messages."

"You're a modern-day Madame Defarge," Effie remarked.

Nell's eyes twinkled. "Except my messages are all for the good."

Effie gave Nell a speaking glance as they ascended the front steps to the house. "*That* remains to be seen."

Like the exterior of the house, the interior of the formal entry hall was composed of aged stone, worn over the centuries to a buttery sheen. Faded carpets covered the floor, and moth-eaten tapestries adorned the walls, along with two large, gilt-framed oil paintings. One was an excellent reproduction of Gentileschi's *Judith Slaying Holofernes*. It had been there since Effie had first arrived at the Academy as a girl. A terrifying painting for a child to behold.

The other painting had been there as well. It was a portrait of a dark-haired woman in a lusterless black dress, standing tall and strong in the silhouette of a doorway. But it was no ordinary rendering, made to flatter its subject. The woman in this portrait had her back to the viewer. Her face was completely hidden from view.

Effie had once heard Miss Corvus offer an explanation of the portrait to a questioning gentleman who had come to inspect the premises on behalf of the parish council. "The modest woman conceals her face," she'd told him.

It was as good a story as any, and one that had well satisfied the pious man. But it wasn't the truth, as Effie would learn.

She deftly removed her bonnet with one hand, still holding her carpetbag in the other. Franc scanned the hall, his liquid brown eyes unblinking as he took in his strange surroundings. He offered another low growl.

There was no one about to inspire it. At this time of day, the inmates of the Academy would all be in their classes, sectioned off into the various rooms of the house like busy little bees in a hive.

But what of the Queen Bee?

When last Effie had faced her, Artemisia Corvus had been in her fourth-floor study—a remote tower room filled with books, antiquated papers corded with ribbons, and a bewildering filing system, the secret of which was known only to its equally secretive inventor.

"Where is she?" Effie asked, moving toward the broad, blackened oak staircase at the edge of the hall. "In her study?"

"Not there." Nell set a hand on Effie's sleeve, gently arresting her step. "She's in her private quarters."

Effie's brows lifted. Miss Corvus never received any of the girls in her private rooms. Not even the teachers. At least, she hadn't during Effie's tenure. Miss Corvus's rooms had always been sealed off, as impenetrable as a tomb, behind an impassable set of tall, iron-banded wooden doors. Not even the canniest members of the Academy had dared attempt entry.

Nell directed Effie down the hall. "She caught a fever some months ago. It weakened her considerably. Stairs have become difficult."

Effie's already uneasy stomach jolted at the news. She couldn't fathom Miss Corvus being weakened by anything. To Effie, the Academy's proprietress had always seemed invincible. "Is she—?"

"She's recovering," Nell said. "But slowly." She guided Effie down the long corridor and through the high stone archways that led past the library and the old conservatory. A right turn into a narrow passage brought them to the very set of iron-banded doors that separated the public rooms from the private.

Nell's expression sobered as she stopped in front of them. "I won't go in. Miss Corvus insists on speaking with you alone."

"Does she, indeed?" Effie lifted Franc from his carpetbag and set him down on the stone floor. He gave a perfunctory shake before springing into motion. Effie caught hold of his lead before he could gallop off. Franc was a loyal companion, but he was also a rogue. He couldn't resist wandering.

She handed the lead to Nell. "If you would be so good as to take him for an airing? And pray don't let him loose. He's swift as a greyhound when he chooses to be. You'd never catch him."

Nell didn't ask any questions. She knew all about Franc's little foibles from Effie's letters. "I shall take him to visit the hedgerow," she said. "Look for me when you're done."

Effie waited until Nell had gone before rapping twice on the door. There was a taut moment of silence before Miss Corvus answered from within.

"Come," she said.

The clipped, frost-edged voice had its usual effect on Effie. It was a reaction borne from a memory too distant to recall as anything more than primitive emotion. It made Effie long to shrink back into herself. To make herself invisible. Maybe then Miss Corvus wouldn't see her. Wouldn't take her away.

But Effie had never excelled at being invisible.

Stiffening her spine, she opened the door.

· · · · ·

Effie was met by the unsettling prospect of a darkened sitting room. The curtains had been drawn shut, and no candles had been lit. There remained only enough light to see the heavy mahogany furnishings, the vases filled with crumbling bouquets of dried flowers, and the shrouds of black fabric that covered the pictures on the walls and the mirror hanging over the fireplace.

For all Miss Corvus's progressive views, for all her insistence on looking to the future, this was a chamber firmly enshrouded in the past. A veiled room, all stale darkness and decay.

Miss Corvus had been similarly veiled the first time Effie had seen her that fateful day eighteen years ago in the London slum of St. Giles.

But Miss Corvus wasn't veiled now.

She sat in a green damask–upholstered armchair by the window, her uncovered face as white as wax. She was clad in stark black, just as Effie was—a plain, but impeccably tailored, silk dress worn over an abundance of petticoats and a formidable wire crinoline. A jet brooch gleamed at her throat, and an embroidered lace handkerchief was clutched in her pale hand.

There was a low inlaid malachite table beside her chair. A tray sat upon it, holding a pitcher of water, a single glass, and a small, stoppered brown bottle with a label pasted on it. Some sort of medicinal tonic, Effie suspected.

Shutting the door behind her, she crossed the room to join her former teacher.

Miss Corvus watched her come with a raptor-like intensity. In appearance, she was all but unchanged from the enigmatic lady who had entered her life when Effie was a child. Only the threads of silver in her hair, the fine lines at the corners of her eyes, and the grooves bracketing her perpetually disapproving mouth betrayed the truth of Miss Corvus's age. She was approaching fifty. A great age for a woman, especially an unmarried one whom the years had made peculiar.

Effie stopped in front of her. She dropped a graceful curtsy, honed to a perfect degree of fashionable elegance in the drawing rooms of Paris. "Miss Corvus."

"Miss Flite," Miss Corvus replied in the same icy tones. "I see my money has not been wholly wasted." She motioned for Effie to step back. "Let me look at you."

Effie remained standing, back straight and chin lifted, silently submitting to Miss Corvus's cold perusal. She examined Effie from top to bottom. The thick ebony hair worn back in a stylish plaited roll. The catlike blue eyes so dark they might be mistaken for violet. The solemn face, with its black arching brows, high cheekbones, and wide, voluptuous mouth. And the figure—lithe and athletic, but not lacking in curves.

Taken along with Effie's striking complexion (a clear rich hue that lingered somewhere between dark ivory and olive), the whole of her appearance made her less a traditionally pretty girl and more a compellingly seductive mystery. People couldn't help but stare. Couldn't help but wonder. *Who was she?* they whispered. *Where did she come from?*

The very questions Effie had begun to ask herself. The ones that had resulted in her being sent away five years ago.

"I rarely get things wrong," Miss Corvus said when she'd finished taking Effie's measure. "But I readily own my mistakes." She signaled for Effie to sit with an impatient flick of her hand.

Effie gave Miss Corvus a sardonic bow of acknowledgment before taking the seat across from her. She was confident enough in her own attributes to recognize the hidden compliment in her former schoolmistress's words.

"You were a pretty child, but had no promise of great beauty," Miss Corvus went on. "Not like Miss Trewlove. It was she who was meant to grow into my Aphrodite incarnate."

"Hence her name," Effie said.

"While you . . . You were meant to soar."

"Hence mine." Effie's voice held no humor. This wasn't the first time Miss Corvus had expressed such sentiments. She'd had fixed intentions for both Effie and Nell when she'd taken them. She was a woman who was rarely without a plan. One for whom an orphan girl was a tool rather than an object of Christian charity.

"Ironic, isn't it?" Miss Corvus mused. "To think, I reared up a falcon who is afraid of heights."

Effie concealed a flinch. She had wondered how long it would be before Miss Corvus brought up her prevailing flaw. The very one that had resulted in Nell being so grievously injured all those years ago.

Suppressing her guilt, Effie affected an air of unconcern. "Even the great Achilles had a single weakness."

"His undoing, as I recall. In your case, it has so far only been the ruin of Miss Trewlove. See that it isn't yours as well."

"Is that why you summoned me back?" Effie asked. "Do you want me scaling walls and peeping into high windows? If that's your grand idea, I take leave to tell you that you have chosen the wrong girl."

"Don't be impertinent," Miss Corvus said. "Remember to whom you are speaking."

Effie fell quiet. She regarded Miss Corvus in mutinous silence.

"That's better." Miss Corvus blotted her lips with her handkerchief. Droplets of perspiration had gathered on her brow, and there was an unhealthy flush in her cheeks, as though the simple act of conversing had overtaxed her.

Nell had mentioned an illness, but she hadn't put a name to it. It occurred to Effie that the complaint might be something rather more serious than a trifling cold or fever.

"Madame Dalhousie has sent regular reports of your conduct," Miss Corvus said, lowering her handkerchief. "She claims you have left your propensity for chaos behind. That you have been a diligent companion; a keen observer and a quick learner. She also says you have garnered a legion of admirers. I trust you have not become entangled with any of them?"

Effie scorned at the suggestion. "Indeed, I have not."

Any flirtation she'd indulged in during her time abroad had been in the manner of practice, not an exercise in passion. She'd been honing her skills, toying with the very gentlemen who sought to heartlessly toy with her. It had been no great feat. Quite the opposite, the male sex made it all too easy. They insisted on underestimating women. On believing young ladies were prey, rather than predator.

"I would expect nothing less," Miss Corvus said. "You were always adept at transforming yourself to suit your company. It will serve you well in your next position."

A flare of disappointment caught Effie unaware. "A new position?"

"You were expecting something else?"

"I have been nearly five years in Paris. I thought—"

Miss Corvus's mouth curved. "That you had earned your stipend?"

Effie didn't answer. It was, in truth, what she *had* thought. She could see now she was stupid to have believed it. Five years spent as a lady's companion wasn't precisely the same as a five-year teaching contract. Naturally, the same terms wouldn't apply.

She felt a fool to have ever supposed they might. Worse than a fool, for she had lately built her dreams on the promise of that elusive stipend. She'd dared to imagine she and Franc might find a place for themselves somewhere. A home that would be theirs alone.

"What have you done to earn it?" Miss Corvus asked. "You have been in school, merely learning your trade."

"I did not attend school in Paris."

"On the contrary. If the Academy was your Eton, then Paris was your Oxford. I'll allow that you have been a most devoted student. But a student is all you have been. It is now your work begins." Miss Corvus looked at her steadily. "What have you to say to that? A position in another household?"

Effie swallowed the surge of bitterness that swelled in her throat. Whatever her private feelings, she refused to allow Miss Corvus to see them. A lady's primary strength lay in keeping her composure. "What *can* I say?" she asked. "As ever, I exist purely at your pleasure."

Miss Corvus didn't dispute the fact. It had been her coin that had enabled Effie's life in France these past five years. Her contacts, too. It was she who had made the arrangement for Effie to act as a companion to Madame Dalhousie.

Purchasing Franc had been Effie's single stroke of independence. Unlike the clothes or the lodgings or even the acquaintances she'd made abroad, Franc belonged entirely to her.

"Then we are agreed," Miss Corvus said. Opening the drawer of the table beside her, she withdrew a note card. A postal direction was written on it in black ink. She handed the card to Effie. "This afternoon, you will travel to London. You will go to that address in Mayfair. I have a contact there, Lady Belwood. She will sponsor your entry into society."

Effie kept her countenance through pure force of will. It was one thing for an orphan girl to move in fashionable society as a lady's companion. It was quite another for her to be introduced into that society as an equal. Such was the fate of the daughters of gentlemen, not former street children from the Rookery.

"To what purpose?" she asked.

"No one is yet acquainted with you in London," Miss Corvus said. "You are a complete unknown. It's why I insisted on you never visiting town before your time. And why I grew so angry when I discovered you'd attempted to do so."

Effie was amazed Miss Corvus was willing to acknowledge the events of five years ago. But if *she* was prepared to reference them, then Effie had no intention of refraining. "I didn't attempt to visit fashionable London. My business was in St. Giles."

Effie had traveled there on the occasion of her eighteenth birthday. She hadn't got far. Miss Corvus had intercepted her within a day.

"Vexing girl!" she'd said furiously during the tense carriage ride

back to the Academy. *"What on earth did you hope to gain from this ill-advised stunt?"*

"I wanted to find out about my past," Effie had answered.

"You have no past," Miss Corvus had told her. *"Only a future. And that future is for me to decide, not you."*

Sitting across from Effie now, a flash of residual anger darkened Miss Corvus's eyes at the reminder of Effie's ingratitude. "A foolish mistake on your part, returning to that place."

"Was it foolish to wonder about my mother?" Effie asked. She had no distinct memory of the lady to call her own, just the faded, dreamlike recollection of a fair-haired woman in a squalid room above a malodorous rag-and-bone shop. A woman who may have been called Grace. The image of her had plagued Effie for as long as she could remember.

"The pitiful wretch who brought you into this world wasn't a mother," Miss Corvus said. "She was a creature of the slums with no means, nor any desire, to support a child. She parted with you willingly. Eagerly. And she was well compensated for it. That you would persist in thinking of her in such romantical terms speaks to your lack of maturity." Her lips compressed. "You disappoint me, Miss Flite."

"And you mistake me as ever," Effie said stiffly. "I have no interest in happy families, nor have I any illusions in that vein. It's knowledge I crave."

Miss Corvus gave a dismissive sniff. "You have it. You know as much as I do."

Effie had her doubts. What she knew was only what Miss Corvus had chosen to tell her. Effie couldn't trust it. Not when she couldn't recollect any of the details for herself. She'd been too young when she'd left the Rookery.

Or rather, when she'd been taken.

The only thing she could recall with any degree of clarity was that one day she'd made the grievous mistake of stealing Miss Corvus's reticule. It had been a sumptuous, velvet article, plump with the weight of coin. Effie had sliced the dangling ribbons from Miss Corvus's wrist with a cutthroat razor as she'd stopped to make a purchase at a Covent Garden flower stall.

Yes, *that* Effie remembered, for that single desperate act had sealed her fate.

As for the rest . . .

"If you don't recall it, why do you wish to?" Miss Corvus asked. "Count it a blessing, and good riddance." She blotted her lips again. "You spend too much time looking backward. It's the future that should concern you."

"A future that you mean to decide for me."

"You are of age. You are free to go at any time."

"But I am *not* free." This time, Effie couldn't keep her frustration from seeping into her voice.

Every article of clothing she possessed belonged to Miss Corvus. Everything she'd ever learned. Everything she was. With each skill she'd acquired, each dress she'd had made for her, and each night she'd spent, safe in a warm bed, she'd racked up a debt. It had never been expressed with pen and ink, but Effie was as conscious of it as breathing.

Miss Corvus appeared to appreciate Effie's dilemma, but she showed no sympathy for it. "Honor is what brought you back. And honor is why you remain."

"A debt of honor," Effie replied. "I mean to discharge it."

"Oh, you shall," Miss Corvus said. "Have no fear of that."

Effie waited with a building sense of apprehension.

"There's a man," Miss Corvus said at length. "Lord Compton." On uttering his name, she broke into a hacking cough. She held her handkerchief to her lips until the fit had subsided. When she drew the lace cloth away, it was stained with blood.

Effie's breath stopped in her chest. She had a vague memory of having seen a similar sight once—a woman, coughing blood into a dingy rag. It had boded nothing but ill.

Miss Corvus continued with an effort. "He's a villain of the worst rank."

"His crime?"

"He snuffed out the life of a girl who was dear to me. Dearer than any creature on this earth. She was like you—strong, beautiful, intelligent. A girl of infinite possibility. Until Compton came along with his flattering words and deceitful kisses. First, he connived to steal her heart, then he stole her fortune. His betrayal was the death of her."

Effie stilled, shocked. "Are you saying he killed her?"

Miss Corvus neither confirmed nor denied the charge. "It was many years ago, long before you came to the Academy. He's never yet been held to account. The girl had no family to seek justice on her behalf, and even if she had . . . no one would imagine Compton capable of such treachery. He was young and handsome then, endearing himself to all."

"And now?"

"He's become old and respectable. A politician who hides his true nature under a cloak of impenetrable piety. His reputation is spotless. Lord Solomon, he's called in the press. A man of rare judgment, decency, and wisdom." Another coughing fit disrupted Miss Corvus's speech.

Effie stood. She went to the table next to Miss Corvus and poured her out a glass of water.

Miss Corvus accepted it gratefully. She wiped the specks of blood from her lips with her handkerchief before taking a drink from the glass.

Effie watched her, frowning. "What has Compton's character to do with you?"

"It has to do with *every* woman," Miss Corvus said, lowering the glass. "A betrayal of one is a betrayal of all."

"But this girl you knew—"

"Long gone, and the evidence of Compton's crime along with her. I've told you, my concern is for the future." Miss Corvus returned her glass to the table beside her. "There is serious discussion about a married women's property bill being brought before Parliament. If passed, it would give a married woman the same rights as an unmarried one. Henceforward, she could keep everything she earned during her marriage. She could retain control of her property. She could exist, in British law, as more than a mere appendage to a husband. It would mean security and independence for countless women throughout the realm. The implications are too great to be ignored."

Effie slowly resumed her seat. She may disagree with Miss Corvus's methods, but Effie's views on the subject of women's welfare had always been as one with her former teacher. They had been ever since she'd first read Miss Leigh Smith's *A Brief Summary, in Plain Language, of the Most Important Laws Concerning Women* at the tender age of thirteen. An illuminating text, and required reading at the Academy, it had revealed, in stark terms, the monstrous legal injustices suffered by women.

"It sounds an excellent proposition," Effie said.

"If Compton has his way, the bill will never see the light of day. He can quash it with a word."

"You're convinced he would?"

"He's already hinted he'll come out against it, whether today or tomorrow or two years hence. When he does, the other lords will follow suit. They take their cues from him. There's only one thing to be done." Miss Corvus's countenance hardened with a dangerous resolve. "Compton must be destroyed."

Effie studied her old schoolmistress. "What do you have in mind? You don't mean—?"

"Don't be ridiculous," Miss Corvus said. "We're not murderesses. We are civilized women in an uncivilized world, acting to balance the scales. When I speak of destruction, I speak of Compton's reputation. *That* is why I summoned you back. No one knows who you are, not of our connection, nor of your dubious beginnings. You have been in Paris, and have become a lady of fashion. Compton has an eye for beauty. Your charms can't compare to Miss Trewlove's, but they're still something out of the common way. He will welcome you into his world. And you . . . you will be the end of him."

Effie began to comprehend her. "You want me to ruin him? But how?"

"Compton is hosting a ball to start the season. Lady Belwood will take you as her guest. Ingratiate yourself with Compton and his wife. Curry invitations to their parties. They entertain widely. You will have ample opportunity to search their house in town and their estate in the country. The evidence of his true character will be there. A leopard doesn't change his spots. Find something we can use against him."

"Anything? Or—"

"Something damning." Miss Corvus's fingers clenched on her handkerchief so tightly her knuckles turned white. "I want Compton's name to become a byword for everything that is low and contemptible in society. I want all he touches to fall to cinders. And all he opposes to rise in triumph over him. His ruination will be the salvation of this proposal. And that ruination depends on you."

"You presume I can do it."

"You *will* do it. And I shall give you ample incentive." Miss Corvus took a rattling breath. Twin spots of color bloomed in her waxen cheeks. "Accomplish this task, and I shall discharge your debt to me. You will be at liberty to leave this place with your honor intact, with all I have given you, and with a modest sum deposited into an account of your choosing. It will be enough to set you safely on an independent path."

Effie's pulse quickened. Such an offer was surely too good to be true. "How much of a modest sum?"

Miss Corvus named a figure.

Effie blinked in astonishment. The amount far surpassed that of the long-ago promised stipend. "And all I must do in return is find the evidence to instigate Compton's downfall?" She could scarcely believe it could be so easy. "Is that all?"

"My dear Miss Flite," Miss Corvus said. "That is *everything*." She reached for her bottle of tonic. "Well, girl? What say you?"

Effie didn't hesitate. She desperately wanted her freedom. She wanted to keep all of her beautiful things, too.

And, of course, there was the money.

"Very well," she said. "I accept your terms."

1

May 1864

Gabriel Royce leaned back in the oxblood leather wing chair behind Viscount Compton's carved walnut desk as though the desk, the library, and the stately Grosvenor Square mansion itself belonged to him. The jacket of his immaculate black-and-white evening suit was open, exposing the white tie and black silk waistcoat beneath. "Seems easy enough to me," he said.

His casual posture was belied by the menace of a Birmingham drawl edging his words. Over the past decade, he'd taken great pains to cultivate an upper-class accent—a necessary skill when dealing with the narrow-minded aristocrats with whom he regularly did business—but whenever his temper threatened, the truth of his origins always managed to seep out.

In those moments, there was no hiding where he came from. Though Gabriel had made a kingdom of St. Giles, it was the Black Country where he'd been born and bred, and where he'd spent the first years of his life. He'd only come to London as a scrappy orphan lad of twelve, eking out a place for himself in the Rookery with his wits— and with his fists.

Lord Compton paced the library carpet in front of Gabriel, his brows pulled into a furious scowl. He was a well-favored man in his middle fifties, with graying brown hair, a full graying beard, and a slightly thickened, but still athletic, figure that spoke of good wine, aristocratic sport, and a life of unutterable privilege. Like Gabriel, Compton was clad in elegant evening wear, though his suit of clothes had likely been made in Savile Row rather than by a struggling back-slum tailor.

"Easy, you call it?" Compton echoed in dismay. "To welcome you into my home? To permit you to associate with my friends? My *family*?"

Gabriel was mildly entertained by the viscount's distress. The man was usually unflappable—a model politician, with a thoughtful tone and a somber manner. "Come now, your lordship. It isn't as though I'm asking to marry your daughter."

Compton turned on Gabriel in the circle of light cast from the oil lamp on the desk. His face was transformed by fatherly outrage. "You go too far, Royce."

"Not far enough, it appears, if you think you have the choice of refusing me."

Compton snorted. "And have you unleash your band of ruffians on me?"

The distant strings of an orchestra drifted from the ballroom above. It was mingled with the muted murmur of voices, and the thump of footsteps as late-coming guests continued to arrive. A polonaise had been playing when Gabriel had first entered the library, followed by a country dance. Another dance was starting now. A spirited galop, which (by the sound of the stomping upstairs) had been joined by a crushing number of couples.

Compton's ball was the first truly tonish party of the social season. The grandest people in London were reputed to be in attendance—illustrious lords, wealthy ladies, and powerful politicians. Compton and his wife had already welcomed most of them when Gabriel had turned up, unannounced and uninvited.

For a few coins, an obliging footman had shown him to Compton's library. The viscount had marched in moments later to find Gabriel seated behind his desk, dressed for the evening's entertainment, and possessing all the deceptive patience of a hungry wolf waiting to strike.

Watching the viscount now, Gabriel's mouth curved in a lazy smile. "If you don't do as I ask, my ruffians will be the least of your troubles."

Compton's expression turned stony. He was no coward. It took guts to walk the reputational tightrope he'd been traversing these many years. But, audacious as he was, he knew his limits. He would do as Gabriel wished in the end. The result was inevitable. It was only the speed at getting to that result that appeared at issue.

Unfortunately for Compton, Gabriel's patience was wearing thin.

"Is it not enough that I keep the law away from your dealings in the Rookery?" Compton asked in a last attempt at reason. "That I protect your interests from those who would drive you out of St. Giles?" He set his hands on the edge of the desk. "You and I had an *agreement*."

Gabriel stood to his full and not inconsiderable height. "Yet still you insult me."

Compton straightened. He took a step backward. It was less out of fear than it was a refusal to submit to Gabriel's physical dominance. The viscount would let no man loom over him, least of all one he considered so far beneath him.

"It's not an insult to insist you and I keep to our proper spheres," he said. "My guests this evening are a different breed from what you're accustomed to. They're gentlemen of influence—"

"Just as I am." Gabriel strolled out from behind the desk. "Which is why you're going to introduce me to them." He smiled again. "I have a sick fancy to become respectable."

Compton's lips flattened. He shot a glance at the closed doors of the library. The music filtered through, an audible reminder of his duties to his guests, and to his position in society. "Your jests are ill-timed, sir."

"It's no jest. I'm formulating a plan for changes in the Rookery. When the time comes, I'll need the freehanded support of wealthy benefactors."

Compton exhaled a contemptuous gust of breath. "Is that what this is about?" Stalking past Gabriel, he jerked open a drawer in his desk and withdrew his checkbook. "If it's money for the poor you're after, your request need go no further than me." He picked up his steel-nibbed pen, poised to dash off an order on his bank. "I'm not opposed to investing in a new workhouse."

Gabriel's jaw tightened on a reflexive surge of anger. Workhouses were the last thing the poor of St. Giles needed. Workhouses that separated mothers from children. That broke up families. Workhouses were where good, decent folk went to sicken and die. As sure a sentence as the hangman's noose, but lacking the dignity of the rope. Unlike a walk to the scaffold, admittance to a workhouse required no judge or jury. It recognized no defense.

After all, what defense was there to the crime of being poor?

No. Gabriel's plans didn't involve workhouses. He had other ideas. A vision for honest, aboveboard reforms to benefit the people of the Rookery and, ultimately, himself.

"I'm not interested in charity," he said.

"Call it a business contract, then," Compton responded.

"A business contract with you?" Gabriel's tone was silky with disdain. "I'd sooner crawl into bed with a scorpion."

Compton's face went rigid. He set down his pen.

"Put away your money," Gabriel told him. "All I require from you this evening are introductions to my betters." He gestured for Compton to precede him to the door. "If you would be so obliging."

Compton thrust his checkbook back into the desk drawer. He

slammed the drawer shut. "Haven't the good people of this city already done enough to clean up St. Giles? And succeeded, too. The slum is all but eradicated."

It was a common misconception among the well-to-do. St. Giles was located in the heart of fashionable London, surrounded on all sides by the wealthiest communities. Many years prior, part of the slum had been cleared away to make room for the construction of New Oxford Street. But the wretches who had formerly occupied those long-removed lodging houses, gin shops, and prostitutes' hovels hadn't miraculously vanished into thin air. They had merely been pressed back into an even smaller area, the squalor of their living conditions now hidden from greater public view.

"Just because you can't see us anymore, doesn't mean we ceased existing," Gabriel said. "The people of the Rookery are still there—only now they're crowded one hundred to a cellar."

Disgust crossed Compton's face. "Such filth and depravity. I curse the day Tobias Wingard ever found his way there."

"But he did find his way there," Gabriel said. "And straight into my betting shop. Quite an impressive stack of papers he had with him, too."

Compton flinched at the reminder. "Very well," he said, coming forward. "I shall do what I can for you." He stopped in front of Gabriel. "But I warn you, Royce. If you at any time expose me to even a hint of impropriety—"

"You're warning *me*?" Gabriel took a step toward the viscount, bringing them face-to-face.

This time Compton held his ground. "Let it be mutual destruction, then."

Gabriel met the viscount's threat with a fleeting smile. "Don't flatter yourself. You might destroy my business, but you could never destroy me. Street rats always survive, one way or another. While fine lords like you—" He gave a humorless chuckle. "There won't be much welcome for Lord Solomon in Whitehall, will there, not once proven accusations of fraud are hung round his neck."

The color drained from Compton's face. "How *dare* you mention such despicable slander in my home, where my wife, or one of my servants might—"

"Rest easy, my lord." Gabriel slapped him hard on the back. "I've no intention of speaking a word of it." Again, he gestured for Compton to precede him. "Not so long as you behave."

Compton glared at him with a flicker of unvarnished hatred before, at last, grudgingly opening the library door. Gabriel had him by the throat and Compton knew it.

Gabriel had no intention of letting him go, not now, nor at any point in future. The viscount's support was too valuable. More valuable yet than Gabriel was willing to admit to the man. A politician in one's pocket was a precious thing. It was in Gabriel's interest that Compton's reputation remained unblemished and intact. The survival of the Rookery depended on it, and Gabriel's survival with it. There was no separating the two.

Together, he and Compton passed from the library to the house's opulent marble-tiled entry hall. A sweeping Italianate staircase led to the first-floor ballroom above. Gabriel climbed the steps alongside his reluctant host.

Two young ladies in full-skirted pastel silk dresses passed them on the ascent. Seeing Gabriel, they blushed and giggled behind their fans, quickening their pace down the stairs. A balding manservant in a plain black suit followed not far behind them. The butler, Gabriel surmised. He was a brawny chap, and one who (judging by the crooked lump masquerading as his nose) wasn't opposed to physical violence.

It was a good thing it had been a pliable young footman who had opened the door when Gabriel had come calling this evening and not this sinister-looking fellow. The outcome might have been very different.

"Do you require assistance, my lord?" the butler asked Compton.

"It's no matter, Parker," Compton said without breaking his stride. "A late-coming guest. I shall introduce him to the others myself."

Parker fixed Gabriel with a suspicious frown as he passed.

Gabriel offered the man a sardonic wink in reply.

Like recognized like. It was a tenet Gabriel had never failed to see proven true, and one that had helped him tremendously in his rise from the slums. He'd learned to recognize a fellow wolf in lamb's clothing.

The butler was one of them.

So was Compton.

Yes, despite the pomp and the pageantry, and the milk-faced young misses giggling behind their fans, Gabriel had every reason to feel at home here.

Upstairs, the ballroom's entrance was marked by two towering marble columns. Footmen flanked the opened doors. They bowed to Gabriel and Compton as they entered.

There were too many couples dancing to count. They moved over the polished wood floor to the strains of the music in a twirl of tailcoats and impossibly wide ruffled skirts, the ladies' jewels shining in the blaze of light produced from the gas wall sconces and the twin crystal gasoliers.

Compton guided Gabriel along the edge of the room, where spectators lined the walls, both sitting and standing. "That's Lord Trefusis," he said, jerking his chin in the direction of an elderly man seated by the bank of green velvet–draped windows. "A charitable gentleman by all accounts. His estates are in Northumberland. And that gentleman, there by the fern, is Sir Newton Cobble, a man of property from Cornwall."

Gabriel registered the two men with immediate skepticism. Aged country gentlemen were something less than the rich London progressives he'd envisioned rallying to his cause.

Compton pointed out another fellow, even older than the first two. "That gentleman with the ear trumpet is Lord Upton-Frye, a Yorkshire baron of good family. If it's alms for the poor you're after, he's the one to speak with." He glanced back at Gabriel with barely veiled contempt. "Well, sir? Which of them shall I introduce you to? I presume they are all of them strangers."

Gabriel coolly returned the viscount's gaze. After their confrontation in the library, he had assumed Compton would fall into line. Instead, the viscount believed he could take Gabriel for a fool. Why else would he be attempting to fob him off on doddering men of little influence, rather than introducing him to those gentlemen with actual power?

The offense couldn't be overlooked. To pardon one affront was to invite a host of others.

Gabriel fully intended to address the issue. To forcibly remind Compton of the very real harm he could do to him. But not here. Not tonight. This evening was for finding benefactors for the people of St. Giles. Not just men of property, but men who understood how to get things done in London, and who had the coin, and the political capital, to do so.

Turning away from his insolent host, Gabriel searched the room for himself.

It was unforgivable ignorance to assume the paths of the poor and the well-bred wealthy never crossed. Indeed, Gabriel himself had placed former denizens of the Rookery in many of the great houses in Mayfair. They worked as scullery maids, stable hands, and footmen, washing pots, mucking out loose boxes, and stoking the fires.

And the flow of cross-class commerce didn't only move in one direction.

The sons of the aristocracy regularly made their way to Gabriel's betting shop in St. Giles. They visited the gin merchants, the flesh peddlers, and the public houses, indulging in all of the worst vices and inventing a few new ones along the way. Often, it had been up to Gabriel to deal with them at the end of their revels, administering his particular brand of Rookery justice.

He recognized some of their faces among the fashionable guests this evening. Upright citizens all, by the looks of them. One would never know that handsome, young Baron Mannering had once wagered the clothes he stood up in on a losing bet, only to find himself spending the night in a Rookery alleyway in nothing but his underdrawers. Or that Lord Powell, heir to the Earl of Ingram, was so deeply in debt to a backstreet moneylender that he'd twice come to Gabriel's betting shop, stinking of cheap wine and sobbing like a baby, begging for Gabriel to intervene.

Which Gabriel had, of course.

Better the young lords were indebted to him than to a poxy wine merchant or moneylender. Influence was currency to Gabriel. He knew how to wield it. To weaponize it. It was invaluable to him, especially now, when the square footage of the Rookery was shrinking by the year. If it shrank any further, the slum threatened to disappear completely. Gabriel had no intention of finding himself displaced and powerless. Not so long as there was something he could do about it.

The orchestra closed the galop with a flourish of strings and horns. Another swirl or two, and a few lively chassés across the room, and the dance was over. Several couples departed the floor and several more came to take their places before the next dance began.

It was then, through a break in the crowd, Gabriel observed two late arrivals enter the ballroom. One was a society matron—blond, buxom, and bejeweled. The other was a younger lady of exceptional poise. Clad in a ball gown of deep blue silk, she stood straight and proud beside her older companion, her chin lifted slightly as she surveyed the room with a dispassionate gaze that spoke more of jaded royalty than of a girl in her middle twenties. So might Cleopatra have regarded a crowd of unruly Romans.

The similarity was only enhanced by the young lady's striking good looks. She had gleaming raven hair, bound in an elaborate roll at her nape, and a flawless expanse of warm, golden ivory skin revealed by the short sleeves and low neckline of her bodice.

Gabriel marked her presence with the same ingrained detachment with which he marked anything out of the ordinary in his environment. He noted her beauty. Her uncommon self-assurance. But he wasn't moved by them. He'd seen countless attractive females in his lifetime. They may differ in their allurements, but one was ultimately interchangeable with the next.

A fair-haired lady in amber silk swept over to greet the late arrivals. It was Compton's wife. Gabriel had never met her formally, but he recognized her pallid face by sight. She'd been an heiress when she and Compton had married, one with a sizable fortune and a notoriously dim intellect. Easy prey for a man like the viscount, on the hunt for money and power.

After an exchange of curtsies, and a short dialogue with the older blond lady, Lady Compton turned to the crowd in search of her husband. She easily found him.

"It seems I'm not the only latecomer," Gabriel said as the three ladies made their way toward them.

Compton followed his gaze. "That is my lady wife," he said tightly, having no idea Gabriel already knew exactly who she was. "And that is Lady Belwood, wife of Sir Walter Belwood. As for the younger lady . . ." This time Compton stared. "I've not yet had the pleasure." He stepped forward. "Doubtless her ladyship wishes to provide an introduction."

Gabriel's expression hardened. He had as little interest in being introduced to society ladies as he had in meeting aged Northumberland squires. But it was too late to avoid the tiresome obligation.

Lady Compton was already bearing down upon them, her two guests in tow.

"My lord!" she said to her husband. "Thank goodness you've returned. I trust this means your business in the library is completed for the evening? You've already missed the arrival of Lord and Lady Martindale, and the Marquess of Whitby. And here is Lady Belwood, just come. She has brought her protégé, Miss Flite, to grace our party."

"My apologies, madam." Lord Compton bowed to the two late arrivals. "Lady Belwood. Miss Flite." His eyes lingered on the younger lady's face for a moment before he grudgingly acknowledged the necessity of introducing Gabriel. "Allow me to present Mr. Royce, an acquaintance of mine. We've been discussing a charitable endeavor, but all is settled now. I've invited him to join us. Mr. Royce? My wife, Lady Compton. And this is our near neighbor, Lady Belwood, and her companion, Miss Flite."

Masking his growing impatience, Gabriel bowed to the three ladies as civilly as if he were a gentleman himself. "Lady Compton. Lady Belwood. Miss Flite."

As he straightened, he held Miss Flite's gaze a fraction longer than was proper. Her eyes were the deepest blue he'd ever seen. More akin to a deep midnight purple in the gaslight.

"Miss Flite has just returned from finishing school in Paris," Lady Belwood said, with a flutter of her ostrich feather fan. "She's staying with me in Brook Street for the season."

"A relation of yours?" Compton asked. "I seem to remember one of your second cousins married an Italian. Or was it a Spaniard?"

Lady Belwood wafted her fan with increased vigor. "Miss Flite is not a blood relation. I was, ah, acquainted with her guardian when I was a girl. I promised, when the time came, I would introduce Miss Flite into society. It is the least I can do for her."

"I'm amazed I've not encountered you before, Miss Flite," Lady Compton said. "Is this your first visit to London?"

"It is, my lady," Miss Flite replied. A faceted glass hairpin in the shape of a dragonfly was nestled in her hair. It sparkled as she moved.

Lady Compton flicked a dubious glance over Miss Flite's elegant face and figure. "You don't strike me as a country girl. But if you've been finished in Paris—"

"Finishing schools accomplish marvelous things these days," Lady Belwood interjected. "The girls they turn out have remarkable polish. One can take them anywhere."

Gabriel directed a cold glare at Compton. It was bad enough to have his time wasted by old country squires and frivolous, fan-fluttering ladies, but now he must affect an interest in *finishing* schools? Until Gabriel had intervened, the children of the Rookery had had no school at all. Boys and girls of five had already been working. The alternative was starvation.

Compton pretended not to notice Gabriel's ire. He kept his attention fixed on his wife—and on Miss Flite.

"You must bring her with you to the musicale next week," Lady Compton said. "My daughter, Carena, will be back from Hampshire. She's to perform an aria for us from *Lucrezia Borgia*. There will be a dinner to start." She touched Lady Belwood's arm. "You *are* still planning to attend?"

Miss Flite exchanged a wordless glance with Lady Belwood.

Lady Belwood appeared distinctly uncomfortable. "Er, yes. That is, I had thought—"

"Oh, but you must," Lady Compton insisted. "We see too little of you. And Miss Flite will certainly wish to make the acquaintance of other young people."

Lady Belwood smiled thinly. "If you insist, then naturally, I shall bring her."

The two older ladies lapsed into a short discussion about the dinner, and about the many events to come before the season's end.

Compton was included by virtue of his wife, who sought his opinion on every subject.

Miss Flite and Gabriel were temporarily left outside the conversation. They stood silent across from each other—Miss Flite attending to what the others were saying, and Gabriel poised to make his exit.

He hadn't come here to engage in polite small talk about dinner parties and musicales. His time would be better spent in conversation with one of those aged country squires. At least then there would be a hope in hell of gaining influence for the people of the Rookery. Here there was nothing.

A civil word or two to Miss Flite and then he would take his leave.

Their eyes met briefly.

"A finishing school in Paris, was it?" Gabriel inquired.

"That's correct." Miss Flite returned her attention to the others.

"And were you?" he asked.

She glanced back at him again, distracted. "Was I what, sir?"

"Finished?"

Her mouth curved into a slow, feline smile. "On the contrary," she said. "I'm just getting started."

Gabriel smiled in return, mildly amused by what he perceived as ladylike flirtation. He was about to reply, when he realized Miss Flite hadn't been looking at him when she'd spoken.

She'd been looking at Compton.

· · · · ·

Effie made her way down the gaslit, richly carpeted corridor on the house's ground floor, her steps unhurried but purposeful. Lord Compton had said the library was where he conducted his business. A fortuitous admission, and one Effie's mind had latched on to like a vise the instant he'd made it.

She'd waited most of the evening to extricate herself. Until now, her dance card had been too full to allow for any moments of freedom, except for a short visit to the ladies' retiring room. A marked success, considering the circumstances. It had been Nell, not Effie, who had been destined to ensnare men with her loveliness. A destiny that had been snuffed out that fateful day on the Academy's roof. If not for Effie's weakness, it would be Nell standing here, preparing to bring about Lord Compton's downfall, not Effie herself.

But so long as Effie *was* here, she was determined to do her best.

She may not be sweet or gentle or possessed of perfect porcelain skin, but five years in Paris had taught her to respect her strengths. What she lacked in classical beauty, she more than made up for with confidence, and with the gift of originality.

The moment the supper dance had ended, and the guests had departed for the dining room, Effie had slipped away to pursue her own agenda.

The enormous skirts of her Parisian ball gown rustled silently over her wire crinoline as she approached the library's double doors. She'd bought the gown at a salon in the Rue de la Paix. It was a beautiful garment, made of Prussian blue silk, with a bodice cut low at the neck and shoulders, and an unforgivingly narrow waist that made a bounty of Effie's modest curves. Along with the distinctiveness of her looks, and the resoluteness of her manner, it had helped her achieve her goal this evening. She'd made herself memorable, a young lady whom Lady Compton, and every other society hostess, would feel bound to invite to all their future events during the season.

It had also ensured she'd caught the attention of the gentlemen in attendance. According to Miss Corvus, Lord Compton was an admirer of beautiful women. It had behooved Effie to at least attempt to appeal to his masculine senses.

A failed attempt, as it happened. The gray-haired viscount hadn't betrayed the least interest in Effie. Neither had he revealed himself to be a particular villain. He'd been excessively civil, addressing her with a fatherly air rather than that of a male admirer. He hadn't asked her to dance. Indeed, aside from a single heated look (which Effie was beginning to wonder if she'd misinterpreted), he'd steered well clear of her.

Unlike the younger gentlemen.

If Effie's aching feet were to judge, she must have danced with every male in attendance between the ages of eighteen and forty.

Well. Perhaps not *all* the males in attendance.

The enigmatic Mr. Royce had stood out among the assembled company as starkly as a feral dog amid a pack of lap spaniels. It wasn't only because he'd failed to beg a dance from her. And it wasn't on account of any deficiencies in his dress. It was something in his posture, and in his pale blue eyes, so cold, hard, and remote.

Effie recalled the way he'd looked at her when they'd been introduced in the ballroom. There had been a certain distance in his gaze. Coupled with the brooding set to his jaw and the skepticism evident across his brow, it had made him appear far removed from the wealth and excess of the glittering lords and ladies surrounding them.

Like Compton, Mr. Royce hadn't shown any marked interest in Effie. He hadn't even bothered to linger in her company. After an introduction, and a fleeting exchange about her time in Paris, he'd disappeared into the crowd. Effie had seen him only once after that, engaged in solemn conversation with a much older gentleman by the ballroom windows.

Pity, he might have made the evening interesting.

As it was, Effie felt tonight's challenge was all too simple. She couldn't believe she'd indulged in any anxiety over it. Those first nights in Lady Belwood's guest room in Brook Street, Effie had fretted for hours in her bed, hugging Franc close and worrying herself to ribbons.

She hadn't been lying when she'd told Nell she hadn't picked a lock in five years. She hadn't crept into any forbidden rooms, either, or stolen anything from anyone. What if . . . ?

But her worries had all been for naught.

Opening one of the wood-paneled doors, Effie passed into the library. Any anxiety she'd had about encountering Lord Compton, or anyone else there, was promptly put to rest. The room stood dark and silent. The gaslights had been turned off, and there was no fire lit in the hearth. The sole source of light came from the tall windows beside Lord Compton's heavy walnut desk. A full moon shimmered through the curtains, shining softly over the inkpots, blotter, and stack of unread correspondence littering the desk's surface.

The rest of the large room was sunk completely into shadow. At one time, that mightn't have been an issue. As a girl, Effie had been accustomed to finding her way without a lamp. It had been one of Miss Corvus's earliest lessons, to master the darkness. An Academy student was never to be dependent on anything, not even a candle. She must find her way, stealthily, fearlessly, with complete self-sufficiency.

But Effie had been too long in the City of Light. Though she didn't fear the darkness, she'd long lost the habit of peering into it like a cat. She exhaled a soft breath of relief to find Compton's desk illuminated.

It was a big piece of furniture, heavily carved, with plenty of drawers, small doors, and other nooks and crannies. She trailed her bare fingertip in a languorous line across the edge of the desk until she reached the stack of letters. Sweeping them up in her hand, she riffled through the envelopes in the moonlight. They were waiting to be posted, addressed to various gentlemen. Not a one of them looked nefarious, but how could Effie tell without breaking their seals?

She quietly returned them to the desk. She was a long way from exposing herself by opening and reading Compton's outgoing post.

First, she would search his desk. If Miss Corvus was to be believed, the viscount's crimes were in the past. It seemed more likely Effie would find evidence of them hidden away somewhere rather than willingly written down in a letter to another person.

Perching on the edge of the leather chair behind the desk, skirts billowing out all around her, Effie's attention was entirely focused on the drawers. The first one she tried was locked. So was the second. She rattled it quietly, privately cursing her luck. Drat Nell! She of the lockpicks and coded samplers. It figured she would be proven right.

Effie reached for her glittering dragonfly hairpin. One of a set of three, it was comprised of faceted glass affixed to a sturdy black wire. Like her dress, it had been made for her in Paris.

She was just inserting it into the lock of the first drawer when the silence in the library was broken by the unmistakable strike of a friction match.

A flame blazed forth from the darkness, illuminating a gentleman's face as he lit his cigarette. He was seated in one of the leather armchairs across the library, his jacket and gloves discarded and his cravat loose at his neck.

Effie went still. It was Mr. Royce. She didn't need a lantern to make out his face. His harshly hewn countenance, with its high cheekbones, sunken cheeks, hard jaw, and coldly piercing blue eyes, was readily identifiable even in the fleeting glow of phosphorus and sulfur.

"Are you lost, Miss Flite?" he asked.

She slowly stood from behind the desk, tucking her dragonfly pin back into her hair. Her composure didn't slip an inch. "Not at all, sir. I was looking for someone."

His gaze held hers. Wafting out his match, he cast it into the crystal ashtray on the table beside him. "Perchance you've found him."

2

Effie took her time coming out from behind the desk, all the while aware of Mr. Royce's unholy gaze fixed upon her. He sat across the library in the glow of his burning cigarette, as dark and dangerous as Hades himself, lounging on his underworld throne.

He wasn't a traditionally handsome man, by any accepted measure. But he was attractive by her reckoning. Clean-shaven, with dark hair cropped close at the neck; a tall, leanly muscled frame; and a face etched with experience. Rather too much experience for a man at his stage of life. He couldn't be much above thirty years of age.

She supposed she should be afraid of him. He was, after all, a male, and one who had cornered her in a darkened room. The prospect of ruination loomed large for any young lady in a situation such as this. Reputations had been lost for far less.

But Effie wasn't frightened. She was too angry with herself to allow room for any other emotion.

Know your surroundings. Know your opponent. Know yourself. They had been the three most important rules Effie had learned at Miss Corvus's Academy. Rules to keep a young lady safe. To assure she was prepared for anything. That she was never out of her element, overmatched, or taken by surprise, left incapable of defending herself.

How could Effie have been so stupid to have fallen at the first hurdle? To have assumed the room was empty instead of conducting an adequate search? She should have checked and double-checked. She should have made certain.

But honestly, she reflected with a private huff of indignation, what kind of gentleman sat alone in a darkened room?

Apparently, the same sort of gentleman who implied she had come here to meet him.

"I think not," she answered him coolly. She crossed in front of the desk to make her exit. The door to the library was but a few yards away.

Mr. Royce observed her progress from within his halo of smoke. "What about this fellow you were looking for? You've not given up on him already?"

Effie regretted having made the excuse. She'd have done better to say she was looking for some*thing*, not some*one*. Especially considering she'd been caught red-handed behind Compton's desk.

But there was no turning back now.

"I didn't say it was a him," she retorted. "And no. I haven't given up. I shall simply search for my friend elsewhere. If you will excuse me?"

"Running away?" he inquired blandly. "How disappointing."

She stopped in front of the desk, nettled. She'd never run away from anything in her life. "If you must know, I dislike cigarette smoke."

He took a deliberate puff of the offending object. "Is that so?"

"Smoking is a filthy habit."

"It's a democratic habit. Unlike pipes or cigars. Where I come from, women smoke cigarettes, too."

Where he came from?

"Aren't you English?" she asked, temporarily diverted.

"As much as you are," he said.

Her eyes narrowed. She might have known he'd be trouble. The interesting men always were. Indeed, that was precisely what made them so interesting. "Why were you sitting here in the dark?"

"I was waiting for you."

"I find that hard to believe. We exchanged all of ten words together this evening, and that was hours ago, and not a very compelling conversation in any case. Why would you ever assume I'd come here?"

"Like recognizes like," he said.

She glanced to the door again, wanting to leave. Curiosity kept her anchored where she stood. "What on earth is *that* supposed to mean?"

He took another slow puff of his cigarette, seeming to privately consider the situation. "Unless I'm mistaken," he remarked to himself. "I suppose there's always a first time."

She exhaled an impatient breath. "I don't have any idea what you're muttering about, sir. I only came to look for someone. I have no reason to—"

"Is it one of those frivolous women's wagers I've heard so much about?" he interrupted. "A lady friend has dared you to steal some bauble of Compton's? His letter opener or his monogrammed seal?"

She glared at him, offended by the suggestion. "Do I *look* like a frivolous young lady?"

He examined her in the darkness. "It's not Compton himself, is it?" He gave a short chuckle as he smoked. "Pity, that."

Effie knew full well what he was insinuating, but most young ladies wouldn't. She feigned ignorance. "I have no business with Lord Compton." She paused, unable to resist adding, "And if I do, it's no affair of yours."

"Oh, but it is, Miss Flite." Putting out his cigarette, he abruptly stood. In three strides he was in front of her, standing so close his legs pushed the enormous swell of her skirts back against her own.

She reflexively backed against the desk. He immediately closed the distance. Her crinoline bowed, sandwiched between them, its metal wires and fabric tape bent all out of shape.

He was a head taller than she was. Broad-shouldered and strong, smelling of tobacco and bergamot shaving soap. They stared into each other's eyes in the moonlight. There was no hint of fear. No threat of violence. Only heat, and something very like recognition.

Effie's fingers curled on the edge of the desktop behind her. It had nothing to do with physical anxiety. Even if he had meant her harm, she wasn't without resource. A swift knee to the nether regions or a solid punch to the throat would have dispatched him in a moment. But she had no interest in causing a scene. Not if she could extricate herself by other means.

She demurely dropped her eyes, throwing in an anxious flutter of her lashes and a slight tremble of her lips for good measure. "You're frightening me, Mr. Royce."

"And yet you haven't gone pale. Your breath is steady." Lifting a hand, he brushed his knuckles very deliberately over the curve of her throat. "So is the beat of your heart."

Effie felt his bold caress like a thunderbolt. Heat shot through her midsection, pooling in her belly with a hazardous simmer. Her gaze jolted back to his.

She was no stranger to the game of flirtation. During her time in Paris, many men had attempted to woo her with sweet words and kisses. But this was different. Mr. Royce was no courtly French gentleman. His touch wasn't sweet. It was incendiary.

His knuckles lingered, a scorching brand at the pulse of her throat. "Though it's not quite as steady now, is it?" he added smugly.

Effie kept her countenance through pure strength of will. Her heart might be thumping like the dickens, but she wouldn't give him the satisfaction of seeing the rest of her melt into a puddle of treacle.

Holding his gaze, she removed his hand from her throat with the same deliberation with which he'd put it there. She pressed her bare fingertips to the inside of his equally bare wrist. His pulse surged beneath her touch. "Refresh my memory, Mr. Royce," she said. "What is it that they say about people in glass houses?"

He made no effort to extricate his large hand from her grasp. "Shall we compare racing pulses, Miss Flite?"

Effie detected a hint of mockery in his deep voice. It was as effective as a dash of cold water. She released him. "You forget yourself."

"Do I?"

"Outrageously so. Is it your habit to insult ladies of brief acquaintance with your forwardness? Or am I to believe I'm a special case?"

He set his hands on the desktop on either side of her. "I'm not sure what you are yet, Miss Flite. But make no mistake, I mean to find out."

"What I am, sir, is a gently bred young lady, here as Lord Compton's guest."

"A gently bred lady who enjoys picking the locks of her host's desk? A lady who didn't run screaming the moment I revealed myself?"

"Perhaps I shall scream now."

"You won't."

"Perhaps," she said levelly, "I shall knock you down."

A slow, distinctly predatory smile curved his lips. He kept her caged against the desk, his eyes locked with hers. "There you are," he said, with a husky scrape of triumph. "I see you now."

Effie's already pounding heart gave a disconcerting double thump. "And I see you," she returned. "You're obviously a good friend of the viscount's. His best friend in the whole world, if your behavior is to judge."

Mr. Royce uttered a derisive snort. "I'm no friend of Compton. But I do have a vested interest in his well-being. Any mischief threatened against him will force me to act." His gaze held hers. "You don't want me to act, my lady."

Effie didn't flinch. "I might say the same to you, sir."

Amusement briefly edged his mouth. "I'm quaking in my boots."

"You should be." Setting her hand flat on his chest, she firmly pushed him back a step. She may as well have been pressing against a slab of solid marble. The muscles beneath his black silk waistcoat were that lean and hard. He nevertheless submitted to the pressure, removing his hands from the desk and backing up just enough to allow her to extricate herself. "Now then," she said calmly, "if you would be so good as to allow me to go about my business?"

"By all means. We wouldn't want anyone catching us alone together."

"They won't." Effie gave her rumpled skirts a brisk shake. Her crinoline sprang back into place. "Indeed, I wager you and I shall never be alone in each other's company again."

Mr. Royce returned to his chair, sinking back into the shadows. Without his cigarette illuminating his face, Effie could no longer make out his features, only the sinister silhouette of him. "I'd take that bet," he said.

It sounded very much like a threat.

Effie refused to acknowledge it. No one was going to intimidate her, this gentleman least of all. No matter that only moments ago he'd made her temperature soar. She crossed to the library door.

This time, he didn't attempt to stop her leaving. But she felt his unsettling pale gaze on her as she exited the room—no longer remote or detached, but distinctly, unmistakably awake.

She had the uneasy feeling that she'd roused a sleeping wolf.

3

Gabriel didn't have a single residence in London. He had three altogether, each placed in locations strategic to his interests. There was the set of rooms he kept in the Rookery, above his betting shop. There were his lodgings by the docks. And there was his newly leased house in Sloane Street—a good-sized premises that had come furnished, and that kept Gabriel at the heart of his operations among the upper classes.

He didn't spend more than a night or two at any given residence. He was a street rogue by birth, unused to having a home of his own, and bearing no attachment to any one place. His predilections were purely based on business.

Tonight, that business brought him to Sloane Street.

He'd staffed the house himself with people he could trust. His butler, Kilby, was chief among them. Born in the West Indies, Kilby had found his way to London in the service of a dissolute nobleman and from thence into the Rookery. He was discreet, loyal, and largely unshockable. Above all, he kept the household running smoothly.

Kilby opened the painted front door, admitting Gabriel into the gaslit hall. His face was dutifully blank as he took Gabriel's hat, gloves, and overcoat. "Will you be requiring anything this evening, sir?"

"Privacy," Gabriel said tersely. He headed for the stairs.

Kilby silently shut the door and locked it, uttering not another word. He and the others knew better than to badger Gabriel when he was in a foul mood. Only one among the small staff would dare.

Ollie O'Cleary was all of fifteen—scrawny, lank-haired, and notoriously incapable of holding his tongue. Newly elevated to the position of valet, he materialized in the hall within seconds of Gabriel's arrival.

"You're back early, Mr. Royce," Ollie said. He trotted after Gabriel, up the central staircase and down the long corridor to Gabriel's bedchamber.

It was a spacious room, sparsely furnished but comfortable, with a thick carpet, a carved four-poster bed, a low mahogany dressing bureau, and an attached bathing room with wood-paneled walls and a large, rolled-rim tub.

"How was the ball, sir?" Ollie asked, shutting the chamber door behind them. He quickly lit the oil lamps. "Did you meet those rich lords what's going to help the Rookery?"

Gabriel stripped off his jacket. "No."

He'd left the ball shortly after parting company with Miss Flite. There had been little point in remaining if Compton was only disposed to introduce Gabriel to aged lords and sirs. The men might well be rich, but the philosophies of Lord Trefusis, Sir Newton Cobble, and Lord Upton-Frye had been firmly entrenched in the past. They were entirely incapable of appreciating the changing landscape of London when it came to the poor and the working classes. Lord Upton-Frye hadn't even been able to get over his aversion to trade.

It benefited those men to maintain the status quo. To keep everyone in their proper place, with none daring to upset the wealthy men's gilded applecart.

Gabriel had a mind to do just that. To break off the wheels of that plump, golden cart entirely, and to smash all its perfect apples into the dirt.

One apple in particular.

He shrugged out of his waistcoat, tossing it onto the end of his bed. Crossing to his bureau, he unfasted his cuff links. His fingers lingered at the pulse point of his right wrist. He was, at once, vividly reminded of another of the difficulties that had plagued him this evening. A difficulty possessed of a lithe figure, with a generous bosom, and a perfect oval of a face, distinguished by elegantly sculpted cheeks, a lush, dusky rose mouth, and a pair of devastating blue eyes framed by thickly arching black brows.

Gabriel hadn't recognized her for what she was when she'd entered the ballroom, but during those moonlit moments in the library, she had revealed herself to him in brilliant color.

"Perhaps I shall knock you down," she'd said.

By God, but she'd been serious.

Ollie collected Gabriel's discarded clothes. He took his new position seriously, despite his endless chatter. "But I thought as how you said they was gonna give you money for building new houses in St. Giles?"

"That was the plan."

"Was?"

"I have another plan now."

Ollie draped the coat and waistcoat over the leather-upholstered armchair beside the bed. "Whatever plan you come up with, Mr. Royce, it's bound to be a good one. I'm keen to do my part."

"You will," Gabriel assured him. "And you'll start at dawn tomorrow. I want you to follow someone."

Ollie's head jerked up. A flash of disappointment darkened his eyes. In his former position as a betting shop runner, he'd frequently been tasked with trailing people. "What about my promotion?"

Gabriel wasn't unsympathetic. Naturally, the lad would rather be acting as a respectable servant than spying on strangers from behind tree trunks and lampposts. But needs must.

"It's not permanent," he said. "You'll be done with the job within a week. After that, you can press all the trousers and brush all the top hats you want."

Ollie's brows knit with suspicion. "It ain't another sporting fella with horses and such? Had the devil of a time keeping up with the last one."

Gabriel inwardly grimaced at the unhappy reminder.

Two years ago, he'd sent Ollie to follow the nephew of another politician. That nephew had been a curricle-driving sporting gent in possession of secrets that could ruin his uncle's career. Gabriel had hoped to use those secrets for his own benefit. He'd known even then it would be useful to have a politician in his corner. And the only way a man like Gabriel could gain such power was by foul means, not fair.

That first scheme had come to naught. The nephew in question had inoculated his uncle—and his family—by revealing his uncle's secret to the world before Gabriel could act.

Fortunately, there was no danger of a similar outcome with Compton. His secret wasn't an illicit love affair resulting in a crop of bastards. If what Gabriel knew about Compton were ever to get out, it wouldn't only mean public scorn, it would mean the man's complete and utter annihilation.

"Not a sporting gent this time," Gabriel said. "It's a lady."

"What lady?" Ollie asked.

"Miss Flite." Gabriel removed his shirt. The looking glass above his bureau reflected his image back at him in the lamplight. It wasn't the face and figure of a gentleman. His features were too hard and hollow. His blue eyes too strangely pale. He appeared menacing, rather than modish.

Up to now, he'd preferred it that way. It was, after all, better to be feared than admired. But after this evening . . .

He ran a hand over the back of his neck. "I don't know her given name."

He'd been excoriating himself over that fact ever since she'd left the library. It didn't seem right for him not to know. Not after he'd stared so deeply into her eyes. Not after he'd seen her. Truly seen her.

She may not be a wolf in sheep's clothing, but she was something in sheep's clothing. An adventuress, he suspected. No other lady could have held his gaze so steadily, could have removed his hand from her throat and pressed his pulse, raising the stakes of his impudent touch with an impudent touch of her own.

He hadn't expected it.

Nor had he expected his physical response.

"Shall we compare racing pulses?" he'd asked her.

Good thing they hadn't. He'd have lost the contest spectacularly. His normally cold heart had been pumping at an extraordinary rate.

"How will I find her?" Ollie asked.

"She's staying with Lady Belwood in Brook Street."

"Not Mayfair again." Ollie's expression soured, recalling his fruitless pursuit of the sporting gentlemen. That fellow had also boasted a Mayfair address. "You sure she don't drive a curricle?"

Gabriel shot the boy an ominous look. "Curricle or no, starting tomorrow morning, you'll be her shadow. I want to know where she goes and who she sees."

"Is that all, Mr. Royce?"

"For now."

"What about them other gents?" Ollie wondered as he collected Gabriel's shirt. "The viscount and his rich friends?"

A muscle ticked in Gabriel's jaw. "I'll deal with them myself."

· · · · ·

The following morning, Gabriel set out to do just that.

It wouldn't serve his interests to ruin Compton outright. What Gabriel required was a hint of a threat. Something only Compton would comprehend, and that would serve to shock him back into line.

There was only one gentleman Gabriel could trust with the task.

Miles Quincey was the editor of the *London Courant*, a smallish newspaper with offices in Fleet Street. It didn't have the circulation of the *Times* or the *Morning Post*, and it wasn't as popular as the *Guardian*, but Gabriel knew for a fact that fashionable people read it.

The *Courant* had made a name for itself in the late 1850s, exposing abuses in private asylums. In the years since, it had published several other highly regarded exposés on affairs both foreign and domestic. But the denizens of Mayfair didn't read the *Courant* for its serious subjects. They read it for its uncannily accurate society column. It was that which kept the paper in business—a fact that infuriated the solemn, stone-faced Miles to no end.

"What the devil does that even mean?" he asked Gabriel.

Miles's office was located at the end of a short hall on the second floor of the paper. Cluttered bookcases lined the wall behind an equally cluttered desk. Miles was seated behind it in his shirtsleeves, ink stains on his fingers and a pen in his hand. He'd been working on editing an article when Gabriel had interrupted him.

Straight-backed wooden chairs were arrayed opposite him, as though he'd just ended a meeting with his staff. A single tall window faced the busy street below. There was a portly black cat with golden eyes perched on the sill, idly swishing its tail.

Gabriel strolled across the office to give the complacent little beast a scratch. He didn't know its name. Miles had too many felines to keep count of. They'd always been his weakness. "What does it matter?" Gabriel asked in return. "It's a few sentences in your society column, not the front page of the paper."

"It matters." Miles sat back in his chair, frowning. He was a taller man than Gabriel, dark-haired and clean-shaven, with the solemn face and lean figure of an ascetic. "That column can be relied on for its accuracy. If I start reporting nonsense—"

"The circulation of the *Courant* will go down exactly zero percent."

Gabriel turned away from the cat to address his friend. "By the by, how are all those ladies' maids and valets on your payroll? Brought you any exciting gossip lately?"

Miles's expression was completely inscrutable. "What you're suggesting would be a reprehensible breach of courtesy, not to mention journalistic malpractice."

"I'm to believe that society scribe of yours finds out the gentry's secrets by other means?"

"Yes. It's called reporting. Now, if you're quite finished impugning my paper and my staff—"

"I don't judge."

"How reassuring, coming from a man who puts his spies in private residences all over the city."

Gabriel sank down in one of the chairs across from Miles with an unapologetic smile. "We can't all be journalists."

"What is it you're playing at, Gabriel?" Miles asked. "We're not two lads in St. Giles anymore, conspiring to steal apples from the costermonger. Those days are long past. You've since gone your way and I've gone mine."

It was an apt assessment of their friendship. Though Miles had spent most of his youth in the Rookery, his mother, Rose, had ultimately found a way to get him out. She'd been a devout, hardworking woman, both whip-smart and determined, with the soul of an academic and the mind of a social reformer.

Gabriel had no mother of his own. None he'd ever known. But Rose Quincey had been something like a mother to him. She had frequently given him shelter as a boy. She'd even taught him to read—a kindness that had paid dividends toward Gabriel's future success.

Rose's aspirations for her own son had been that much greater. On Miles's thirteenth birthday, she had arranged an apprenticeship for him with a printer in the West Country. It was there Miles had resided for the remainder of his childhood. He'd finally returned to London years later, a sober, educated gentleman determined to become a newspaperman.

He had come to see Gabriel then, the friendship of their youth unforgotten. As boys, they'd been as close as brothers. But there was no denying their differences as men. They had little in common anymore, save for memories of their past.

"I told you when I came to work at the *Courant* that I wouldn't permit you to make use of it," Miles reminded him.

"Always so cynical," Gabriel said. "It's not as if I'm asking you to divulge the secrets of the nation."

"No, only that I print some dross about a man named Wingard who's rumored to be in possession of important papers." Miles tossed aside his pen in a rare burst of temper. "Who the hell is Wingard? And what papers? And why should anyone care?"

Gabriel had no intention of enmeshing straitlaced Miles in his web any more than was necessary. And to tell him the tale would be to ensnare him utterly. No one except Compton need know about that fateful day Tobias Wingard had stumbled into Gabriel's betting shop, wasting with fever and desperate for coin to pay his debts.

Why Wingard hadn't gone to Compton directly, Gabriel could only guess. He suspected it was because the two men's lives had diverged so dramatically after their joint venture in defrauding Wingard's vulnerable half sister.

Compton had used his part of the fortune they'd stolen to set himself up in London as a gentleman of means. There, he'd married a wealthy heiress, biding his time in luxury until his father and older brother had died and he'd inherited the title. From thence, a career in politics, and a lofty position in society, his slate wiped clean of any trace of the evil he had done.

Wingard had, meanwhile, squandered his portion of the fortune on gaming. Addicted to drink and drug, and ailing from a rotting liver, he'd had no position in society to speak of. No friends or connections he might turn to in his time of need. All he'd had were a few damning documents, and a handful of mightily compromising letters Compton had penned to Wingard's half sister.

You must trust me to manage the funds for you, my sweet, Compton had written in one of them. *Such things are a husband's privilege. As we are to be married, and the right will soon be mine by law, there can be no objections in it, only the easing of a burden which I know has weighed too heavily on your delicate shoulders since the loss of your estimable father.*

The letters had been stained with Wingard's sister's tears. To hear Wingard tell it, Compton had had everything from the girl—her fortune, her reputation, her heart. What had become of her afterward, Wingard hadn't known. Gone abroad, he'd surmised, very probably determined to make an end of herself.

As for Wingard himself—

Gabriel stood. "Wingard's dead. I have the papers. And only one man will care. That's more than enough for me." He pressed Miles's shoulder hard before taking his leave. "Print it, old friend. And if anyone comes inquiring, send them to me."

4

Sun streamed through the gold silk–curtained windows of Lady Belwood's well-appointed guest room. It was a beautiful morning in London, neither damp nor excessively chilly. The perfect day for an excursion.

Effie buttoned her black velvet mantelet over her plain black silk walking dress, preparing to go out. There had been no opportunity for her errand yesterday. The day after a ball was always a busy one, especially if a young lady had made as great an impression as Effie had.

Large bouquets of flowers had arrived throughout the morning, sent by the gentlemen she'd danced with. The generous tributes had been followed by afternoon calls—more gentlemen, and some ladies, too, paying their respects, issuing invitations, and assuaging their curiosity.

Lady Belwood hadn't been best pleased. Indeed, from the moment Effie had appeared in Brook Street ten days ago, with Franc and her trunks in tow, her ladyship had exhibited a pronounced anxiety. Whatever connection she had to Miss Corvus, it clearly wasn't one based on friendship. Lady Belwood had made it plain from the first that Effie was less of a guest and more of an unwanted charge on her dwindling good humor.

She had nevertheless sat beside Effie for every call, spine rigid and lips pinched, an unwilling participant in Effie's deception.

Meanwhile, Effie had done her duty. She'd transformed herself according to her company, one moment smiling and conversing, the next blushing and demurely batting her lashes, and all the while desperately impatient to get back to the Academy to inform Miss Corvus that there was a decided complication to their plan.

A very large and very sinister complication. Effie could still feel the brush of his fingers over her throat.

At the ball, Mr. Royce had come closer to her than any other gentlemen in attendance. Yet, he'd sent no bouquet the following morning. And he hadn't appeared in Brook Street later that afternoon to pay his respects along with the rest of Effie's callers.

Doubtless it was for the best. Lady Belwood was apprehensive enough without the likes of Mr. Royce darkening her doorstep. She'd spent the whole of last evening at dinner with Effie, pale and silent at the opposite end of the long mahogany table, drinking glass after glass of Burgundy wine.

Sir Walter had been absent from the table as usual. Older than his wife by some twenty years, he suffered from various ailments that often kept him confined to his rooms. Effie had met the man only a handful of times since she'd come to stay. When first introduced to him, she'd been both surprised and relieved by his lack of interest in her.

He was, it transpired, working on a lengthy tome cataloguing the rich history of the Belwood line, which he claimed could be traced back, undiluted, to the reign of some antiquated king or other. The social affairs of women held little fascination in comparison.

Would that Lady Belwood were as indifferent to Effie's presence as her husband.

"She'll be happier with us today, won't she, Franc?" Effie remarked as she retrieved her veiled black bonnet from the foot of the cherrywood four-poster bed. "We shall likely be gone until supper."

Franc frisked about Effie's wide skirts in anticipation of their departure. He'd found the house's small back garden a dull respite from the confinement of the guest room. Like Effie, he was eager to venture further.

She was just fetching his lead when a soft tap sounded at the door. "Yes?" Effie called out.

Lady Belwood entered, shutting the white-paneled bedroom door behind her. She was a handsome blond lady of passing middle age, attractively plump, and smartly dressed in a ruffled muslin morning gown. "Miss Flite, I must tell you—" She stopped, registering Effie's bonnet and gloves. "Are you going out?"

Effie pasted on a smile. "Indeed."

"Dressed like *that*?"

"As you see." Widows rarely inspired attention. Clothed all in black, with a net veil shielding her face, Effie could go where she pleased and no one would question her. That is, if they noticed her at all.

She held Franc's lead, preparing to fasten it to his collar. He trotted out of her reach to sniff the blue-and-yellow floral carpet and the pooling hem of the draperies. Effie prayed he wouldn't be indiscreet. Despite his continental origins, Franc couldn't always be trusted to behave in a civilized manner.

Lady Belwood followed his progress with uneasy eyes. "I don't care for dogs."

It was the same sentence she'd uttered when Effie had first arrived, and one she'd repeated at least a dozen times since.

Effie answered just as she had on each previous occasion. "Franc isn't a dog. He's a poodle."

"You *are* taking him with you on your outing? My servants can't always be watching him, you know."

"I am." Effie caught up with Franc by the washstand. Sweeping him into her arms, she fixed his lead to his collar.

"Wherever can you be headed?" her ladyship asked. "Not Bond

Street or Hyde Park, I trust. Not in those garments. And not without a maid to accompany you."

"I've no need for a maid where I'm going."

A pained expression puckered Lady Belwood's brow. "A lady *must* have a maid. I should be lost without mine."

Effie didn't doubt it. Most fashionable females in Lady Belwood's position felt the same. But poor women must shift for themselves. So, too, the girls of Miss Corvus's Benevolent Academy.

The gowns Effie had commissioned in Paris had all been made with front fastenings, the same as the dresses she'd worn at the Academy. Miss Corvus believed in self-sufficiency. The strongest lady was an independent lady, and that independence began with her toilette.

Effie had long grown accustomed to dressing herself and tending to her own coiffure. She was nimble fingered with curling tongs and pins, and she counted herself quite skillful when it came to sponging and pressing her gowns. No one who saw her would ever find her wanting.

"You may rest easy, ma'am," Effie said. "I shall do nothing on my outing that will cause remark."

"Your very presence is causing remark!" Lady Belwood walked to the window. She twitched the curtain, as though someone might be peeping up at them from the street. It was all of a piece with her strange behavior since Effie had arrived. She'd been nervous as a cat, jumping when servants entered the room, and whispering when it wasn't strictly necessary.

Was it fear? Effie suspected it might be.

"I expect you're bound for that . . . that *place* at the edge of the Epping Forest," Lady Belwood said.

Effie wondered that the woman couldn't bring herself to say the Academy's name. "I wouldn't be surprised if my travels took me in that direction."

Lady Belwood let the curtain fall. "But this is all very distressing!" She paced to the bedroom's small fireplace, and from there to the double wardrobe. "I was assured, if I did as she wished, if I introduced you into polite society, there would be nothing connecting me to that . . . that *place*. And now, here you are, darting off there at the first opportunity!"

"No one will notice me," Effie said.

"*Everyone* has noticed you, Miss Flite, from Lord Mannering and Sir Newton to Lord Compton himself. I'd no notion attending his ball would lead to an invitation to dine at his home. He's such a good and decent gentleman. I shrink at deceiving him."

Effie gave her hostess an interested look as she returned Franc to the ground. Lady Belwood was ignorant of Effie's true purpose in attending Compton's ball. Her ladyship thought it merely an introduction to society. She had no idea that Compton himself was Effie's goal, not a successful London season.

"Is he likely to interrogate you on the subject?" Effie asked.

Lady Belwood batted the suggestion away with a wave of her hand. "Lord Compton is far too important to trouble himself with the pedigree of every young lady who crosses his path. He will doubtless take me at my word. But that's beside the point." She returned to the window. "It's been lie upon lie for decades. If only I hadn't—" She broke off, folding her arms as though she had a chill. "That woman contacted me three weeks ago with her request. I knew the day would come. I daren't refuse her. Giving you a season is an easy enough task, after all. But if you should bring my name into disrepute—"

Effie indicated her sober countenance and unassuming black clothing. "Do I *look* like the sort of young lady who would bring someone's name into disrepute?"

Lady Belwood frowned. "No, I-I don't suppose you do."

"Well, then." Effie walked to the door, Franc dutifully at her side. "If there's nothing else, ma'am, I had best be off."

Bidding a brisk farewell to her hand-wringing hostess, Effie departed the house in Brook Street with a purposeful stride. Franc pranced alongside her at the end of his lead, his small black nose to the wind. They walked for several blocks until they reached Claridge's Hotel. From there, Effie hailed a hackney to take them to the railway station. An omnibus ride to the station would have been cheaper, but this wasn't the time for economy. Miss Corvus's Academy was some seventeen miles away. The faster Effie got there, the more swiftly she could return and resume her work.

One rail journey, and another hired hackney cab ride later, Effie and Franc arrived at the Academy's imposing black iron gates. They were admitted by an older student in a plain stuff dress. The girl goggled at Effie unrepentantly as she showed her to one of the anterooms off the Academy's central hall.

Effie wasn't there above five minutes before Nell came to join her.

"Miss Corvus can't see you today," Nell informed Effie. "Will I do?"

Effie gave her friend a brief but heartfelt hug. "On any other occasion, yes. But today's errand is rather delicate. I must meet with Miss Corvus privately. She wouldn't appreciate me speaking out of turn."

Nell drew back to look at Effie. Her mouth tilted with sympathetic understanding. "Is it about Lord Compton?"

Effie's brows lifted in surprise. "You know?"

"Some of it, yes. Miss Corvus occasionally lets me into her confidence."

"Then you comprehend why I must see her."

"Indeed. But she's in no condition to receive you. The doctor's just been, and she's had a double dose of morphine. She'll sleep until dinner. I've been deputized to act in her stead." Nell gently slipped her hand under Effie's arm. "Come with me."

Effie could do nothing but obey. Collecting Franc under one

arm, she numbly trailed after her limping friend, visions of a gravely ill Miss Corvus plaguing her footsteps. Whatever her history with the woman, Effie couldn't accept the idea of her dying. A world without Artemisia Corvus was a world that didn't make sense.

"It's all in hand," Nell promised her. "You needn't fret."

"I'm not fretting," Effie lied. "Not with you in charge."

"Hardly that. To be in charge would be to know all of Miss Corvus's secrets. I haven't yet reached that exalted stage."

Ahead of them, girls in coarsely woven gray dresses with full skirts worn over wire crinolines hurried through the corridors on the way to their classes. They cast Effie startled glances as they passed her in the hall. Their young faces lit with excitement.

"That's *her*!" one declared. "Euphemia Flite!"

"I thought she would be older," another whispered.

"I thought she would be taller," her friend replied archly.

The girls burst into giggles as they strode away.

Franc curled his lip at their retreating figures. He didn't like being laughed at, even if that laughter was kindly meant. Effie soothed his offended dignity with an absent scratch.

"Your exploits are legendary among the girls," Nell said.

"I daresay," Effie replied dryly. It was those very exploits that had earned her a reputation for chaos.

"Do you remember the time you stole all the sugar from the pantry and replaced it with salt?"

"How could I forget?" Effie had eaten most of the sugar, making herself sick in the process. She'd had to spend two nights in the infirmary.

"Or when you smuggled that aged dog into the dormitories and persuaded the rest of us to help you hide it and care for it?"

"Dear old Max," Effie murmured. He had ultimately found a good home with Miss Sengupta, one of the Academy's visiting instructors.

"And what about the duel you fought in the forest with that vile farm boy from the village? Foils at dawn, or some scandalous thing." Nell chuckled. "You were always creating disorder for poor Miss Corvus to put right. No one else has ever vexed her so."

"I'm not particularly proud of my behavior then. I'd prefer the girls didn't know of me at all rather than know me for my worst conduct."

"They know you as the best and brightest among us."

Effie found the prospect of that no more reassuring.

She'd spent thirteen years at the Academy. More than a decade, marked by rebellion and catastrophe. Her triumphs at languages, fencing, and self-defense paled in comparison to the cloying sense of alienation that had daily eaten away at her soul. In the end, not even Nell's friendship had managed to blunt the pain of it. Effie had never felt she belonged here. She'd never felt she belonged anywhere.

"I was neither the best, nor the brightest," she said. "I was only the first."

"Yes, but you went to Paris. Your life has been something for them to aspire to." Nell guided Effie up the stairs, past the student dormitories and onward to the staff rooms.

The third door at the end of the hall had a painted placard hanging on it that proclaimed its occupant: MISS P. TREWLOVE.

"You have a private room," Effie said rather unnecessarily.

Nell unlocked the door. She ushered Effie into the dark, quiet chamber. "So might you have had if you'd remained."

"*Have* you decided to remain?" Effie asked. "Your five years are nearly up. You might go anywhere."

Nell shut the door behind them. She lit a glass lamp. The small room was illuminated in a rosy glow, revealing a neat little bed with a quilted coverlet, a dainty writing desk, and a high-legged wardrobe painted a beguiling shade of pink. A round needlepoint cushion was propped in a spoon-back chair in the corner. It was embroidered with the Academy's unofficial symbol—a black raven with a white-tipped wing.

"Not all of us desire to go away from this place," she said. "Some of us are committed to the mission of the Academy."

Effie didn't believe it for a moment. If Nell had truly decided to stay on permanently, it wasn't because of any philosophical leanings. It was because of her injuries. As a girl, she'd been self-conscious of them. Fearful of how the world might perceive her outside the safety of the school's gates.

"How can you know what you desire if you've never been any-where?" Effie asked her. "If you've never had any experience of so-ciety?"

"Through books," Nell said. "Through scholarly journals, and the daily papers. I keep abreast of what's going on in the world. I don't need to see it for myself to know which way my conscience tends."

It was a logical enough answer. Inherently plausible. Fundamen-tally Nell.

Looking at her beautiful friend—so clever and compassionate—a surge of guilt seized Effie by the throat. "This is my doing," she said. "My weakness has robbed you of your free will."

Nell flinched. "Don't be absurd."

"If I hadn't been so determined to master my fear, you'd never have been obliged to come after me that day. You'd never have fallen from the roof and—"

"It was my choice," Nell said. "*That's* free will, Effie. Being young. Making reckless decisions. Risking it all for your friends—your family." She smiled softly. "You're my sister, you know that. I'd have done anything for you. I still would."

"And I for you," Effie said. "Always."

"There you see? Free will. Though we neither of us fully contemplated the risks, did we? We thought ourselves invincible. Too much Aristophanes, I daresay."

"'There is no animal more invincible than a woman,'" Effie quoted. "'Nor fire either, nor any wildcat so ruthless.'"

"Exactly," Nell said. "I wish it had been otherwise. Of course I do. My leg aches in poor weather, and I'm not as nimble as I once was. But this is who I am now. I wouldn't change it."

Effie set Franc on the ground, leaving his lead attached. With the door shut, he couldn't wander, but it was always better to err on the side of safety. He dragged the light length of velvet behind him as he explored the room.

"You needn't change," she said. "You're perfect. I only ask that you venture outside the bounds of the school before you commit yourself to remaining here forever. Go to the theater or the symphony. Visit the dressmaker. Kiss a handsome fellow."

Nell's cheeks went pink. "Really—"

"*That* you can't get from books."

"Nonsense," Nell replied, still blushing. "Novels hold plenty of kisses. And more if I wish. A girl need only know the right titles, and romance is hers for the taking."

"Is that enough for you?" Effie asked, taking a seat on the edge of Nell's bed.

"For now," Nell replied. Her smiled dimmed. "You could always come back."

"To be a teacher like you? I don't know what I could teach that would be of value."

"English and art. Globes and grammar. Dining etiquette, deportment, defense."

"Do they all study defense now?" Effie asked. In her day, such classes had been limited to Miss Corvus's special girls. The ones who had shown themselves to be cleverer than the others, astute with their lessons and skilled at sport, with valiant hearts and independent spirits.

"Miss Corvus determined it essential not long after you left for Paris," Nell replied. "I confess, I encouraged her in that regard. Every girl should know how to defend herself from encroachments."

"I thought that's what our crinolines were for," Effie said, only partially in jest.

Nell sank down beside Effie on the bed. "Fashion is fleeting, but a well-timed right cross is forever." She added wryly, "To paraphrase *The Oracle of the Ring.*"

Effie's lips tipped in a reluctant smile, recalling the dry text on the history of pugilism that she and Nell had been assigned as girls. "Is it still required reading when one is learning the rudiments of boxing?"

"I should say not. Miss Sparrow prefers application over theory, and it's she who has taken over teaching defense since Miss Corvus retired from teaching it herself."

"Gemma Sparrow? Good gracious."

"I know. She is rather fierce. Miss Corvus thought it best for her to channel her fury."

"On the younger girls?"

"Don't be silly. We have a sandbag."

Effie refrained from comment. She'd been friendly with wild, impetuous Gemma as a girl, but Gemma was too many years younger than Effie for them to be true friends. Effie had preferred keeping her own counsel. For those moments when she'd needed someone to lean on, there had always been Nell.

"Dining etiquette is the only class I remember with any degree of fondness," Effie said. "And that's simply because Miss Pascal permitted us to eat the cakes afterward."

Like Miss Sengupta, Miss Pascal had been one of their many visiting instructors. Strong, eccentric ladies hailing from all corners of the globe. They came for a term or two, but never lingered. Most were women Miss Corvus had known during her time abroad. A bold contingent of females, with singular looks and decided views.

"Macarons, if I recall," Nell said. "You always did have a partiality for elegance. Delicate sweets, beautiful clothing, adorable little dogs." She leaned down to give Franc a gentle scratch of acknowledgment. "You're far better suited to go after Compton than I would have been."

"I'm not," Effie assured her. "I failed at the first challenge." She gave Nell an abridged description of what had happened in the library the night of Compton's ball. She didn't mince words when it came to Mr. Royce. This wasn't the time for girlish secrets.

Nell listened in silence, a thoughtful line etching her brow. "He unnerved you," she concluded when Effie had finished.

"He did, rather."

"And that's a problem because . . . ?"

"It's not a problem in itself. The issue is that he's set himself up as some manner of guardian at Compton's gates. The night of the ball, he distinctly warned me off. That's why I'm here today, to discover what's to be done. Or, more to the point, what I'm *permitted* to do. For if I must get through him to bring down Compton, then Mr. Royce will need to be dealt with."

"Then deal with him," Nell said. "You've never had any difficulty before."

"He's not like the men I've met before," Effie said. "He's . . . I don't know what he is."

"Is he dangerous?" Nell asked.

Effie recalled the strangely detached look in Mr. Royce's eyes. That cold way he had of surveying the room around him. Of surveying *her*. "I suspect so."

"More dangerous than you are?"

Effie huffed. "I'm not so dangerous anymore."

"Perhaps that's the problem," Nell said. "In all your efforts at refinement, you've forgotten who you are."

Effie gave Nell a speaking look. "I've never forgotten who I am, *or* where I came from. It's why Miss Corvus sent me away in the first place."

"You're forgetting it now." Nell took Effie's hand. She pressed it firmly. "You're one of us."

A rush of unexpected emotion caught Effie off her guard. "An Academy girl? It's not an identity, Nell."

"But it is! Far more than the facts of your parentage are. We none of us can be distilled to the circumstances of our birth." Nell again squeezed Effie's hand, taking the sting out of her words. "You're too bitter, that's the trouble. You persist in blaming Miss Corvus for the conditions that brought you here. And she's accepted that blame—foolishly, I feel—in the mistaken belief that your anger would fuel you. Instead, all it's done is cloud your judgment. It's made you suspicious of everything you've learned. Perpetually dissatisfied, imagining there's something better waiting just around the corner, if only you could be free of this place."

A knot formed in Effie's stomach. She hated that Nell could read her so easily.

"If you must be angry," Nell said, "be angry at men like Lord Compton."

Effie met Nell's eyes. It was difficult to reconcile the picture Miss Corvus had painted of the viscount's misdeeds with the gray-haired fatherly figure Effie had met at the ball. "What do you know about him?"

"I know of his opposition to reforming the women's property law, and . . . I know he once callously destroyed the hopes and reputation of a vulnerable young lady."

"Then it's true, the things Miss Corvus told me?"

"Yes." Releasing Effie's hand, Nell stood from the bed. She

limped to her desk. "I can't be entirely certain, but . . . I suspect the young lady was Miss Corvus herself."

Effie stared after her friend, stunned. *"What?"*

"It must have been decades ago," Nell said. "Long before she started the school. Indeed, it may well be the *reason* she started it. Unless I'm mistaken, she went abroad for a time, her reputation in tatters, and came back quite another person. But she hasn't forgotten what he did to her. And she won't allow him to do the same to all women—to prevent us having our measure of security and independence in this world. It's important someone stop him."

Effie shook her head in reflexive disbelief. "How do you know all of that? Has Miss Corvus told you—"

"No. She keeps that part of herself a mystery. But since her illness has worsened, I've had to assume some of her duties. She was constrained to explain the fundamentals of the filing system in her study. I've seen things there which I daresay I was never meant to."

"What things?"

"Old letters she wrote to her half brother, returned to her unread. They paint a damning picture. The rest of the tale I've pieced together myself."

"Is it a very dreadful one?"

"As dreadful as it is commonplace. Men take advantage of women every day. The worst was that Miss Corvus had no one to defend or protect her. Only the same dissolute half brother who, from what I can discern, was all but complicit in Lord Compton's crime. It was he who took the evidence away before she could use it. She said as much in one of her letters to him."

"Her own brother betrayed her?" Effie was appalled.

Franc uttered a yip of complaint from across the room, interrupting their conversation. He had unwittingly wrapped his lead around the leg of the wardrobe. A frequent complaint of his. In Paris, he'd often tangled his lead on the cluttered furnishings in Madame Dalhousie's apartment.

Effie had taught him a command for the purpose. "*Faire le tour*, Franc."

The little poodle immediately obeyed, turning three times around the wardrobe leg in the opposite direction. His lead came free.

"*Bon travail*," she praised him.

Franc's tail quivered in response. He trotted to Effie, his lead trailing behind him.

"That's a useful trick," Nell remarked.

"It is," Effie agreed as she picked Franc up. "And for more than unwinding his lead." She pressed a distracted kiss to his beribboned head, her thoughts returning to the subject at hand. "I didn't even know Miss Corvus *had* a brother. Or any family, come to that."

"Nor did I," Nell said. "I'd always imagined she'd sprung fully formed from Zeus's head, like the goddess Athena."

Effie smiled slightly. "In battle armor, as well."

"Quite so," Nell said. "Speaking of which . . ." She extracted a folded newspaper from a drawer in her secretary. "There's a report in this morning's *Courant* that troubles me." She returned to Effie, pointing to the offending lines as she passed her the paper. "Just there, at the bottom of the society column."

Effie read it, frowning:

Whispers about the affairs of the late Mr. Wingard have lately reached your humble correspondent's ears. Rumors of a trove of important documents, which, if made public, could cause trouble for more than one of my gentle readers. Old sins, it is said, cast long shadows, and never more so than when those sins have been set down in ink and paper.

"Who is Mr. Wingard?" Effie asked, lowering the newspaper.

"I don't know who *this* Mr. Wingard is," Nell replied. "Only that Miss Corvus's half brother bore the same name."

"Perhaps it's a common one?"

"What I fear it is, my dear, is another complication." Retrieving the paper, Nell took it back to her desk. "If the need arises, you shall have to deal with it, just as you'll have to deal with this Mr. Royce fellow. We can let nothing stand in the way of toppling Compton."

"Given her supposed history with the man, I wonder that Miss Corvus trusts me to do it."

"Naturally, she does." Nell remained on the opposite side of the small room, facing Effie. "Who better to represent her than the girl she made in her image?"

Effie glared at her friend in the lamp's glow. "I'm not surprised you put distance between us if you're going to spout such nonsense."

"It isn't nonsense. You and Miss Corvus are essentially the same. I daresay that's why you were constantly at odds with each other. She sees herself in you, and you in her—the good *and* the bad. But she believes in you for all that. She'd have given this task to no one else."

"We both know that's not true," Effie said. "It should have been you."

"It would *never* have been me," Nell retorted with an edge of uncharacteristic sharpness. "Despite what you believe about my falling from the tower roof, or about the part you played in it. You were always meant to be her avenging angel. She's counting on you. So are we all."

Effie's fingers tangled in Franc's curly black coat. She didn't have the heart to argue with Nell on the subject. Not when Nell was already showing signs of annoyance. She so rarely exhibited anger or bitterness over the past. To be sure, Effie had rather she would.

"*The Oracle of the Ring* says the first blow is half the battle," she replied instead. "By that measure, I'm halfway to being finished."

"Then make the second half count," Nell said. "Remember yourself, Effie. And remember the rules."

"Know my surroundings. Know my opponent. Know myself." Effie heaved a sigh. "I used to think Miss Corvus the veriest hypocrite for the first rule, considering she never permitted me to venture further than the bounds of the school."

"Miss Corvus is too ill at the moment to prevent you doing anything," Nell said. "Go where you will. Learn what you can. *Anything* is permissible if it achieves our goal. And, Effie? Whatever happens . . . don't come back here again."

Effie couldn't conceal the flash of hurt provoked by Nell's words. She rose, Franc cradled in her arms. "In other words, I'm on my own."

"Never. You must simply be more careful." Nell returned to her. "I don't know everything about Compton's crime, or how deeply he injured Miss Corvus, but I know he has a great deal to lose. Assume the worst—that he's having you followed, that he's intercepting your letters, that he's peering into keyholes."

Effie found it hard to imagine any of those things given the viscount's seeming lack of interest in her. Then again . . . now she thought of it, she *had* seen a similar-looking boy more than once during her journey to the Academy this morning. She'd scarcely registered it at the time. It hadn't occurred to her then that she might have been being followed.

Just as it hadn't occurred to her that a wolf might be lurking in the darkness of Lord Compton's library.

"I shall be on my guard in future," she vowed.

"See that you are," Nell said. "If you need to reach us again, send a sampler."

A sampler?

"Joy," Effie muttered.

5

Gabriel's betting shop was located at the dark heart of the squalid maze of narrow, intersecting alleyways that characterized what remained of the Rookery. It was an outwardly unobtrusive building, faded and splintering, crammed between the sagging facades of a gin shop and a brothel.

Unlike its neighbors, Gabriel's shop bore no markers to identify its purpose. There were no staggering drunkards or dissipated former soldiers lined outside, and no bawdy working girls plying their trade. There was only a single guard—one rough-looking and exceedingly large man employed to keep watch over the door.

Inside the shop was another matter. Amid the smoke, the sweat, and the shouting, a disparate and ever-changing crowd of men gathered around long slips of paper nailed to the back wall. These were the all-important betting lists. Each race had their own, which stated the odds against the horses. There were other lists, too, on everything from boxing matches to the inane wagers of private gentlemen. If a contest was involved, Gabriel was generally offering odds on it.

As a consequence, his shop attracted men of every stripe; tradesmen, clerks, aristocrats, and rascals. After studying the lists, they lined up at the large desk in the front of the shop to lay their bets. And if any of those fellows lost and couldn't pay up, Gabriel dealt with them the same, whether they were landed gentry or the lad who emptied chamber pots at the local lodging house.

None of it was strictly legal. The 1853 Act for the Suppression of Betting Houses had seen to that. But Viscount Compton kept the law from Gabriel's door. There was no need any longer to bribe the police, or exert pressure on the local watch. With Compton in his pocket, Gabriel conducted business just as he always had, only now entirely free of interference.

Well, not *quite* as he always had.

With the size of the Rookery rapidly decreasing, Gabriel's only hope of retaining some semblance of power was to rebuild the fading slum into something like a respectable neighborhood. A man touting reform couldn't be seen resorting to physical violence. For that, Gabriel now relied on his men. It was they who dealt with the fellows who fell behind in paying their debts, while Gabriel himself remained above the fray, holding court from his private office at the back of the shop.

It was there he'd retired this morning, to the chair behind his heavy oak desk, temporarily abandoning his fashionable premises in Sloane Street. Miles had done as Gabriel requested. Yesterday's edition of the *London Courant* had contained the vague lines about Wingard in its society column. Now all that remained was for Compton to formulate his response.

Gabriel was confident one was forthcoming. Until such time, he had plenty to occupy himself—odds to make, bills to settle, and neighborhood disputes to mediate. Conducting business in the Rookery kept him grounded. It reminded him who he was, obliterating any delusions of grandeur.

He'd seen too many men who, once quit of the slum, were ashamed to reveal the truth of their origins. He refused to be one of them, no matter how much money he made. There was no point in his trying to forget where he came from when no one else ever would.

Unlike Miles, Gabriel hadn't any formal education or training to fall back on. He was someone important purely because the residents of the Rookery recognized him as such. Take that away, and what was left? A handful of nefarious investments? A sparsely furnished house in Sloane Street and a half-empty set of rooms by the docks?

Gabriel had no real home. Nowhere he truly belonged except here.

Money hadn't changed that. Not the fine clothes he wore, the expensive stable of horses he kept, or even the cultivated accents he spoke. He would always be a street rat at heart.

The door of his office opened. One of his men—a hulking brute named Liam Murphy—popped his head in. "There's a man what wants to see you, Mr. Royce. Come from your house in town."

Gabriel looked up from his papers. He removed the round, gold-rimmed spectacles he wore when he worked, casting them aside. "Send him in."

Murphy ushered through the liveried footman from Sloane Street. The footman hastened to Gabriel's desk. "Mr. Kilby sent me, sir." He extracted an envelope from his coat and handed it to Gabriel. "This was delivered by one of Lord Compton's servants but half an hour ago."

Gabriel took the envelope, breaking the monogrammed seal. "What servant did he send?"

"An older man with a crooked nose, Mr. Kilby says."

"His butler, Parker," Gabriel mused. No doubt Compton meant it as a message. A counterthreat to Gabriel's threat in the *Courant*. Parker was a villain, after all, and one who wasn't a stranger to using his fists.

Gabriel was amused rather than intimidated. If Compton believed implied threats of violence would work to keep Gabriel silent, the man was in for a very rude awakening.

He extracted a cream-laid note card from the envelope. It was a printed invitation to a musicale at Compton's home next Monday evening. The same musicale to which Gabriel had overheard Lady Compton inviting Lady Belwood and Miss Flite. The viscount had appended the card in black ink:

Lord Haverford will be in attendance. He is a gentleman worth knowing.—C

Gabriel chuckled. "That's more like it." He addressed the footman. "I'll be returning to Sloane Street on Sunday. Tell Kilby to have all in readiness."

"Yes, sir." The footman retreated. As he exited the office, another, much smaller figure pushed passed him to gain entry.

Murphy grabbed the lad by the back of his coat.

Ollie slipped free of the garment without losing a step. "Mr. Royce!" he panted. "Beg pardon, but—"

"O'Cleary." Gabriel tucked Compton's invitation back in its envelope. "You shouldn't be here."

"I know, sir, but—"

Murphy caught hold of Ollie's shoulder. "Out you go, runt."

Gabriel flashed Murphy a look. Murphy immediately released the lad, backing out of the room and shutting the door.

"When I give you a job," Gabriel said to Ollie, "I expect you to do it."

"I am doing it, sir."

"You're supposed to be following Miss Flite."

"I did," Ollie said, harried. "I *am*." He pointed wildly to the closed door of the office. "She's here!"

Gabriel stared at him for a split second, uncomprehending. And then he surged to his feet. "In my bleeding betting shop?"

Ollie followed Gabriel to the door. "Not in the betting shop, sir. In St. Giles. She's at Mother Comfort's."

"The devil she is." Gabriel pushed through the crowd of men outside. "With an escort?"

"She don't have any servants with her, only a fluffy little dog," Ollie said, running after him.

Gabriel muttered a violent oath. Mother Comfort's gin shop had once been a thriving concern. But not anymore. Now, it was a desperate place, one of the lowest and most disreputable gathering spots in St. Giles.

Miss Flite hadn't struck him as a stupid woman, but she must be lacking something in the upper story if she'd come to the Rookery alone. A well-to-do young lady like her would be easy prey for every rogue, pickpocket, and procurer.

Pushing open the door of his shop, Gabriel bounded down the steps to the alleyway. He belatedly realized he'd left his coat and necktie in his office. It mattered little. This wasn't a social call in Mayfair. Indeed, he'd be lucky if this wasn't Miss Flite's funeral.

He strode past the brothel, turning right down the next alleyway and then left down the one after. The passages of the Rookery were dark and narrow, a fetid warren filled with a suffocating expanse of humanity at its lowest ebb. Drunkards retched into corners, slatterns sagged against walls in various states of undress, and squalling, red-faced babes clung to the soiled skirts of drink-sotted mothers.

Scattered among them were the true victims of the slum—the hardworking poor struggling to survive with some measure of dignity. Costermongers, rag merchants, and washerwomen; bakers' assistants, publicans, and children selling flowers from trays. Many of them acknowledged Gabriel as he passed, calling out his name or doffing their caps in respect.

Gabriel hardly noticed. His sights were firmly fixed ahead of him. Mother Comfort's wasn't much further. If he could get there quickly enough, Miss Flite wouldn't come to harm.

Ollie chattered on breathlessly as he kept pace with Gabriel's long stride. "I've been following her just like you told me, sir. She didn't go out the day after the ball, but she had loads of callers, and more deliveries of flowers than I could count. And then yesterday, she suddenly comes out of the house, all in black like a widow, and she takes a train to the Epping Forest."

Gabriel flashed him a sharp glance. "Where in the Epping Forest?"

"A big stone house with an iron gate around it. There weren't no way for me to get in. But the gates had a name over 'em."

"Which you couldn't read," Gabriel concluded.

Ollie reddened. "No, sir," he admitted, abashed.

Gabriel's brows sank with displeasure. There was no excuse for the lad's ignorance. Not now the Rookery had a semblance of a school. Gabriel subsidized it himself. His desire to reform the slum might be rooted in self-interest, but he wasn't without vision. He was determined every child be given the same opportunity that Rose Quincey had given him. A chance to learn to read and to write. To better themselves.

Ollie had flat-out refused to attend. He'd claimed he was too old to learn, preferring instead to devote the whole of his attention to his new role as a gentleman's valet. It was a long-standing bone of contention between them.

"But I did ask at the public house in the village," Ollie continued. "The barman said as how it was called the Crinoline Academy."

"The Crinoline Academy," Gabriel repeatedly flatly. He very much doubted that was the place's official name. "A girls' school, was it?"

"Something like. Miss Flite returned to Brook Street after. Then, this morning, she comes out again, dressed all in black like yesterday, and she comes here, sir. Straight to St. Giles!"

Gabriel scowled. What the devil could she be up to?

Another turn down an alleyway brought them to a small, crooked building with dirty plate glass windows patched with soiled rags. The premises appeared quiet enough. The sun was shining, and the worst of the slum's residents hadn't yet emerged from the shadows. That didn't make it any safer of an establishment for a young lady.

Gabriel entered the dank interior of the shop, letting the door slam loudly behind him. The shop's customers looked up as one. There weren't many of them at this time of day, only a scattering of hard-faced, gin-soaked ruffians, hunched around small wooden tables, nursing their drinks amid a cloud of pipe and cigarette smoke.

Miss Flite stood at the shop's filthy counter. A pair of large, unshaven men in threadbare coats and sweat-stained breeches loomed on either side of her, watching her from beneath the brims of their low cloth caps the way hungry sharks might watch an oblivious seal frolicking to its doom.

She was dressed all in black, just as Ollie had described. An ebony parasol was tucked under her arm, and a tiny black dog danced at her feet, constrained by the slim velvet lead she held in her black-gloved hand. The fine veil of her bonnet had been drawn back to reveal her face as she spoke to the barman, old Ned Scrimple.

Ned was staring at her with an expression that—when coupled with the lascivious stares of the other men—had Gabriel reflexively clenching his fist. He forced his fingers to loosen. Things could easily escalate. There was drink involved, and there was an uncommonly attractive woman. A few more swallows of liquid courage and one of these louts would willingly start a brawl over her.

"What's this, Ned?" Gabriel asked with deceptive casualness. "A party?"

Miss Flite turned. Her dark blue gaze flicked from Gabriel to Ollie and back again. If she was surprised to see them, she didn't show it. "Good morning, gentlemen."

A glass of spirits sat on the counter beside her, so far untouched.

"A bit early in the day for a drink, is it not, my lady?" Gabriel inquired, coming to join her.

"Oh, that isn't for me," Miss Flite said. "It's for him." She smiled in Ollie's direction. "I thought you might be thirsty, young man. You've kept such a brisk pace these past two days."

Ollie paled. He was usually more effective when following people, blending in easily with his surroundings and remaining invisible. If Miss Flite had spotted him, it could only be because he'd been careless.

Gabriel stepped up to the counter, putting himself squarely between Miss Flite and the larger villain on her right. He stared down at her, as close to her as he'd been in Compton's library. This time, his pulse was unaffected. His blood pumped cold and steady, fully aware of the danger, even if she wasn't.

"Is that what's brought you here today? The impertinence of this young lad?"

Ollie flinched to hear Gabriel's Birmingham accent emerge, knowing that it never boded well.

Ned, the barman, was equally aware. He took a step back from the counter, holding his hands up in apology. "She were asking about the old days, Mr. Royce, some two decades past, long before I took up shop. I meant no disrespect. I didn't know she were one of yours."

"The old days," Gabriel repeated. "Ah. But they're dead and gone, aren't they, Ned?"

"That's what I told her, sir."

"She's looking for someone named Grace," the man on the right said. "Knew a whore named Grace once." He craned his head around Gabriel to leer at Miss Flite. "Not as pretty a whore as you are, but—"

In one lightning-fast movement, Gabriel grabbed the man by his greasy hair and slammed his face down on the bar. There was a crunching sound, followed by a vigorous spurt of blood.

"My nose!" the man bellowed.

Ned rushed to the man's aid, dirty bar cloth in hand. "Shut up," he growled as he cleaned up the blood. "You want it to be your neck?"

"That's Gabriel Royce, you lummox!" one of the drunkards called out from a table nearby. "Him who runs St. Giles. Best shut your mouth if you know what's good for you."

Miss Flite gave Gabriel an interested look. One would never guess by her expression that there was a man bleeding copiously not six feet away. "Is it true?" she asked. "*Do* you run St. Giles?"

Gabriel motioned to the door. "Shall we?"

"I don't mind a little blood."

"Nor do I. But I do recall your aversion to smoke."

Her lips compressed. For a moment it seemed she would refuse. "Very well," she said at last. "How could I refuse such gentlemanly consideration?"

With that, she picked up her little dog—a black, curly-coated bit of fluff with a red satin ribbon bow on its head. The tiny beast fixed Gabriel with a surprisingly fearsome glare as Miss Flite conveyed it from the shop.

Gabriel strode after her. When Ollie moved to follow, Gabriel jerked his head back to the bar. "Drink your drink," he commanded.

Outside, Miss Flite continued carrying her dog as she proceeded down the refuse-strewn alleyway. The skirts of her plain, black silk day dress were nearly as wide as the skirts of her ball gown had been. They swayed about her in a seductive swish of fabric, at once protective and provocative.

Gabriel stalked along at her side, as closely as the circumference of her hem would allow. His blood was pumping harder now. By God, but he'd lost his temper. And the man hadn't even touched Miss Flite, or offered her violence. All he'd done was call her a whore. As professions went, it wasn't even the worst one. Gabriel's chest still tightened with fury to recall it.

He couldn't think why. Miss Flite was nothing to him. Just a comely female he'd met under unusual circumstances at a ball. A lady who had intrigued him, yes. But a lady nonetheless. He had no use for such refined creatures.

"What a knight in shining armor you've turned out to be, Mr. Royce. First sending that boy to follow me, and now coming to my rescue." She bent her head to briefly nuzzle her dog. "He *is* yours, isn't he?"

"He works for me, yes." Gabriel expected her to react with anger. Instead, a fleeting glimmer of relief crossed her face. "That doesn't trouble you?"

She huffed. "I thought Lord Compton had sent him."

He narrowed his eyes at her. "Why would Compton have you followed?"

"Why would *you*, more to the point?"

He felt the brush of her full skirts whispering against his trouser leg as they walked. The Crinoline Academy, Ollie had called the school Miss Flite had visited. And she was surely wearing a formidable crinoline now.

Gabriel pushed the image out of his mind. The last thing he needed was to be envisioning Miss Flite in her underclothes. "Perhaps I wanted to keep you out of trouble," he said. "If Ollie hadn't come to fetch me—"

"I was perfectly fine as I was."

"You were five minutes away from being grievously insulted by any one of those blackguards. Or worse. And you with what—a parasol to defend you? A little scrap of a dog?"

"His name is Franc," she informed him.

"Frank?"

"Franc," she corrected him, with no discernable change to her pronunciation. "He's French."

Gabriel's mouth tugged into a reluctant smile. "A French franc, eh? Fancy that." He reached to give the little dog a scratch.

"I wouldn't," Miss Flite warned. "His bite is worse than his bark."

"Is that a fact?"

"And so is mine," she added.

This time Gabriel grinned.

"My parasol is tipped with steel, by the way," she said. "It's sharp as a razor's edge. I was in no danger in that place, and I certainly didn't require rescuing."

Gabriel glanced at her black-ruffled parasol. He hadn't noticed it before, but looking at it now . . .

It was, indeed, tipped with steel. The silver-sharp edges gleamed treacherously in the sunlight.

His brows lowered. He'd seen many a knife or razor secreted on a woman's person, but he'd never observed a fashionable silken accessory made up with such lethal intent. What sort of woman carried such an article?

"On the contrary," Miss Flite continued, "you interfered at the very moment I might have learned something useful."

"About a woman named Grace?" he asked.

"That man said he knew her."

"And old Ned said you were asking about someone from two decades past. That idiot who made the mistake of addressing you is all of twenty himself if he's a day. Unless he was an infant when he met this woman—"

"Yes, yes. Very well. But still, it really *is* none of your business, Mr. Royce." She paused. "Or should I say Gabriel?" Her eyes betrayed a flicker of curiosity. "Is that really your Christian name?"

"You don't approve?"

"It isn't that. It's only that you don't seem very angelic." Stopping at the end of the alleyway, she bent to place her dog on the ground. "And you run St. Giles, do you?" she asked again as she straightened. "What does that even mean?"

"What about *your* name?" he countered. "Am I not to have the pleasure?"

She looked straight ahead for a moment as they resumed walking down the alleyway to the right. Her dog trotted in front of her at the full length of his lead. "Euphemia," she said.

"Euphemia," he repeated.

"You don't approve?" she tossed back at him.

Gabriel fell silent for the space of a heartbeat. "Quite the opposite. It suits you."

Even now, clad in unrelieved black, as respectable as a fashionable English widow, there was something of the continental about her. A mysterious quality, conjured by her raven hair and olive-tinged skin, that spoke of warm weather and sultry climes. Gabriel didn't wonder Compton had assumed she was the offspring of some Spaniard or Italian.

"That doesn't sound very complimentary," she remarked.

"Blame the messenger. I'm not one of those fine lords you met at Compton's, waltzing with you and paying you pretty compliments."

"No, not waltzing with me, only sending your minions after me for God knows what reason."

Gabriel thrust his hands into his pockets. "When did you notice the lad? He'll want to know where he erred."

"Yesterday at the station. I saw him twice, once at the bookstand, and again at the cabstand. After that, it was easy to spot him." Her gaze fell to Gabriel's neck and shoulders. "By the by, you seem to be absent your coat and cravat."

"Noticed, have you?"

"No lady could fail to. It's positively indecent."

An unaccountable flare of heat ignited in Gabriel's veins. He ignored it, just as he ignored the brush of her skirts. "Violence doesn't offend you, but my shirtsleeves do? You fascinate me, Miss Flite."

"What can I say? I'm a fascinating creature."

Another smile threatened. He ruthlessly suppressed it. "Why were you visiting a school near the Epping Forest? I thought you'd been finished in Paris, not educated in some British girls' academy."

She didn't bat an eye. "I *was* finished in Paris. That place near the Epping Forest isn't a school. It's an orphanage. I'm charity minded—a laudable inclination. It's the same reason I came to St. Giles today."

"Not because of Compton?" he asked. An endless pause. "And not because of me?"

She gave him a sidelong look. "I didn't know you were from here, did I?"

"I'm not originally. I was born in the Black Country. In Birmingham. I came here when I was a lad." Gabriel heard the gruff-edged words emerge as though they'd been uttered by another person. It was far too much information to share with a female. Personal, and nonessential. His jaw tightened, mouth clamping shut before he could give in to the unaccountable impulse to tell her anything more.

"Now you rule over everyone, is that the story? How enthralling." She paused before adding, "And no, my visit here hasn't anything to do with Compton. It's a benevolent concern, merely. Someone my family knew long ago. I'd like to discover what happened to her."

"Her given name was Grace? What was her surname?"

"I can't recall. But I believe she had fair hair, and that she at one time lodged over a rag-and-bone shop. Surely, someone must remember her. It would only have been seventeen or eighteen years ago."

"Only that?" He scoffed. "The slums were cleared in the forties to make room for expanding the road. Thousands were evicted. Many others left for Church Lane or Devil's Acre. Even if you could find someone who remembered her, the likelihood of them still being in St. Giles is next to nothing."

Euphemia's face fell. Her footsteps slowed as they turned down another alleyway. Franc pulled impatiently at his lead, urging his mistress forward. She didn't attend him. "I hadn't any idea."

Gabriel regarded her with nagging concern. She'd shown little authentic emotion since the night they'd first met. Not a flinch when he'd caught her at Compton's desk, and not a start when Gabriel had bloodied the scoundrel's nose in front of her at Mother Comfort's. But this—this was genuine.

"Sorry to disappoint you," he said.

She didn't appear to hear him. She lapsed into silence for several seconds. And then: "Are Church Lane and Devil's Acre very far from here?"

He frowned, discerning her intention. "If you've got any idea of turning up there as you did here today, you'll do me the courtesy of putting it straight out of your head. I've no interest in you being murdered."

She adjusted her dog's lead, reeling the little beast closer. "I shan't be murdered. Have no fear."

"Forgive me if I fail to be reassured by your French poodle or the pointy tip of your silken parasol." Removing his hands from his pockets, he caught her by the arm, arresting her step as they approached Oxford Street. "If it's charity that interests you, there are plenty of other ways to exert your finer instincts than imperiling yourself to find this Grace woman. Did you look around the streets of the Rookery? Did you see the state of the people there?"

The slum was behind them now, masked by the bustling street ahead. Only someone who navigated the narrow maze of Rookery passages could find the sink of iniquity within—a rotten cancer in London's West End, its acreage diminished, but its character unaltered.

"I could hardly miss them," she said. "If you do run the place, why haven't you done something about the conditions of it?"

Her silk-clad arm was slim and strong beneath his fingers, with a hint of feminine softness to it. His fingertips itched to caress the delicately rounded underside. A fierce temptation. He released her before he could give in to it.

"Do you think I was attending that ball for my own amusement?" he asked her. "I was looking for patrons. Men of influence who could help reform the slum into something like a livable neighborhood, instead of what it's become since the clearances."

"How would that benefit you?"

"It would benefit everyone," he said. "I've already sponsored a school for the Rookery children, and paid for repairs to some of the roofs, and renovations for a handful of the dwelling houses. But I'm only one man, not a public works committee. Large-scale change requires large-scale measures."

She gave him a look that was hard to read. "*You* begin to fascinate *me*, Mr. Royce."

The heat in his veins suffused into his midsection. He returned her opaque gaze, wishing like mad that he knew what she was thinking.

But it was impossible.

An empty hackney cab rolled down the street. Gabriel summoned it with a shrill whistle. The driver responded, pulling his horses up in front of them.

Gabriel gestured to the cab. While it wasn't as luxurious a vehicle as she was likely accustomed to, the four-wheeled carriage was roomier and less perilous than a two-wheeled hansom. "If you would oblige me."

Euphemia stopped and folded her arms. Her tight silk bodice strained over the voluptuous swell of her bosom.

He inwardly scowled with the ferocity of a baited bear. He was noticing too much about her, and far too keenly. The turn of her countenance. The excellence of her bosom. The softness of the underside of her arm, by heaven! And those perfections didn't begin to touch the courage she'd exhibited or the cleverness of her mind—allurements against which he had even less defense.

She needed to go before he said something—or worse, *did* something—stupid.

Stalking to the door of the hackney, he jerked it open. "Brook Street," he said to the jarvey. And then to Euphemia: "Miss Flite?"

At length, she grudgingly obeyed him. "I'd planned to leave in any event, once I'd questioned the men at the gin shop. I must go home and change. I'm expecting callers at one."

Gabriel had no doubt she was. It didn't make the statement any more pleasant to hear. He offered his hand to help her into the cab.

She ignored it. Picking up her little dog, she climbed in all on her own and sat down.

Gabriel shut the door after her. He didn't back away immediately. The cab's window was down, her face mere inches from his.

She set a hand at the open window, fingers curling over the top of the door. "That's not to say I'm finished with my inquiries."

"As I recall. You're just getting started. But if you take my advice, you'll refrain from starting anything here. The slums are no place for a lady."

"If that's the case, will you do me the favor of asking your acquaintances in Church Street and Devil's Acre about Grace?"

"I shall," he said.

"How will I know if you discover anything?"

"I'll tell you myself."

"I can't think when. We're not likely to see each other again anytime soon."

"Sooner than you might imagine," he said, thinking of the invitation he'd received to Compton's musicale. "Now, if you will be so good? I have work to do."

"Yes, of course," she said. "Good luck with your endeavors, Gabriel."

"I'd wish you the same, Euphemia, if I had any idea what the devil you were up to."

She smiled at that. It wasn't the catlike smile he'd seen at Compton's or the hint of a smug smile she'd given Ollie at Mother Comfort's. It was a real smile, both at her mouth and in her eyes. Seeing it, the heat in Gabriel's midsection roared into a furious blaze.

He impulsively caught her hand through the cab's open window. Raising it to his lips, he pressed a kiss to the curve of her kid-gloved knuckles. Her eyes widened, her fingers tightening on his in a startled clasp.

Franc instantly shot forward, baring his teeth at Gabriel.

Gabriel's mouth hitched with amusement at the protective display. Releasing Euphemia's hand, he chucked the little dog gently under the chin. Franc ceased snarling. He stared at Gabriel, stunned.

Euphemia was staring at him, too. Gabriel thought he detected a slight flush in her cheeks.

Then again, it was entirely possible the mere kiss of her gloved hand had robbed him of his senses.

He backed away from the cab as the jarvey started the horses. "Careful how you go, Miss Flite."

She didn't reply, only looked at him, a shadow of bewilderment in her gaze, as the hackney rolled off with a rattle, merging with the traffic of the busy street and soon disappearing from view.

6

E ffie sagged back in the seat of the hired cab as it jolted down the
  street. She held Franc tightly in her arms, her heart beating
swiftly and her head buzzing as though she'd just received a fearsome clout from an opponent in battle.

The sensation was nothing to the queasy trembling in her
stomach.

Nell had said anything was permissible. *Go where you will. Learn
what you can.* The words had unleashed Effie. This morning, on
setting out from Brook Street, she'd used them to rationalize a visit
to St. Giles. She must know her surroundings, mustn't she? And the
Rookery was as much a part of London as any other neighborhood.

But she hadn't reckoned for how the experience would affect her.

As she'd ventured down the labyrinthine alleyways, questioning
the slum's few sober-looking residents and ultimately finding her
way to Mother Comfort's gin shop, Effie had outwardly maintained
her composure. Her determination to find out something about her
mother had superseded all other concerns. There was generally some
older person in a place who possessed the community's collective
memory. Surely, one of them would remember a fair-haired woman
named Grace who had once given up her child to a sinister lady in
black.

But with every alley Effie had traversed, she'd been drawn further and further back into that same murk of memory—too far away to touch or recall, but close enough to feel.

And goodness, how she'd felt it.

Even now, safely ensconced in the hackney cab with Franc, the foul sights and smells of the Rookery lingered, leaving their grim stamp on her soul.

She hadn't anything to show for it, either. Indeed, rather than finding the needle she had sought, all she'd discovered was an ever-growing collection of haystacks.

And that wasn't even the worst of it.

Effie's fingers tangled in Franc's curls, the wild buzzing in her head and chest only increasing as she recalled the sight of Gabriel Royce entering the gin shop.

Never in her life had she seen a man so utterly in charge of his environment. King of all he surveyed. And not a kindhearted king, either. A cold and implacable one, who had dispatched a man who had outweighed him by at least five stone as easily as if he were swatting a bothersome fly.

He'd been in his shirtsleeves, too. And without a cravat! The neck of his shirt had gaped, revealing the strong column of his throat.

Effie supposed she shouldn't have noticed it. Then again, knowing one's surroundings meant noticing *everything* in them, even if that everything included the bare neck of one's brooding would-be rescuer.

The entire episode had been as breathtaking as it was baffling. The way Gabriel had behaved. Smashing that man who had insulted her against the gin shop counter. Clasping her arm so gently. Kissing her hand!

What had he meant by it all? He wasn't, it was to be hoped, interested in her romantically, was he?

She couldn't credit it. Not given the actions that had preceded today's encounter.

Gabriel had warned her away from Compton. He'd even had her followed. That boy of his had seen her visit the Academy, for heaven's sake! Effie couldn't believe she hadn't spotted the lad earlier. She felt a fool not to have done so. And now Gabriel knew of her connection with the place. Whether he believed it was one wholly based on her charitable instincts, Effie took leave to doubt. The man didn't strike her as being stupid. Calculating, yes. Foolish, never.

No, she decided firmly. His attentions, such that they were, weren't inspired by romantic attraction. They were fueled by self-interest. He was her opponent, nothing more.

Recognizing that fact put all the rest in its proper perspective.

Nevertheless . . .

Effie gave Franc a look of gentle reproof as the hackney clattered on toward Mayfair. "You didn't bite him."

Franc's shrewd brown eyes blinked up at her without apology. He bit anyone he deemed a threat. When it came to judgments of character, his intuition was as reliable as clockwork.

She frowned down at him. "Don't say you like the man."

Franc's pom-pom tail quivered faintly in answer.

"If that's the case," Effie said, "you're in trouble, my friend."

And so am I, she added silently.

· · · · ·

There was much to be done in the lead-up to the dinner at Lord Compton's house next week. Effie couldn't afford to be idle. The following day, she embarked on another series of errands, this time appropriately garbed in a morning dress of lavender-sprigged white grenadine and properly chaperoned by one of the Belwoods' housemaids. Their first stop: a chemist's shop in Bond Street.

Effie settled Franc more firmly under her arm as she entered. She'd had no choice but to bring him. The only servant in Brook Street she trusted to look after him was the upstairs maid, Mary—a sensible girl, and the very one Lady Belwood had commanded to accompany Effie this morning.

Mary dutifully followed as Effie examined the displays of glass bottles, potions, and plasters. "What are you looking for, miss?" she asked. "P'raps I can help."

"Vesta matches," Effie said. "And a case."

The young maid was too well trained of a servant to question the purpose of either item. She assisted Effie in locating them, and then waited while Effie made her purchase from the linen-smocked proprietor.

An oil and candle shop was next, followed by a stationer's, and then a draper's shop where Effie bought a ball of sturdy twine.

Having satisfied herself that she had all she required for the next stage of her mission, Effie's thoughts turned from practical preparation to intellectual necessity. "Hatchards Booksellers in Piccadilly," she told the coachman as she and Mary climbed back into the Belwoods' carriage.

Hatchards had the reputation for being one of the best stocked bookshops in the city. Effie had often read about the place, but she'd never been herself. So much of London was still a mystery to her. She was uncovering it by degrees, with the aid of a good map and the guidebook she'd purchased on her arrival, both eager and wary, lest the city's much-vaunted attractions should prove to disappoint.

The coachman set them down in front of the famous shop not ten minutes later, amid the teeming traffic of the busy street. Its entrance was flanked by two large mullioned windows featuring colorful arrangements of the latest works of poetry and prose.

Effie passed through the shop's dark painted door, with Franc in her arms and Mary close behind her. Inside, several ladies and gentlemen were perusing the expansive shelves and examining the offerings on the strategically placed table displays. A few people glanced up, but most paid Effie no heed.

"You may look about at your leisure," Effie told Mary. "Or remain here if you prefer."

A row of wooden chairs was arrayed by the door. Another female servant was seated there, awaiting her mistress. Mary bobbed a curtsy before joining her.

Effie approached the shop counter, her ruffle-trimmed grenadine skirts rustling softly over her petticoats and crinoline.

A mustachioed shop assistant in a plain cloth suit came to assist her. Spying Franc, his mouth formed a moue of distaste. "May I help you, miss?"

"I hope you can," Effie said. "I require this quarter's edition of the *Westminster Review*."

The shop assistant promptly retrieved it, passing it to her across the counter. "Is that all?"

Effie flipped through the journal, distracted for a moment by the articles it contained. It was a publication known for its radicalism. Among other beliefs, it endorsed the principle of universal suffrage. "No indeed," she said, at length, recalling herself to the present. "Will you point me to your philosophical section?"

"Greek philosophies or Roman?"

"Women's philosophies," Effie replied matter-of-factly.

The shop assistant directed her toward a single shelf at the very back of the shop. Effie was thankful he didn't escort her to it himself. She required no guidance on her reading material. She knew exactly what it was she was looking for.

Her tastes had been cultivated at the Academy. The library there was filled with volumes of every sort. Miss Corvus had urged the girls to read widely and often, everything from Aristophanes and Herodotus to Machiavelli, Astell, and Wollstonecraft.

"Knowledge is your greatest weapon," she'd told them. *"And books are knowledge made manifest."*

Effie had found it to be true. Books enlarged one's mind. They encouraged one to think. To feel. To understand. They could be more than that, too, when the occasion called for it. In the absence of community, books could be companions. They could be friends.

And Effie would need friends on the lonely road she must travel to bring down Compton. Particularly now, after being barred from returning to visit Nell.

It hadn't mattered so much in Paris. There, at least, Madame Dalhousie had permitted Effie to attend women's talks on equality and education. Here in London, however, Effie had no such diversions. She was too busy keeping up an appearance of fashionable sameness to risk exposing herself as a budding revolutionary.

But the soul required sustenance, however sparse the fare.

And here at Hatchards, it appeared to be very sparse, indeed.

Effie drew her fingers over the scant collection of titles on the shelf. It was but five books altogether, one of which she'd already read, and three of which were written by men. Was this meager selection meant to represent the whole of women in London? And this at one of the largest bookshops in the city?

It was a disgrace.

She withdrew the copy of *A Practical Illustration of Women's Rights* by Mrs. Endicott. It was a recently published work. A thin volume, but it would have to suffice for now. Effie was just tucking it under her arm along with her copy of the *Westminster Review* when a shadow fell over her. A low growl vibrated in Franc's throat, announcing the presence of danger.

"Miss Flite? What a charming coincidence."

Effie froze where she stood, recognizing the gentleman's suave, almost fatherly voice. She took a split second to collect herself before lifting her gaze to Lord Compton's face.

He stood over her, dressed in an elegant wool topcoat and expensive-looking silk hat, his gray beard combed into meticulous order. The same inexplicable glitter of heat was evident in his eyes as had been there when she'd been introduced to him at the ball. This time there was no mistaking it for anything other than what it was.

Her skin crawled.

Good heavens. Had he followed her here? Had he been following her all along?

Surely not. It was a popular bookshop on one of the busiest streets in London. His presence here was likely the veriest coincidence, just as he'd said. Still . . . Effie had promised Nell she would remain on her guard.

Maintaining her composure, she bestowed the viscount with a warm smile. "My lord." She curtsied. "I did not see you there."

He bowed to her. "You were examining that book with unduly rapt attention."

"Yes, I was. It's sometimes difficult to choose a good title, is it not?" Her attention fell to the volume he held in his gloved hand. "Though you appear to have been successful."

He lifted the book briefly. It looked to be an expensive one, bound in shining green leather, its title engraved in gold. "A history of music. It is a gift for my daughter, Carena." His expression warmed with paternal fondness at the mention of the girl. "She returns from Hampshire tomorrow."

"I look forward to making her acquaintance."

"You shall meet her when she performs at our musicale." He glanced at the items Effie had chosen. "And your book? A similarly edifying text, I presume?"

"I hope it will be."

He extended his free hand to her. "May I?"

Effie's smile turned quizzical. But she could hardly refuse the man. She passed him the book, inadvertently revealing the title of the journal tucked beneath it.

His brows lifted slightly. "The *Westminster Review*?" He gave a cluck of disapproval. Turning his attention to the book, he scanned the thin spine before thumbing through the pages. "And this—a piece of radicalism if I've ever seen it."

Effie affected surprise. "Radicalism, my lord?"

"Any reasonable man would agree with the assessment." He snapped the book shut. "Does Lady Belwood know you're purchasing such subversive materials?"

"Educating myself can surely do no harm, sir."

"Publications like these are a contagion. They pollute the minds of ladies. Once inflicted, it is impossible to repair the damage." Lord Compton's tone took on a condescending edge, as though he were speaking to a child. "A girl's education is a subject for her father, and later, her husband, to decide. It is not a self-guided endeavor. Such a course would be folly for any female."

Effie inwardly recoiled at every pompous word the man uttered. If she weren't pretending to be a genteel young lady, she would know how to answer. But these were early days yet. She couldn't afford to expose herself.

"Forgive me," she said meekly. "I haven't a father."

"Your guardian, then. Lady Belwood mentioned the man." Lord Compton placed Effie's book back on the shelf. "You must leave it with him." He reached for her copy of the *Westminster Review*. "Allow me to return that rubbish to its place as well."

Franc's teeth flashed, narrowly missing the viscount's fingers.

Effie hastily stepped back before the little dog could inflict any damage. "Do take care, my lord. My poodle is rather protective of me."

Lord Compton stiffened. Withdrawing his empty hand, he dusted it on his trouser leg, as though the barest contact with Franc had sullied his glove. "That dog would benefit from a muzzle."

"Doubtless you're right," Effie said, even as she took another step backward, the swell of her skirts enforcing distance between them. Muzzle Franc? The very notion!

"A dog that bites a man is liable to be destroyed. The law permits it."

Her blood ran cold. "I couldn't bear to contemplate it. Franc means more to me than anything in the world."

"Then you must enforce civility on him."

"I shall," she lied.

The viscount's mouth curled in a thin smile. "Less radicalism and more obedience, that's what I recommend, Miss Flite. You will find it a suitable recipe for young ladies—and for dogs." He bowed to her, his eyes lingering for an extra moment on her face. "Until we meet again, my dear."

She inclined her head, her mouth gone dry. "My lord."

The viscount strolled off, heading for the counter to purchase his daughter's book. Effie was left standing in front of the ragtag shelf of women's philosophy books, her nerves all ajangle.

She'd been warned Compton was a villain, but to threaten Franc? That was taking things rather too far. Indeed, the odious man had just made things personal.

Effie gave Franc a reassuring kiss on the head. "Dreadful man," she murmured to him. "You were exactly within your rights."

"Excuse me." A woman approached the shelf behind Effie. "If you wouldn't mind?"

It was a young lady, somewhat older than Effie in appearance. She wore a plain gray dress and was possessed of an unusually serious air. The impression was aided by the glass in her silver-framed spectacles. It was surely over an inch thick.

Effie moved out of her way. "I beg your pardon. Is it these titles you're interested in? I fear the selection is rather scant."

"So I discern." Reaching up, the young lady selected the book Lord Compton had just returned to the shelf. She offered it to Effie. "I believe this is yours."

Effie met the young woman's eyes behind her spectacles. She

wondered just how much the girl had overheard. "Thank you," she said.

"Not at all."

"Ruth! Oh, there you are." A slim, handsomely dressed gentleman came to join them.

Effie recognized him at once. It was Lord Phillip Mannering, one of the young men who had danced with her at the ball and sent her flowers the day afterward. He'd returned to Brook Street once more since then, calling on Effie yesterday afternoon. A harmless enough fellow—unobjectionable in appearance, courtly in manner, and just amusing enough not to be a bore.

His face spread into a grin to see her. "Miss Flite!" He swept off his hat, sketching her a bow. "How do you do?"

"Lord Mannering."

"I see you've met m'sister. Ruth? This is Miss Flite."

Effie exchanged curtsies with Miss Mannering. "I wasn't aware Lord Mannering had a sister."

Miss Mannering gave her brother a pointed look. "I'm not surprised. My brother rarely recalls my existence himself."

Lord Mannering flushed. "Ruth's been in the country, at Luxford Place, with m'mother. She's only returned to town yesterday evening. Had to come straight to the bookshop, didn't you?"

"I've exhausted my reading material," Miss Mannering said. "I had hoped Hatchards would offer replenishment. Alas."

"Alas," Effie agreed.

Miss Mannering's eyes smiled, though her mouth remained set in a neutral line. "Farrer and Devonport in the Strand stocks a greater number of titles on the subject. I shall visit them myself when I'm not pressed for time." She turned to her brother. "Philip?"

"Yes, yes. We must dash. We're due for tea at my old aunt's house in Green Street. Can't miss it, you know. She's a right old tartar." He bowed to Effie once more. "Until we meet again, Miss Flite."

Effie bid them both good day. She was heartened to have met a fashionable young lady with some level of fellow feeling. Granted, it wasn't enough to offset the unpleasantness of her exchange with Lord Compton, but given the circumstances, Effie must take success where she could find it.

As for the viscount himself . . .

She could no longer deny that he might be capable of the things Miss Corvus had accused him of. There was something in his eyes. That odd flicker of heat when he looked at Effie. As though, deep under his mask, beneath the scrupulously crafted veneer of wisdom and civility, he was not an honorable man at all.

Today he had betrayed but a glimpse of his true nature.

Effie had marked it. For the moment, it was more than enough to spur her on. Any gentleman who compared women to dogs was long overdue for a comeuppance.

It seemed only proper that she should be the one to give it to him.

7

The following Monday evening, as Effie dressed in a dinner gown of violet foulard to attend the Comptons' musicale, she kept her mission firmly in mind. Nothing else signified, not her long-lost mother, not Gabriel Royce, and certainly not the people of the Rookery. Only the Academy mattered, and only the destruction of Compton.

She strategically placed her three glass dragonfly hairpins in the base of her rolled coiffure. Then, lifting her skirts, she used the ball of twine to secure the few small items she'd purchased to the wire and tape cage of her crinoline.

During her days at the Academy, Effie had often employed the frame of her crinoline to disguise various odds and ends. Miss Corvus had initially disapproved of the practice, bristling as she'd always done at Effie's tendency to break the rules. But Miss Corvus's disapproval hadn't lasted long. In time, she'd come to support Effie's methods, and had even encouraged the other special girls to follow her example.

Crinolines, it had transpired, were more than armor—more than a means of protecting a lady from encroachment or of asserting one's right to take up space. They were yet another method of concealment.

Lowering her petticoats and skirts back into place, Effie gave her hips an experimental shake. Her violet silk skirts swung about her in a voluminous swell of fabric. The items tied to the inside of her crinoline didn't budge.

Excellent.

Gathering her cloak and her gloves, she joined Lady Belwood in the drawing room for a preprandial drink while they awaited the carriage.

Decorated in shades of apple-green silk and antique gold brocade, the room was notable for its heavy gilt-framed portraits of grand-looking ladies and gentlemen in powdered wigs and lace. Belwood ancestors, presumably. They peered down at the present occupant of the room with expressions of well-bred disdain.

Lady Belwood's fair cheeks were already quite red. She appeared to be on her second glass of wine. "Sir Walter regrets he is unable to join us," she said from her seat on the tufted velvet settee. "His gout is paining him worse today."

Effie was unsurprised by his absence. "Was Lady Compton expecting him?"

"I should think not. Sir Walter rarely troubles himself attending society gatherings. He prizes the purity of his bloodline to such a degree, it pains him to fraternize with those of less dignified pedigree." Lady Belwood drained her glass. "Yet another reason you must refrain from inspiring talk. To learn of my connection to that *place* would likely send my husband to an early grave."

Effie withheld comment as she finished her own small glass of sherry. She could think of only one possible connection between a titled lady of esteemed pedigree and a remote orphanage for girls.

Was it possible Lady Belwood had, at some time, given up an illegitimate child to Miss Corvus's care? It would certainly explain the power Miss Corvus held over her ladyship, and her ladyship's uncommon anxiety in relation to it.

Effie's suspicions were only enhanced a few moments later when she and Lady Belwood were comfortably ensconced in the Belwoods' sumptuous coach-and-four, making the short journey to the Comptons' house in Grosvenor Square.

"Were you, ah, very young when you found your way to that place?" her ladyship asked as the carriage rolled away from Brook Street.

Effie drew her thin black velvet cloak more firmly about her. Outside the window, the cold night sky was illuminated by the silverlight glow of a waning gibbous moon. "Quite young, yes."

"And may I ask—" Lady Belwood bit her lip. "Were you orphaned by tragedy? Or were your parents—"

"My mother was very poor," Effie said. "She surrendered me to Miss Corvus."

For a sum, Effie might have added.

Or, possibly, for a bottle of gin.

That's what a girl at the Academy had said once (seconds before Effie had slapped her in response, earning yet another punishment for herself). Though how the girl would have known anything about her mother, Effie hadn't the slightest idea.

It ultimately made no difference. Whether Effie's mother had sold her for coin or for drink, the result had been the same.

"How distressing," Lady Belwood said.

"Not at all," Effie replied. "I hardly remember it." That much was true at least, unless one counted the nagging murky memories that still plagued her heart and, occasionally, her dreams.

Lady Belwood regarded Effie from her seat across the carriage. "That place has been your life, I gather. I expect you have many friends there."

"Not as many as you might imagine," Effie said.

She was in no mood to be questioned about her past. Not after her visit to St. Giles last week. And not by this fine lady who looked as though she'd never known a day of want or desperation in her life.

For as long as Effie could remember, she'd felt the ache of having been given up by her mother. It was more than a feeling of abandonment. It was a keen sense of betrayal. If Lady Belwood did have a child at the Academy, she didn't deserve to know anything about her. Not if her ladyship had chosen a life of luxury over the life of her own helpless daughter.

A pitiless reaction, perhaps, but there it was.

"You are certainly making friends here," Lady Belwood went on. "The gentlemen especially seem to admire you. If it's an offer of marriage you're seeking—"

"I am not," Effie assured her.

Marriage was the last thing she wanted. Only a fool would aspire to it. To marry was to give up one's power.

Granted, if it ever passed into law (a very big *if* in Effie's estimation), a married women's property bill would provide some protection. But it still wouldn't give a woman the same freedom she'd have if she remained unwed. Without a husband to encumber her, Effie could go where she wished and live as she chose. She envisioned a snug little flat for her and Franc when all this was over. A place entirely their own.

Lady Belwood looked at her, perplexed. "Why else would a girl of your age take part in the season?"

"To enlarge my acquaintance," Effie said vaguely.

"I see. And do the other girls . . ." The bouncing lights from the carriage lamps danced over Lady Belwood's unusually tense face. "Do any of them go into society as you have been doing?"

A rogue glimmer of compassion stirred in Effie's breast. "No, my lady. None."

Lady Belwood's countenance softened with something like relief. "Yes, well, I had thought—" She broke off. "That is, I should never have expected—"

The carriage slowed.

Her ladyship looked gratefully to the window, leaving her sentence unfinished. "Ah. I perceive we have arrived."

Effie followed her gaze as the carriage came to a halt. The

Comptons' stately white-stuccoed house was lit with torches. A liveried footman awaited them on the front step. No other carriages were lined up ahead of them. It appeared Effie and Lady Belwood were the first to arrive.

"You're a little early, my dear," Lady Compton said, greeting them in the hall. "My husband and daughter aren't yet down."

"Oh, are we? How embarrassing." Lady Belwood tittered nervously as she received a kiss on both cheeks from her hostess.

"Not at all," Lady Compton said. "This will give Miss Flite an opportunity to become acquainted with my daughter. Parker?" She caught the eye of her butler. "Show Miss Flite to Carena's room." She turned to Effie. "My daughter's maid is putting the finishing touches on her toilette. Her friends are with her—Lady Lavinia and Miss Whitbread. I'm sure they would be glad for you to join them."

"It would be my pleasure, ma'am," Effie said.

"And don't let them tarry overlong," Lady Compton added. "I can already hear the other carriages arriving."

"This way, miss," the butler said to Effie. He was a large, balding man with hard eyes and a crooked nose that appeared to have been broken several times. He motioned to the central staircase.

Effie allowed one of the footmen to take her cloak before obediently following the butler up the marble steps. She'd hoped to have a moment before the evening's activities commenced to revisit Compton's library. Then again, a connection with the man's daughter might prove useful. Either way, the acquaintance was unavoidable.

The family's apartments were on the second floor of the house. Effie followed the butler up another staircase, and down a wide, carpeted hall illuminated by wall sconces. She subtly scanned the layout of the floors as they went, taking mental note of the entrances, alcoves, and exits.

Every inch of Compton's home was a testament to his wealth and position. Rich surfaces, shimmering crystal, gilt-framed oil paintings, and sumptuous Aubusson. The house even had indoor privies, one on each floor, as Effie had learned at the ball. A single indoor privy was a luxury. But several? It was an unmeasured extravagance, the likes of which Effie had never seen, not even in Paris.

How much of Miss Corvus's fortune had gone to fund such well-bred excess? And just how had Compton managed to steal it from her? Miss Corvus was no fool to be tricked by a man, no matter how handsome he was, or how skilled at flattery.

But perhaps she hadn't been as shrewd then as she was now. Rejection and betrayal changed a person. Effie knew that firsthand.

Parker knocked on a gold-and-cream-painted door halfway down the hall. It was cracked open by a black-aproned lady's maid of indeterminate years.

"Lady Compton has sent Miss Flite to join the young ladies," Parker said to her.

The maid opened the door wider. She dropped a curtsy. "Do come in, miss."

"Thank you," Effie said.

The lady's maid admitted Effie into a luxurious sitting room decorated in shades of pink and rose. "Right this way," she said. "Miss Carena and the other young ladies are in her dressing room."

She escorted Effie through another door. It opened to a candlelit room as spacious as a dressmaker's shop. There, two young ladies in pastel silk gowns lounged on velvet-upholstered couches arrayed around a dais, sipping champagne from crystal flutes. A third young lady stood on the small platform, also drinking champagne, while two kneeling housemaids hastily mended the hem of her enormous ruffled pink skirts.

This lofty creature was surely Carena Compton.

She turned to the door as she took another drink of her champagne, ignoring the poor maids at her feet who were obliged to crawl hastily about her, reconfiguring their positions at her swirling hem.

Her white-blond hair and milky pale skin were luminous in the candle-light.

"Who is this, Meacham?" she demanded imperiously.

Effie knew better than to make impromptu judgments about people. Categorization led to sloppiness. It prevented one from seeing the facts. From observing the truth. All the same . . .

Here was a young lady Effie recognized at once for exactly what she was. A girl for whom wealth and privilege were more than a birthright. They were an identity. An unpleasant kind of girl.

Truth be told, Effie was rather relieved to discover it. She wouldn't have enjoyed ruining the father of a girl she actually liked.

"Lady Compton has sent Miss Flite to join you, miss," Meacham said.

"Miss Flite," Miss Compton repeated with a ring of disdain. "The French girl? Yes, Mama did mention something about you. As did Lord Mannering and Lord Powell. You've been entertaining them all in our absence, I hear."

"She's not French," one of the lounging ladies said with a hiccup and a giggle.

"No indeed," Effie said. "Though I have been in Paris for a long while."

"A finishing school, isn't that right?" the other lounging lady asked. "My brother heard it from one of his friends at his club."

"That is Miss Whitbread," Miss Compton said, briskly introducing the giggler. "And that is Lady Lavinia Bulstrode."

Miss Whitbread was a short, pale girl, with light brown hair and sharp, pinched features softened only slightly by the effects of her champagne. Lady Lavinia, by contrast, was tall and slim. Her profile was decidedly Grecian—an effect aided by her ribboned coiffure. Like Miss Compton, the two girls wore rich silk dresses weighted with tassels and trimmings, the cost of which would have beggared the average female.

Effie acknowledged them in turn. "A pleasure to meet you."

"Lady Lavinia and Miss Whitbread have been with me at Rawdon Court since Easter," Miss Compton said. "I never come to town for my parents' opening ball. A stuffy event. No one of importance ever attends."

Effie smiled. "I found it a fine enough affair."

"Compared to all the balls you attended in Paris?" Lady Lavinia asked.

"Nothing compares with Paris," Effie said. "Have the three of you been?"

"Steamer travel is death on one's complexion," Miss Whitbread replied. "I shouldn't like to become sallow."

"You're very tan, Miss Flite." Lady Lavinia examined Effie down the length of her aquiline nose. "Do they not use Gowland's in Paris?"

Effie's smile remained undimmed. She wondered how many young ladies their tactics had served to oppress and intimidate? To be sure, in the secret heart of her—that small, vulnerable part that beckoned back to her childhood—it was impossible for Effie not to feel a bit daunted herself. In her early years, she had often been made to feel wanting. To feel *other*.

But that was a very long time ago. Since then, she'd learned the true weakness of bullies. They were frightened creatures, really, emboldened in a group, but not undefeatable. It was rather satisfying to see them scatter.

Though she couldn't enjoy that satisfaction today. She wasn't here to score points. She was here to ingratiate herself.

"The French concept of beauty is very different from the English one," she said. "It's little surprise we Britons ape our Gallic sisters. They're years ahead of us. May I?" Effie helped herself to a flute of champagne from the tray. "I understand you will be honoring us with an aria this evening, Miss Compton."

Miss Compton pursed her lips. Swishing her skirts, she resumed her original position. The seamstresses crawled quickly to keep up. "Do you sing, Miss Flite?"

"I don't possess that gift, no." Effie sat down on a tufted pink velvet chair beside Miss Whitbread's sofa. "I prefer athletic endeavors."

"Riding?" Miss Whitbread asked.

"Target practice," Effie said, taking a sip of her drink.

She was only half in jest. The Academy had focused little effort on equestrienne activities. Horses were exceedingly expensive. Whereas archery, knife-throwing, and fencing required only the use of non-sentient implements that could be shared by all.

"The gentlemen sometimes enjoy target-shooting at Rawdon Court," Miss Compton said. "We ladies never participate. It is unbecoming to be always competing."

Effie refrained from pointing out that they were surely competing now. "How do you occupy your time instead?"

"With music and flower arranging," Miss Compton replied. "Rawdon is at its most beautiful in the spring."

"This house is quite lovely, too," Effie said. "I'm given to understand it has an extensive library."

"Does it?" Miss Whitbread asked with a dubious expression. "I never noticed."

"My father has a complete set of thirteenth-century books." Miss Compton adjusted the fluttering lace trimming on her neckline. "He collects old texts. It is his prevailing passion."

"I should like to see them, given the opportunity. Perhaps after dinner?" Effie raised her glass to her lips with studied casualness. "Unless it would disturb Lord Compton's work."

"Why should it?" Miss Compton asked.

"I recall he was conducting charitable business there during the ball last week," Effie said. It had been something to do with Gabriel. Lord Compton had mentioned it when Effie had been introduced to him. "I daresay there are many such demands on his time."

Miss Compton brushed the concern aside. "Papa never conducts important business in his library. That's only where he receives the begging public. Clergymen, social reformers, and the like, who come to plead for his aid. It's his study where he deals with affairs of true consequence."

Effie gave her an alert look.

"But not tonight," Miss Compton went on. "Mama has absolutely forbidden him from slipping away from the party since I will be singing."

Effie mentally abandoned her plans to investigate the desk in the library. The monstrous piece of furniture could wait for another day. Tonight, she would search Lord Compton's study instead. Wherever *that* was.

"If you wish to see the library, I will show it to you when the ladies retire after dinner," Miss Compton offered with the grandiosity of a medieval princess bestowing her largesse on a ragged serf. "But we cannot linger. I must have time to prepare for my solo."

"Thank you," Effie said. "I shall look forward to it."

Rising from her sofa on unsteady feet, Miss Whitbread teetered to the silk-draped window. She peered down at the street. "I knew I'd heard carriages. Lord, but it's a crush out there."

"Shall we go downstairs?" Lady Lavinia asked.

"Not yet," Miss Compton said. "Let my parents welcome the guests. I shall see them in the salon."

Lady Lavinia leaned back on her sofa with a sigh as she finished her drink. "Your father and mother have a marriage to aspire to. She is one of the most acclaimed hostesses in town, and he is so handsome and commanding."

"Handsome?" Miss Whitbread giggled from the window.

"He was," Miss Compton snapped, provoked. "Only look at his portrait in the gallery at Rawdon. He could have had anyone."

"So could your mother have had," Miss Whitbread said. "The

fortune her father left her was nearly as great as mine. And don't tell me it doesn't weigh with a gentleman."

"Do you agree, Miss Flite?" Lady Lavinia asked. "Is a fortune enough of an inducement for a gentleman seeking a wife?"

"It may not be sufficient for marriage," Miss Compton pronounced, "but it's obviously necessary. No man of our acquaintance would wed a church mouse."

Effie felt the scrutiny of the young ladies fixing upon her, equal parts curious and mean-spirited. They were plainly eager to know if *she* possessed a fortune. Under other circumstances, it would be impolite for them to ask outright, but champagne was involved, and they were in a dressing room, not a drawing room.

Miss Whitbread was the first to summon the courage. "I expect Lord and Lady Belwood have settled a goodly sum on you," she said. "She and her husband have no children of their own, and childless people must find some person on whom to bestow their fortune. As you're the only child of Lady Belwood's closest friend—"

"Oh, do be quiet, Patricia," Lady Lavinia interrupted. "Must you give voice to every vulgar thought in your head?"

"I meant no offense," Miss Whitbread said. "I'm only repeating what I've heard."

"Cease repeating it in my hearing," Miss Compton retorted, glaring at her tipsy friend. "And do turn the subject before I expire from boredom."

Effie smiled into her champagne, neither confirming nor denying the rumor.

It was all to the good if people thought her an heiress. She needed them to believe she was one of them. And to be one of them, one must have money. Not the kind earned through honest labor, but the kind bestowed on one through the privilege of one's birth and connections. *That* was the only variety of money that mattered to people like these.

The conversation resumed in another direction, with the three ladies lapsing into a discussion about their gowns, and about the gentlemen who would be in attendance at the dinner that preceded the musicale.

Soon, the small porcelain clock on the mantel was chiming the hour.

"I must go down," Miss Compton said. She pulled her skirts away from the maids around her hem. "Enough fussing. If you haven't finished by now, you're not worth your positions, and I shall tell my mother so."

The maids hastened to their feet with their sewing boxes, knees cracking and stays creaking. They were older women, their brows dotted with perspiration, and their eyes shadowed with unease.

Effie regarded them with an intense throb of fellow feeling. Servants relied on the goodwill of their employers. Any one of them was only ever a position or two away from the gutter. An unexpected dismissal or a lack of a good reference could be as damning as a death sentence, especially for female servants without family or connections.

"It's excellent work as far as I can see," Effie said to Miss Compton. She turned to the maids, smiling. "How talented with a needle you both are."

The older of the two servants remained expressionless, but the younger gave Effie a grateful look. "Thank you, miss."

Miss Compton waved them off. "Go on!" She turned to Effie before the maids departed. "Madame du Champs had her seamstresses working to finish this dress for two days and nights straight. And now to find that one of my own servants has torn the hem as they were pressing it?" She stomped down off the dais. "That I should have to tolerate such incompetence!"

"Yes, it is rather frustrating," Effie agreed. "Putting up with people one would rather send straight to the guillotine."

"They don't still guillotine people in France, do they?" Miss Whitbread asked with a horrified giggle.

"Only the ones who are very bad," Effie replied.

Miss Compton flounced to the door. Lady Lavinia and Miss Whitbread hurried to accompany her. Their backs were to Effie as they passed.

Setting aside her champagne, Effie took the opportunity to discreetly withdraw one of her dragonfly hairpins from her coiffure. She slipped it into the side of her seat cushion, obscuring it from view. Having done so, she rose to follow the young ladies down to the Comptons' palatial crimsin-and-blue salon where the guests had gathered before dinner.

The drawing room was being used for this evening's performance, and was presently off-limits to them. It was there they would congregate after their meal to hear Miss Compton and the others perform. Lady Compton had invited even more guests to enjoy that distinguished spectacle. Dinner itself was to be attended by a far more exclusive group. It was still a large one—some twenty-four people altogether. They gathered around the salon, ladies in shimmering gowns and gentlemen in pristine evening wear, engaged in varying degrees of polite conversation.

Effie's gaze immediately homed in on Lord Compton.

The gray-haired viscount stood by the enormous baroque fireplace, sober-faced and dignified, in company with two other gentlemen. One was a broad, bespectacled fellow with a crop of blazing red hair. The other—

Effie stared.

It was Gabriel Royce.

8

Gabriel had told himself he'd come to Grosvenor Square this evening purely to make the acquaintance of Lord Haverford. But the instant he set eyes on Euphemia Flite, he knew it to be a lie.

The care he'd taken when he'd dressed this evening, the onyx cuff links, the perfectly pressed suit, and even the new variety of expensive pomade in his hair, hadn't been for Haverford's benefit. They had been for *her*.

It was a bitter realization. One that prompted a sardonic smile to twist his mouth at the sight of her. Like it or not, he'd been moved to present himself as a gentleman for her sake. To show her he wasn't the brawling, bare-necked brute she'd encountered in the Rookery.

She arched a mocking brow at him in return. No longer clad in unrelieved black, she wore a short-sleeved evening gown of deep violet silk, her raven hair twisted into a roll at her nape and secured with two sparkling pins in the shape of dragonflies. It wasn't as luxurious an ensemble as those worn by the three young ladies she'd entered the room with, but there was an elegant subtlety to Euphemia's appearance that put her friends in the shade.

It took an effort not to stare.

Lord Compton's face darkened with displeasure. "My daughter, Carena," he said, wrongly presuming it was she who had caught Gabriel's attention. "If you will excuse me?"

Lord Haverford murmured his assent as their host headed away.

Compton crossed the room to greet the young ladies. On reaching them, he pressed a kiss to his daughter's cheek. A pasty girl with a haughty air about her, Miss Compton endured his tribute with the jaded insouciance of an empress receiving homage from a subject. She gestured to the young ladies surrounding her. Her court, as it were.

Compton bowed to them. His eyes lingered on Euphemia just as they had at the ball last week. She gazed up at him in response, her face lighting with a luminous smile. The viscount was visibly jolted by it.

Gabriel observed his reaction with a flare of scorn. Bloody fool. Couldn't he see when he was being manipulated by a woman? Euphemia wasn't interested in Compton. Not that way. Gabriel would wager his last farthing on it.

She was toying with him like a cat, for some unfathomable reason of her own, and doing so with extraordinary ease. The more Gabriel saw of her, the more he recognized it. She possessed the uncanny ability to turn up the flame of her beauty the way others might turn up the flame of an oil lamp. She dimmed it or brightened it according to her company—shaping the effect to her mysterious will.

But it wasn't genuine for all that. Gabriel recognized that, too.

Last week, he'd been the beneficiary of one of her authentic smiles. It had been as unlike the expression she was bestowing on Compton as a blazing summer day was to the blackest night. Nothing else could have prompted Gabriel to behave as he had.

"Do you know that young lady?" Lord Haverford asked. Barely forty years of age, he was a younger man than Gabriel had expected— stout and ginger-haired, with a serious aspect about him.

"Miss Compton?" Gabriel answered, purposely misunderstanding him. "I've not had the pleasure."

"Not her," Lord Haverford said. "The young lady Lord Compton is speaking with. The one with the diamond dragonflies in her hair."

They weren't diamonds. Gabriel could identify paste when he saw it. Euphemia had worn the same hairpins to the ball—false stones in a false setting. They struck him as more a personal peculiarity than a flawed attempt at exaggerating her wealth. Nothing else in her person would lead one to believe she was lacking in money.

"That lady is Miss Flite," he grudgingly admitted. "Lady Belwood's ward."

"You must introduce me," Lord Haverford said. "The fresh crop of eligible misses each season is the only thing that makes these society events interesting."

Gabriel had about as much intention of introducing Haverford to Euphemia Flite as he had in becoming an aeronaut. But he wasn't about to let his personal inclinations get in the way of his business aims. "If it's diversion you require, you'll want to hear my plans for St. Giles."

Haverford's attention returned to Gabriel. He gave him an indulgent smile. "Compton mentioned you were interested in charity."

"Is that all he's said?"

"The substance of it."

Gabriel concealed a flare of irritation. He had some idea of what Compton had told Haverford. Something about Gabriel's distasteful origins, very likely, and how Gabriel had managed to rise above them to find himself here tonight—less a guest than an object of Compton's generosity.

The mention of Wingard's name in the *Courant* may have served to force the viscount back into line, but he was still far from being a willing partner. There had been a furious glint in his eyes as he'd welcomed Gabriel this evening. A look that made it clear he'd far rather see Gabriel dangling from the end of a rope than entering the Comptons' Grosvenor Square mansion with the other guests.

"Not charity," Gabriel said. "What this project requires is someone with foresight."

"I've frequently been called progressive in my views," Haverford acknowledged. "I presume that's why you asked Compton for an introduction."

"St. Giles needs progressive thinking. With adequate housing and sewage in place, the Rookery would cease to be a bed of indigence and disease. It could become a respectable neighborhood."

"You're talking about reforming the slum."

"I am."

"Most would rather eradicate it."

"They haven't succeeded yet."

Haverford chuckled. "No, indeed. Despite all efforts." He leaned back against the mantel, examining Gabriel. "What's your interest?"

"I spent most of my youth there," Gabriel replied frankly. He expected Haverford to recoil, but the man only looked at him with increased attentiveness. "I know firsthand what the good people of the Rookery must endure, living in such vile conditions."

"And you raised yourself up from those conditions, did you? But you must have done to find yourself in our company. Compton doesn't invite just anyone to his parties."

"I've made something of a name for myself, yes."

"Yet still you concern yourself with the Rookery? Most men wouldn't have looked back."

Gabriel smiled wryly. "An error on their parts. Men who don't look back never see what's coming for them."

Haverford laughed again before growing serious. "I take an interest in slum conditions. Especially now, with the threat of another cholera epidemic. The sickness finds a ready home in filth and squalor. With the Rookery located in the center of our finest neighborhoods, it puts us all at risk. It doesn't make sense not to either reform it or to wipe it out completely. Many gentlemen prefer the latter solution."

"As I said," Gabriel repeated, "they haven't succeeded yet."

Haverford nodded, frowning. "It's a complex issue. The St. Giles district is governed by a Board of Works. It's they who are charged with overseeing new construction, sewage, and paving."

Gabriel had some familiarity with the Board. It was an elected body of gentlemen of the civil parish, covering not only St. Giles, but the larger area of St. George Bloomsbury. "None of them have an interest in preserving the Rookery. I'd say the opposite."

"That may be true, but the Board is a changeable body. One third of the men are replaced every year. Which makes your timing somewhat fortuitous. Elections for the vacant seats are to be held at the end of this month. It could bring in new blood. New ideas."

"Or more of the same."

"That depends on the men who are running," Haverford said. He gave another thoughtful nod. "We should discuss this more, but not here. No one wishes to hear about sewage plans at a gathering of this sort. Shall we withdraw to the library during the musical portion of the evening? Unless you have a great desire to hear Miss Compton perform."

"No desire at all," Gabriel said.

The next moment, a footman materialized at the entrance of the salon to announce that dinner was served. Lady Compton fluttered about, making certain the order of precedence was maintained as the guests made their way to the Compton's expansive, wood-paneled dining room.

A low-hanging chandelier illuminated a long, damask-covered table laid with a lavish display of china, crystal, and plate. Flower arrangements ran down the table's center—pink roses and ferns spilling over the gold epergnes that held them. Footmen stood on either side in the shimmering candlelight, silently waiting to do their mistress's bidding.

Gabriel presumed that, given his pedigree, he would be seated miles away from Compton and the other high-ranking lords and ladies. He wasn't wrong.

"I've put you here, Mr. Royce," Lady Compton said, ushering him to a seat at the bottom of the table. A raven-haired lady in a violet dinner dress was standing near it, her shapely back to them. "Ah! And here is your charming seat partner, Miss Flite."

Euphemia turned.

Gabriel's heart thudded hard.

"You have already been introduced, as I recall," Lady Compton said before floating away to see to her other guests.

Euphemia stood by her chair for a moment, looking at him in silence.

"I told you we'd meet again," he said.

"Did you know then that you would be here tonight?" she asked.

"I did." He pulled out her chair for her before the footman could do it.

She sat down. "You might have said."

"Do you suppose I'm here for you?" he asked, pushing in her chair.

"I wouldn't be so presumptuous," she said.

Gabriel sat down beside her. Catching the soft fragrance of her perfume—some maddening decoction of honey and black currants—his heart gave another heavy double thump. Stupid. They were dining together, yes, but not alone somewhere, just the two of them. There were countless other people stretching down the length of the table. Lady Belwood, Lord Haverford, and Compton himself. And yet . . .

There was a kind of privacy at a party of this size. Amid the overlapping voices and the clink of crystal and cutlery, one could address one's seat partner as candidly as one chose. Providing they didn't betray that frankness by their expression, no one would be the wiser.

"Though you did say we'd meet again when you had information for me," she reminded him. Her voice sank, adding, "About Grace."

"So I did." He'd also kissed her hand—an equally inane action.

His blood had been up after the incident at Mother Comfort's, and he'd been battling the influence of a mighty attraction.

Her face lit with guarded expectation. "And do you?"

"No," he said bluntly. Once out of her company, common sense had prevailed. He'd come to regret both his promise and his reckless tribute to her. Who knew where either might lead?

"But you *did* make inquiries?" she asked.

"It's been less than a week."

"Ample time, surely."

Gabriel flashed her a dark look. She was a lady used to twining idiotic men around her finger. Despite recent evidence to the contrary, he refused to be one of them. "Do you imagine I have nothing else to occupy me? I've a business to run, and my own affairs to see to." He draped his napkin on his lap. "Church Lane and Devil's Acre aren't going anywhere."

The faint glimmer of hope in her face flickered out. "In other words, you intend to prioritize all your other commitments ahead of the one you made to me."

"I prioritize them according to importance."

"Their importance to *you*."

"Who else?"

He may as well have told her *she* wasn't important. She reacted just the same.

The mask of impenetrable composure she so often wore slipped back into place. She was in every appearance ladylike. Untouchable. Only the faint thread of disappointment that seeped into her voice hinted at her true feelings. "That's the precise trouble with relying on other people. If they don't let you down outright, they take their sweet time in doing so, wasting your own time in the bargain."

He regarded her with mild amusement. "I didn't take you for a cynic."

"A realist. I could more easily have gone myself."

"I wouldn't advise it," he said. "Your parasol notwithstanding."

"If you believe a parasol is the only weapon I have in my arsenal, Mr. Royce, allow me to say you don't know me at all."

Gabriel's mouth tugged reflexively at one corner. He didn't allow himself to crack a smile. He had no intention of encouraging whatever self-destructive madness it was that compelled her to venture into the London slums. "If your interests lie elsewhere, why are you here tonight?" he asked. "Looking to burnish your acquaintance with Compton?"

"Is that so objectionable?"

"What was he saying to you earlier?"

"He was describing the size of his book collection. Did you know he collects medieval texts?"

"I neither know, nor care." Gabriel's brows sank with sudden suspicion. "You're not planning to visit his library again, I trust."

She unfolded her snowy white napkin and placed it on her lap as the footmen began serving dinner. "I shall soon be well acquainted with the place, never fear. Miss Compton is giving me a tour of it after dinner."

He dropped his voice. "All the easier to search it when everyone's distracted at the musicale? Don't bother. Lord Haverford and I will be using it then."

"Oh?"

"We have business to discuss about St. Giles."

Her dark blue eyes flicked to his with a spark of genuine interest. "Is he going to help you implement your ideas for reform?"

Gabriel was caught by her gaze. "I'm reserving hope."

With all the guests seated, the soup course was served. The footmen started at the top of the table, and worked their way down, ladling out potage à la julienne into each of the guests' dishes. Parker moved among them, pouring out the wine.

Gabriel kept an eye on the man as he came to fill his glass. Parker's face tightened as he poured. It plainly rubbed him on the raw to be serving a man like Gabriel. Servants were often as arrogant as their employers when it came to questions of rank, but Parker was more than snobbish. There was a ferocity to him that made every movement feel a threat. At least, where Gabriel was concerned.

Where had Compton found him? And what was he using him for? It couldn't only be for pouring wine and conveying cream-laid invitations to parties.

Turning his head, Gabriel caught Euphemia observing the man, too. For a split second he had the uncanny impression that she was wondering the same thing he was. She had a thoughtful frown in her gaze as Parker poured her wine. Only when he, and the footman who served her soup, had passed on to the gentleman on her opposite side (Lord Mannering, by God!) did she resume the conversation she and Gabriel had been having.

"How would you do it?" she asked, picking up her silver soup spoon. "Reform St. Giles, I mean."

He downed a swallow of wine. It was pale ruby in color, delicately fragrant and smooth as silk, with no trace of sourness to it. As ever, nothing but the best for Compton. The man had a weakness for fine things.

"Did you attend the Great Exhibition?" Gabriel asked abruptly.

Euphemia's lush mouth quirked at the brusque change of subject. "No. I was but a child of ten or eleven then, and not at liberty to do as I pleased."

"I was a bit older," he said.

The Great Exhibition had taken place in 1851. Housed in the Crystal Palace—a sparkling cast iron and plate glass building erected in Hyde Park—it had showcased the finest Britain had to offer in the way of industry and design. It had also presented the art and inventions of other nations. People had traveled from all over to goggle at the displays.

Gabriel had been seventeen at the time, swiftly rising through the ranks of Rookery villains. Miles had gone away for his apprenticeship. Rose Quincey had died. There was no one to soften Gabriel's hard edges any longer, and nothing to stand in the way of his worst instincts.

With its ever-changing crowds of tourists, the Crystal Palace had been a prime spot for thieving. It was what had brought Gabriel there on that particular day, but it hadn't been what had possessed him to linger.

"Prince Albert had a model lodging house on display," he said. "It was built full scale beside the Crystal Palace. A structure of red brick, made large enough for four families, with windows, insulation, and other necessities. It sparked my imagination."

Euphemia sipped her soup. "You must have seen many similar houses in London."

"Not in the Rookery. The dwellings there were in a deplorable state. They still are, what remains of them. Imagine the improvement if those old buildings were replaced with brick lodging houses like the ones from the Exhibition."

Her brow furrowed. "You believe that would solve the Rookery's problems?"

"Many of those problems arise from overcrowding. Not only disease and despair, but drunkenness as well."

"How do one's living conditions affect one's sobriety?"

"When too many people lodge in a single room, the inmates fall prey to thieving. Rather than see their wages stolen while they sleep, they drink their earnings."

"You're jesting."

"I'm not. It happens with unfortunate regularity. Fear of theft leads to drunkenness, and drunkenness leads to every other vice. Men lose their jobs, they lose their wages, and they end up in even more degraded circumstances."

The phenomenon wasn't limited to the Rookery. It happened in every slum, in every corner of the realm. Gabriel had experienced it firsthand in Birmingham. His miserable wretch of a father had drunk away the last of their meager savings on a three-day binge that had ended with him stumbling into the cut and drowning. Only eleven at the time, Gabriel had been called to identify his father's gin-soaked carcass the following morning. In that case, it hadn't only meant the loss of Gabriel's lodgings. It had meant the loss of everything.

Gabriel had eventually stolen enough coin to get him to London. At the time, he'd believed he might have an uncle living there who would take him in. It had proven to be another of his father's many lies. There had been no uncle, only the same brutal existence Gabriel had endured in the Black Country, this time suffered entirely on his own.

He'd come a long way since then. All the way here to a viscount's table, sitting beside Euphemia Flite. It was a great deal too far to fall. Gabriel had no intention of doing so.

Raising her spoon, Euphemia took another dainty sip of her soup. "What of the women?"

Gabriel attended to his own soup. Like the wine, the creamy blend of potatoes, butter, and vegetables was silky and rich with flavor. Yet another testament to Compton's wealth. There was no blandness or bitterness in his fare.

"What about them?" he asked.

"When men fall into vice and degradation, every woman with whom they're connected must partake of it, too. Their wives, their daughters. Even women unknown to them. Only consider how that lout behaved toward me last week."

Gabriel's jaw tightened briefly at the reminder. If not for Ollie coming to fetch him, Gabriel would never have known Euphemia had gone to Mother Comfort's. She'd have been trapped there on her own, with only her parasol and her dog to protect her. Her seemingly bottomless well of self-confidence notwithstanding, Gabriel doubted she'd have walked out of the place unscathed.

"And that was nothing compared to what the man's wife must endure," Euphemia said. "He only insulted me. He didn't have a legal right to my earnings or my property."

Gabriel seemed to have lost the thread of the conversation. *Had* that ruffian been married? And if Gabriel didn't know the answer, how in the hell did Euphemia? "I don't follow," he said. "What does the man's wife have to do with it?"

"Not just his wife, but the wives of all men like him. A man who drinks his wages, and who shortly finds himself unemployed, will inevitably turn his eye to his wife's earnings. He'll soon run through those as well, impoverishing them both. The law allows him to do so."

Gabriel looked at her in dawning realization. This time his heart did more than beat heavily. It seemed to stop beating entirely. "Good God," he uttered. "I might have known you were a bluestocking."

The signs had all been there. Her confidence. Her singularity. The way she spoke and moved, with such uncommon sense of purpose. He felt a fool not to have recognized it before.

Strong, intelligent women had always been his weakness. He blamed it on the example set by Miles's mother, Rose. She'd been something of a bluestocking, too, with her forward-thinking ways, and her determination to better herself and her son despite all the odds against her.

The granite wall of Gabriel's already weakened defenses began to crumble.

Euphemia smiled slightly. "Label me what you will, the facts remain the same. If it's reform you're after, you must consider the women's situation as something distinct from the men's."

"You presume this won't help them, just because it helps the men as well?"

"I make no presumption. I only ask—"

"Many a widow with children to raise would benefit from decent housing. The mother of one of my friends had to bring him up in a room no larger than a cupboard. They froze in winter, and near suffocated from the stench in the summer. The rotting walls were thin as paper, and the street outside a cesspit. And she was one of the fortunate ones."

Euphemia's spoon stilled halfway to her mouth. She lowered it back to her soup dish untouched.

"I can't speak to the laws governing women," he said. "All I can do is try to help the people of St. Giles. Adequate housing would have a favorable impact on men, women, and children alike. Not to mention the drainage issues in the Rookery and the refuse—" He stopped himself.

Bloody hell. Was he seriously telling her about drains and cesspits?

Her honest interest in his plans had set him talking unguarded, just the way he might talk to Lord Haverford or another man of his ilk. But Euphemia wasn't a gentleman reformer. She was a lady. And while Gabriel may not be a gentleman, neither was he an idiot.

He set down his soup spoon. "Forgive me. For a moment, I forgot whom I was addressing."

Euphemia didn't appear offended by the turn their conversation had taken. "What does it matter whom you're addressing? If people can endure living in such conditions, the rest of society can certainly endure hearing about them."

"But not, I should imagine, at a dinner party."

Again, a hint of a smile touched her lips. The subtle expression went through Gabriel like a lightning strike.

"Perhaps that's exactly the trouble," she said. "This persistent unwillingness to see or hear anything unpleasant. As though if we don't know about a problem, the problem doesn't exist. I find that very small-minded. It's far better to face a thing head-on."

"I agree," Gabriel said. "It's what I mean to do in St. Giles." That it would benefit him personally didn't negate the rightness of it.

She hesitated a moment. "May I ask . . ."

"Ask anything you like."

"Very well." She looked into his eyes. "Just how is it you run St. Giles? You never answered before."

"No, I didn't."

"Well?" she pressed him. "Did the residents employ some mechanism to elect you as their spokesman? Or is your role self-appointed?"

Gabriel's heart took on a leaden weight. No longer thumping erratically, it was a millstone in his chest, sinking straight to the dark abyss of his soul.

She didn't know who or what he was yet. Despite having met him in St. Giles. Despite having seen him dispatch that drunkard in Mother Comfort's. She was under the illusion, just as Lord Haverford seemed to be, that Gabriel was simply a man of humble origins who had, with hard work and honest effort, managed to rise above the bleakness of his circumstances.

But there was no hiding the truth.

Even here among the guests tonight, sprinkled amid the lords and ladies to whom Gabriel's name was unknown, there were plenty who knew firsthand of his brutality. Gentlemen who had regularly visited Gabriel's betting shop. Some who still owed him money.

He raised his wineglass. "Both," he answered. "I run St. Giles because I'm the most powerful man in it. My betting shop is at the heart of the Rookery. It's how I've earned my fortune, *and* my reputation. Ask any number of the young gentlemen here tonight. They've all been at my mercy at one time or another." His mouth curled in a humorless smile. "And I've precious little mercy, Miss Flite, as anyone who crosses me soon discovers."

9

Effie spent the next several courses in conversation with Lord Mannering. It wasn't by preference. Talking to each of one's seat partners was a polite requirement at a dinner party. That much had been drilled into Effie's head during Miss Pascal's classes at the Academy.

"One must never commit the sin of speaking to only one seat partner all evening," Miss Pascal had said. *"Vary your partner, just as you vary your conversation."*

"If our seat partners are all men," Gemma Sparrow had retorted with a mutinous scowl, *"what conversation can possibly be had?"*

"You may discuss the weather," Miss Pascal had replied, unruffled. *"Or the character of the wine."*

"Or the character sitting on your opposite side," Gemma had said under her breath.

"On no account," Miss Pascal had shot back sternly. *"Never talk about other people. It is the mark of a small and common mind. And never discuss religion or the politics of the nation. Your opinions on such weighty subjects are your own concern. Don't inflict them on strangers through the vehicle of speech. Your power lies in your ability to conceal."*

By that reckoning, Effie had just spent the first half of her meal giving away her power to Gabriel Royce. She'd been so thoroughly engaged in speaking with him, she hadn't thought to conceal her feelings at all. Not on the subject of women's welfare. She'd spoken to him candidly, honestly, and with a distinct lack of self-restraint.

If not for Miss Pascal's dratted rules for dining etiquette, Effie would be speaking to Gabriel still. Indeed, their conversation had just started to get interesting.

He was, it transpired, exactly what she'd suspected him of being: a dangerous man. Worse, even. A merciless man, as he'd confessed himself.

And yet, nothing so straightforward as that. A true villain wouldn't be attempting to reform the Rookery. He wouldn't be here at all, subjecting himself to the snubs and slights of his supposed betters, all so he might gain influential patrons to affect his ideas for reform.

"A betting shop," Lord Mannering confirmed in a low voice in Effie's ear. "What does Compton mean by inviting him here? He may as well have invited my tailor and bootmaker as well."

"You object to keeping company with working men?" Effie asked as she finished her small portion of curried lobster.

"I'm no relic," Lord Mannering said. "I'm as open-minded as the next fellow. But I say . . . one doesn't expect to meet a villain of that sort across the table. It puts a man off his feed."

Effie hadn't noticed any lack of appetite on his lordship's part. He'd eaten everything placed in front of him with remarkable gusto. Effie herself had taken only a light sustenance. She didn't want rich sauces and heavy starches weighing her down as she embarked on her mission this evening.

A gentleman's study could be located anywhere in a house—downstairs, upstairs, or even in the attic. Time would be of the essence. Though Miss Compton had claimed her father would remain in the drawing room for the entire musicale, the viscount was only guaranteed to be fully occupied for as long as his daughter took to perform her aria. Any additional minutes after that would be a gift.

Effie would have to work quickly.

It was some relief Gabriel would be engaged in the library with Lord Haverford once the music started. Effie didn't much fancy a repeat of what had happened when she was searching Compton's desk during the ball. As it was, her path would be almost entirely clear. She'd only have to manage the servants, and that should be easy enough. Providing one of those servants wasn't the Compton's butler, Parker.

"Good thing m'sister didn't come tonight," Lord Mannering went on. "Shouldn't have liked her to be exposed to the lower orders. Not that she'd object, mind. Always going to lectures and radical whatnot, she is."

"Was she otherwise engaged this evening?" Effie asked.

"Some committee meeting or other. Claimed it couldn't be missed. Not as if she'd be performing in any case. Ruth don't like singing to people. She prefers talking at them."

"I'm sorry not to see her again." Effie meant it. It would be nice to have a like-minded acquaintance or two in town. Someone to talk to with something like candor. Thus far, she'd only revealed her views to Gabriel. A bluestocking, he'd called her. The name was surely tame in comparison to Effie's and the other Academy girls' true predilections.

"Will you be performing this evening, Miss Flite?" Lord Mannering asked.

"Indeed not," Effie replied. "I rarely perform for strangers."

As she spoke, she felt the weight of Gabriel's gaze. He'd looked at her more than once since she'd turned her attention to Lord Mannering. Doubtless he was bored. The lady on his left was Miss Whitbread. What they could have to converse about was anyone's guess.

"But you do play and sing?" Lord Mannering asked.

"A very little," she said. "I prefer needlework."

It was lately the truth. On the rare nights when she and Lady

Belwood weren't engaged elsewhere, Effie had been spending her evenings working on a series of samplers. They contained the alphabet in neat lines at the bottom, various scenes from town at the top, and the requisite raven with its white-tipped wing.

Effie didn't enjoy the exercise as much as Nell surely did, but the samplers were ready should Effie require them. All that remained was to add in the necessary code. It could be numbers stitched outright, or numbers displayed in the form of a flock of birds, depending on the length of the message. To make it less easy for strangers to solve should the sampler fall into the wrong hands, the special girls at the Academy knew to transpose threes and sixes, nines and twelves, and the letters E and W.

With luck, Effie would be sending off a sampler to Nell within a day. It all hinged on what she might find in Compton's study.

After the final course had been served, and the guests had partaken of even more wine, Lady Compton rose from her place at the top of the table and signaled for the ladies to join her in retiring to the salon for coffee. The gentleman stood, remaining on their feet until the ladies had withdrawn from the room. As Effie passed Gabriel, their eyes met. There was no sign of warmth or familiarity in his gaze. To be sure, he looked at her rather as he had on the first occasion they'd met. There was a certain coldness and distance about him, which she hoped was more for the other guests' benefit than it was for her alone.

Either way, it was the least of Effie's concerns. She had her visit to the library with Miss Compton to get through, and then a short period spent with the other ladies in the salon, before she could set her plan in motion.

Miss Compton dutifully—and rather impatiently—collected Effie on the way out of the dining room. "We don't have long," she said.

True to her word, her tour of the library was both brief and perfunctory. Effie had expected nothing less. She wandered obediently behind her young hostess, taking private note of the room's cabinets, corners, and groupings of overstuffed leather sofas and chairs. Among them was the same chair Gabriel had been seated in last week, watching her from across the room, his face lit by the infernal smolder of his cigarette. A prickle of awareness lifted the fine hairs on the back of Effie's neck to recall it.

But the library wasn't dark this time, and there was no ravening wolf lurking in the shadows. The gaslights were turned up, revealing a room that was, in essentials, no different from the libraries in dozens of other fine houses.

"These are the books you were asking about," Miss Compton said boredly. She indicated a single row of ten large, flat-spined leather volumes lining a shelf near the fireplace. "Dry old things, and all in Latin. Heaven knows what they're about. Some long-dead flora or fauna, I'm told."

Effie joined Miss Compton at the shelf. She didn't have to feign interest. Old books were a subject of fascination to her. "May I?" she asked.

Miss Compton granted her permission with a flick of her white hand. "If you wish."

Effie carefully extracted one of the tall books from the shelf. The medieval binding was sewn on with some manner of cord. It was infinitely fragile in her hand as she opened it. The book's thin vellum pages were equally fragile—as delicate as butterfly wings. She handled them with care, turning to the book's first page. It contained a small illumination. Time had faded it, but the image of a man, a snake, a raven, and a lion was still discernable. The illustration was surrounded by handwritten text.

Effie had been taught enough Latin at the Academy to decipher some of the words. "It's a translation of Aristotle's *Historia Animalium*."

Miss Compton lifted her brows. "I wouldn't know."

Effie turned another dry page and another, examining the images and the words. A faint fragrance stirred from within the bindings. The smell of ash, smoke, and leather. And something else.

It was a scent Effie knew, but couldn't seem to recall. A trace of dusky floral intrigue, edged with the unmistakable sweetness of decay.

"Where did your father find such treasures?" Effie asked.

Miss Compton was occupied in smoothing her skirts. She cast the book a disinterested glance. "They've been in our family for generations."

"Hmm." Closing the book, Effie slowly returned it to the shelf. Whatever the fragrance was that had tugged at her memory, it was of little consequence at present. She had a more important mystery to solve. "I'm astonished your father doesn't keep them in his study," she said, "as precious as they are."

"It would hardly be convenient for guests to view them there," Miss Compton replied as though Effie were a half-wit.

"Oh?" Effie gave her young hostess a suitably guileless look. "Is his study so far removed from the rest of the house?"

"It's adjacent to his bedchamber." Miss Compton moved toward the door with sharp impatience. "If you're quite finished?"

Effie's mouth curved into a slow smile. "Not quite. But don't worry. I shan't keep you any longer." She followed Miss Compton into the hall.

Miss Compton looked back at her with grudging civility. "If those old books truly interest you, you may come again another day. My father wouldn't mind it, and I daresay you and I will be seeing more of each other during the season. The connection is scarcely avoidable."

Effie registered the insult, but took no offense from it. She must have a reason to return here, and no number of balls or dinners would ever provide sufficient enough excuse. For that, she needed to cultivate an acquaintance with Compton's daughter. "I should like that very much," she replied.

She and Miss Compton returned to the salon. By that time, the gentlemen had joined the ladies, along with dozens of other guests who had come expressly to hear the music.

Effie didn't see Gabriel in the crowd. Nor could she find Lord Haverford. She presumed they had already taken themselves off to have their discussion about St. Giles.

That was one problem dealt with.

She accompanied Lady Belwood to the drawing room for the musical portion of the evening. Best to keep near her hostess for this part. It was less risk than sitting with Miss Whitbread or Lady Lavinia, either of whom might take undue notice when Effie slipped away.

The Comptons' large, Japanese silk–papered drawing room had been transformed for the event. The doors between it and the connecting room had been thrown open, making one enormous, high-ceilinged space. Row upon row of upholstered chairs were arrayed around a makeshift stage on which stood a piano and a harp. Two footmen at the entrance of the room distributed printed programs to each of the guests as they entered.

Effie urged Lady Belwood to a pair of straight-backed chairs near the exit.

"So far from the stage," Lady Belwood said. "Should we not sit closer?"

"No indeed," Effie replied, taking her seat. "These chairs are perfect."

Lady Belwood appeared doubtful, but she didn't argue. Sitting down beside Effie, she opened her program. "Oh, look! Miss Compton is singing 'Com'è bello! Quale incanto.'"

"How delightful." Effie opened her own program, perusing the order of pieces to be performed. Four young ladies were preceding

Miss Compton with lighter works, and several more would come after her, singing both classical and popular pieces in solos and duets.

Glancing up from her program, Effie scanned the crowd for Lord Compton. She found him by the door on the opposite side of the room. He appeared just as solemn and respectable as on the previous occasions they'd met. There was no sign of the monster lurking within. Except . . .

Except that earlier, when he'd come to greet his daughter in the salon, he'd given Effie the same variety of ominous, glittering look he'd bestowed on her at the ball and at Hatchards. A look that only seemed to increase in heat each time Effie crossed his path.

Whatever else he was hiding, Lord Compton couldn't hide he was attracted to her.

It wasn't a crime in and of itself. Still, it was something.

He stood across the room, the gracious host, poised next to his fashionable wife as she smiled and fluttered her fan. They remained on their feet until all their guests were seated. Only then did Lord Compton sit down in the first row.

Effie breathed an inward sigh of relief. There would be no missing him there. So long as he remained as he'd promised his daughter, Effie would count it safe for her to leave.

Lady Compton mounted the stage, her crystal-beaded silk dinner dress glimmering in the candlelight. She introduced the first performer—an insipid-looking child barely out of the schoolroom. Her accompanists joined her on the stage, one on the piano and one playing the violin. Her stilted performance was followed by another young lady and then another, possessed of varying degrees of talent.

Effie bided her time. Only when Carena Compton was standing atop the stage, and her three accompanists along with her, did Effie prepare to make her move.

The first notes of the aria from *Lucrezia Borgia* sounded, and Miss Compton's mouth opened in impeccably trained harmony. She had a fine soprano voice. Rather more than fine, if Effie was being generous. The guests sat up straight in their seats, some leaning forward, listening to the hypnotic notes of the aria with rapt attention.

Effie chose that very moment to touch a hand to her hair. "Oh no," she breathed.

Lady Belwood gave her a distracted glance. "Is something wrong?"

"I've lost one of my hairpins," Effie said.

Lady Belwood flashed a dubious look at the cut glass dragonflies in Effie's hair. "Have you?"

"I had three of them and now there are only two." Effie lowered her voice to an urgent whisper. "I believe I know where I left it. If you will excuse me?"

"Must you go looking for it *now*?"

"I won't be five minutes." Clutching her skirts in her hand, Effie stood and, as Miss Compton hit a high note, slipped silently out the doors of the drawing room.

A small crowd of servants had gathered in the hall to listen to the music. At the sight of Effie emerging, they scattered like a herd of frightened deer. Parker wasn't among their number. Effie's heartbeat quickened. If he wasn't here, where was he?

There wasn't time to discover it.

She walked purposefully toward the stairs. As she moved to ascend them, she was nearly bowled over by a harried housemaid racing down the steps with her sewing box.

"Beg pardon, miss!" the servant gasped, coming to an unsteady halt.

Effie recognized her. It was the younger of the two maids who had been attending to Miss Compton's torn hem earlier. "Not at all," she said. "Where are you off to in such a rush?"

"The ladies' retiring room," the maid replied. "Lady Fiona is performing after Miss Compton, and she's just discovered that the trimming on her sleeve has come loose."

"An emergency to be sure." Effie mounted the stairs. "Don't let me keep you."

The maid flashed a desperate look toward the ladies' retiring room as she followed in Effie's wake. "Do you need help with something?"

"Nothing to trouble you." Effie glanced back with a smile of explanation. "I believe I may have left my jeweled hairpin in Miss Compton's room."

"Shall I send Miss Meacham to assist you? She's in the retiring room, but—"

"No, indeed. I can retrieve it easily enough myself." Effie paused. "Providing you remind me which door it is?"

The maid's brow puckered. "Fourth from the right, miss."

"Thank you." Effie affected a look of relief as she entered the upstairs hall. "I thought I'd recognize it myself, but you know how it is in a house of this size. All the doors look alike." She again smiled back at the maid. "I shouldn't like to wander into his lordship's room by mistake."

The maid gave a weak smile in return. "No danger of that, miss. The master's room is at the end of the hall." She hovered at the top of the steps. "Are you certain you don't need—"

"Never mind me," Effie said. "Hadn't you best make haste to Lady Fiona? She'd never forgive either of us if she was obliged to perform with a loose piece of trimming."

Relief washed over the maid's worried face. She bobbed a curtsy. "Thank you, miss," she said gratefully, and turning, she dashed back down the steps with her sewing box clasped in front of her.

Effie waited until the maid was gone from sight before continuing down the hall. If Lord Compton's private study was adjacent to his bedchamber, the door to that chamber was the obvious point of access. She headed for it with single-minded intent. It was a large door. One that rather put her in mind of the door to Bluebeard's chamber.

And well it should.

Herein slept the man who had stolen Miss Corvus's fortune. Who had tricked her and betrayed her, and who—if permitted to—might use his position to affect the safety and security of all women. Effie had her own private reasons for wishing his destruction, but she was still keenly sensitive to the larger picture.

She stopped at the door and listened, one hand resting lightly on the doorknob. There was no sound from within. If Parker or his lordship's valet were inside, they were taking pains to disguise their presence, and Effie knew of no reason why they should.

Steeling herself, she opened the door to Compton's room and entered.

10

Lord Compton's bedroom was awash in darkness. Effie stopped inside, the door clicking shut behind her. She blinked into the murk, willing her eyes to adjust.

This time, there was no Gabriel Royce to light a friction match. Fortunately, Effie hadn't come unprepared. Raising her skirts, she felt for the small taper candle she'd tied to the wires of her cage crinoline. It was still there, along with the small candleholder, and the silver vesta case.

Unlike regular friction matches, vesta matches were made of wax, with red phosphorus tips. One could strike them anywhere. Effie waited to do so until she was certain there was no one else in the room. Only then did she light her candle. It produced just enough of a flame for her to see in front of her.

Like his daughter's bedroom, Lord Compton's chamber was of an enormous size. In the dim glow of the candle, Effie beheld a monstrous mahogany four-poster bed, several towering wardrobes, and a full-sized sofa and chairs arranged around a marble fireplace. A bank of windows lined the opposite wall, the glass covered in thick folds of velvet draperies.

Effie moved past them toward the open door across the room. It led to his lordship's dressing room and bathing chamber, the luxury of which seemed to her even greater than in his bedroom. But Effie didn't have time to reflect on Compton's propensity for extravagance, nor on the possibility that some of that extravagance had been funded by Miss Corvus. She kept her eyes ahead of her, scanning every surface as she went, lest—like that night in the library—she should be taken unaware.

She found Compton's study on the other side of his bathing room. Entering it in the tiny halo of candlelight, Effie's already fizzing pulse surged with a mixture of anxiety and anticipation. She couldn't think when she'd have another opportunity such as this. She was determined to make the most of it.

The study was small in comparison to the other rooms. It contained a secretary desk, a chest of drawers, and several leather chairs. Two bookcases rose on either side of the desk. They held row upon row of thick, leather-bound volumes, their titles stamped in gold on the spines. No medieval texts, these. They were books on geography, history, and law.

Effie skimmed the titles on her way to the desk. Were these books more personal to him than the ones in his library? If they were, it wasn't readily apparent why.

She sat down in the chair in front of his desk. Placing her candle atop the surface, she quietly began testing the drawers. To her surprise, many of them were unlocked. Surprise swiftly gave way to disappointment as she searched each one, finding nothing but tradesmen's bills, a few dry letters from Compton's colleagues in Parliament, and a document that appeared to be the lease agreement on a house.

Hope sprang anew with the next drawer. It was located behind a small door on the side of the desk. Unlike the other drawers, this one refused to open.

Removing her two remaining dragonfly hairpins, Effie set to work. She inserted the first hairpin into the lock until she felt resistance from the lock pins. Using that hairpin as leverage, she slid the second hairpin into the lock and manipulated the tumbler. It took a bit of doing, but after a few nerve-racking minutes, Effie felt the unmistakable click as the lock opened.

Satisfaction flared in her breast. Next time she saw Nell, Effie looked forward to informing her that she hadn't, in fact, forgotten everything she'd learned at the Academy. After returning her hairpins to her hair, Effie slid out the small drawer. It contained a stack of loose papers that smelled faintly of violets. Withdrawing them, she quickly ascertained that they were handwritten notes, all penned in the same script and signed with the same initial—*D*. Effie pored over them in the candlelight. They didn't contain anything damning in regard to Miss Corvus, but neither were they entirely innocent.

My dearest, what pleasure you gave me (one of the notes read). *My poor body has not yet recovered.*

And . . .

How virile and strong you were yesterday afternoon. Shall we repeat the performance Thursday morning next?

The more Effie read of the notes, the more she became convinced of two things: 1) Compton had a mistress; and 2) he and that mistress had a regular appointment on Thursday mornings.

But where did they meet? The letters didn't specify. Effie presumed it was a prearranged location. A hotel room or a house, perhaps.

Her thoughts instantly returned to the lease agreement. She removed it from the desk again, this time examining it more closely. The house was located in Ellis Street. Had Compton let it for his mistress? Effie suspected he might have done. She committed the address to memory.

"Lord Solomon, indeed," she murmured disdainfully as she returned the lease to its place. She put the letters back in their drawer and locked it.

Evidence of a mistress wasn't what she'd hoped to find, but it wasn't nothing. For now, it would have to do.

Rising from the desk, she paused to blow out her candle. Once the wick was sufficiently cooled, she resecured the taper and the holder to her crinoline and prepared to make her exit in the darkness. She'd already been away from the performance too long. Any longer and her absence would be remarked. A lost hairpin could only explain so much.

She was just making her way back through Lord Compton's bedroom, preparing to slip out the door, when a male voice sounded in the hall.

Effie froze where she stood. Her heart leapt into her throat. Good lord. It was a servant!

Her gaze darted about the darkened room. With only seconds to act, she did the only thing she could. She dashed behind the heavy curtains, hoping against hope that there would be a window seat she could squeeze into. It was the only way to disguise the fullness of her skirts.

But there was no window seat.

And the windows weren't windows, either. They were tall glass doors leading out to a stone terrace.

Effie tried the handle of the first one. Relief flooded through her to find it unlocked. Pulling the door open, she slipped out onto the terrace. There was no time to shut it, for in that same instant, the door to Compton's chamber opened and a servant entered the room.

Cold night air washed over Effie. With the moon hanging overhead, it was lighter outside than it had been in Compton's room. Anyone might see her. She hastily backed to the edge of the terrace, as far away from the open glass door as she could, until she felt the low stone railing press at her back.

A cool breeze passed over her, stirring her skirts. The same breeze rustled the velvet curtains, catching the servant's eye.

"Now who left that open?" the man muttered to himself.

Effie held her breath, listening to him cross the room to the terrace doors. She waited for him to pop his head out. To see her and sound the alarm. A dozen excuses for her presence ran through her head in a furious rush.

But the servant didn't look outside. He only pushed the glass door shut. There was a dull clunk as he locked it.

Effie's hands gripped the railing behind her. Minutes later, she heard the man depart. Only then did the reality of her position hit her. The terrace doors had no proper handles on the outside. She'd been locked out here. *Left* out here.

She cast a look of cold panic at the moonlit gardens below. Her stomach plummeted. For a moment, it was as if she'd already fallen, down, down, down, to the paving stones. It was that real. That visceral. The terrace floor seemed to shift beneath her feet. She squeezed her eyes shut as a wave of dizziness assailed her. It was coupled with the same wash of clammy perspiration she'd felt that day so long ago when she'd been trapped on the tower roof of the Academy. Then, Nell had climbed up to save her. But Nell wasn't coming this time.

No one was coming.

· · · · ·

Gabriel strolled down the secluded tree-lined path that ran along the edge of the Comptons' expansive gardens. The tip of his half-finished cigarette glowed in the darkness. Along with the moon and a blanket of shimmering stars, it was the only light to guide his way. No lanterns or torches had been set out for the evening. Lady Compton had doubtless anticipated her guests remaining inside.

Inside was the last place Gabriel wanted to be.

He'd just been discussing the rot and disease of the Rookery. To go from that to the cloying luxury of the drawing room, with its passel of rich young ladies singing in Italian, was too bitter a contrast. In his present frame of mind, Gabriel knew it would only fire his temper.

Instead, on leaving the library after his talk with Haverford, Gabriel had withdrawn to the gardens for a smoke. With luck, a cigarette and some fresh air would restore his equanimity.

Music drifted over him as he walked—the faint sounds of the piano and violin accompanied by a feeble contralto. The musicale was still in full swing. There was no hope of avoiding the whole of it. He would have to return eventually, if for no other reason than to show himself amenable to society's rules.

And to see Euphemia again.

It was a damnable urge. An unwelcome attraction all mixed up with his growing feeling of frustration and disillusionment. He had no place in this world. *Her* world. And it wasn't some mistaken sense of inferiority that compelled him to acknowledge it. It was the grim understanding that these people—these illustrious lords and ladies of London—would never change.

They existed in a sphere too far above the struggles of the common man and woman to ever comprehend them. For them, charity was entertainment. Compassion a performance. To gain their fickle attention, humble working people had to debase themselves, exposing their misery and abdicating their pride for the merest chance at a few scraps from the rich man's table.

There was no dignity in it, this glorified begging. Especially for Gabriel, who scorned to ask anyone for anything. He'd had to swallow his rancor to talk with Haverford. Whether or not the sacrifice had been worth it, Gabriel didn't yet know. Haverford hadn't spoken in terms of swift reforms. He'd approached the matter legally and theoretically, referencing scholarly reports, parliamentary opinions, and possible amendments to the 1855 Metropolis Management Act.

Haverford had also discussed the upcoming elections to the

St. Giles District Board of Works. The character and opinions of the newly elected board members would have an outsize impact on the Rookery's future. As much of an impact as that of Compton and politicians like him.

Whatever action was taken, it would depend on them to implement it. Which meant that, soon, Gabriel would be even more reliant on Compton than he was already. And Compton would know it.

Gabriel took a scowling drag of his cigarette. He was in a foul mood, that was the trouble. He had been ever since dinner, when he'd been obliged to tell Euphemia that his lofty position in St. Giles had originated not by order of his birth or connection or honest hard work, but by virtue of being a bookmaker—a glorified Rookery villain, who had risen to his current status through violence and intimidation.

He wasn't ashamed of what he was or where he came from. But in that moment, seated next to her in the candlelight, he'd felt something resembling regret. An earnest, elegant young lady like her—one who had been finished in Paris, by God—was so far removed from a man like him she practically existed on another planet. It didn't matter that she had the heart of an adventuress. That he'd seen in her eyes, that night in Compton's library, a spirit as fierce and formidable as his own. He could still never hope to reach her. To touch her. Not if he made another fortune for himself and bought half a dozen properties in Mayfair.

That didn't mean he relished the idea of her enjoying the remainder of the musicale with a witless arse like Lord Mannering or a self-righteous hypocrite like Lord Powell.

Better it should be Gabriel sitting beside her.

With that in mind, he finished his cigarette and headed back. The enormous white stucco house loomed ahead, towering over the neatly trimmed rosebushes and perfectly manicured grass of the formal gardens. A massive wisteria climbed up the walls, thick, woody, and drooping with heavy clusters of pale lilac flowers. Its branches stretched up to the high windows above where shadows moved and lights glimmered.

He avoided the main path, opting instead for a secluded track that ran alongside the house. There was a door there that led to the hall by the billiard room. It was the way he'd come out. As he approached, he paused to put out his cigarette, tipping his head back to take one last look at the waning moon.

It was then he saw it.

Or rather, *her.*

The distinct flash of violet silk was unmistakable. It shone briefly in the moonlight, a fleeting glimpse of color through the stone railing of a small terrace three floors above.

Gabriel's body went still.

For the barest moment, he wondered if he'd imagined it. It couldn't be her. That wasn't the ballroom terrace. It was the balcony of someone's private quarters. And she wasn't standing there, as any sane person would do. She appeared to be seated on the ground, her skirts billowing about her in a heap. What the devil was she—

There was a faint shudder of a tremulous breath.

His heart lurched. He took a sharp step forward. "Miss Flite?"

There was no response, only the same soft, unsteady gasping. It sent a jolt of apprehension through him. "Euphemia?" he said, raising his voice. "Is that *you?*"

A slim, ungloved hand slipped out of the terrace railing, gripping the stone pillar in reply. "Gabriel?" Her voice was a mere thread of sound. "I can't . . ."

"You can't what?"

"Move." The bewildering statement was followed by a pitiful breath of unsteady laughter.

The sound squeezed Gabriel's already quaking heart in a viselike grip. "Good God. Are you hurt?"

She uttered another short laugh. It had more in common with a whimper. "Scared," she breathed. "S-Stupid of me."

He didn't require any other explanation. What would be the point? She couldn't move. She could barely talk. And she'd just admitted to being frightened. Her situation must be alarming indeed.

His reaction to her distress was no less alarming.

Shedding the close-fitting constraints of his evening jacket, Gabriel strode to the wall of the house. He gripped the thick branches of the aged wisteria. Whether it could hold his weight on its own was debatable. He didn't pause to test it. Impelled by the sound of her whimpering breaths, he hoisted himself up.

He had some experience in climbing. In his youth, he and the other street children had often broken into houses searching for food and coin. Back then, Gabriel had become adept at shimmying up vines and running along rooftops.

Granted, it was decades since he'd last attempted it. He was much bigger now, and far broader of shoulder. Maneuvering his weight took some doing. The branches made ominous creaking noises beneath him, and he muttered more than one curse before he reached the terrace. But reach it he did. Gripping the edge, he hoisted himself over the railing like some demented Romeo.

He found Euphemia hunched in the corner in a cloud of violet silk. Her face was waxen in the moonlight, her lips bloodless and her forehead damp with perspiration. Her bosom rose and fell with every rapid, shuddering breath.

The vise on Gabriel's heart squeezed tighter still, making it difficult for him to think or to breathe. He could only react. Sinking down next to her, he took her face in his hands, forcing her to look at him. She met his burning stare with wide, panicked eyes. "Scared," he repeated. "Of heights?"

Tears started in her gaze. They shimmered there, unfallen, turn-

ing the dark blue of her eyes to the same deep shade of plummy violet as her gown.

"It's all right," he murmured gruffly. "You're all right." His thumbs
moved over her cheeks in an achingly gentle caress. "I've found you."

She nodded mutely as her teeth began to chatter. Her neck and
arms were bare, but he doubted the reaction was from the cold. She
appeared to be in some kind of terror-induced shock.

He continued stroking her, staring into her eyes, compelling her
to focus on him—only him—until he felt her breath coming easier.
The full skirts of her dress bunched between them. "Daft woman,"
he said softly. "Why didn't you just go back inside?"

"Locked out," she managed in a whisper.

His thumbs stilled on her cheeks. He shot a narrow look at the
glass doors. "Whose room is this?"

"C-Compton's."

Gabriel suppressed a swell of masculine outrage. What in the hell
could she possibly be doing in Compton's bedchamber? And how
had she found herself locked outside of it?

"What was your plan?" he demanded in a low growl. "To remain
here all night?"

"B-Break the window."

"Which you would have explained exactly how?"

"Past explaining. Too . . . too frightened."

A disconcerting wave of tenderness washed over him. It sank into
his soul, overwhelming his defenses—*and* his better judgment. "All
right," he muttered, half to himself and half to her. His fingers gently
cradled her jaw, his thumbs sliding over her cheeks. "This is what's
going to happen, sweetheart. I'm going to rescue you."

Her gaze turned toward the railing. A quaver of fear went through
her. She huffed another whimpering laugh. "Impossible."

"Come." He brought her face back to his. "I'd never have taken you for a defeatist." The rough edge of his Birmingham accent emerged, turning his a's into ai's. This time, it wasn't anger that summoned it, but another, more powerful, emotion. He didn't stop to examine it.

"A realist," she replied, just as she'd said at dinner. "There's only one way down." She trembled. "Down."

"Quite. We'll use those branches. It's what—three floors? That's nothing. All you have to do is calm yourself sufficiently enough to hold on to me."

She shook her head. "I can't."

He stroked her face. They didn't have time to linger. At any moment, a servant might enter Compton's room or one of the guests might wander out into the garden. "What? Don't you trust my climbing ability? I've got nine lives, me."

"One of us will fall."

"Neither of us is going to fall." He bent his head to hers, still holding her face in his hands. "Do you want to know the secret to it? Don't think of how high up you are."

She gave him a pained look. A tear spilled from her brimming eyes to slide down her cheek. "I can concentrate on nothing else."

Gabriel brushed the hot tear away with the pad of his thumb. His face was inches from hers. He felt her sweet breath puffing softly against his lips. She smelled of honey and black currants. Of everything he'd ever wanted in life but never received. Never deserved. He bent his head closer, his voice deepening to a husky scrape. "Concentrate on this," he said.

And his mouth captured hers.

11

Effie's fear-paralyzed brain registered Gabriel's intention a split second before he acted. She inhaled a startled gasp. The faint trembling sound was muffled by his mouth claiming hers.

He kissed her gently to start. As gently as the way he had held and caressed her face to reassure her. But finding her willing, the tame character of his kiss transformed in a quicksilver instant. The intensity increased by dizzyingly swift degrees. No longer soft and searching, his mouth took hers with a hungry desperation, kissing her fiercely, deeply, urgently.

A rush of yielding warmth flooded through her. Her brow creased and her eyes fell closed. The frozen panic that had immobilized her only seconds before burned away at the edges. The cool night around them was reduced to a single pulse point. To the two of them here, on the terrace floor, his knees crushing her skirts, and his large, calloused hands framing her face. And his lips—

His lips.

They angled over hers, engulfing her in an all-encompassing heat.

Her heart thumped wildly and her blood ignited. She'd been kissed before, but never like this. There was no calculation in it. No chaste deference or rakish strategy. Only the barely leashed passion of a man who had resisted the desire for too long. A man who wanted to touch her, to taste her, to breathe her in.

She surrendered to the scorching pressure of his mouth, her lips softening and parting beneath his. Fear was eclipsed by the heart-quaking sensation of their mingled breath. A soft moan escaped her throat as she kissed him back.

It was ill-advised. Nonsensical. But a small, distant voice in the furthest recesses of Effie's soul whispered that this was where she belonged. Not on the terrace, but with him, this dangerous, merciless, unfathomable man who had climbed three stories to save her.

Releasing her grip on the stone pillar, she brought her hand to cover his on her cheek. It wasn't to stop him. It was to keep him there, prolonging the tender intensity of the moment.

But there was no prolonging it.

At length, he drew back, his brow resting on hers. His breath was unsteady. "Still scared?"

She curved her fingers around his. He pressed her hand in response. "Yes," she admitted, her breath as woefully uneven as his. "But I'm no longer frozen with fear." Her voice sounded quite unlike her own.

"Good." He pulled back further so he could search her gaze. There was something different in his face—a line of deep consternation etching his forehead and a frowning shadow of baffled vulnerability flickering at the back of his eyes. It was only a crack. A glimmer. But Effie registered it just the same.

She had the uneasy sensation that the fundamental topography of their acquaintance had undergone a seismic shift. It was more than a change of perception. It was an alteration to the very ground on which they stood.

But they weren't on the ground, she reminded herself.

A flush of cold air kissed her cheeks as Gabriel removed his hands from her face. "We need to get out of here," he said.

She nodded her assent.

He stood all at once. Still holding her right hand in his, he pulled her up along with him.

Effie rose on quivering legs. The sight of the dark garden stretched out beneath them, unobscured by the terrace rail, sent another tremor of fear through her. She clung to Gabriel's sleeve. "I don't think I can do it."

"Yes, you can." Gently extricating himself from her grasp, he went to the stone railing. "I'll go over first, and then I'll help you. We're not debating it."

With that, he swung over the side.

A reflexive scream bubbled in Effie's throat. She ruthlessly stifled it, hating that her fear of heights should make her so weak and irrational. Gabriel hadn't leapt to his doom, for heaven's sake. He was safe on the other side of the terrace rail.

"Lift your skirts out of the way," he said.

Still trembling, Effie caught her petticoats and crinoline up as best she could, revealing a glimpse of her stocking-clad limbs.

That wasn't all she revealed.

The moonlight glinted on the implements tied to her crinoline.

Gabriel shot them an inscrutable look. Whatever his thoughts, he appeared to comprehend she was in no position to hear them. His gaze returned to hers, commanding all her attention. "Take my hand," he said. "And don't look down."

Staring steadily back at him, she obediently accepted his out-stretched hand. Her heart was racing and her palms were damp, but what else could she do? There was no other way out of this. She was going to have to trust him.

He helped her swing one leg over and then another, first holding her hand and then holding her waist. He then edged her to the wis-teria, step by careful step, along the outside of the terrace. His booted foot found a knot in the branches and he pulled himself over.

His arm was still around her waist. "Look at me," he said when her eyes drifted. "We're almost there. All that's left is to move your foot onto that branch."

Again, Effie obeyed him. Some of her hair had come loose from its pins. It fell in her eyes but she couldn't brush it away. She was gripping the wisteria with both hands, and Gabriel was gripping her.

"We'll go down together," he said, his big body half covering hers. He was protecting her. Ensuring that, so long as he didn't fall, she wouldn't fall.

It was cold comfort, given what had happened to Nell.

Effie moistened her dry lips. "Gabriel——" She looked at him over her right shoulder. His face was only inches from hers. "You should know that the last person who attempted to help me down from a great height ended up grievously injured."

He stared at her a moment. "The last person——?" His brows snapped together. "Are you telling me this has happened to you *before*?"

"Yes," she confessed. "Though, it wasn't a terrace. It was the roof of a building."

His arm tightened reflexively around her, strong as a band of iron. "Bloody hell, Euphemia."

Her fingers clenched tight to the branches. "Considering what's just transpired between us, I had rather you called me Effie." She paused. "It's what my friends call me."

His expression was at once unreadable. "We're going to be friends, are we?"

"I believe so."

"Do you kiss all of your friends?" he asked in a peculiarly neutral tone.

"I didn't kiss *you*," she pointed out. "You kissed *me*."

He helped her descend another branch. His low voice was a rough growl in her ear. "When you and I get down from here, we're going to have a serious conversation."

But by the time Effie's feet were safely on the ground, she was in no position to discuss anything. The distant sound of music carried on the evening breeze. It was "All Through the Night"—the penultimate piece of the evening. Effie remembered seeing it on the program.

No longer in danger of falling, she quickly regained her senses. She had a purpose in being here. One that wouldn't be aided by the loss of her reputation.

She hastily smoothed her hair and skirts back into some semblance of order. "I must return at once," she said. "The concert's nearly over and Lady Belwood will be concerned. I don't want her sending the servants to look for me."

Gabriel's own hair was uncharacteristically disheveled. He retrieved his coat from the ground and wordlessly put it on.

Effie went to him without thinking and reached to neaten his cravat. "I can tell you're aching to lecture, scold, or interrogate me, but I trust it can wait until a more convenient time. Later this week, perhaps?"

He didn't reply, only stared down at her in brooding silence. A lock of dark hair had fallen across his brow. Effie brushed it back. It was surprisingly thick and silky under her fingers, tamed by an expensive pomade. She'd caught the elusive fragrance of it as he'd helped her down the wisteria—bergamot and spices, like his shaving soap.

Gabriel was uncommonly still as she fussed over him, uttering not a single syllable. But a strange look had come into his pale blue eyes. Effie couldn't interpret it, but something inside of her warned her to cease her ministrations. One shouldn't be petting a wolf as though he were a spaniel.

Dropping her hands, she backed away. "Forgive my presumption," she said. "I abhor a wrinkled cravat."

"Miss Flite—"

"And rumpled hair," she added. "It's so untidy."

His brows sank. "Euphemia—"

"You shall doubtless want to return to the musicale as well. May I suggest you wait five minutes so we don't appear together?"

"Effie."

She stopped. Her heart fluttered madly. "Yes, Gabriel?"

"You can expect me later this week," he informed her.

She took another unconscious step back. "In Brook Street?" Lady Belwood would have ten fits.

"Not in Brook Street," he said.

"Where, then?" Another step backward. "I have an exceedingly busy schedule. It would help if I knew when and where to antici-pate you."

She still had the offices of the *London Courant* to visit, and Ellis Street to surveil, not to mention her inquiries into Devil's Acre and Church Lane. Gabriel's presence would be less than desirable at any of those places, especially if he was going to interfere with her methods or attempt to stop her from conducting her inquiries alto-gether.

He'd rescued her, yes. And he'd undisputedly made her heart beat faster. Still . . .

Just because a lady shared a deep, smoldering kiss with a gentle-man didn't mean that gentleman need be privy to all that lady's business.

Gabriel observed her steady retreat as if he could read her mind. "I'll find you again," he promised darkly. "You may depend on it."

· · · · ·

Gabriel didn't return to the musicale that night. After Effie fled the garden, he remained for nearly half an hour, pacing the darkened grounds like a restless tiger, waiting for his blood to cool.

It didn't.

He could still feel her. Still taste her. Still smell the fragrance of her perfume on his clothes—a heady mixture of warm floral spice and sweet, dark berries. It was undoubtedly French. Undisputably her.

A scowl contracted his brow. He should never have kissed her. He certainly hadn't planned to. But the moment had been too fraught with emotion to allow for anything like concrete plans. For the first time since he'd met her, she'd been vulnerable. Frightened, trembling, and in need of reassurance. That's all it had been to begin with, an effort to reassure her.

Until Gabriel had taken it further.

He blamed the circumstances. The moonlight, the music, the fact that he'd just climbed to her aid.

And he blamed himself.

He'd spent the better part of the evening vowing that he wouldn't be twined around her finger like the other hapless men in her wake. And yet, when it came to the point, the temptation of her soft, trembling lips had proved too great to resist.

In that moment, Gabriel had succumbed to the same bewildering, overpowering desire that had caught him in its grip the night he'd loomed over her in Compton's library. Then, it had been only his pulse that had reacted. This time it had been every part of him.

He scrubbed the side of his jaw as he walked, forcing himself to think with his head.

She'd been on the terrace outside of Compton's rooms. *And* she'd had a small taper candle and a silver match case secured to the tapes of her wire crinoline. Gabriel had caught a brief glimpse of them as Effie had lifted her skirts to climb over the rail.

She was up to something—had been since the first night he'd met her. Something sinister by the looks of it. Doubtless she'd been searching Compton's bedchamber the same way she'd attempted to search the man's desk. To what purpose? And what had she meant that someone had once been grievously injured rescuing her from the roof of a building? A *roof*, by God!

His chest constricted. The thought of her falling—

But no.

No.

He was determined to approach this logically.

As he continued alone through the moonlit garden, he catalogued what he knew about her. It was precious little, and most of it hearsay. She had been finished in Paris, and was by way of being Lord and Lady Belwood's ward. Her instincts were charitable, as illustrated by her visit to St. Giles and to an Epping Forest girls' orphanage. And she had a bluestocking spirit, as evidenced by the conversation they'd shared at dinner.

But though she spoke, dressed, and moved like a lady of the first rank, she regularly engaged in distinctly unladylike activities. Searching gentlemen's desks and bedchambers. Dressing in widow's weeds and traveling about the city without a maid. And who could forget the razor tip on her parasol?

What it all meant, he didn't know. But as he departed Compton's house that evening, Gabriel was determined to find out.

12

E ffie posted her first sampler to the Academy the following morning. It contained no lengthy message, only a single line that could be deciphered in code: **HE HAS A MISTRESS.**

Even as she dispatched the parcel to the London post office with one of Lady Belwood's footmen, Effie knew the effort to be in vain. What man of rank didn't keep a mistress? So long as he was discreet, his peers forgave him the sin.

Then again, not every man was known as Lord Solomon.

Effie was resolved to go to Ellis Street on Thursday to confirm her suspicions. She would see if there was any intelligence there worth relaying to Miss Corvus. In the meanwhile, Effie had other lines of inquiry to pursue, both for the Academy and for herself.

She was in her bedroom, collecting her hat and gloves, preparing to leave Brook Street with Franc, when one of the Belwoods' house-maids tapped on the door. It was Mary.

"Beg pardon, Miss Flite," she said, "but you have a caller."

Effie paused in the act of putting on her little jet-trimmed black velvet hat. "At this hour?" It was half past ten in the morning. She wasn't accustomed to receiving callers until one. "Who is it?"

"It's Miss Compton," Mary said. "I've put her in the drawing room. Shall I bring in tea for you?"

Effie frowned. Carena Compton? What on earth could *she* want? And why could it not wait until normal receiving hours?

But there was no avoiding the troublesome call. To be sure, Effie might well turn such an inconvenience to her benefit. She was, after all, at pains to cultivate an acquaintance with the arrogant girl.

"Tea would be excellent," Effie said. "Thank you, Mary. Please tell Miss Compton I shall be down directly."

"Yes, miss." Mary curtsied before withdrawing, closing the door after her.

Casting aside her hat and tugging off her gloves, Effie unclasped Franc's lead from his collar. The little poodle looked up at her with profound disappointment.

"I'm sorry," she told him. "Our outing will have to be postponed."

His lips quivered in a semblance of a snarl.

"My thoughts exactly," Effie said. She picked him up and placed him on the bed. "Perhaps a nap until I return?"

Franc grudgingly went to Effie's pillow.

"Faire le tour," she encouraged him.

He obediently turned three times in a circle before lying down. His sides heaved with a weary sigh.

Effie felt the sentiment echo in her own weary soul. Too many of the preceding days had been spent in stifling drawing rooms, parlors, and ballrooms, cramped together with other ladies and gentlemen under the gaslights.

It hadn't been without purpose. With every introduction made to her, every conversation she had and every dance she shared, Effie was gaining a greater and greater foothold into London society. People were beginning to see her as one of them. To accept her and—more importantly—to include her.

This was why Miss Corvus had summoned her back from Paris. Not because Effie was the most impressive of the girls at searching rooms or breaking into locked desks, but because Effie knew how to be a lady. She could blend in with the fashionable elite, move among them, be one of them.

For now, it was as much her job as it had been being lady's companion to Madame Dalhousie. Effie consoled herself that at least this position had a worthy prize at the end of it—her complete independence. It was no minor thing. On the contrary. It was *everything*.

She gave Franc a consoling scratch on the head. "One day soon," she promised him, "you and I will be at liberty to do as we please."

But not today.

Smoothing her cherry red caraco jacket and giving her black poplin skirts a shake, she departed her bedchamber and descended the stairs to the drawing room.

Miss Compton was seated on the tufted settee, clad in a berry-colored silk dress trimmed with a staggering amount of pink chenille fringe. She stood when Effie entered.

"Miss Compton," Effie said, exchanging a curtsy with the girl. "This is a surprise."

Miss Compton's beautiful face was unsmiling. She opened her fringe-trimmed reticule. "I came to return this to you." She extracted Effie's dragonfly pin.

Effie affected a look of relief, even as her senses sharpened with alertness. "You found it? How splendid." Taking the pin from Miss Compton, Effie blithely tucked it into one of the side rolls of her upswept coiffure, placing it alongside the dragonfly hairpin that was already there. She was never without one. "Thank you for returning it to me." She gestured for Miss Compton to sit. "But you needn't have brought it yourself, surely."

Miss Compton resumed her seat on the settee. "I presumed it was something of value to you, else you wouldn't have been searching my rooms for it during the musicale."

Effie smiled. She had nothing to hide in that regard. It was the whole reason she'd left the hairpin behind. Its presence had given her an excuse to poke about upstairs during the musicale. "It's of great value to me." She sat down across from her. "I was quite distressed when I couldn't find it."

"Sentimental value, I expect you mean. For it's only cut glass." Miss Compton's eyes took on a spiteful gleam. "Or perhaps you weren't aware?"

Effie's smile remained, undimmed. Of course, she knew it was glass. All of her hairpins, brooches, and ornaments were similarly made. She could afford nothing else.

It didn't mean she must forsake her love of fine things. Even if it *was* only playacting at being a lady of wealth and refinement. The desire was no less real. To be a well-to-do lady was to have beautiful clothes. To eat delicately iced petits fours and pastel-colored macarons. To smell of French parfum and to ride in lacquered carriages with velvet-upholstered seats. Being a lady meant safety, satiety, luxury.

If Effie hadn't a weakness for the accoutrements of the role, she wouldn't be here. Miss Corvus had recognized that weakness only too well. It's why she'd promised that, if Effie was successful in her mission, she could keep all of her clothes.

"Sentimental is exactly how I would describe my attachment to it," Effie said. "I was certain it must have fallen on the floor of your dressing room. Is that where you found it?"

"It wasn't on the floor. It had slipped between the cushions of a chair. My maid, Meacham, discovered it last night before I retired."

"Then you must convey my thanks to Miss Meacham." Effie paused for a long moment, still holding Miss Compton's challenging gaze. "Is that the only reason you've come?"

"No," Miss Compton said, raising her chin a notch. "It is not." She said nothing more, only glared at Effie with a look of kindling fury.

She plainly expected Effie to question her further on the subject, or—more likely—for Effie to offer up some clumsy, premature apology for whatever imagined offense she'd caused.

Effie did neither.

A taut silence vibrated between them.

Effie felt no great urgency to fill it. There was power in saying nothing. It generally prompted one's opponent to stumble into the conversational breach, saying too much. *Revealing* too much.

In the end, Miss Compton couldn't resist.

"You left the drawing room during my performance," she said accusingly.

Effie's brows lifted slightly.

"And I know you weren't searching for that hairpin, for you didn't return until the end of the musicale." Twin spots of color blazed in Miss Compton's cheeks. "Neither did Lord Mannering."

Ah.

Effie began to understand. "Oh?" she replied. "Were we the only ones absent?"

Miss Compton's gloved hands clenched into fists on her lap. "There were others," she acknowledged. "But you and Lord Mannering have a prior connection. You were sat next to him at dinner."

"For that, you must blame your mother. I had no control of the seating arrangement."

"It isn't only his placement at the table. It's what's been happening while I've been in Hampshire."

Effie recalled Miss Compton referencing Lord Mannering and Lord Powell when Effie had come to her dressing room. Something about Effie entertaining the two gentlemen in Miss Compton's absence. Then, Effie had presumed the comment to be cattiness. Now, she recognized it as jealousy.

"Do you deny that he's called on you here?" Miss Compton asked with building impatience. "And more than once?"

"Cordial visits made during Lady Belwood's receiving hours,"

Effie said dismissively. "There have been many such calls since I arrived in London."

"Doubtless there have been. And doubtless someone will have told you that Lord Mannering and I have had a secret understanding for nearly a year."

Effie resisted remarking that it couldn't be very secret if everyone knew about it. "Indeed, they have not," she said instead. "And even if they had, it wouldn't have changed my behavior."

The color in Miss Compton's cheeks darkened. "So, you admit it."

"That I've met the gentleman? Yes. It doesn't follow that I have designs on the poor man."

"Then where did you go during the musicale? Where did *he* go?"

"Perhaps he went to play billiards?" Effie suggested. "Or to smoke a cigar? Or perhaps he was availing himself of the necessary?"

Miss Compton flushed scarlet. It was the height of indelicacy to mention anything even remotely related to the privy.

Effie gave her a faint look of sympathy. There was no point in baiting the girl. And no sport in it, either. Miss Compton may have wealth and power, but in this moment, she was wholly at the mercy of her own emotions. It didn't serve Effie's aims to prolong her misery.

"I can think of a dozen reasons he might have left the drawing room, and none of them have anything to do with me searching for my hairpin," Effie said. "Indeed, if I were a betting sort, I'd wager he was in the library with Mr. Royce and Lord Haverford, discussing their charitable endeavors."

"Mr. Royce?" Miss Compton was incredulous. "That strange man my father invited? The one with the pale dead eyes?"

A twinge of indignation took Effie unaware. She had thought the same about Gabriel's eyes on first meeting him. His gaze had been so cold, glassy, and distant—almost cruel in its detachment. But she didn't like to hear anyone else describing him so, particularly this spoiled young lady. Not now that Effie knew him better. And not after what had happened between them on the terrace.

Effie had been up half the night replaying the kiss they'd shared. And not only the kiss.

She had relived the way he'd rescued her, too, both cursing her helplessness and puzzling over his gentleness. The way he'd braced her with his body on the wisteria. The strength of his arms. The fierce burr of his voice in her ear as he'd returned her safely to solid ground.

She hadn't seen him after they parted in the garden. He'd never returned to the musicale. He'd simply gone, leaving behind his ominous promise: *"I'll find you again."*

Even now, it made her knees quiver to think of it. Her *knees*, for heaven's sake!

"Is that man involved in a charitable scheme with Lord Haverford?" Miss Compton asked.

"I believe he is," Effie said. "Is Lord Mannering a charitable fellow? You know him far better than I."

"He concerns himself with charitable matters, naturally."

"There you are, then."

A frown creased Miss Compton's brow. "I suppose you might be right."

Mary silently entered carrying the tea tray. It held a silver tea service, a set of painted porcelain cups and saucers, and a plate containing what appeared to be a small seedcake. She brought it to them.

Effie smiled again. "Thank you, Mary," she said. "You may put it down here."

"Yes, miss."

"I hadn't intended to linger," Miss Compton said after the maid departed.

"Nonsense," Effie replied. "You must tell me all about your

understanding with Lord Mannering." She reached for the silver tea-pot to pour out their tea. "Do you know, I suspected he had a prior attachment. On the few occasions I met him, he had a faraway look in his eyes, as though he was thinking of someone else."

Some of the tension left Miss Compton's face. "Did he?"

"Assuredly so. But tell me, why such a long engagement?"

Miss Compton's hands slowly unclenched. "Papa doesn't approve of him for me," she said. "Something about Lord Mannering having unfavorable vices."

"Oh?" Effie passed her a cup of tea. She remembered Gabriel saying that Lord Mannering had once been at his mercy. If that were so, his lordship's vice must have to do with gambling. "I wouldn't have believed so."

"Nor do I believe it," Miss Compton said, accepting the cup. "And nor does my mother. She agrees that someone as handsome and affable as his lordship is would never behave in an ungentlemanlike manner."

Effie wasn't sure what handsomeness had to do with it. "So, you continue to hold out hope?"

"I see no reason I shouldn't." Miss Compton took a sip of her tea. "Do you expect him today?"

"I don't expect anyone," Effie said. "I'm still so very new here. Every visit is a surprise."

Miss Compton's eyes narrowed. "If he does come—"

"I shall talk only of you," Effie promised.

"And if he should ask you to join him for a drive or a walk in the park—"

"I shall suggest we make a foursome of it with you and . . ." Effie stopped. "Who else should I mention inviting?"

"Mr. Royce or Lord Haverford, I daresay, if they're involved in a charity together." Miss Compton lowered her cup. "I far prefer Lord Haverford, though he is old and stuffy."

"Excellent," Effie said. "We have a plan."

Having satisfied herself that Effie was in some small degree an ally rather than an out-and-out rival, Miss Compton soon departed. Effie bid her good day with a sense of accomplishment. She was gradually managing to assemble the necessary pieces on the board. One of the most important of those pieces was Carena Compton.

A friendship with her would enable Effie to visit Lord Compton's house in Grosvenor Square with regularity. It would also, with a little strategy, result in Effie obtaining an invitation to Rawdon Court. All Effie had to do was use Miss Compton effectively. It shouldn't be difficult, given the lady's weaknesses.

After finishing her tea, Effie returned to her room, where she donned her hat, gloves, and mantle, and collected Franc. Within ten minutes, they were out the door, walking down Brook Street together, Effie's hat ribbons fluttering and Franc prancing ahead of her at the end of his lead.

She turned down Park Street, and from thence to Upper Grosvenor Street, avoiding the necessity of passing Grosvenor Square. From there, she hailed a hackney to take her and Franc as far as the Strand. Their destination was some three miles distance. Effie had studied the route on her map this morning before getting dressed. On arriving there, she and Franc disembarked from the hackney, heading toward Fleet Street with a purposeful step.

She was gradually learning her way about London. That was the first rule nearly fulfilled. *Know your surroundings.*

And she already had the third rule mastered. She knew herself. Her strengths, her weaknesses, her prevailing desire. She wanted to secure a decisive victory for women. What Academy girl didn't? She also wanted—*desperately* wanted—a home of her own, safe and snug somewhere with Franc, beholden to no one.

It was the second rule that was proving difficult. *Know your opponent.*

But just who was her opponent? Was it Lord Compton? Or was it Gabriel Royce?

After their kiss last night on the terrace, she'd been too flustered to consider the matter properly, but the stark light of morning had brought cold common sense. He'd kissed her, yes. And he'd enjoyed kissing her, obviously. But that didn't preclude him being her enemy. Indeed, the kiss itself may have been the first shot fired in the battle to come.

"You don't want me to act, my lady," he'd warned her that night in Compton's library.

Had *this* been the action he'd been threatening? But if it had, why had she seen a crack in his cold facade? That brief, flickering glimmer of baffled vulnerability? It made her stomach tremble to recall it.

She shook off the feeling, refocusing her attention on the task at hand. Tipping her head back, she gazed up at the gray stone building ahead. A painted sign proclaimed its name: THE LONDON COURANT.

"Ah," she said to Franc. "Here we are."

13

May was derby month and, with Epsom drawing closer, Gabriel had his hands full at the betting shop. It was there he could be found the day after the musicale, laying odds, calculating wins and losses, and dealing with the endless procession of men crowding the floor to examine the lists.

There was no help for it. Business must come first. But even as Gabriel dealt with the chaos that accompanied the spring racing meets, Effie Flite was never far from his mind.

On returning from his house in Sloane Street that morning, he summoned Bill Walsh to his office. Walsh was, like Murphy, one of Gabriel's chief enforcers—a big, ugly bruiser of a fellow, accustomed to using his fists. But unlike Murphy, Walsh possessed a modicum of intelligence.

"I have a job for you," Gabriel said from behind his desk, barely looking up from calculating figures in his ledger. "And I want no violence, only results."

"Anything, Mr. Royce," Walsh replied.

"Go to Church Lane. Go to Devil's Acre. Find me a fair-haired woman by the name of Grace who lived above a rag-and-bone shop in the Rookery seventeen or eighteen years ago. If you can't discover her outright, then find someone who remembers her. When you do, bring them to me."

"Is that all, sir?"

Gabriel flicked him a cool glance through the lenses of his round, gold-rimmed spectacles. "For now."

Effie had claimed that this Grace person was someone her family had known long ago. A servant, Gabriel suspected, or some old retainer whose fate was a matter of sentiment. Regardless of the person's status, she was important enough that Effie had risked a visit to the Rookery to find her. Important enough that Effie had asked Gabriel for help.

He recalled the queer, lost look in her eyes that day when he'd told her the slum had been cleared and its residents scattered to the four winds. Her face had fallen and her footsteps had faltered. She'd stared about the alley with a vague expression of devastation.

This Grace woman meant something to Effie. She may not be a key in herself, but if she could provide the smallest insight into Effie's past, or offer any illumination on her present aims, Gabriel planned to find her. And he intended to find her first.

It wasn't the only action Gabriel had contemplated after his and Effie's interlude in the garden. He'd seriously considered having her followed for a second time, if not by Ollie or Walsh, then by another of his men. He'd nearly done it, too, for no other reason than to ensure her safety. The devil only knew what mischief she might be getting herself into. Another venture into Compton's bedchamber? Another balcony? Another roof, by God?

Gabriel had ultimately abandoned the idea. What would have been the point in having her followed again? She'd spied Ollie quickly enough. It stood to reason that she'd spot anyone else Gabriel sent just as easily.

In any event, the odds she'd ricocheted straight from her disastrous near miss on Compton's terrace to another reckless attempt at whatever it was she was doing were slim to nothing. It had been—what?

All of twelve hours since he'd rescued her? Hardly time to fall victim to another mishap.

Chances were, she was safe in Brook Street, still recovering from the episode at Compton's. Either that or she was occupied with some tedious society event. The season was packed to bursting with balls, routs, picnics, and every other variety of fashionable party.

Gabriel didn't like to think of her in company with the rich, blue-blooded gentlemen that populated Compton's world. Still, it was some consolation to know she was out of danger as he attended to shop business.

He would find her in the coming days to have that talk he'd promised her. Tomorrow or the day after, perhaps. Then, he could confront her rationally, logically, without the vivid memory of that blasted kiss seeping in to rob him of his senses.

Until then, diversion was what he needed, and the betting shop offered plenty of it.

He was still there hours later, coatless and rumpled in the main room, discussing the lists with Murphy, when Miles Quincey surprised him with a visit.

Gabriel's mouth curved into a smile to see his old friend. "Miles. Don't say you're looking to place a wager?"

Miles stood apart from the rough and unshaven fellows who crowded the shop. He'd never approved of the turn Gabriel's life had taken. Indeed, clad all in black, with a frown darkening his brow, he looked more like a disapproving clergyman than an intrepid newspaperman known for employing daring methods to get his stories.

"I never wager with my money," Miles said.

"Only with your life, is that it?" Gabriel was but half in jest. Despite appearances, Miles was no bookish, untried gentleman. He had been quite lethal in their youth, and even beyond that, if the tales about his adventures abroad held any truth.

"Rarely even that anymore," Miles said. "May I have a word with you outside?"

Gabriel slapped Murphy on his brawny arm, dismissing him as he joined his friend. "The air inside not refined enough for you?" he asked, accompanying Miles to the alley. "You'll find it worse out here."

"It's not fresh air I want, but privacy." Miles peered up at the sagging buildings that lined the alley. One stood out among them. Unlike its dilapidated and decaying brethren, it showed signs of having lately been repaired. "Tindall's Lodging House has a new roof, I see."

"It needed one. There are more families living there now."

"You paid for it, I gather."

"I wouldn't have had to if anyone else gave a damn."

Miles walked with Gabriel to the end of the alley. "I understand you're attempting to find a few who will."

Gabriel flashed him a look.

"My sources tell me you've lately been in society, meeting with Lord Compton and Lord Haverford," Miles said.

"Your sources," Gabriel repeated flatly. "Do you have spies in Viscount Compton's house, too?" Even Gabriel hadn't gone that far.

"I've told you. I don't need to resort to spies. But I do have my ways of learning things." Miles returned his look. "Am I wrong?"

"I did speak to them both about reforming the Rookery," Gabriel said. He relayed the substance of his conversation with the two men.

Miles didn't appear impressed by Gabriel's efforts. "You do realize that, if they rebuild the Rookery, it will no longer *be* the Rookery. Once there's decent housing and adequate plumbing, a better class of people will move in. The ones you're trying to save will end up even worse off than they are now."

Gabriel regarded his friend without expression. "And here I thought you were the more optimistic of the two of us."

"I would be if it were anything else." Miles's expression was somber. "What you're trying to perform is akin to those fables my mother used to read to us from that old mythology book of hers. The one with Sisyphus."

Gabriel's brows lowered. "That poor chap with the boulder?"

"Exactly. Always attempting, never succeeding. You should take a lesson from it."

Gabriel had never much liked morality lessons. "There are more improvements hereabouts than a new roof on a lodging house."

"Yes, you mentioned them last time I came. There's a school, isn't there? Run by the publican's widow?"

"She's teaching the children to read, just as your mother taught us."

"It's admirable," Miles said. "Still . . . you've set yourself an impossible task. If you do manage to accomplish sweeping change, it will sweep those people away in the bargain. You'd do better to chuck the place in altogether and start somewhere new. You surely have the coin now to set yourself up."

Gabriel walked alongside his friend as they doubled back toward the betting shop. His already perilous mood was souring at a rapid rate.

Miles had been gone from the Rookery too long to ever understand. And even if he'd remained there as a lad instead of going to take up his apprenticeship, he'd still fail to grasp it. He'd had a mother. A family. An identity of his own.

Gabriel's identity had, by contrast, been knitted entirely from the soiled and bloody threads of the slum. A borrowed slum at that. He hadn't even been born here. He was a usurper. A cuckoo in the nest. What power he wielded here had been taken, not given to him by birth. Without it, he had nothing. He *was* nothing.

"Set myself up as what?" he asked in a voice of deceptive calm.

"I wouldn't presume to tell you. All I know is that every time I see you, more of the life has gone from your eyes."

Gabriel didn't reply. He knew what he was. Knew what he saw in his shaving glass each morning. The hollowness. The emptiness. Miles wasn't wrong. That didn't mean Gabriel had to admit it to him.

"Go to that house of yours in Sloane Street," Miles advised. "Find yourself a wife. Exert yourself toward teaching your own children to read. Generational change is the only kind of change we have any control over. The rest . . ." His gaze drifted over the Rookery. He shook his head. "This place killed my mother. It kills everyone in it eventually, if not from dissipation and disease, then from outright despair. Better it should shrink away to nothing, than have you attempt to revive it."

Gabriel stopped outside of his betting shop. There was a guard on the door—a big brute of a man named Digby. He was still admitting men with regularity. "Is this what brought you here?" Gabriel asked Miles. "You felt the need to deliver a sermon? A waste of your time, I should've thought."

Miles sighed. "No. That isn't why I'm here. I came for another reason. You said to tell you if anyone came asking after those lines about Wingard in the *Courant*."

Gabriel gave him a sharp look. "Someone came?"

It made no sense. Why the hell would Compton send someone inquiring when he already knew Gabriel was behind the threat?

"They did," Miles said. "Or rather *she* did."

Gabriel stilled. *"She?"*

"A woman. A lady, as it were. She visited the *Courant* not an hour ago. She had a little black poodle with her. My clerk made the mistake of admitting them into my office. My cats—"

"Never mind your bloody cats. What did the lady want?"

"The obvious. She wanted to know where I obtained my information. Asked if I knew how she could contact this Wingard fellow's family. Claimed he was a relation of hers."

Gabriel's blood went cold as ice. This was a possibility he hadn't considered, that Effie was connected in some way to Compton's past. Not with Compton alone, but with Wingard and the fraud the two men had perpetrated against Wingard's sister. "What the devil did you tell her?"

"What *could* I tell her? That dog of hers had my cats on the run. There was so much hissing and spitting it was all I could do to keep my office from being destroyed. I managed to get her out the door with the help of my clerk, muttering something about protecting my sources, and then——"

"And then you came here," Gabriel concluded. His gaze shot to the entrance and exit of the alleyway. He half expected to see Effie emerge, triumphant, having successfully used Miles to make the connection between Wingard, Compton, and Gabriel. "Bloody fool. Did it not occur to you that you might have been followed?"

"By whom?"

"By *her*," Gabriel said.

"The lady with the poodle?" Miles looked at Gabriel as though he'd gone insane. "Let me guess, she and her little dog are a pair of dangerous villains?"

Gabriel didn't know about the villainous aspect to Effie Flite, but he was beginning to suspect that dangerous was precisely what she was. If she was looking through Compton's things, if she was asking about Wingard, she could only be after the documents that proved the two men's crime.

Documents that Gabriel currently had under triple lock and key.

Was she truly a relation of Wingard and his ill-fated sister? If she was, her search could have but one purpose. She must want to bring Compton to justice. Little did she realize that she'd destroy Gabriel in the bargain. Without Compton's support, neither Gabriel nor the Rookery had any future at all, only an unchecked free fall toward complete obliteration.

Gabriel stalked back to his shop. He had thought his and Effie's positions at odds before, but this revelation put them squarely on opposite sides of the battlefield. Their interests were that diametrically opposed. There would be no reconciling them.

Miles followed after him. "Where are you going?"

"To fetch my coat," Gabriel snarled. "And then to bleeding Mayfair."

14

Effie had never been fishing herself, but she knew a thing or two about baiting hooks. A few calculating inquiries here, a few pointed remarks there, and something was bound to stir from the murky depths of London in answer. All she must do is wait. She was confident that, with time, one of her lures would get a bite. If not from the whale-sized Compton himself, then from a useful sort of game fish.

She hadn't anticipated reeling in a shark.

"Miss Flite." Gabriel Royce stepped in front of Effie on the tree-lined path in Hyde Park where she was walking Franc. His face was somber, his eyes blazing.

Effie came to a surprised halt beneath the silver birches. Her heart gave a girlish flutter, even as her other senses vibrated in re-sounding warning. "Mr. Royce," she said with creditable calm. "What an unexpected pleasure."

It was nearly half past two, and the sun was shining brightly in a clear aquamarine sky. The fashionable hour was still many hours away. Ladies and gentlemen of every stripe were nevertheless out in force taking advantage of the fine weather—riding, driving, and walking along the avenues below.

Unlike the other gentlemen strolling in the park, Gabriel had no hat, gloves, or walking stick. He wore a plain black three-piece suit, the single-breasted coat open to reveal the gold chain of his pocket watch. There was a rumpled, impatient air about him, rather like an attorney or other busy professional who had been prematurely called away from his office.

In that taut moment, her thoughts already occupied by the latest lure she'd cast, Effie could think of only one thing that would have dragged him from his betting shop. And it wasn't the kiss they'd shared. It was her visit to the *London Courant* this morning.

Her heart ceased its fluttering. It sank into her stomach like a stone. Was it possible that Gabriel was in some way connected to Mr. Wingard?

He appeared provoked enough for it. To be sure, he was looking at her just as he had that first night in Compton's library in the seconds before Effie had removed his hand from her throat—cold, implacable, dangerous.

Franc didn't register the threat. At finding Gabriel blocking their way, the little poodle gave only the faintest tail quiver of recognition before he resumed pulling on his lead, demanding Effie continue their walk.

Effie obliged him. Deftly sidestepping Gabriel, she proceeded down the path, letting Franc lead the way. The swell of her poplin skirt brushed Gabriel's leg as she passed him. "However did you find me?" she asked.

He came alongside her, his face hard as granite. "Lady Belwood's footman directed me."

Effie somehow managed to keep her countenance. "You called in Brook Street?"

"I did."

"You must be keen to see me indeed if you were willing to pay a formal call."

"Keen," he repeated. "That's one way of putting it."

The alarm bells in Effie's head grew louder. "Whatever can have prompted such eagerness?"

"Need you ask?"

Effie cast him a veiled glance. He wasn't going to make this easy for her, neither for her mission to the Academy, nor for her pride. Of the two, she knew which was the more dispensable. The Academy must come first.

"Yes, I see," she said carefully. "I confess, I did think you might come today."

He returned her opaque glance with an enigmatic look of his own. "Did you." It wasn't a question.

They were far from the busy promenade now. No one was likely to remark them walking together unchaperoned. Even if they did, they would think them no different from any other courting couple who had broken away from the ranks for a private stroll.

"Perhaps not in the park," Effie said. "And not in this informal manner. But . . . yes. After what happened between us last night, a gentleman would waste no time in calling to pay his respects."

He held her gaze. Something in his face made Effie's breath constrict. "You believe I'm here because I kissed you?"

The air crackled around them. Effie ignored it as best she could, recognizing the tactic for what it was. He was attempting to put her on the back foot. To provoke her into saying or doing something that would reveal her secret objectives.

It was the same thing Effie was doing to him.

"You did promise that we were due a serious conversation," she reminded him. "I presumed it must be about your intentions." She conjured a tremulous smile. "If you mean to court me—"

He muttered something under his breath. It sounded like an oath.

"You do, don't you?" Effie pressed him. "Indeed, most fashionable people would agree that, after the intimacies you inflicted on me, a proposal of marriage would be—"

Gabriel caught her arm, cutting off her speech. "You infernal minx," he said in a low growl, bringing her around to face him in a swirl of her poplin skirts. "It would serve you right if I did propose to you."

Effie's heart leapt. She was briefly startled into a genuine smile. She swiftly disguised it.

But it was too late.

His cold expression softened a fraction. So did his grip on her arm. "And I inflicted a kiss on you, did I?"

She lowered her lashes. "As to that . . ."

"I seem to recall you getting into the spirit of it."

Heat crept up her throat. She prayed it wouldn't seep into her face where he could see it. "I obviously wasn't thinking straight. That was the whole reason you were there."

"And why were *you* there?" he demanded. "And what were you up to today when you were meant to be safe in Brook Street recovering from your ordeal last night?"

She lifted her gaze in bewilderment. "Whoever said I would be remaining indoors for the day?"

"Any other lady would have—"

"What? Taken to her bed? Called for her sal volatile? You must think me a very poor-spirited female."

"What I think," he said, "is that you might have at least done me the courtesy of staying out of trouble for the next twenty-four hours after you left me last night."

Effie stared at him. Is *that* what this was about? He'd presumed she would be safe in Brook Street, but instead he'd discovered that she'd put herself in some kind of danger? Was that why he'd come all this way, absent his hat and gloves, even going so far as to call at the Belwoods' residence to find her? Because he was *concerned* about her?

The possibility warmed her to her silk stocking–clad toes. An inconvenient reaction. She didn't need any more reason to like the man.

"I'm not in trouble," she said in an effort to reassure him.

"If that's what you believe," he replied without a hint of sentimentality, "you're either woefully overconfident or spectacularly ignorant—or both."

Her mouth compressed in a tight line. She instantly discarded the ridiculous notion that he was driven by concern. Her suspicions reverted to their original course. He wasn't here for her. He was here for himself, and—very probably—for Compton.

Effie pointedly removed her arm from his grasp. "I'm glad you didn't come to court me," she informed him as she resumed walking with Franc. "A union built on insults and underestimation would never have worked."

Gabriel overtook her. His glower was palpable. "This isn't a jest, Effie."

"I'm not jesting," she said. "Though I am pleased to see you've dispensed with the needless formalities."

Last night they had used each other's given names. It had felt as though they'd drawn closer. As though they were halfway to being friends.

But he wasn't her friend today, whatever name he chose to call her.

"Well? Pray, don't keep me in suspense," she said. "We've already established that you're not here to court me. And you obviously aren't here out of any gentlemanly concern. Not for me, anyway. So, who is it that's caused you to come and see me in all this state? Shall I hazard a guess?"

"I warned you," he said. "I told you I had a vested interest in Compton's well-being."

"Because you need his money to reform the slum? Surely, one rich man's pocketbook is as good as another's."

"Compton isn't only wealthy. He holds influence in Parliament. Reforms require changes to laws. He can do that—*and* convince the other politicians to follow his lead." Gabriel flashed her a blazing look. "So, whatever it is you've been looking for in his library, in his bedchamber, and at the offices of the *London Courant*—"

Effie's gloved fingers tightened reflexively on Franc's lead. She'd suspected her visit to the paper was Gabriel's motive for being here, but hearing it confirmed nevertheless provoked a private flinch. "Are you having me followed again?" she asked before he could finish.

He didn't deny it.

She racked her brain, trying to recall any faces she'd seen more than once during her journey to and from the *Courant*. But there hadn't been anyone. Effie would have known if there had. She'd been that careful.

"I understand you caused quite a furor," he said.

Effie switched Franc's lead to her opposite hand so he could wander among the shrubs on the left side of the path. She wondered just how much Gabriel knew about her visit to the paper. Everything, presumably, if he was referencing the commotion Franc's presence had caused.

"How was I to know the editor of the paper kept cats in his office?" She added tartly, "And I wasn't asking about Lord Compton, for your information. I was inquiring about someone else."

Gabriel once again lapsed into silence. Effie felt the weight of it as they walked. She knew he was waiting for her to fill the void, just as she was waiting for him.

This time, she broke first.

"Aren't you at all curious who that was?" she asked. "But I suppose you already know that, too, else you wouldn't be here."

"Is your name really Flite?" he countered.

Effie stiffened. She understood what he was referring to. She'd told the editor of the *Courant* she was a relation of Mr. Wingard. There had been but one purpose behind the lie—to discover if the Wingard mentioned in the society column was the same man as Miss Corvus's half brother. The editor had offered no answer in that regard.

But Gabriel had.

"For as long as I can remember," she replied truthfully. And then: "What connection has Mr. Wingard to Lord Compton?"

Gabriel stopped on the path beneath the birch trees. His face was wiped clean of expression. "Who says he does?"

She turned on him. "Your presence here tells me so. If you've come all this way to warn me off, I must be perilously close to something damaging to the viscount."

He shook his head. "You're clutching at straws. Just because you didn't learn anything at the paper—"

She gave him a calculating smile. "Who says I didn't learn anything?"

· · · · ·

Gabriel looked at her steadily, betraying nothing. She was still difficult to read, but less difficult than she'd been on the first occasion they'd met. He saw her now, the real Euphemia Flite, shimmering beneath her elegantly crafted facade, as uncertain of him as he was of her.

It did nothing to ease the tightness in his chest.

He'd sought her out in a hot burst of fury—angry with her for meddling with things she didn't understand and even angrier with himself for underestimating her. But when he'd seen her walking Franc beneath the silver birches, time had slowed. His temper had cooled and something else had come to take its place. An odd warmth. A strange softness.

He'd thought of holding her again. Of kissing her in the moonlight.

But not now. Once again, his temper threatened to get the better of him.

"What did you learn?" he asked.

Effie lifted her shoulder in a careless shrug. She wore a voluminous black skirt and a close-fitting red velvet jacket. A little jet-trimmed velvet hat was perched atop the plaited rolls of her ebony hair at a rakish angle. One of her dragonfly hairpins twinkled from beneath it.

She was equal parts dark and bright. Like a sleek, jewel-eyed wild cat on the hunt—every twitch and every movement a study in panther-like grace.

"After I left the offices of the *Courant*, I naturally withdrew to a shop across the street and waited," she said as if it were the most obvious thing in the world.

Gabriel's vitals twisted into a knot. He'd known it would be something of the sort. It was the very reason he'd anticipated seeing her in the Rookery in the moments following Miles's arrival. "And?" he asked.

"The editor of the paper emerged from the building not twenty minutes later. He got into a hansom cab."

"You followed him."

"I did," she said. "Alas, I lost him in the traffic on the Strand. There were too many hansoms, and my hackney driver became confused about which one he was meant to follow. He ended up taking me all the way to Camden Town. Franc and I only returned to Mayfair a short while ago."

The knot in Gabriel's chest didn't ease. It wasn't enough to know she hadn't discovered Miles's destination. There was more to this. Gabriel sensed it as surely as breathing. "What's your interest in Compton?" he asked. "And please don't insult me by lying."

"I have no reason to lie," she said. "I'm interested in the viscount for the same reason you are—for his ability to influence laws."

Gabriel searched her eyes. "What laws?"

"Laws that affect women." Her expression became serious. "There's been talk of a married women's property bill. Have you heard of it?"

He shook his head, a line etching his brow. There was doubtless discussion of a great many bills among members of Parliament and those who influenced their decisions. Gabriel wasn't party to it. He hadn't that kind of power, or that level of learning. The only laws he was familiar with were the ones that impacted his business, and those that Haverford claimed could possibly help the Rookery.

"You must know that married women have no rights to their own funds," she said. "Everything they have and everything they earn belongs to their husbands. Indeed, once wed, a woman ceases to exist as an individual. Only the husband's rights remain."

"I know of it in practice," Gabriel acknowledged. Growing up in the slums, he'd frequently seen dissolute men living off the earnings of their hardworking wives.

"Then you realize how important it is that women have a legal right to keep what's theirs. For many of them, it would mean the difference between life and death." Her solemn words took on an edge of passionate earnestness. "Money is independence. And independence is the only thing worth having. A woman who can't keep what she earns can't support herself outside of her marriage. She becomes her husband's captive. If her husband is a brute, what recourse does she have? None in law. Not currently."

Gabriel's frown deepened. Is this all this was? Effie's fervent bluestocking ideas about women gaining equality in the law? It was plausible on its face. Even so . . .

An unsettling possibility took hold of him.

He cut her a sharp glance. "You're not married, are you?"

Effie was surprised into a short laugh. "Goodness, no. I never will be, either. I am resolved upon it."

Gabriel felt a disturbing flash of irritation. Her disdain for marriage shouldn't make a difference to him. He had no vested interest in her matrimonial state. All the same . . .

"What do you plan to do with yourself, then?" he asked, nettled. "Live alone for the remainder of your life, subsisting on your vast fortune?"

"I won't be alone," she said. "I'll have Franc."

The indefatigable black poodle gamboled at the end of his velvet lead, sniffing here and wandering there, all the while endlessly pulling at Effie with the strength of his impatience to be off. She resumed walking, letting the little beast take her further up the path.

Gabriel cast a narrow look back in the direction of Rotten Row as he followed. The horses and riders were mere specks in the distance. "Do you often walk him this far alone?"

"It's not so very far. In Paris I used to take him out for hours at a time. We were frequently on our own in the parks or wandering along the Seine."

A seed of suspicion took root in Gabriel's mind. "The finishing school allowed you such freedom?"

Effie fell quiet for several seconds. "Yes." She paused. "That is . . . in my final year in Paris, I was a . . . a sort of companion to a French lady. She didn't rise until the late afternoon. Most of the day was mine alone. Indeed, that's how I came to meet Franc. I stopped at the Dog Market one Sunday in the Boulevard de l'Hôpital. A woman was selling poodle puppies from a basket. Franc was the last of them. I daresay I should have walked on, but he gazed up at me with his big brown eyes and . . ." A soft smile touched her lips. "I knew we were meant for each other."

"That's all it takes, is it?"

Her gaze met his. "In that instance it was."

Warmth infiltrated Gabriel's veins. *What about when we met?* he wanted to ask her.

But he wasn't some green lad begging reassurance from his first woman.

And she wasn't his woman at all.

"Madame was taken with an apoplexy when I returned to the apartment with him," Effie continued. "But Franc and I weren't to be separated. He was mine, and I was his, and that was all there was to it."

Franc bestowed a phlegmatic sniff on a clump of weeds as his mistress finished her tale. He was far ahead on the path, at the very end of his lead, seeming to pay her no attention at all.

"Not the most fearsome protector," Gabriel observed.

"On the contrary," she said. "Franc could disarm anyone who attempted to harm me. I've taught him a great many commands for the purpose."

Gabriel chuckled. "I'll bet."

Effie arched a brow at him in challenge. "Franc?" She whistled. *"Faire le tour."*

The poodle's small head jerked up. He at once sprang into action, tiny paws flying as he returned to Effie at a gallop. Still attached to his long velvet lead, he circled Gabriel three times, wrapping the lead around Gabriel's legs and effectively bringing him to a halt. After the third revolution, Franc stopped and looked at Effie in canine expectation.

"Bon travail," Effie told him.

Franc's tail quivered with pleasure.

Gabriel dropped a sardonic look at his bound limbs. "Is that all? Or does he do something else?"

"Franc? No." Effie stepped forward. Her full skirts pressed against the front of Gabriel's legs. "But *I* can do anything." She brought the flat of her hand to his chest, giving him a light push. "See? You're my prisoner."

Gabriel gazed down at her. A peculiar heaviness formed in his breast.

The sun shone through the tree branches, streaking the landscape in dappled warmth. Its rays kissed her upturned face, turning her skin to gold.

He was struck, all at once, by the visceral memory of how she'd looked on the terrace. She'd had no mask to protect her, then. No clever quips or catlike smiles to shield the rawness of her soul. Only an aching vulnerability too cumbersome for her to carry.

Once seen, it couldn't be unseen. Even now, when she stood so straight and strong, with her little dog beside her, willing to take on Compton. Willing to take on Gabriel, too, if it came to that. The vulnerability was still there, a shadow beneath the surface of her.

It provoked an answering ache of vulnerability in Gabriel.

He set his hand over hers. His heart beat heavily beneath her palm. He was certain she felt it. "Surprisingly effective," he said.

The triumphant gleam in her eyes dimmed. It was replaced by something watchful and uncertain. For all her boldness, she was still a young lady.

And he was still a man.

"I seem to be at your mercy," he told her.

"Exactly my point." There was a forced briskness in her voice, underscored by a trace of breathlessness. Slipping her hand from beneath his, she quickly slid Franc's lead free of Gabriel's legs. "Size isn't everything. There's intelligence, inventiveness, and loyalty. Not to mention the power of surprise. Any one of them is more valuable than brute strength."

Gabriel's mouth quirked. He'd succeeded in flustering her. There was some satisfaction in it. He had no desire to be the only one affected by this growing attraction between them. "So that's to be the culmination of your London season, is it? A retired life somewhere with your dog?"

"If I can clear a path for a married women's property bill, yes." She took a step back from him, adjusting Franc's lead. "I shall go away somewhere, far from here, where Franc and I can live in happy obscurity."

Gabriel's expression sobered. He liked the idea of her disappearing into some invisible existence even less than he liked the idea of her risking her neck. "How does searching Compton's bedchamber help your cause?"

"Not his bedchamber. His study." She paused again. "I have it on good authority that Lord Compton stands in the way of the bill being introduced into Parliament."

Gabriel's brows lowered. "So, you intend to compel his support through . . . what? Blackmail?"

It was the exact course Gabriel had chosen himself. A hazardous course. The thought of Effie—

"Don't be ridiculous," she said. "Blackmail is a loathsome business." She smoothed her gloves. "I intend to remove Compton from the board entirely."

Gabriel stared at her, both impressed and astounded by her audacity. He'd thought her an intelligent woman, not a simpleton. "Do you imagine you can move a man like Compton about like a token on a game board?"

"I don't presume it will be easy," Effie said. "He is, by all accounts, a powerful man."

"A *very* powerful one," Gabriel returned. "And one who's essential to my business."

She gave him a curious look. "I thought you only required him to help reform St. Giles? Are you saying he's involved with your betting shop as well?"

"Not involved, no. But he keeps the wolf from my door."

A wry twinkle flickered in the depths of her violet blue eyes. "Funny. I thought *you* were the wolf."

His heart thumped hard. He ignored it. "There are all manner of wolves in London. The trick is learning how to tell the useful ones from the ones who'll rip your throat out."

"No one is going to rip my throat out. Indeed, I'd like to see them try. But I appreciate your warning." She smiled again, this time with a trace of regret. "I suppose this means we must be enemies. Pity. I'd rather hoped we might be friends."

"I'm not your enemy, Effie," he said.

"Yet here you are, not two hours after I inquired about Mr. Wingard." She held his gaze. There was no softness this time. No smiles. Only an implacable resolve as mighty as his own. "Do you know what became of the documents mentioned in the paper? The ones that might pose a danger to someone in society?"

An image of those tattered, tearstained documents entered Gabriel's mind. They were dangerous, to be sure, and not only to Compton. Without them, Gabriel and all the rest of the people in the Rookery stood to lose everything that mattered to them.

"What I know," he said gravely, "is that powerful men will do anything to protect their secrets. Gentlemen of Compton's rank aren't to be trifled with. Forget him and move on from this mad quest while you still have the chance."

Color crept into her cheeks. It wasn't a blush. It was building fury. "Forgive me, but that sounds rather like a threat."

Gabriel wasn't sure that it wasn't. "Take it how you will. If you continue to act against the man, I'll have to stop you."

Her eyes blazed. "You're welcome to try, sir. As for myself, I intend to go on about my business, just as before. If you plan on checking my every move, you'll have to look sharp. I won't be retiring with my smelling salts anytime soon." She picked up Franc. "Good day to you." She dropped Gabriel a mocking curtsy before striding back down the sunlit path in a flourish of black skirts, her little dog cradled safely in her arms.

Gabriel was left there amid the silver birches, staring after her with a brooding frown. Unless he was mistaken, Effie Flite had just declared war.

On him.

15

Effie sat alone in the back of the hired hackney at the corner of Ellis and Sloane Streets. The thought of how much money she was expending in cab fare ticked steadily at the back of her mind. But there was nothing for it. She didn't know the precise time on Thursday mornings that Lord Compton arrived at his mistress's house for their weekly tryst. Indeed, she wasn't even entirely sure this *was* his mistress's house.

It stood at the end of the street, as commonplace as the homes that surrounded it. None were too grand, neither were they overly modest. They were just the sort of respectable, vaguely elegant brick homes one would expect on the fringes of fashionable London. A perfect place for a busy politician to house his mistress. It was but two miles from Westminster.

Effie had already been watching the house for nearly an hour, waiting for the viscount's carriage to arrive. It was a good thing she'd hired a hackney rather than resorting to her original plan—strolling the street with Franc. While it might have been nice to obtain a closer view, one couldn't walk a poodle up and down the same street for an hour without drawing unwanted attention.

As it was, Effie hoped to remain invisible. She'd worn her widow's weeds and veil again. And there was enough through traffic, both by riders and passing carriages, that a hackney parked at the end of the street shouldn't draw too much notice.

She was just beginning to doubt her plan when a glossy black carriage entered the street. Leaning forward in her seat, Effie peered out the greasy window of the hackney. The carriage had no crest or other insignia on its side. It was unmarked—and unidentifiable. It was an expensive vehicle for all that, from the luster of its paint to the sheen on the copper coats of its perfectly matched set of bays.

Effie knew how much Compton enjoyed his luxuries.

She held her breath as the carriage slowed to a halt at the end of the street, stopping in front of the very address Effie had found in the lease agreement. She tried her best to discern the carriage's occupant. Drat it! They were too far away.

There was no time to waste. Coming to a swift decision, Effie pulled the black net veil of her bonnet down over her face, collected her parasol, and opened the door of the hackney. "Wait for me," she said as she stepped down into the street unassisted.

"Right-o, ma'am," the aged jarvey said with a weary tip of his hat.

Effie crossed to the same side of the street as the house. She walked toward it with an even step—neither too fast, nor too slow. There weren't enough other people out strolling to hide her presence, but there was some activity. Children were playing nearby under the care of a pinafore-clad nurse, and several footmen were busily occupied sweeping doorsteps and polishing brass knockers.

Still a distance away, she watched as the hulking driver of the luxurious carriage jumped down from the box. He shot a look up and down the street before turning to open the carriage door.

Effie's heart stopped beating. It was Parker, Compton's butler. She'd know his ogreish countenance anywhere. She came to an immediate halt.

Good gracious. Had he seen her?

He undoubtedly had. But he hadn't appeared to recognize her, *or* register her as a threat. If he had done, he wouldn't be helping his master down from the carriage.

Compton emerged, the high collar of his wool overcoat pulled up to shield his face, and the brim of his gray silk top hat tugged down over his eyes. Despite his efforts to obscure his identity, it *was* indeed the viscount. Even a glimpse of his profile was enough for Effie to identify him.

Like his manservant, Compton cast a glance up and down the street.

In the same moment, Effie opened her parasol and, tilting it to camouflage her upper body, turned toward the brick residence next to her. It was but five houses away from where Compton stood. A young footman holding a broom was at the top of the steps. A cloud of dust billowed around him.

"Did I get you, ma'am?" he asked anxiously.

Effie smiled up at him from behind her veil. "Only a little," she lied. "My skirts can withstand it." As she spoke, she tipped her parasol back an inch, just far enough to watch Compton walk to the door of the house.

"I didn't see you there," the footman said, "or I'd never have swept at you."

Compton rapped on the door. It was at once opened—and not by a servant. A striking lady in a lace-trimmed peach morning gown leaned out to greet him. Her hair was black and her skin porcelain pale. She grasped the lapel of his coat with one ruffle-draped hand, drawing him into the house. The door shut behind them. Parker returned to the carriage, still surveying the street with a scowl.

"Pray don't regard it," Effie replied to the footman absently. She turned her head to him. "Indeed, perhaps you might help me."

The young footman came down the steps to join her, still holding his broom. He was in his shirtsleeves. An intelligent-looking lad, but rather young for his position. "Yes, ma'am?"

"I fear I've got my street numbers turned around. Does the house at the end of the street not belong to Mrs. Gibbons?"

"No, ma'am."

"I was sure the lady I just observed was she."

"No, ma'am," the footman said again. "That's Mrs. Naismith."

"Not Debra Naismith?" Effie asked, taking a stab in the dark.

"Can't say for certain," he replied, chewing his lip. "But I think it's Dora, not Debra. I can ask the housekeeper—"

"No, no," Effie said hurriedly. "It's my mistake." She cast a lost look back at the hackney. "I seem to be at the wrong end of Cadogan Place."

The young man's face lit with understanding. "There's your trouble, ma'am. This is Ellis Street. Cadogan Place is that way." He pointed in the opposite direction.

"Good heavens," Effie said. "My driver must have misunderstood my directions." She withdrew a coin from her reticule, placing it into his hand. "I'm obliged to you."

"Happy to help." He doffed his cap to her.

Effie felt Parker's gaze burning into her back as she returned to the corner. It wasn't because he knew her, she told herself; it was merely that she was an object of curiosity. Her pulse nevertheless jumped with every step, fully expecting that Parker would overtake her and—

She knew not what.

All she knew was that she had no desire to find out.

She could defend herself well enough, it was true, but even so . . . Parker was a large man, and despite her exhortations to Gabriel about the value of inventiveness and the power of surprise, brute strength at its utmost was still a force to be reckoned with.

The jarvey awaited her ahead, hunched on his perch. He appeared to be dozing.

Effie strode up to the door of the hackney. She was just about to open it when she caught sight of a familiar figure strolling past on

Sloane Street. It was that odious boy! The one who had followed her to the Rookery that day.

Her temper flared.

"Another moment," she said to the jarvey. He snuffled in reply as she marched off after the lad.

He was wearing dark trousers and a neatly buttoned dark coat, and held a brown paper–wrapped parcel in his hand. He wasn't doing a very good job of following her this time. If he were, she wouldn't have been able to get behind him.

"Well, well," she said quietly, overtaking him halfway down Sloane Street. "If it isn't my chivalrous St. Giles shadow."

The lad spun around with a start. He gaped at her. "Miss Flite!"

"I thought it was you," she said. "No, don't run. I'm not going to hurt you. Though I do have a mind to box your ears."

He flinched, backing up a step.

Effie closed the distance. "How *dare* your master send you to follow me again? I should have thought he'd learned his lesson."

"I'm not following you! I swear it. I *work* here." He jerked his head in the direction of a handsome red brick house with a black-painted door. "I've just come from fetching a new pair of gloves for Mr. Royce in Bond Street. I didn't even know you was anywhere near here!"

A dawning suspicion came over Effie. She stared up at the tall house. "That isn't . . . ?"

"Mr. Royce's residence in town," the lad confirmed. "He ain't there now, but he'll be back this evening."

Effie's gaze drifted over the elegant brick facade. A strange tremor went through her—the slightest trilling of butterfly wings. It was an odd sensation, and one totally incongruous to her present occupation. But to think that this was his *home*. Where he entertained his friends. Where he dined. Where he *slept*.

She hadn't really imagined Gabriel living anywhere. Certainly not someplace as traditional as this. He was so vital. So dangerous. And yet, he doubtless maintained the same habits as other gentlemen, reading the paper over his morning coffee or indulging in a glass of port after dinner. He obviously shaved over a washstand at the start of his day, and he inevitably retired at night to a bed somewhere. If not here, then—

No.

No.

She didn't wish to think of him in someone else's bed. Not after the kiss they'd shared, and the friendship they'd almost had.

But almost was as bad as never. The end result was precisely the same.

Effie willed the butterflies in her stomach to cease fluttering their wings. They went still at her command. She had the grim idea that she'd killed them.

Oh, why must she be at odds with him when she liked him so much? Why must he be Compton's protector, and not the viscount's enemy like she was?

It wasn't fair.

But nothing was fair.

Effie collected herself. "You're his house servant, are you?"

"His valet. And I truly ain't following you," he said again. "Not after you spotted me like you did."

"No, I suppose not," she allowed. "Your master will have sent someone else to do the job."

Gabriel had admitted as much two days ago during their confrontation in Hyde Park. How else could he have known that Effie visited the *Courant*?

The lad lowered his eyes with a sheepish flush. "I don't know about that."

"Forgive me if I take your professed ignorance with a grain of salt." She looked the boy up and down. His hair was lank, and his face slightly spotty, but he didn't appear neglected. "What's your name? Ollie, isn't it?"

"Ollie O'Cleary, miss."

"Well, Ollie O'Cleary," she said, donning her most severe expression. "You be sure to tell anyone else your master sends my way that I see *everything*, and I don't take kindly to spies."

"Yes, miss." Ollie shifted from foot to foot, looking decidedly uncomfortable.

"That's all," Effie said, adding ominously, "For now."

Ollie immediately bolted off to Gabriel's house.

Effie didn't remain to watch him go in. She returned to the hackney on the corner, settling safe in the cab. She could just make out Parker at the end of the street, still waiting with the carriage while Compton finished his lascivious business.

The swine.

Effie leaned back in her seat as the jarvey returned her to Brook Street. She was in a foul mood. Both frustrated and heartsick. Angry, too, though she didn't know at whom.

Still, the morning hadn't been a complete waste of her time. She'd learned the name of Compton's mistress, as well as the lady's address and the time of their weekly assignations. Mrs. Dora Naismith, a woman with the same striking coloring as Miss Corvus. Apparently, Compton had a weakness for raven-haired beauties. Which put Effie in a strong position, all things considered.

And Mrs. Naismith's name wasn't the only information Effie had garnered.

Like it or not—useful or not—she now knew where Gabriel lived.

· · · · ·

Gabriel's address proved to be of value to Effie much sooner than she had anticipated.

Later that afternoon, during Lady Belwood's receiving hours, Lord Mannering called with his sister, Ruth.

Effie had just completed her latest sampler and sent it off to the Academy. It had spelled out Dora Naismith's name in code. Whether that name would mean anything to Miss Corvus, Effie could only guess.

After straightening her skirts and smoothing her hair, she joined Lady Belwood to greet their guests in the drawing room. Her ladyship was often present when Effie had visitors. It was as much out of anxiety, Effie suspected, as out of a desire to provide proper chaperonage. She sat down beside Effie on the settee as Lord Mannering and his sister took their seats on the brocade sofa opposite. Formal calls were brief affairs, lasting only between ten and twenty minutes. Most visitors didn't even remain long enough for a cup of tea.

"We've come on a mission," Lord Mannering said, his hat and gloves in hand. "Tell her, Ruth."

Miss Mannering was sensibly clad in a plain brown wool dress, with no visible sign of a wire crinoline. The older of the pair, she had the look of a girl who had been cursed with far more intelligence than her male relations and had long been obliged to endure their prattling with good grace. "My brother has got it into his head to attend Mr. Galezzo's high-wire performance at Cremorne Gardens tomorrow evening. Perhaps you've heard of it?"

Effie wasn't acquainted with Mr. Galezzo's act, but she'd often read about Cremorne Gardens. It was a famous twelve-acre pleasure garden located on the northern bank of the Thames. The newspapers regularly featured stories on the entertainments offered there, everything from its famous Chinese dancing pagoda to concerts, balloon ascents, and military exhibitions.

"A high-wire act," Lady Belwood murmured. "How thrilling."

"The fellow traverses a six-hundred-foot wire suspended fifty feet in the air," Lord Mannering relayed eagerly. "There's a ballet afterward, and a supper. Fireworks, too, if you and Ruth aren't done in. That is . . ." He bestowed a sheepish smile on Effie. "If you'll consent to come."

"Is it safe, sir?" Lady Belwood asked. "One hears things about Cremorne. Alarming tales of what goes on after dark. One wonders if it's still quite a respectable place?"

"It's safe enough with an escort," Lord Mannering said. "I wouldn't let the ladies out of my sight." He looked to Effie. "Do say you'll join us. I'm told that Galezzo crosses the wire both forward and backward. Imagine!"

Effie recalled her promise to Carena Compton—*and* her reasons for making it. "Lady Belwood is right. It does sound thrilling. But surely such a death-defying display deserves a larger party?" She brightened. "I know! We could invite Miss Compton."

Miss Mannering's thin brows lifted at the suggestion. She noticeably refrained from comment.

Lord Mannering shifted in his seat. "Don't mean to be ungracious, but . . . not much fun for a chap to host a large party of females. Hadn't we best keep it just you, me, and m'sister?"

"Yes, I see." Effie nodded in thought. "Naturally, we shall have to add two more gentlemen to the group to even the numbers."

Miss Mannering's mouth curved with quiet understanding. She doubtless suspected that Effie desired to convert a potential tête-à-tête with Lord Mannering into a less intimate affair, without outright rejecting the man. "Lord Powell might be willing," she said. "He and my brother often go about together to these sorts of events."

"Not quite the same, Ruth," Lord Mannering said under his breath.

"Lord Powell will do nicely." Effie's thoughts turned to the red brick house in Sloane Street, with its black-painted door. To the way she'd felt looking up at it this morning. A wild idea took hold of her. "And I know just the gentleman to complete our party," she said. "Miss Compton mentioned him particularly."

"A gentleman for Miss Compton?" Lord Mannering perked up. "Oh, well that's all right."

"You'll join us then, Miss Flite?" Miss Mannering asked.

"I would be delighted," Effie said.

She told herself later, as she wrote out the invitation to Gabriel, that she was only doing it to vex him. It was important to keep one's enemies close. More important still to keep them off-balance. If she played her hand well, a visit to Cremorne Gardens tomorrow night would do both.

But as she sealed the envelope and rang for a footman to deliver it to Sloane Street, Effie knew herself to be a liar. There was only one reason for inviting Gabriel. It had nothing to do with strategy, and everything to do with her heart.

16

On returning to Sloane Street that evening, after a day spent in meetings with Lord Haverford and his influential friends, Gabriel was met in the hall by Kilby, Ollie O'Cleary, and Bill Walsh. The three hovered as Gabriel divested himself of his hat, coat, and gloves.

Gabriel's already grim mood took a turn for the worse. "Not at the door," he said before stalking into the gaslit dining room. There, he poured himself a glass of whiskey from the bottle on the mahogany sideboard and downed it in one swallow. If there was one thing he couldn't tolerate, it was being met at the door with bad news. And by the looks on their faces, Gabriel was in for a parcel of it.

Setting down his empty glass, he rested his hands on the sideboard, head bent.

He counted himself a skillful businessman when it came to running the betting shop and dealing with the fraught politics of the Rookery. The complicated mechanisms of government involved in improving a London neighborhood, however, were another beast entirely.

Ensconced with Haverford and several other gentlemen in a smoke-filled room at their club, Gabriel had listened as the men talked about forming a committee, in consult with Lord Compton, to write an impartial report on conditions in St. Giles. Haverford had also suggested that Compton might pen a newspaper article in support of reform to be published in the *Times*. There had been other proposals, too—nearly half a dozen altogether—but however well-thought-out and well-intentioned, they all bore two things in common. Each required Compton's unequivocal support, and each required time—an abundance of it.

Gabriel had no desire for the former. As for the latter . . .

The Rookery was running out of time. Which meant Gabriel was, too. He had no patience for lengthy studies, detailed reports, or pious editorials. The people of St. Giles needed change now, not in some unreliable, indefinite future. Without it, the already dwindling slum wouldn't survive another year.

He poured himself another glass of whiskey. Kilby, Ollie, and Walsh waited in the dining room doorway. Kilby was unshakable as ever, his posture unbending, and his lined face a study in butler-like reserve. His stillness cast an unflattering light on Ollie's and Walsh's restlessness. The two shifted from foot to foot with nervous apprehension, the soles of their shoes squeaking in protest.

"Walsh," Gabriel said, taking a drink. "Speak to me."

Bill Walsh stepped forward. He held his cloth cap in his meaty hands. What remained of his hair was ruthlessly slicked down with a heavy application of bear grease pomade. "I found someone, Mr. Royce. An old woman what knew Grace."

"Did you," Gabriel said in a flat monotone. "And yet . . ." He cast a dispassionate glance around the dining room. "I see no old woman here. Do you, Kilby?"

"No, sir," the butler replied.

Gabriel took another drink. "I distinctly recall telling you that if you found someone you were to bring them to me."

"Yes, sir," Walsh said.

"Yes, sir," Gabriel murmured. "Yet, here we are."

Walsh drew closer. "Thing is, Mr. Royce, I did try to get her to come, but the old woman—Mrs. Young, she calls herself—she weren't having it. Says she won't travel outside Hertfordshire on no account. And seeing as how you said I wasn't to use violence—"

Gabriel leveled a look at him. "Hertfordshire? Is that where you've been since Tuesday?"

Walsh nodded. "A blacksmith chap in Church Lane directed me. Claimed this Mrs. Young knew everyone from the old days in St. Giles. She lived in the same lodging house as him 'til five years ago when she moved to Trowley Green—a village outside Sawbridgeworth—to lodge with her widowed sister."

"And she knew Grace, did she?"

"She says she knew *of* her."

Gabriel exhaled a weary breath. It appeared he would be making a journey to Trowley Green.

The timing was scarcely convenient. Sawbridgeworth was over thirty miles away. He'd lose nearly a day traveling back and forth on the train, and for what? A few very likely useless scraps of information about someone else's aged family servant?

But not someone else's. Effie's.

He straightened from the sideboard, leaving the rest of his drink unfinished. "Give Kilby the address."

"Yes, Mr. Royce." Walsh bobbed his head.

"Kilby?" Gabriel summoned the butler next. "I presume you have something pressing to tell me?"

The butler approached. "A footman delivered this for you earlier this afternoon, sir. He claimed it was important." Kilby handed Gabriel a white envelope sealed with a pale violet wafer.

"From Compton?" Gabriel asked as he took it.

"The footman was from the Belwoods' residence in Brook Street, sir."

Gabriel stilled. He stared at the envelope in his hand. The direction had been written in a firm but delicate hand. *His* direction.

He didn't wait until he was alone to open it. While the three men stood back, with varying expressions of unease, Gabriel broke the seal on the envelope. The letter inside was short and to the point—only a few lines, penned in the same elegant hand as the one that had written out his address.

Dear Sir,

I shall be visiting Cremorne Gardens tomorrow evening, along with a small party of friends, to view Mr. Galezzo's high-wire act. We would be pleased if you would join us.

We depart Brook Street at eight o'clock. Meet us there, if you are so inclined.

Yours etc.,
E. Flite

Gabriel read the message twice through before folding it back into its envelope and thrusting it into the pocket of his waistcoat. He was aware of his heart beating rather more heavily than it had a moment ago. It did nothing to improve his mood.

How the devil had she obtained his address? And what friends? Gentlemen ones, no doubt.

Scowling, he picked up his glass again. "What about you, Ollie?" he asked crossly. "Anything you want to add?"

"Only that Miss Flite were here earlier, sir."

Gabriel dropped his glass back onto the sideboard with a heavy clink. He turned on the lad. "*Here?* In my *house?*"

Ollie took a reflexive step backward. "Not inside it, Mr. Royce. On the street. She came up on me, like. Thought I were following her again."

"Miss Flite was in Sloane Street?"

Ollie nodded rapidly. "She were angry at me. Said I was to tell anyone else you sent to follow her that she sees everything and she don't take kindly to spies."

"And somewhere in this brief and riveting exchange, you told her this house belonged to me." Gabriel felt the bitter urge to laugh. And not with humor. In dismay at the extent of his own masculine naivete.

Had he really thought that his warnings to Effie in Hyde Park would have any appreciable effect on her? That she'd seriously consider backing off of Compton?

No, Gabriel hadn't thought she would. Neither had he thought that she'd turn her sights on him.

Look sharp, she'd told him.

And Gabriel hadn't. He'd been too busy being pulled in twenty different directions. Too distracted with trying to save himself, all the while confident in the fact that Effie would never find Wingard's documents, not if it was Compton she was chasing.

But she wasn't chasing him any longer, was she? Not exclusively.

Gabriel saw it now quite clearly. Effie Flite was chasing him.

17

Effie stole another wary glance at Gabriel as she, and the rest of their party, passed through the wrought iron gates that marked the King's Road entrance to Cremorne Gardens. The sun was setting, but one would never know it. Gaslights and colored oil lamps illuminated the lush, tree-covered landscape, lending a magical air to the ornamental fountains, variegated flower beds, and classically styled statuary.

Music floated on the evening breeze, drifting down from the orchestra pavilion to the ever-increasing clusters of newly arrived visitors near the gates. People of every class were here to see Mr. Galezzo's famed performance. Fashionable ladies and gentlemen in evening clothes, who had come straight from the theater or opera house, entered alongside bawdy women, shabbily dressed men, and common working folk with their entire families in tow.

The atmosphere buzzed with excitement. Everywhere one turned, people were smiling, laughing, and making merry.

But Effie wasn't attending them. Try as she might to maintain an air of polite disinterest, her attention kept returning to Gabriel.

He had appeared in Brook Street promptly at eight, looking devastatingly handsome in a black three-piece suit and plain black wool overcoat. An understated ensemble, transformed into the devil's raiment by Gabriel's stark features, cold eyes, and menacing figure.

The faces of Lord Mannering and Lord Powell had both drained of color to see him. The ladies had been only slightly more welcoming. Miss Compton had stiffly inclined her head, and Miss Mannering had offered a rigid curtsy.

Gabriel had endured their snobbery with his usual air of detachment. The only glimpse of emotion he'd shown was when he'd turned his sinister sights on Effie. To everyone else, the expression in his icy blue gaze had doubtless been as remote as it was before. But not to her. She'd seen a flicker of smoldering challenge.

"You asked and I came, mortal," that blazing look seemed to say. "Behold what happens when you summon Hades up from the underworld."

Too late, Effie realized she'd made a grave miscalculation.

When she'd written to Gabriel yesterday, she'd known he would be provoked by her effrontery. However, she'd presumed that, on his arrival, his aggravation would be tempered by his usual sardonic humor. That they'd spar the way they had in Hyde Park, when he'd covered her hand with his atop his heavily beating heart. A confrontation edged with a hint of sweetness, just like every other encounter they'd had.

Instead, Gabriel's irritation appeared to have festered into something unpredictable and dangerous.

Registering his granite-hard countenance as he walked beside her, Effie's pulse trilled an unmistakable warning. He was angry, to be sure. But she couldn't yet discern whether that anger was directed at her, or at himself.

"The wire walker's act commences at nine o'clock," Lord Powell said, leading them along the gravel path that cut through the park's green velvet expanse of lawn. He was a stocky, fair-haired gentleman of modest height, with a neatly trimmed beard and mustache. Not as dashing a man as Lord Mannering, but attractive enough, given his pedigree. For the moment, he only possessed a courtesy title. On his father's death, however, Powell would inherit an earldom.

Miss Compton walked between him and Lord Mannering as though it were she who was hosting the party and not Lord Mannering and his sister. A costly strawberry pink silk cloak floated over her equally expensive evening dress. She cast her eyes over the raucous crowds with a disdainful air. "It appears all of London has come to see him perform his wire walk."

"Cremorne requires no test of pedigree," Miss Mannering replied. Like Miss Compton, she wore an evening dress, though hers boasted slightly less in the way of trimmings. "If it did, it would quickly go out of business."

"No danger of that," Lord Mannering said. He cast a wistful glance at Effie in the lamplight. It wasn't the first such look he'd aimed at her since they'd arrived. "You're not too cold, Miss Flite?"

"Not at all." Effie's black velvet cloak was thin, but the Parisienne evening dress she wore beneath it was warm enough on its own. Made of midnight blue grosgrain silk, the tight, round-waisted bodice was cut low at the neck and shoulders, culminating in delicate cap sleeves, and the passementerie-trimmed skirts were abundant. Paired with the glittering glass dragonflies in her hair and the dainty grosgrain belt circling her midsection, the whole of it presented a striking picture.

Effie had intended it so as she'd dressed this evening. At the time, she'd been thinking of Gabriel's reaction rather than her work for the Academy.

Another amateurish mistake.

Had her head been less in the clouds, she'd have listened to the cautionary voice in it telling her that she ought not risk outshining Miss Compton.

Effie still needed the girl. She required continued access to Lord Compton, especially now. This afternoon's post had brought a sampler from Nell. It had contained two terse words in coded reply to the sampler Effie had sent about Compton having a mistress: **NOT ENOUGH**.

As if Effie hadn't known that!

She obviously had much more to learn. Much more to prove.

"You've never been to Cremorne before, have you?" Miss Mannering asked. She walked beside Effie and Gabriel, a few steps behind Lord Mannering and the others.

"I've not had the pleasure," Effie said.

Lord Mannering looked back at her. "It's a delightful place. They have countless fantastical exhibitions in the spring and summer. Tonight, the high wire, and next week there's to be a balloon ascension by the aeronaut Mr. Chapin."

"My brother enjoys death-defying displays," Miss Mannering said.

"Do you attend them as well?" Effie asked her.

Light from one of the torches lining the path shone over Miss Mannering's solemn face. "But rarely. My taste doesn't run to popular entertainments. I favor more scholarly pursuits."

Lord Mannering laughed. "Give Ruth a lecture over a feat of derring-do any day. She vastly prefers them, and the drier the better."

Miss Mannering endured her younger brother's gibes with good humor. "Phillip only thinks the lectures I attend are dry because they have to do with the affairs of women."

"I rather enjoy a good lecture," Effie said. "In Paris, I regularly attended talks at the Institut Historique and the École des Beaux-Arts."

Miss Mannering's mouth curved with approval. "I had a feeling you were sensible."

Effie smiled. "What gave me away?"

"Your choice of reading material at Hatchards, to start." Miss Mannering dropped her voice. "And your kindness to my brother. Any other lady would have brutally dispatched him by now."

"Perhaps rejection would be a kindness in itself," Effie replied quietly. "But I have few enough friends in London without dispatching the ones who actively seek my company."

"If you have a mind to make more, you might be interested in attending a talk with me next Wednesday morning in Kensington. Lady Bartlett has invited a prominent Manchester teacher to speak about the education of girls. It's open house. Everyone is welcome."

"I'd like that very much," Effie said. "Thank you, Miss Mannering."

"Please, call me Ruth."

"Euphemia," Effie offered in reply. She felt Gabriel's cool gaze briefly touch her face.

She knew what he must be thinking. She'd given him leave to call her Effie, while Ruth Mannering was denied the privilege.

It wasn't the same.

Ruth may be the sort of girl that, under other circumstances, Effie would have been friends with, but they *weren't* friends. They would never *be* friends. How could they when Effie was here under false pretenses?

Given her mission, it was safer to refrain from forming intimate connections. A friend could be hurt by Effie's deception. An acquaintance could only be disappointed.

As for Gabriel, Effie saw him for no more and no less than exactly what he was. And, despite the fact he knew nothing of her past, he saw her, too. Like recognized like, he'd told her the night they'd met. There was no question of betrayal between the two of them. They knew what they were.

Which is why he had no right to be angry with her. Not on any account. She'd told him flat out that she intended to continue about her business. If Gabriel was foolish enough to stand in her way, he had only himself to blame.

Miss Compton glanced at Effie over her shoulder. "Don't let fashionable society hear of your attendance at one of Lady Bartlett's gatherings, Miss Flite. You wouldn't like to get a name for yourself."

"Is that name bluestocking?" Ruth retorted, seeming to be only half in jest. "There are worse names for women."

"Only one name is worthy for females of *my* acquaintance," Miss Compton said. "That name is lady."

"Well put," Lord Powell said. "A true lady, with all her delicacy, is a creature to be revered." He offered Ruth his arm as they ascended the gentle slope toward the exhibition grounds. "If you'll permit me, Miss Mannering?"

A blush pinkened Ruth's cheeks as she accepted his arm. It was she who had suggested including Lord Powell in their party, and it was now apparent why. She plainly had a soft spot for the man. "Thank you, my lord."

Miss Compton took the opportunity to take Lord Mannering's arm. It was the work of a moment. She'd already asserted her claim over him by her proximity. She'd scarcely left his side since she'd arrived in Brook Street.

Lord Mannering flashed another regretful look in Effie's direction before resigning himself to Miss Compton's maneuverings.

Effie fell in beside Gabriel as the others pulled ahead of them. His head was bent, his jaw set hard, as he walked. His thoughts seemed to have turned inward, leaving his outward aspect as impenetrable as armor. Only a muscle ticking in his cheek betrayed the war he was battling within.

"You haven't had much to say to me, sir," she remarked.

"I have a great deal to say to you, and none of it fit for company." His deep voice was completely without inflection.

A prickle of anxiety traced down Effie's spine. He was behaving much as he had when she'd first met him. That distant gaze, and that cold, remote manner, with no emotion to soften it. Then, it had intrigued her. Tonight, it set her on edge.

This, she recognized, was the ominous calm before the storm. And a storm was coming; she could feel it. She nevertheless affected an air of unconcern. "Oh?"

"You might have mentioned that Mannering and Powell were to be in your party."

"You don't approve of them?"

His face was impassive. "They both owe me money."

Effie recalled how the two men had reacted when Gabriel had arrived in Brook Street. "Goodness. That certainly explains a lot."

"So, it wasn't part of your plan?"

"To make them miserable? Of course not."

"To make me miserable, then."

"Are you?" She smiled. "I'm sorry to hear it."

"Now why do I have difficulty believing that?" he murmured.

Effie refused to be intimidated by his mood. Never mind that her insides were starting to tremble and her palms were growing damp beneath her evening gloves. She'd never shrunk from a challenge.

Drawing closer to him, she tucked her hand in his arm uninvited. Gabriel stiffened at her touch, but he didn't withdraw from her. Effie didn't know what she would have done if he had. It was difficult enough pretending they were on civil terms this evening without having to deal with an outright rejection.

"You're here, aren't you?" she said. "It can't only be to punish me for my impertinence."

"Impertinence, you call it, coming to my home? Threatening Ollie? Writing to me at my address?"

"How dastardly you make me sound."

"Dastardly," he repeated. "That's a word for it."

"I can think of a few others—bold, clever, inventive." Effie paused. "Why do you keep such a fine house in Sloane Street?"

He gave her a look that was hard to read. "You thought it fine?"

"Anyone would. It's a handsome home in a good neighborhood, well suited for a gentleman of means and his family." An alarming thought entered her head. "You don't *have* a family, do you?"

He'd asked her if she was married, but it had never occurred to her that he might be married himself. Not until this instant.

Gabriel's silence did nothing to quell her uncertainty.

"Do you?" she asked again.

He was quiet another moment before answering. "Not a soul."

"No wife?" she clarified. "Someone waiting at home for you in that fine house?"

"It's as empty as I am, Miss Flite," he said without a trace of humor.

Miss Flite? They had regressed. She opened her mouth to tell him so when he forestalled her.

"Do you take me for a fool?" he asked.

Her already uneven pulse skittered with apprehension. "I wouldn't dream of—"

"Perchance you've mistaken me for some untried youth you can make dance on a string?"

The beating of Effie's heart drowned out the music and conversation that surrounded them. The crowds faded into the background. She and Gabriel might have been alone. "Really," she said. "That's flattering to neither of us."

"But accurate, I discern." He leveled her with a glare. "What did you suppose would happen when you sent for me?"

"I didn't *send* for you. I merely—"

"That I'd come on the trot like that little dog of yours?" No longer emotionless, his words had begun to take on the same dark edge she'd heard that day in Mother Comfort's. A flat drawl, with a downward intonation.

Effie suspected it was the lingering trace of his native accent. Birmingham, he'd said. She recalled how Ollie and the barman had recoiled to hear it, as though it were a sign of terrible things to come.

Did Gabriel imagine he could intimidate her in the same fashion? Send her cowering back in fear like he did those men in the Rookery? She wasn't his underling, by heaven.

And she was no man.

She met his cold gaze and held it, unflinching. "I assure you, Mr. Royce," she replied gravely, "I would *never* mistake you for Franc. One of you is a loyal and courageous companion, while the other . . ."

Is only a lapdog, she nearly said.

But she wasn't an idiot. Despite her desire to nettle him, she retained some small sense of self-preservation.

It made no difference in the end. She may as well have uttered the inflammatory words aloud. Gabriel as good as heard them.

Something perilous flickered at the back of his eyes. The barest crack in his armor. A glimmer of scorching emotion broke through. For an instant, he looked as though he wanted to seize her and shake her.

Or perhaps seize her and do something else.

Effie's breath stopped as apprehension was overpowered by a wild, and wholly nonsensical, rush of anticipation.

"Mind how you go, Miss Flite," Lord Mannering called back. "It's a bit of a crush up ahead."

Effie tore her gaze from Gabriel's. The giddy rush she'd felt only seconds before was snuffed out as swiftly as a candle flame doused with cold water.

Good heavens. She'd very nearly forgotten they were in company with other people. Not only Lord Mannering and his party, but the countless strangers who, like them, were making their way to the exhibition grounds.

It was precisely the problem. Effie's fascination with Gabriel Royce was clouding her judgment. So long as her head and her heart were caught up with him, she would never be able to think clearly enough for the task at hand. And Effie's future—*and* Franc's— depended on her thinking clearly.

She removed her hand from Gabriel's arm. "I shall stay close to you, my lord," she called back to Lord Mannering. "Have no fear."

Gabriel dropped a brooding look to his sleeve, where her gloved fingers had rested only seconds before. After a taut moment, he returned his attention to the gathering crowd ahead.

Hundreds of people had already congregated on the lawn in anticipation of Mr. Galezzo's performance. Gasps emerged from Miss Compton and several of the others walking nearby as the high wire came into view. Startlingly thin, the wire cable twinkled silver in the torchlit sky, stretching from a stand of old elm trees, beneath which a wooden platform had been erected, all the way to the top of the building opposite. Six hundred feet altogether, or so Lord Mannering had claimed.

Effie's stomach jolted on an expected roil of trepidation. She didn't see how it was possible for anyone to traverse a wire so fine, even a celebrated Italian ascensionist. Not unless the man weighed less than a sparrow.

"Most everyone else will be standing," Lord Mannering told them as they approached the front. "It will be better if we do as well, else we risk the chance of being unable to see."

"Mr. Galezzo will be fifty feet above us," Ruth pointed out. "We can hardly miss him."

People pressed in on them on every side as new arrivals joined the crowd on the lawn.

"It's so loud." Miss Compton wrinkled her nose at a humbly dressed party of ladies and gentlemen on their left. "And what is that appalling odor?"

Lord Mannering patted her hand in reflexive consolation. "I've procured a table for us at the restaurant afterward. You'll feel brighter when you've had some lobster salad and champagne. We can dine at our leisure until the fireworks begin at eleven."

Gabriel drew closer to Effie, wordlessly staking out his place amid the chaos.

Effie felt his presence beside her, less reassuring than simmering with unspoken promise. She chanced a fleeting look at him in the colored light. He wasn't interested in the high wire, nor in the prospect of lobster salad and champagne. His attention was entirely fixed on her.

"I'm not finished with you," he informed her darkly.

Effie's heart pounded an erratic rhythm. "Nor I with you," she retorted, sounding braver than she felt.

There were indeed going to be fireworks this evening, she thought grimly. And not only the kind in the sky.

· · · · ·

Gabriel had no liking for dangerous acts performed for entertainment's sake. Where he came from, life and death were serious matters. That very seriousness was doubtless the reason such displays drew enormous crowds. People thrilled to see wire dancers and aeronauts putting their lives in peril. The prospect of death was a heady liqueur. To cheat the devil even headier. It made the viewing public feel as if they, too, possessed some measure of immortality.

For Gabriel, it only made him impatient.

He'd come here tonight for Effie. To confront her, he'd thought. To show her that he was a force to be reckoned with. And yet, when he'd seen her in the drawing room in Brook Street, standing among her newfound friends of the fashionable elite, violet eyed and mysterious, with her glass dragonflies twinkling in her hair . . .

He'd been lost.

The realization brought him no pleasure.

It was, along with the increasingly tangled plans to reform the Rookery, yet another example of an improbable future. A glittering possibility that lingered just out of his reach. It was affecting his sleep. Making him restless. Making him weak. Gabriel's only hope was to rid himself of this frustrating attraction to Euphemia Flite completely. He was resolved to do it tonight.

There was but one way to go about the business. He would force her to admit her true intentions. To reveal herself as a mercenary jade who was using him, just as she was using Mannering and Compton's daughter, and God knows who else.

Gabriel's blood boiled to think of how easily she'd baited him. She'd practically called him her lapdog, by heaven! He wasn't stupid. He knew she'd only said it to provoke him. The infuriating point was how admirably she'd succeeded. And to what end? They were all of them nothing more than interchangeable pieces on her infernal board, necessary in her game to ruin Compton.

Gabriel had no intention of letting her succeed. Despite his attraction to her. Despite his heart (or any less noble organs he'd lately been thinking with). Nothing could be allowed to jeopardize his plans for saving the Rookery. And Compton's reputational well-being was an essential component of those plans. Too much depended on his support. Without it, everything else would crumble. Haverford and his influential friends would fall away. So, too, would the protections Gabriel enjoyed for his betting shop. There would be nothing left. Compton would see to that. And it would all be because Effie couldn't leave it alone.

And because Gabriel couldn't leave *her* alone.

He stared straight ahead, his mood darkening by the second. The crowd around them increased in size, the people growing raucous and impatient. It must be nearing nine o'clock. Gabriel was reaching for his pocket watch to confirm the time when a portly gentleman in garish plaid trousers and a velvet top hat came out to address them.

"Ladies and gentlemen!" the man announced in a booming voice that carried over the assembled throng. "Esteemed guests! You are about to witness a feat so daring, so extraordinary, that it defies belief. A rare and astonishing act performed by a man whose name is spoken with reverence all across our great realm. I present to you the renowned wire dancer himself, magician of the rope and acclaimed Italian ascensionist, the one and only, Carlo Galezzo!"

A small dark-haired man bounded out onto the green. He was dressed in a pair of garish gold-embroidered red silk trunks, worn over a full body leotard. Not more than one and twenty if he was a day, he sketched flamboyant bows to his audience in every direction before gracefully climbing the ladder attached to the wooden platform by the elms.

When he reached the top, he stepped to the edge of the platform. The thin cable stretched ahead of him. Lanterns had been positioned at various angles beneath it to illuminate his progress. The crowd collectively held its breath as he extended his leg and set his foot on the wire.

Gabriel heard Effie inhale sharply. Glancing down at her, he found her pale and still, staring up at Galezzo with a rapt, vaguely terrified expression. Gabriel's brows sank in a frown. She'd owned to being afraid of heights. Did that fear extend to seeing others in high places? He suspected it did.

The little fool. Hadn't she realized the effect Galezzo's performance might have on her?

But it was too late for Gabriel to draw her away from the spectacle. They were boxed in on three sides, the full force of the crowd pressing against them as Galezzo took his first steps out onto the wire.

He swayed back and forth, drawing gasps from the crowd, but he didn't falter. Knees bent and eyes fixed straight in front of him, he placed his right foot at an angle directly in front of his left, advancing slowly but surely to the midpoint of the wire.

A hum of amazement passed over the audience. There were more gasps and whispers, along with a few murmured prayers for the wire dancer's safety.

Effie's hand crept into Gabriel's. She was still staring at Galezzo, seemingly unaware that she'd reached out to Gabriel for reassurance.

But Gabriel wasn't unaware. His chest tightened as his fingers engulfed hers.

He was still going to rid himself of his attraction to her, but not now. Not yet. In this moment, Effie was in his care. Vexing as she was, Gabriel didn't take the charge of her lightly.

"How does he do it?" Miss Compton whispered to Lord Mannering. "Why doesn't he fall?"

"He never falls," Lord Mannering said under his breath. "The man's a marvel."

Galezzo continued across the wire, grinning broadly. He seemed to draw confidence from the astounded murmurs. He'd just reached the opposite side, and was preparing to retrace his steps backward, when the iron hook that secured the cable to the tree gave an ominous screech.

Time stood still—hundreds of people frozen to the spot, looking up with matching expressions of horror. Effie's hand clenched Gabriel's spasmodically as a woman's shrill cry pierced the silence. The man in the plaid trousers sprinted to the platform in company with several workmen. But it was all too late.

Metal scraped against metal as the hook broke free of its chain moorings.

Galezzo's face betrayed a split second of dismay before the wire slackened under his feet and he plummeted forty feet to the ground, landing on the gravel promenade.

Screams rent the air, and the crowd rushed forward. Gabriel pulled Effie in front of him, shielding her with his body. Someone shoved him hard in the back, and another nearly trampled over Miss Compton. She appeared to have fainted dead away on the grass. Beside her, Miss Mannering turned an odd shade of green before sinking down into her skirts. Powell staggered, white-faced, to help her, looking as though he might be sick himself.

People were crying and shouting on every side, their attentions scattered between the surfeit of collapsing ladies and the broken and bleeding body of the lifeless Galezzo.

"Somebody help him!" a man cried.

"A doctor! Is anyone a doctor?" another called out.

"I'm a doctor!" someone replied. "Out of my way!"

Effie's knees buckled. Gabriel swept her up into his arms before she could fall. He had a vague impression of Mannering and Powell crouched down, tending to Miss Compton and Miss Mannering. Gabriel didn't pause to inquire after the ladies' welfare. He was thinking of only one lady.

"Is Galezzo dead?" someone cried out amid the shouts and screams.

"If he isn't, he soon will be," an unhelpful male voice replied. "He's broken his head."

Effie moaned softly. "Oh God."

"Don't look." Gabriel pressed her face into the curve of his neck. Turning from the gruesome scene, he carried her away, shouldering a path for them back through the crowd.

"I saw him fall. I saw his face—"

"You're safe," Gabriel said. "I have you." He conveyed her down the path, leaving the chaos behind. Leaving *everything* behind. He strode toward the tall trees and rolling lawn that lay away from the orchestra pavilion, the restaurants, and the colorful lights of the exhibition grounds. He didn't stop until they were exactly where they needed to be.

Alone.

18

After eleven, the densely planted tangle of trees off the main avenues of Cremorne Gardens became the preferred haunt of prostitutes. There, dark walks abounded, and foliage provided ample cover for illicit dealings. But not now. It was hours until the fireworks, and the sordid elements hadn't yet staked their claim. Until they did, the woods were merely secluded, and comparatively quiet. A place one could catch one's breath.

Gabriel set Effie down on the ground beneath an enormous oak. Colored glass oil lamps illuminated its heavy branches in soft shades of yellow, red, and green. She offered no objection, merely slumped there, pale and trembling, in her thin velvet cloak.

She'd witnessed a man's death. That alone was a debilitating enough shock for a lady. But this man hadn't just died. He'd met his end falling from a great height. It was Effie's worst fear in the world, Gabriel suspected.

Taking off his coat, he draped it over her shoulders. "Don't move," he commanded.

He strode off to the nearest restaurant tent where, for a few coins, he procured a bottle of cheap champagne and an empty glass. Promptly bringing it back to Effie, he filled the glass and pressed it to her lips. "Drink."

"I don't—"

"Drink."

A line formed between her ebony brows as she obeyed him. She began with a small sip. He tipped the glass, encouraging her to swallow the whole of it. She grimaced, turning her face away. "It's dreadful."

"It's swill," he allowed. "But it will do the trick." He waited until she'd finished and then, casting aside the glass, sank down on the ground beside her.

She bent her head, her eyes squeezing shut. "I feel as though I'm going to be sick."

"Give it five minutes."

"You imagine strong drink will make things better?"

"It generally does."

She buried her face in her gloved hands. A sob emerged from behind her fingers. "I can't get his face out of my head."

Gabriel's chest constricted at the sound of her tears. He set his hand on the narrow curve of her back. "Don't think about it."

"Was he—"

"The doctor is with him. There's nothing we can do."

"He can't have survived, can he?" Her quaking voice choked with emotion. "That poor man. He wasn't much more than a boy."

"It will have been quick," Gabriel said. It was a small mercy. He'd seen Galezzo's body lying twisted on the bloodstained gravel. Doubtless the man's back had broken, along with his head.

Effie's shoulders shook as she wept for him.

Gabriel encircled her with his arm, drawing her firmly against his chest. She came to him willingly, dampening his shoulder with her tears as he held her.

The situation was far from ideal. He in an agony of frustration at his inability to protect and console her, and she overcome with emotion at having seen the wire walker fall. Some rogue, treacherous part of Gabriel's brain nevertheless marked how perfectly they fit together. It whispered in his ear and in his heart, a devil come to tempt him, telling him that she had been fashioned just for him. That she was his missing piece. The other part of his soul.

Despite her tears, despite the circumstances, he was overcome by a powerful feeling of rightness.

He turned his face into the raven coils of her hair, inhaling the intoxicating fragrance of honey and black currants. He was no good at comforting people. But this was important. *She* was important. "It's all right," he said. "It's over. I have you now."

The storm of Effie's tears slowly subsided. Gabriel held her until she grew still and quiet, rubbing her back and murmuring into her hair. She took a deep, unsteady breath. Her tears had ceased, but she made no attempt to withdraw from him.

Gabriel supposed he should have acted for both of them, setting her away from him and speedily returning her to her friends. But decorum counted for nothing when weighed against the sensation of Effie in his arms.

The faint strains of violin music floated over the darkened gardens as the orchestra resumed playing at the pavilion. Gabriel recognized the melody of Schubert's "Serenade." It felt leagues away, somewhere in the vast distance, far removed from the darkened, tree-shrouded sanctuary where he and Effie had withdrawn.

"Mannering shouldn't have brought you to such a display," he said.

"He wasn't to know what would happen."

"What do you imagine becomes of wire dancers, sweetheart? They inevitably fall. It's a danger of the job."

She murmured something in reply. Gabriel couldn't fully hear it—her voice was muffled against his chest—but it sounded as though she'd said, "I feel as though it was me who fell."

His jaw tightened, recalling her face as she'd watched Galezzo take his first steps out onto the wire. "You should never have been here in the first place," he said. "What madness compelled you to accept Mannering's invitation?"

"I promised Miss Compton I'd include her the next time he invited me anywhere."

A frown darkened Gabriel's brow. "You and your scheming. Look where it's ended you."

She didn't reply, only slipped her arm around his midsection.

His heart contracted painfully. Still scowling, he enfolded her in a fierce embrace. Soft tremors were coursing through her body in waves. "You require a new cloak," he said crossly.

She nestled closer in response.

He tucked her head under his chin. One of her ever-present glass dragonfly pins scraped his jaw. His scowl deepened. "And someone must buy you proper jewels for your hair."

She didn't inquire as to who that someone might be. "These *are* proper jewels."

"Glass," he scoffed. "You should have diamonds."

"The man I bought them from in Paris said that dragonflies symbolize transformation. He told me they'd bring me luck."

"*Bad* luck. Where I come from, they're called the devil's darning needles. Parents warn their children that, if they tell lies, a dragonfly will sew their mouth shut."

Effie glanced up at him with concern through her tear-damp lashes. "Did *your* parents tell you that?"

"I had no parents," he said. "None who would take the trouble to tell me fairy stories."

"Your mother and father—"

"Just a father, and only in name. He drowned in the cut before I left Birmingham."

"Oh, Gabriel." Her arm tightened around him. "I'm sorry."

"So am I—that he didn't die sooner. I'd have been vastly better off."

She stilled in his arms. "How can one be better off with no parents? Without them . . . where do you belong? You have no home. No true connection."

"You have what you make."

"It isn't the same."

His brows notched. He remembered Lady Belwood saying something about having been close friends with Effie's guardian. But what of Effie's mother and father? Had they gone the way of Gabriel's own parents?

"You speak as though you're familiar with the condition," he said.

She fell quiet. "No," she replied at length. "But I read things. I feel things. It seems to me—"

"I've lived it, love," he said. "There's no use mourning the loss of something you never had. If you want to survive you have to keep moving."

Effie again lapsed into silence. And then: "Don't you ever look backward?"

"I don't care about that part of my past." He gazed down at her. "Your past, on the other hand . . ."

She bent her head. "Mine is of no interest."

"It is to me." He paused. "Have you always been afraid of heights?"

She settled her cheek back against his breast, directly atop his beating heart. "As long as I can remember."

"Why?" he asked.

"Common sense. Look what happens when you ascend too high."

Her answer rang hollow in Gabriel's ears. It wasn't a lie, as far as he could tell, but neither was it the whole truth. "You said you'd been on a roof once. That someone was injured."

"Yes." She took her time in continuing, as though pulling the story from the dark depths of her soul. "She came to my rescue, like you did on the terrace. But we were children. She was smaller than me, and I was too frightened. She was attempting to help me down when she lost her grip."

He drew back to glare at her. "What in blazes were you doing up there in the first place?"

"Facing my fears," she said. "I believed it was necessary to overcome them."

"On the roof of a blasted building?"

She was unrepentant. As if it were perfectly normal for girls in finishing schools to be cavorting about on rooftops. "Haven't you any outsize fears?"

He snorted a derisive breath. "You imagine I'd confess them to you?"

"I wouldn't use it against you."

"I'm sure," he said dryly.

"I mean it." She toyed with one of the cloth-covered buttons on his waistcoat. "It seems only fair you should tell me. You already know my greatest fear."

"A fear for a fear?" Gabriel uttered a low huff of amusement. "Very well, if it will keep you from dwelling on that cursed wire walker." He thought about it a moment before answering. "I expect, if I'm terrified of anything, it's of being still."

"Being still?" she echoed doubtfully.

"Stay too long in one place, let your defenses down, and someone's always there to get the better of you. Rob you. Kill you. A lad has to stay alert, keep moving, if he wants to survive."

"Everyone must sleep eventually."

"Some people sleep with one eye open."

Effie gave him a thoughtful look. "Some people must be very tired."

Gabriel's mouth hitched wryly. "Exhausted."

"That's why it's important to have a true friend. Someone you trust with your life. You can sleep in turns."

"You speak from your vast experience?"

She settled back against him. "I have friends who look after me."

"And to think," he said into her hair, "I might have been one of them."

"A pity, as I told you."

Her hand found his. She didn't take it outright, but her fingers twined idly with his own.

There was a casual possessiveness in her touch, as though he belonged to her alone. She'd touched him just the same that night in Compton's garden, smoothing his hair and adjusting his cravat. Gabriel had held himself still for her, drinking in every second of her tenderness, parched for the lack of it.

He wasn't accustomed to intimacy. Not this variety. He had the uneasy premonition that, when it came to her, he would never get enough of it.

"Why does your accent come and go?" she asked him.

He toyed with her fingers. "I try to prevent it."

"Why?"

"It's uncouth," he said. "People of your class take me more seriously when I talk like them."

"Did you teach yourself to do so?"

"Not well enough. My old accent always comes back when I feel too much."

She went quiet again. And then: "Do you feel too much for me?"

He couldn't deny it. Not when she was in his arms. "I suppose I must, else I wouldn't be here."

"I'm glad you're here," she said softly. "Glad you can be still with me."

"Is that what I'm doing?"

"Aren't you?"

Gabriel hesitated to give voice to his more cynical thoughts. To ask the question that had been plaguing him since he'd received her invitation. He knew it would spoil whatever was happening between them. This fragile spun-glass illusion of closeness and warmth, so far untouched by the realities that separated them in the daylight. He had no wish to shatter it. Nevertheless . . .

"Why did you invite me to join Mannering's party?" he asked.

She said nothing.

Gabriel's mood dipped. She was soft and pliant in his arms. A fragrant bundle of black currant–perfumed femininity, trusting him, all but embracing him in return here in the lamplit darkness. But he couldn't allow himself to forget what she was. Even at her most vulnerable, Euphemia Flite was still a panther on the hunt. He wouldn't make the error of mistaking her for a harmless tabby.

"You don't have to answer," he said. "I already know why. You believe you can play with me like you're playing with Compton."

"Why would you imagine I'd deal with you as I intend to deal with him?" she asked. "Are you the same as he is?"

Gabriel bent his head closer to her. His lips brushed the silken shell of her ear. "Darling, I'm worse."

Effie's mouth curled up at one corner, threatening a smile. "How much worse?" she wondered. "Have you ruined many ladies?"

Gabriel's own brief smile faded.

"Have you broken their hearts?" she asked.

He thought of the emotionless liaisons he'd had in his youth. Cold, transactional encounters with no warmth or affection to them. "The ladies I've known were already ruined when they met me," he said. "And there was no question of hearts."

"What about their money?"

Gabriel scorned at the suggestion. "I don't take money from women."

"Just from men."

"Men who know what I am when they meet me. If they owe me anything, it's because they choose to take the risk. That's the nature of gambling." He caught her chin with his fingers, gently forcing her to look at him. Her blue eyes were still tear-damp, glistening up at him like dark violet jewels beneath the glow of the colored lamps.

"What about you, minx?" he asked. "Ruined any men lately? Broken any hearts?"

"No, not yet." She smiled. "But the night is young."

· · · · ·

Effie knew very well what she'd done. Her teasing words had been akin to throwing down a gauntlet. Being the man he was, Gabriel had no choice but to pick it up. She watched, heart beating hard, as a dozen conflicting emotions crossed his face at once. He was plainly at war with himself—half of him desperately wanting to resist her, and half of him wanting her full stop.

There was no question which half would prevail.

His expression became dangerously intent. No longer pale as ice, his blue eyes burned with an unmistakable fire. Still holding her chin in his grasp, he bent his head and kissed her.

Effie's eyes closed as his mouth claimed hers. The last time they had kissed, she'd been overcome by sheer panic on the terrace. This time was different. Despite the terrible events that had preceded him taking her into his arms, she was in full possession of her wits.

Or as much in possession as she could be, given the circumstances.

She was alone with him in the darkened woods, far from the interference of chaperones or well-intentioned companions. He'd brought her here himself. Stolen her away to protect her from harm, just like some hero in a fairy tale.

Or possibly the villain.

Her unruly heart made no distinction. It threatened to leap

straight out of her chest. She sensed the ragged grip he had on his control. Could taste his desire for her. It was there, in his touch and in his breath. A fierce, wild thing—ungovernable, unstoppable.

Her lips yielded eagerly to his. This was no time for calculated coquetry. Not after what they'd shared this evening. Indeed, the tragedy seemed to unleash something in them both, making them reckless, desperate.

How else to explain her feelings? She *wanted* him. Not just him holding her and resting his cheek against her hair. Not even him calling her love, or sweetheart, or darling—though her heart had marked every endearment. She wanted *him*. And why shouldn't she have what she wanted for once? Why shouldn't they both have it? Life was woefully short. It could all end in an instant.

He released her chin. His large hand curved around the back of her neck. His mouth was hot on hers, his kiss almost bruising.

Effie felt it everywhere, igniting her blood and turning her limbs to melted treacle.

She had read about kisses like these in novels. The sort of desperate, all-consuming kisses that made respectable young ladies shed their inhibitions and rush wantonly to their own ruination. But Effie wasn't one of those passive, proper damsels. Despite her inexperience, despite the effect of his sinful mouth on her heart, her head, and even her knees, she had a keen sense of her own power in their embrace.

Leaning into him, she kissed him back as passionately as he kissed her.

The remaining thread of Gabriel's control snapped in spectacular fashion. A tremor went through him. He took her mouth harder, held her tighter, lost whatever semblance he'd had of strategy or finesse.

Effie gave herself over to the tender assault. This was exactly what she needed; this scorching, possessive heat. She yearned to be consumed by it. To let it burn, unfettered, until all the wrongness in her world had been extinguished by the rightness of whatever this was between them.

It was a hazardous alchemy. Ladies were taught to abhor a loss of control. Excess passion, they were told, was undignified and unseemly. But there was nothing insulting or undignified in Gabriel's embrace. They had found each other; that's all that mattered.

For the first time in memory, the loneliness Effie had always felt subsided. It was replaced by something else—deep, elemental, powerful.

Gabriel must have felt it, too. "What have you done to me?" His voice was a husky, baffled rasp against her mouth.

"*I?*" She slid her fingers in his hair, wishing she could feel the thick locks between her fingers. There was already so much between them. She couldn't tolerate anything more. "Drat these gloves," she muttered.

He chuckled. The sound turned into a low groan as she deepened their kiss. "*Effie*—"

"It wasn't a game," she said.

His breath came hard. "What?"

"Inviting you here. I wanted to see you again so much." Her half-parted lips clung sweetly to his. "Though if you ask me tomorrow, I shall deny it."

He pulled back a fraction to meet her gaze. The expression in his eyes was strangely serious, oddly vulnerable. "I wanted to see you, too," he admitted. "Since the night we met . . . not a day has passed that I haven't thought of you."

Effie's heart clenched. She smoothed the hair at his nape. "Not all happy thoughts, I'd wager."

"Have your thoughts about me all been happy ones, then?"

"Bewildered ones. I don't know quite what to do with you."

"I have a few ideas." He kissed her again.

She sighed against his mouth, returning his kiss. For a moment, she lost herself in the searing honeyed heat of it. The first real intimacy they'd exchanged, their defenses down, and their longing for each other partially laid bare. He'd been thinking of her every day. He'd been wanting her, too. The knowledge had the power to strip away the last of her inhibitions.

But even in the aching midst of it, there in his arms, her breath mingling with his, Effie retained a particle of awareness. All women must do so. Like it or not, in this world, a lady's reputation was currency. Once lost, there was little that could be done to redeem it.

Music reached her ears from the orchestra pavilion, reminding her that they were not alone, no matter how much it felt they were. Their embrace could go no further. Most would say it had already gone too far.

Inwardly cursing the necessity of it, she broke their kiss. Her cheek came to rest against his, her hands drifting to his shoulders. "Would that there was nothing at issue between us but this," she said softly. "We could happily cry friends."

His hand stroked over her back in a slow caress. "There needn't be anything between us."

"No, indeed. If you'd abandon your allegiance to Compton and help me instead—"

"Compton again?" Gabriel's hand stilled on her spine. He drew back from her with a scowl. "Do you never cease thinking about the blasted man?"

Effie's hands slipped from his shoulders. "You know he's a villain, yet still you protect him."

"I'm not protecting him. I'm protecting myself—and the Rookery. While rich, fashionable ladies like you are playing at politics, I'm fighting for survival."

"I'm not playing," she replied, offended. "And it has nothing to do with being rich or fashionable. A married women's property bill would change the lives of countless women of every class."

"Strangers. They're nothing to you. While the people of the Rookery—they're all I have. All I've known." Releasing her from his arms, he abruptly stood. He paced to the edge of the small clearing, raking a hand through his hair. "If I do nothing, the Rookery will be gone within a year. Its size is already diminished. My betting shop won't last."

A chill settled over Effie. She still had his overcoat around her, but without the furnace-like heat of his body, the night became far colder. She felt, all at once, very much on her own. "You would value a gambling enterprise over a bill that would save thousands of women from being used and exploited by their husbands?"

"A bill we both know will never pass," he said.

Her temper rose. It may well be so. There had been previous attempts to reform the married women's property law. All of them had failed. Why should this attempt be any different?

"What about Compton's other crimes?" she asked. "Is he never to be held to account for those?"

"What crimes?" Gabriel returned. "What proof do you have that he's done anything illegal—or immoral?"

Effie gave an eloquent huff, thinking of Mrs. Naismith's ruffle-clad arm pulling Compton through her door. Exposing the viscount's immorality wouldn't be any trouble. As for uncovering the rest of Compton's villainous deeds . . .

"The proof exists," she said. "Those papers the *Courant* referred to, for starters. You know where they are, don't you?"

He shook his head, refusing to be drawn on the subject.

Gathering her skirts, Effie moved to stand. Gabriel was back at her side in an instant. The fearsome glower he wore was belied by the tenderness with which he assisted her to her feet. He remained close to her after she stood, his hand lingering on her elbow.

A dreadful thought occurred to her.

"Is it you who has them?" she asked.

Gabriel's hand fell from her arm as though he'd been scalded. He took a step back. His face went suspiciously blank, just as it had when she'd questioned him about Wingard and Compton that day in Hyde Park, but not before Effie saw the terrible truth in his eyes.

Her stomach plummeted. Her question had been impulsive conjecture at best. She hadn't really thought it could be true.

But it was, wasn't it?

Effie understood it in that bleak moment with absolute certainty.

The papers proving Compton's crimes against Miss Corvus weren't in the viscount's desk, or in his study, or anywhere in his house in town or at his grand estate in Hampshire. They were in Gabriel's keeping. They had been all along.

19

Effie had dealt with many unexpected events in her life and managed to maintain her composure through most of them. She took pride in her sense of self-possession. It was one of her particular skills. Even Miss Corvus had been impressed by the degree to which Effie could keep her countenance. Self-control was a powerful tool in an Academy girl's arsenal of concealment. The less the world knew what a lady was thinking, the more dangerous she became.

But standing by the oak tree where she and Gabriel had just kissed so passionately, glaring at his suddenly expressionless face, something inside of Effie crumbled. She no longer cared about power, and she didn't give a fig for concealment.

Her throat clogged with acrid emotion. "I want them," she said.

Gabriel didn't reply. His harshly hewn features were coldly stark, the colored lanterns in the tree casting shadows over his high cheekbones and sunken cheeks. He was at once so remote. So ruthlessly detached. He might have been the devil himself standing there, willfully deaf to the entreaties of some hapless mortal maiden.

Effie was too upset to be ignored. Closing the distance between them, she gripped the lapels of his jacket in her fists. Her crinoline was crushed between them as she gave him a shake. "I *want* them."

A flicker of some unnameable emotion crossed his face. If Effie didn't know better, she'd think he was experiencing something like regret or remorse.

As if that were possible!

She shook him harder. *"You liar."* Raw hurt vibrated in her quaking voice. "You knew about Mr. Wingard. You knew about all of it. And you let me—"

He covered her hands with his. "Effie—"

"I should have recognized it from the beginning. Why else would Compton be helping you? Why would you be protecting him? All for your mercenary, selfish—"

"I need him, Effie." He pressed her hands. "I *need* him."

She jerked away from him, wrenching her hands free. Tears smarted in her eyes. The sting of them only served to stoke her temper. That she would cry over a man! And not a man who had perished like poor Mr. Galezzo, but a man who had tricked her and, very probably, laughed at her.

Turning her back on him, she marshaled her senses. It took a Herculean effort. The entirety of their acquaintance was flashing through her brain at lightning speed, every move he'd made cast in a new light. A *damning* light.

"For your betting shop," she said flatly. "Of course. How silly of me." She wrapped her arms around herself, feeling colder by the moment. "How did you gain possession—"

"Wingard gave them to me himself. He was dying of drink. He needed someone to settle his debts, and to pay for a doctor."

"And you naturally obliged him."

Gabriel advanced on her slowly. *"Was* he a relation of yours?"

"He was no one to me. But I know who he was. I know what he did. He was as vile a man as Compton. But villains will find each other, I daresay, and help each other, too. It's ever been thus among men."

"Effie—"

234 · Mimi Matthews

"The *Courant* said there were rumors circulating about his papers. Other people must know of them."

"There have been no rumors. I'm the one who had Miles Quincey put those lines in the *Courant*. They were meant to be a warning to Compton. It never occurred to me that anyone else would even notice them."

Effie was jolted anew by this latest revelation. She flashed him a stunned glance over her shoulder. "You're acquainted with Mr. Quincey?"

"We grew up together in St. Giles. It was me he came to see after you left him that day in Fleet Street. That's how I knew you'd been there, not because I had you followed." He paused, adding, "I haven't, by the way. Not since Ollie failed so abysmally."

His assurance did nothing to mollify her.

"Your ideas for reform must be dreadfully important to you if you've gone to such trouble," she said bitterly. "Blackmailing Compton? Using your friends?"

"Whatever you're thinking—"

"I'm thinking that I'm a colossal fool. What else could I be thinking?"

He reached for her arm. She pulled away from his touch. "I didn't lie to you," he said. "I warned you from the first that you had to leave Compton alone."

"Yes," she replied. "You've been strikingly honest."

"I've been as honest with you as you've been with me."

Effie absorbed his words in silence, grudgingly acknowledging the truth of them. Her entire identity here in London was a lie. And before that, too, for as long as she could remember. How could it be otherwise? She didn't know who she was herself, or who she'd been in those years before Miss Corvus had found her in the slum. How could anyone else?

It was why Effie and Franc had to have a home of their own. Somewhere they could truly belong. That was all that mattered, not this. Not *him*.

"What's to prevent me from taking the documents from you?" she asked.

Gabriel fell quiet for a moment behind her. "You could try," he said, "but I wouldn't advise it."

It didn't sound like a threat. Effie registered it as one nonetheless. Gabriel had power in his world. More power in his way, she suspected, than Compton himself. At least with the viscount there was a veneer of civility. One must maintain outward standards and observe proper decorum. With Gabriel, there was no such veneer. No game board. No rules. She couldn't simply waltz into his betting shop or his fine house in Sloane Street on some social pretext.

Unless . . .

She briefly considered obtaining the documents by other means, only to discard the idea. She was no seasoned seductress. Despite her skill at flirtation, she'd never truly been with a man. The stolen kisses she'd shared with Gabriel had been the closest she'd come. She couldn't imagine taking things further, certainly not for mercenary gain. Not when her heart was so much engaged.

Gabriel seemed to sense the wretchedness of her dilemma. He reached for her again. This time she didn't flinch. His fingers curled around her upper arm. He turned her to face him. "Don't be angry."

"I'm angry at myself."

"For ever thinking well of me?"

"Yes, quite. For imagining that we—" She stopped before she could finish. She had no desire to make herself even more weak and pitiable in his eyes than she doubtless already was.

Gabriel's face was no longer cold. There was a brooding look about him—a guarded concern in his eyes, coupled with some troubling emotion she couldn't interpret. "May I kiss you again?" he asked.

"No."

He nodded solemnly, taking the rejection in stride. "That's fair," he said. And then: "Shall I tell you something that might cheer you?"

She looked up at him mulishly. She hated this feeling. It was anger and mortification all rolled into one. While she'd been sparring with him, imagining that she had the upper hand, he'd been in control the whole time. It made her wonder, were women ever in control? Or was the control they wielded only an illusion permitted by men? If so, it wasn't any kind of control worth having, not as far as Effie was concerned.

"Shall I?" he asked again.

"If you must," she said sullenly. "But it won't change anything between us. You and I will never—"

"I found someone who knew your friend Grace," he said.

Nothing else on earth could have distracted Effie from her misery. She stepped forward with a start. "*What?* When?"

"I made inquiries, just as I told you I would. My man discovered a woman in a village outside of Sawbridgeworth who used to live in St. Giles before the clearances. She claims to have known her."

Effie searched his face, almost afraid to ask. "What did she say?"

He ran his hand up and down her arm in a slow, reassuring pass. "I haven't spoken to her yet. She won't come to London. She expects me to call on her in Hertfordshire. I mean to go next week, before the Epsom Derby."

Effie recoiled at the thought. He couldn't go. Not if there was a chance the old woman would reveal something about Effie's mother. Or worse, about Effie herself. "No," she objected. "I must go myself. If you'll give me her direction—"

"I'm going." Gabriel's tone left no room for argument. His hand moved on her arm again, both gentle and unmistakably proprietary. "If you'd like to accompany me—"

"To Hertfordshire? Are you mad?" It was miles away. An even greater distance than the Academy. "An unmarried lady can't travel alone with a gentleman. It would be scandalous."

Not to mention the risk to Effie's heart. She was furious with Gabriel, yes, but that didn't mean she had the strength to resist him. Not if they were on their own together for a prolonged period, and not if he would insist on stroking her and cajoling her like some fractious wild creature.

"Traveling alone with me is taking things too far, is it? After rooftops, terraces, and a jaunt through the slum? After this evening?"

"Yes," she said. And then more emphatically. *"Yes."* Her voice splintered. "I have no desire to see you again."

He shook his head. "You don't mean that."

"I do mean it." It didn't feel like a lie, though the words nearly stuck in her throat. "I don't know why you should care about the fate of my old servant in any case."

His eyes kindled. "It's not your old servant I care about."

Effie's injured heart gave a traitorous thump. The implication was clear. She refused to let it soften her resolve against him. She was too hurt and disappointed. "If that's true, then you'll give me the woman's direction so I can go alone. You won't force me to forgo this chance merely to avoid being in company with you."

He stared down at her for an endless moment. A muscle flexed in his jaw. "Very well," he said. "If that's truly want you want."

A queer burning sensation prickled at the back of Effie's eyes. Again, she feared she might cry. "It is."

The truth was, she didn't know what she wanted anymore. Her head and her heart were in a terrible muddle. She'd seen a man die tonight. She'd learned that the gentleman she was coming to care for had lied to her. The same gentleman she'd shared intimacies with that she'd never shared with anyone before.

She needed to think. To gather her wits and regain her composure. Until such time, she needed to be as far away from Gabriel Royce as possible.

20

Gabriel was accompanying Effie out of the woods and back onto the main promenade of the Gardens when Mannering intercepted them. Seeing the young lord step into their path, Gabriel's already dangerous mood took a sharp turn for the worse.

He might have known Mannering would come searching for Effie. The idiot was plainly infatuated with her. He'd been pursuing her doggedly enough with all his formal calls and bloody invitations.

Gabriel should have been amused. But he was no fool. For all Mannering's faults, he was still in possession of an estate and a title. The woman he married would become *Lady* Mannering. She would have a position in society that demanded respect. While the woman who married Gabriel . . .

But Effie didn't want marriage—or so she'd claimed. And Gabriel didn't know what he wanted anymore.

He had begun the evening determined to rid himself of his attraction to her, but he was ending it in a far different frame of mind. Perhaps it was because of how well she fit in his arms. Perhaps it was because of how she'd returned his kisses. Whatever the reason, in those moments after Effie had discovered the truth about Wingard's documents, knowing that she was about to walk away from him forever, Gabriel would have done anything—*said* anything—to keep her there.

He'd had but one final card in his favor—the location of the old woman in Hertfordshire. He hadn't intended to play it. When he had, it had been less out of strategy than desperation.

A novice mistake. A desperate card player was a losing card player. Everyone associated with the world of betting knew it. When the stakes were high, a man had to remain cold and emotionless in order to win.

For Gabriel, the stakes had never felt higher.

He supposed he was infatuated with Effie, too, in his way. How else to explain the fact that he couldn't stop thinking about her? That he wanted to see her every minute? Kiss her, talk to her, make her smile one of her genuine smiles?

But infatuation was too small a word.

When a man contemplated giving up everything he held sacred for a woman, it surely must be love.

Once acknowledged, the emotion surged in Gabriel's veins, as irksome as it was unmistakable. He recognized it with a grim sense of certainty. He was in love with Euphemia Flite.

He and every other gentleman in London.

Unlike them, Gabriel had nothing tangible to offer her. Not a title. Not a vast fortune. Not even the distinction of formal education. He had nothing save himself.

It wasn't enough.

Indeed, judging by the fleeting glimmer of relief in Effie's face when she saw him, Mannering was, at the moment, a far preferable alternative.

It was some consolation that the dapper young baron wasn't at his best. His hair was rumpled, his cravat unknotted, and his coat missing a button. "Miss Flite," he said with evident relief. "Thank God you are safe."

Effie still wore Gabriel's heavy black coat draped over her shoulders. She slipped it off, returning it to him without a word.

He took it from her, equally silent. The interior was warm to the touch. A whisper of her fragrance lingered where the collar had brushed her bare skin.

"I'm quite well," she said to Lord Mannering. "And the others? Are they—"

"Miss Compton was in a bad state. Powell has taken her and my sister home in the carriage. I saw them off before coming to find you. Someone said that Royce had carried you away from the fray." He looked to Gabriel. "I owe you a debt, sir."

"You do," Gabriel agreed without inflection. "But nothing on her account." Standing half a step behind Effie in the shadow of the trees, he exercised a ruthless control over his emotions. The same control that had allowed him to relinquish her in the woods. It wouldn't take much to break it. A word from her. A look. A touch.

"May I kiss you again?" he'd asked her only minutes before.

But she hadn't wanted him then, and she didn't want him now. She'd scarcely even looked at him since they'd emerged onto the path.

If Mannering suspected anything, he didn't show it. The events of the evening had been too fraught to allow for a strict enforcement of any social rules. Gabriel had spirited Effie to safety; that was all his lordship seemed to care about.

"I shall take charge of her now," he said manfully. "I have a cab waiting." He approached Effie, proffering his arm. "Miss Flite?"

Gabriel's jaw hardened. If he insisted on escorting Effie home himself, it would only put her in the position of refusing him again, just as she'd refused his request to kiss her. She'd made it perfectly plain that she never wanted to see him again.

But though she may not want him in this moment, Gabriel still wanted her to be safe, even if that meant he must relinquish her to another.

He remained unmoving as she took Mannering's arm.

"Are you coming with us, Royce?" Mannering asked.

"I'll make my own way," Gabriel said.

At last Effie looked at him. There was a glint of uncertainty in her face. Doubtless she was thinking of his promise to provide her with the location of the old woman in Hertfordshire.

It was better than her not thinking of him at all.

"I'll send word to you tomorrow," he said. And then to Mannering: "You should reach Brook Steet within the half hour. See that nothing delays you."

Mannering's throat bobbed on a swallow. He mumbled an acknowledgment to Gabriel's unspoken warning before leading Effie away back toward the gates of the Gardens. She walked alongside him without looking back, the glass dragonflies in her hair twinkling in the lamplight.

Gabriel watched her go, a bloodless stone settling in the place where his heart should be.

There was a good chance he'd lost her this evening. That any flicker of fondness or friendship she'd felt for him had died the moment she'd learned he had Wingard's documents and was unwilling to give them to her.

Perhaps she truly did wish never to see him again.

The prospect left him empty. Numb. The only feeling he could summon as her black-cloaked figure disappeared into the crowd was something very close to despair.

"What have you done to me?" he'd asked her.

He still didn't know the answer. All he knew was that she'd been a bright, dazzling light in his dark world. Not a remote, beautiful creature to put on a pedestal, but an equal. A second self. If he wanted her, he was going to have to win her.

And he wanted her like mad.

Never mind that the odds against him were rising by the second. Gabriel was a bookmaker. He made his own odds. So long as he did, this game wasn't over. Not until he said it was.

. . . . .

Effie exchanged all of five words with Lord Mannering during their journey to Brook Street. She was in no mood for conversation. All she desired was the comfort of Franc and the warmth of her borrowed bed.

Lord Mannering seemed to comprehend the situation. He promptly delivered her to the Belwoods' door, stopping only long enough to explain the situation to her ladyship.

Effie didn't remain to hear their conversation. She headed straight upstairs to her room. The lamp had been left on low for Franc at her insistence. He was curled up on her pillow, having put himself to bed for the night. He appeared so small and helpless. Just a tiny black ball of fluff with his little black nose and diminutive paw pads.

Her throat closed on a raw swell of emotion. It was the final straw, seeing Franc looking so much at the mercy of the world. He was wholly depending on her. They had only each other. There was no one else to rely on. No one else to trust.

She crossed the room to him. Hearing her familiar tread on the carpet, Franc roused himself from his slumber. His pom-pom tail quivered. Effie picked him up, allowing him to lick her face in greeting. She kissed his head in return.

"It was dreadful," she told him. "The wire walker fell, the Gardens were in chaos, and Mr. Royce—" Moisture burned in her eyes. "He is *not* our friend."

Franc licked the hot tear that rolled down her cheek.

"I have been unforgivably stupid," Effie said, struggling not to cry. "But no longer."

Franc blinked up at her in canine inquiry.

She forced back her tears. She'd already wept once this evening over poor Mr. Galezzo. Her own troubles were minor in comparison.

She refused to cry over them. "I shall formulate a new plan," she said. "Tomorrow I shall start anew."

"Miss Flite?" Lady Belwood entered, not bothering to knock. "Oh, but it is insupportable. I don't wonder you are in tears. That you should have been exposed to such a sordid and gruesome scene! Cleeves? A hot bath for Miss Flite. And Mary? Fetch the bottle of laudanum from my dressing table."

"I thank you," Effie said. "I don't want a bath. Nor do I want any laudanum."

"You cannot know what is best in your current state. A lady isn't meant to endure such troublesome sights. It can have a grave effect on her constitution."

"But I am not a lady," Effie said.

Lady Belwood recoiled at the unwelcome reminder.

Effie held Franc tight. "All I require is my bed. If you please, ma'am."

Lady Belwood pursed her lips. "If that is what you wish."

Mary appeared at the door with the laudanum.

Her ladyship waved her out. "It won't be necessary, Mary. You may go." She turned back to Effie with stiff dignity. "Sleep well, Miss Flite."

Effie waited until Lady Belwood had gone before setting Franc back down on the bed. While he returned to the warmth of her pillow, Effie stripped out of her evening dress, petticoats, corset, and crinoline. She unpinned her hair, placing her glass dragonflies on the dressing table as carefully as if they'd been diamonds.

All of her clothes were similarly disposed, skirts and bodice draped with exquisite preciseness over a chair and stockings meticulously rolled. It quieted her mind, going through the motions required of any woman acting as her own lady's maid. She couldn't allow her clothing to wrinkle, else she'd be the one obliged to press it. And she couldn't leave her hair unbrushed or it would fall to her to unsnarl the tangles in the morning.

She did it all herself, every painstaking step helping to mute her heartsickness and misery.

When at last she'd finished, she turned down the lamp and climbed into bed. Franc curled up against her. His small body was a warm, solid weight at her bosom, lending her comfort where there otherwise would be none.

With everything in its proper place, her thoughts settled into something like order.

She had a job still to do, and she must take her injured heart well out of the equation, along with her wounded pride. Neither could serve her now. What she required was ruthless pragmatism.

Gabriel had Mr. Wingard's documents, it was true, and he didn't intend to part with them. But Effie hadn't been sent to London to find those specific documents. Indeed, Miss Corvus hadn't even known they still existed.

No.

She had tasked Effie with discovering evidence of *other* crimes.

"A leopard doesn't change his spots," Miss Corvus had said. *"Find something we can use against him."*

Discouraged as Effie was, she had no reason to give up. If Lord Compton had wronged someone else in the intervening years, if he'd stolen any money or taken advantage of some woman, the evidence of it was sure to be out there somewhere. All Effie had to do was find it.

As for Gabriel Royce . . .

He was a distraction, that was all. One best forgotten.

Never mind that he'd found someone who knew Effie's mother. That he'd caught Effie when she swooned. That he'd kissed her so sweetly, and had, for a few all-too-brief moments in his arms, made her feel safe, and wanted, and cared for.

Such things must count for nothing when weighed against his treachery.

Tomorrow, he would send her the old woman's direction in Hertfordshire, and then Effie would communicate with him no more.

The bleak prospect was enough to resurrect her tears. No longer capable of preventing them, she buried her face in Franc's curly coat and wept.

21

The following day, Effie presented herself at the Comptons' house in Grosvenor Square, armed with a renewed sense of purpose.

Miss Compton was, as ever, the likeliest means of gaining access to the Comptons' residences in London and Hampshire. If Effie had any hope of searching those places, she would need to maintain favorable relations with the girl.

Last night's events had been an unfortunate setback. Miss Compton would almost certainly have heard by now that Lord Mannering had escorted Effie home. It was precisely why Effie had wasted no time in coming to pay her respects.

Parker admitted Effie into the marble-tiled hall. "Lady Compton is out this afternoon," he informed her. "Miss Compton is receiving."

"How fortunate," Effie said. "It is Miss Compton I have come to see." She waited for Parker to take her up, but the butler didn't move. Not immediately. He lingered a moment in the hall, regarding her with a troubled frown.

Effie had worn a violet-sprigged white organdy day dress with a ruched bodice and dainty pearl buttons. It was as unlike the black mourning garb she'd donned in Ellis Street as day was to night. She nevertheless felt a quiver of anxiety, fearing Parker might recognize her. "Is anything the matter?" she asked.

"No, miss," he said. But his troubled aspect remained as he escorted Effie to the drawing room. He glanced at her several times as they ascended the stairs, eyes lingering on her face and figure as though struggling to recall a fact just out of his reach.

Effie prayed he wouldn't make the connection between her and the veiled widow he'd observed outside Mrs. Naismith's house. If he did . . .

But there was no point anticipating trouble. Not when Effie had trouble enough already.

Bringing her to the door of the drawing room, Parker announced her name in dour tones: "Miss Flite."

Miss Compton sat on a lavish sofa upholstered in crane-and-pagoda-embroidered Japanese silk. She wasn't alone. Ruth Mannering was seated across from her. She was still in her bonnet and gloves, a brown cloth paletot buttoned over her modest gown. She rose as Effie entered.

"Euphemia," she said. "I was just taking my leave. You were to be my next stop."

Effie exchanged curtsies with her before warmly taking her hand. "And you were to be mine."

Ruth scanned her face with concern. "How are you faring after last night's events?"

Effie was conscious of her appearance. She'd cried too much yesterday, and this morning, when she'd risen from bed, her looking glass had showed the proof of it. There were dark smudges under her eyes and a certain paleness beneath her golden ivory complexion.

It wasn't only on account of the tragedy. It was owing to Gabriel. He hadn't yet sent the old woman's direction. Effie had found herself anticipating his message far too much. And not just because of the implications about her mother, but because of her feelings for him. Try as she might, she couldn't simply shut them off like a water tap.

"I slept very ill," she admitted. "And you?"

"I'm bearing up." Ruth gave Effie's hand a squeeze before releasing it. "Would that I could say the same for Miss Compton."

Miss Compton remained seated, a look of displeasure on her beautiful face. The folds of her ruffle- and lace-trimmed day dress billowed around her in a cloud of lustrous pink silk.

Effie went to her with a show of concern. She took her hand, just as she'd taken Ruth's. "You poor thing. I heard that you'd fainted."

Miss Compton's hand remained limp in Effie's. She tugged it away at the first opportunity. "Any lady of refinement would have been similarly affected."

"Many women fainted," Ruth said. "According to this morning's paper, some were so much afflicted they had to be conveyed to St. George's Hospital. And that is not all." She lowered her voice. "Mr. Galezzo expired last night, not long after he was removed from the Gardens."

Effie had seen the report in this morning's edition of the *Courant*. It had said the man had been conveyed to his home in Chelsea, where he had lingered for hours in an unconscious state before finally succumbing to his injuries.

"A tragedy, to be sure," Effie said. "He was so young and so very talented."

"Must the two of you speak of it in front of me?" Miss Compton whisked open her painted fan. She wafted it rapidly in a burst of pique. "It's a miracle I'm not still confined to my bed after what transpired. I shouldn't have bothered to come down at all if not for so many people calling to ask after my welfare." She gave a petulant sniff in Ruth's direction. "Though some have been markedly absent, I must say."

Ruth's sober expression took on a consoling air, even as her eyes glinted with impatience at Miss Compton's affected invalidism. "My brother sent me in his stead. He meant no offense. Indeed, I thought it showed uncommon delicacy on his part. He had no desire to remind you of the events of last night."

"As if any lady could forget!" Miss Compton turned her hostile glare on Effie. "I notice that you seem to have recovered with remarkable ease, Miss Flite."

"Not at all," Effie said. "I'm sure I shall be having nightmares for weeks."

"I feel the same," Ruth said. "One must soldier on, of course, but . . . I find myself in need of peace and quiet after yesterday's events. My brother is escorting me home to Luxford Place for a brief respite. He's making the arrangements as we speak."

Miss Compton ceased fluttering her fan. "Lord Mannering is leaving London?" She sat up straight in her seat. "For how long?"

"We shall be back Wednesday afternoon." Ruth turned to Effie. "Regrettably, it means I must miss that morning's lecture at Lady Bartlett's house."

"I'm sorry to hear it," Effie said. "I was looking forward to attending."

"You needn't forgo the pleasure on my account. Her ladyship welcomes all comers. You have only to show your face and her butler will admit you. Bring a friend, if you like."

"Are you quite sure Lord Mannering will be coming back?" Miss Compton asked.

"Of a certainty," Ruth said. "He is intent on attending Mr. Chapin's balloon ascent at Cremorne Gardens. It's set for two o'clock if the weather is fine. Philip is confident we can make it if we depart Luxford Place by ten. I'd have thought, after last evening, he would have lost the taste for such spectacle, but he claims balloons are in a different category from high wires."

Effie smiled. "I admire his sagacity."

"That's one word for it," Ruth said. Curtsying to them both, she took her leave, promising to call again on her return to London.

Effie was left standing alone in front of Miss Compton, like a wayward schoolgirl in anticipation of a dressing-down. There appeared little hope of being invited to sit.

It wasn't the time to show weakness. One could be amenable—conciliatory, even—and still be decisive.

Effie helped herself to a seat beside Miss Compton on the Japanese sofa. Their skirts bunched against each other. "I gather you're upset that Lord Mannering escorted me home," she said, unprompted. "Pray, don't be. He only exerted himself because he sincerely promised Lady Belwood he'd guarantee my welfare. Had he lost me in the Gardens—"

The entirety of Miss Compton's body stiffened. "But you weren't lost, were you? You were with that Royce fellow. Lord Powell said the man carried you away. Meanwhile, I was on the grass, in fear for my life, with no one to attend me."

"We both know that isn't true," Effie said gently. "Lord Mannering didn't leave your side until he was assured you were safe in the carriage with his sister and Lord Powell. Indeed, anyone would say he showed more care for your welfare than he did for mine. I was but an afterthought to him."

A pucker formed in Miss Compton's brow. "I hadn't thought of it that way."

"That's understandable. You were distraught. So were we all."

"It was a dreadful spectacle," Miss Compton said. "I shall never forget the gruesomeness of all that blood."

Effie couldn't forget it, either. Mr. Galezzo had been performing for them. Risking life and limb for their coin, and their amusement. Yet, now he was gone, people like Miss Compton were more concerned with the harm they'd suffered in witnessing the tragedy of his death than they were with Mr. Galezzo actually having died.

Was it any wonder Ruth required a respite in the country?

In that moment, Effie wished she might follow her example. She was tired of fashionable London. Tired of pretending to be something she wasn't.

But there would be no withdrawing from the field—and no money with which to do it—until her job was finished.

"Poor thing," Effie murmured again, far more sympathetically than she felt. "You must give it time. The memory is still very fresh."

"Everyone else has had the grace to call and offer their consolation," Miss Compton said. "Lady Lavinia, Miss Whitbread, even Lord Powell. But not Lord Mannering. Oh no, not him."

"He did send his sister," Effie reminded her.

"A likely story! He should have called on me himself. He should have known what was due to me." Miss Compton's eyes glimmered with angry vulnerability. "That I must be left to wait upon him, never knowing if he'll grace me with his presence or if he'll slight me—" She stopped short, fingers clenching the sticks of her fan. "He never used to be so cruel."

Effie studied her face. Reluctant compassion stirred at the genuine torment she saw there. "If the acquaintance pains you so, why do you put up with it?"

"It wasn't always so. He was exceedingly attentive to me at Christmas. We spent two weeks in each other's company at Orleigh Park with Lady Lavinia's family in Devonshire." Miss Compton fidgeted with her fan. "She claims we were *too* much in each other's company. She says that, perchance, his lordship has grown tired of me."

"Perhaps he's merely recognized you're ill-suited," Effie suggested.

Miss Compton's eyes flashed to hers. "Has he said so?"

"Not to me. But once a gentleman's affections turn cool . . ." Effie hesitated.

She was meant to be using Miss Compton, not offering the girl heartfelt advice. The two of them weren't friends, nor anything approaching that state. Indeed, they didn't even *like* each other. Still . . .

The indelible bonds of sisterhood compelled Effie to speak honestly.

"You don't want to wed a man who isn't besotted with you," she said. "Distance can only grow after marriage. If that union begins with coldness and disregard, what do you imagine will come in the years that follow? It can only lead to unhappiness."

Miss Compton stared at her. "You would advise me to give him up? After I have been secretly attached to him for nearly a year?"

"Count yourself lucky that is all it's been. You're still very young. In time, you'll find someone you like better."

"There is no one I will *ever* like better," Miss Compton declared.

Effie's heart thumped in bitter accord with the assertion. She thought of Gabriel. Of the pain that came when one's tender feelings were so drastically at odds with the realities of life. "You feel that now, I don't doubt it. But it doesn't change the fact that you deserve a gentleman who will put you first. *All* women deserve it—if it's a gentleman they want at all."

"What else should they want?" Miss Compton asked, perplexed. "The alternative to marriage is . . . *spinsterhood*."

The thread of disdain in her voice as she uttered the word provoked a faint smile from Effie.

How ignorant some women could be about their own source of power!

"Spinsterhood is a contradictory state," Effie said. "Both most maligned *and* most desirable. In the absence of marriage, a woman retains her freedom, in law as well as in fact. She can do as she likes."

Rather than intrigued, Miss Compton appeared appalled by the idea. "What is there worth doing without the protection of a gentleman?"

"Women don't require a gentleman's protection. They're perfectly capable of protecting themselves. All they lack is the knowledge to do it." Effie gave her a curious look. "Hadn't you a governess to tell you so?"

"If that is what your governess taught you," Miss Compton said repressively, "she was a very different breed from mine."

Effie's mouth curved with bittersweet memory, recalling Miss Corvus's strident lectures on feminine independence. *An Academy girl must be armed for the battle of life. She must know how to read and to think. She must be equipped to defend herself.*

"When all the world deserts you, you will have no friend but yourself to rely on," Miss Corvus had told them. *"See that you are a fierce and competent friend. A friend to be reckoned with."*

"Yes," Effie agreed quietly. "She was, rather."

"My governess believed young ladies should be educated only so far as required to be a suitable helpmeet to their husbands," Miss Compton said. "My father believes the same. It is the common way of things among girls of my class."

My class, not *our* class.

Effie didn't fail to note the distinction. Even at her most defenseless, Miss Compton was still in possession of as many barbs as a hedgehog. "Then you must educate yourself," Effie said. "There's no good reason why learning should stop at the schoolroom. Not when there are books, and women's salons, and—"

"Really, Miss Flite. After last night, education is the last thing on my mind."

"Quite so," Effie said, undeterred. "You require diversion." She paused to consider. "Perhaps you might accompany me to the lecture at Lady Bartlett's on Wednesday?"

Miss Compton blinked. "To hear some frumpy bluestocking talk radical nonsense?"

"Miss Mannering doesn't consider it nonsense. If you intend a long-term association with the family, I should think it well to culti-vate those interests that—"

"Yes, I see." Miss Compton gave a thoughtful flutter of her fan. "I suppose I *might* make an effort, even though I find such radicalism to be—"

"What's this about radicalism?" Lord Compton's voice sounded from the entrance of the drawing room.

Effie's gaze jolted to the doorway. Her pulse quickened on a rush of trepidation. She hadn't anticipated encountering his lordship today. And certainly not like this.

He was dressed for home in a pair of charcoal gray trousers and a burgundy smoking jacket with a velvet shawl collar. A disconcerting sight. Effie had never seen him so casually attired.

She stood as he entered, offering a flawless curtsy. "My lord."

"Miss Flite." He bowed to her, smiling suavely. "You are not, it is to be hoped, corrupting my daughter."

Effie summoned a smile in return as she resumed her seat. He was teasing her, she could tell. The fine hairs on the back of her neck nevertheless lifted in warning. "Impossible, sir. You must know your daughter is incorruptible."

"I should hope so." He bent to press a kiss to Miss Compton's cheek. "How is the invalid today? Not overexerting herself, I hope?"

Miss Compton dutifully accepted her father's tribute. "Mama said it was better I should receive callers than languish alone in my rooms."

Lord Compton straightened. "Your mother is still out?"

"She's visiting her dressmaker." Miss Compton settled back on the sofa. "Miss Flite has asked me to accompany her to one of Lady Bartlett's meetings."

"I see." Lord's Compton's attention returned to Effie. His gaze held the same gleam of simmering interest he'd betrayed on the previous occasions they had met. "Tell me, how has a lovely young lady like you found herself caught up in Lady Bartlett's toils?"

"Miss Mannering invited her," Miss Compton replied before Effie could answer.

Lord Compton cast a repressive look at his daughter. "Miss Mannering would do better to direct her attentions closer to home."

Miss Compton flushed deeply.

Effie recalled Miss Compton having said that her father disapproved of Lord Mannering's gambling habits. Doubtless he knew Mannering was indebted to Gabriel. "Is Lady Bartlett an objectionable person?" Effie asked.

"She meddles in the affairs of men," he replied.

"The education of British girls?"

"Quite so. The subject is best left to the childrens' parents."

"Not every girl is fortunate enough to have parents," Effie pointed out.

"In which case her learning must be guided by her betters," Lord Compton said. "I have several gentlemen acquaintances who sit on the boards of charity schools. The girls within are brought up in accordance with their prospects."

"While girls of good family—"

"Must be trained to be good wives and pleasant companions. It is a husband's privilege to manage the other aspects of their lives."

"Finances and so forth?" Effie queried, thinking of Miss Corvus.

"Among other things." Lord Compton smiled at Effie again with fatherly condescension. It was an expression at odds with the one that continued to glimmer at the back of his eyes. "I despair of seeing genteel young ladies trouble their heads with such matters. Pray don't tell me you are one of them, Miss Flite?"

"Miss Flite is a bookish sort of person," Miss Compton said. "She has a great interest in your library."

"Ah yes. My daughter informed me that you perused one of my medieval texts the night of our musicale. I trust you found it sufficiently enlightening?"

Effie wondered if Miss Compton had shared everything about that night with her father. If she had . . .

It would mean that Lord Compton knew about Effie's lost hair-pin. That he knew about her disappearing upstairs during the performances.

Despite his outward civility, despite his fatherly air, she would be a fool to underestimate him.

This was the man who had bested Miss Corvus. If Effie was going to take him on, she'd have to remain on her guard.

"I did, sir," she said, choosing her words with care. "Regrettably, I only had but a few moments to admire your collection. I have been anxious to see it again ever since."

"I would be pleased to show it to you now," Lord Compton said. "If you can spare the time."

Effie's senses trembled a warning. She had eagerly anticipated perusing the viscount's library again, but not with the villain himself as her guide. Still . . .

The opportunity of being in company with the man was too great to refuse.

"I would like that very much," she said. "Thank you, my lord."

Miss Compton moved to rise.

"No need, my dear," her father told her. "You must rest from your ordeal. I shall take charge of your charming guest." He gestured to the door of the drawing room. "After you, Miss Flite."

22

Effie stood beside Lord Compton as he extracted the first volume of his medieval collection from its shelf near the fireplace. The library was empty at this time of day, sun filtering in through the half-closed draperies, capturing dancing dust motes in its rays.

This was but the third time Effie had entered the vast book-lined room. On her first visit, she'd encountered Gabriel in the darkness (a memory that still made her heart quicken). On the second, she'd been in company with Miss Compton. And now, here she was again, this time with the man she'd been pursuing from the beginning.

Gabriel would assuredly *not* approve.

He'd warned her away from the viscount countless times since they'd met. *"Gentlemen of Compton's rank aren't to be trifled with,"* he'd said. *"Powerful men will do anything to protect their secrets."*

But Effie had power, too. Hers lay in the fact that she was a woman, and in this world, by this man, women had always been underestimated. Whoever Miss Corvus had been when Compton had robbed her and betrayed her, she hadn't been the fierce and formidable female she would later become. It was *that* woman who had brought Effie up. Who had, as Nell claimed, raised Effie in her image.

Let Compton underestimate her at his peril.

"My daughter tells me you read Latin," he said, passing her the book.

Effie managed a small, self-effacing smile. "Only a very little, my lord."

He studied her face. "I wasn't aware French finishing schools were in the habit of teaching Latin to their students. Not even a very little of it."

"I have always been precocious when it comes to learning. Some of my teachers were disposed to encourage me."

"And your parents approved?" His expression transformed into a sly mockery of paternal concern. "But you are without parents, I recall."

Effie cradled the book in her hands. She was navigating a treacherous path. If she took a step wrong, the ground would give way beneath her feet. There would be no way of recovering it. She would be lost.

This was why, from the beginning, it had been important not to tell outright lies. A successful fabrication was always daringly close to the truth.

"They have been gone since I was a small child," she said. "I was raised by my guardian."

"A relation?"

"No, but she knew my mother, and was disposed to act in my interests."

"She?" His brows lifted. He had presumed her guardian to be a man.

"Quite," Effie said. "She saw I was brought up in accordance with my prospects."

His smile thinned to hear his own words quoted back at him. "What female can ask for better?" He pulled out a chair at an inlaid drum table nearby. "Miss Flite?"

Effie sat down, permitting him to push in her chair. He stood at her back for a moment, uncomfortably close. She felt his hot breath, and smelled his sandalwood cologne. Her pulse skittered with anxiety as he took the chair beside her.

She focused on the book. Opening the cover, she found the first illumination—a man, a snake, a raven, and a lion. It was the same illumination that had graced the first page of the volume she'd perused the night of the musicale, only this one was far more vivid. The snake had been tinted in green, the lion in saffron yellow, and the raven was solid black.

She traced them with her fingertip. "Miss Compton said these books had been in your family for generations. They must be very precious to you."

"They are." Lord Compton brought his fingers to rest on the image of the snake, mere inches from her own. "I prize the rare and beautiful. When the two meet, you will not find a more diligent and appreciative custodian than I."

Effie moistened her lips. Her mouth was suddenly dry. "What of the content of the book itself?" she inquired with a creditable degree of composure. "Do you not care what lies within the pages?"

"The substance of it is negligible. One might read a translation of Aristotle's text on zoology anywhere these days." His finger drew closer to hers on the page. "No, my dear. The value of this collection lies in its rarity. Its price cannot be measured."

She gave him a frowning look. "But . . . you *have* read it?"

His lips flattened. "For the most part."

Effie began to understand. She thought of his house, and all the vast extravagances within it, from the Japanese drawing room and the Italian marble floors, to the imported crystal chandeliers, the towering oil paintings, and the quality of the wine served at his table. She had long recognized that Compton enjoyed luxury, but she realized something else now.

For all his lofty reputation as a gentleman of wisdom, Compton was only a dilettante. A man who dabbled at refinement, unwilling to put in the actual work of reading a book or learning a language. A man who, when given the choice between the difficult path or the easy one, would always choose the latter. It was why he hadn't set out to make his own fortune, preferring instead to steal one from Miss Corvus.

Effie hadn't thought she could like him any less. But to have books such as these, and to never read them? It was practically criminal.

She slowly turned the next page, and then another. The same faint fragrance stirred from within the leaves that she'd caught when she'd looked at the previous volume. Ash, smoke, and leather, coupled with flowery sweetness and decay. The oddly familiar scent tickled at the back of her mind. She knew this smell. Not the decay, but something else . . .

The more pages she turned, the deeper it lured her into its flowery complexity.

"Are you searching for a particular passage, Miss Flite?"

Effie started. She hadn't intended to let the silence stretch so long between them. And all the while he'd been watching her, weighing her expression and measuring her responses. "I only read a little Latin, as I said," she answered with a rueful smile. "I have just realized this volume is the one about human animals."

"You don't care for human biology?"

"I'd prefer to read about wild creatures. Their behavior is far more interesting."

"As a student of human behavior, I must disagree."

"Yes, but you boast a vast and varied acquaintance, my lord. While I . . ." She glanced at him through her lashes. "I have only the experience of young people like myself."

"Young men," Lord Compton said derisively. "Immature bucks like Lord Mannering will doubtless bore a lady of your discernment. I beg you would not judge the rest of my sex by his example."

"You don't care for Lord Mannering? That is unfortunate, given Miss Compton's feelings."

"My daughter will soon get over this ill-advised infatuation. She is destined for greater things." His lips curled into another patronizing smile. "You, on the other hand, appear to be meant for greater still." He turned the next page of the book, his finger brushing slowly over hers. "I have been making inquiries about you, Miss Flite."

Effie stilled. "Oh?"

"Contrary to what is believed, Lady Belwood has confided that you are in no expectation of an inheritance from her and her husband."

Effie met his eyes. "I was unaware that anyone thought I was."

"Many have presumed it to be the case. As it transpires, you are wholly reliant on the generosity of your sponsor." Again, his fingers brushed hers. "Do you plan to marry?"

Her skin crawled at his touch. "I have no firm plans."

"How, then, do you propose to support yourself when the season comes to a close?"

"I have not thought that far ahead, my lord."

"You will naturally be in want of someone to look after you once you have left Lady Belwood's care. For a young woman with no family or connections, the world can be a dangerous place."

"Yes, quite dangerous," she said solemnly. "People should really take care, shouldn't they?"

His expression glinted with dry amusement. "You aren't afraid of the future?"

"I have no reason to fear it. I've done no wrong, and I've made no enemies."

"Show me a man with no enemies, and I shall show you a man who hasn't truly lived," his lordship quipped.

"Yes," Effie agreed. "But I am not a man, my lord."

He chuckled. "No, you most certainly are not, are you?" He touched her hand again. "If you find yourself in need of a protector, you must allow me to advise you."

Effie's stomach clenched. She had known the viscount capable of veiled flirtation, but she hadn't anticipated an implied offer of his protection. It was an insult disguised as an honor. One she would never have been subjected to if she were truly a lady of wealth and breeding.

But she wasn't.

Lord Compton believed she was unprotected. Entirely without resource.

He leaned closer, his breath a hot puff against her cheek. "A man like Mr. Royce may appear exciting on first acquaintance, but you would be wise to keep your distance from him."

A flare of alarm took Effie unaware.

Good lord. How much did Compton know about what she'd been up to these past weeks?

"I have no interest in Mr. Royce," she said evenly.

"You were observed leaving my library on the night of the ball," Lord Compton replied. "He came out after you."

Observed by *whom*? Parker, Effie presumed. How much else had the butler seen?

She shook her head. "It isn't what you—"

"And my daughter mentioned that you and Mr. Royce were both absent again during the musicale. Not to mention his behavior toward you at Cremorne Gardens. He carried you off, my daughter claims." He patted Effie's hand. "You wouldn't like to have your name linked to his, would you, my dear?"

"Rather it should be linked to someone else's?"

"If you are so inclined," he said. "You're a charming girl. Choose your course correctly, and the future will be yours to make."

"A tempting proposition," Effie murmured. "I shall certainly think on it." With that, she deftly slipped her fingers free of his, reaching to turn another page. The same fragrance stirred. But this time it wasn't the bewilderingly familiar scent that demanded her attention.

It was something else. Her eye was caught by a scrap of Latin at the top right corner of the page.

It was no medieval text. It had been added much later. The ink was still dark, the handwriting starkly familiar.

> *Donum meum tibi*
> *in coniugii nostri vigilia.*
>
> —*E.W.*

Effie's gaze jerked to Lord Compton's face. He was staring at the inscription, too, a deep groove forming between his brows. He appeared as confounded by its presence as she was. Indeed, if his expression was to judge, he had never seen it before in his life.

And perhaps he hadn't, if he'd never read the books in their entirety.

If he had, he would have found Miss Corvus's message to him years ago. She had obviously expected him to. She'd likely assumed he would treasure this collection, would read it from beginning to end multiple times, just as she had assuredly done. For they were her books, weren't they?

Effie recognized it in the exact instant she recognized the elusive fragrance. It was the same faint scent that had lingered among the black cloth–draped surfaces and crumbling dried flowers of Miss Corvus's private quarters at the Academy. The perfume of a long-ago sweetness turned acrid by betrayal.

"*My gift to you on the eve of our marriage,*" Effie read aloud in a tone of affected bewilderment. "*Signed E. W.*"

They were the same letters the Academy girls had been taught to transpose in their samplers. Remnants of who Miss Corvus had been before Compton had destroyed her. The *W* was surely for Wingard. Effie could only guess at what the *E* might stand for.

"Was this written by one of your distant ancestors, my lord?" she asked.

"Yes," he said after a tense moment. "Someone long dead, presumably. I shall see about having it expunged."

"You don't approve of sentiment?"

"I don't approve of someone defacing my books," he said tightly.

But the medieval collection wasn't his. It had never been his. Miss Corvus had given it to him as an early wedding gift, hadn't she? And he had kept it, the blackguard, just as he'd kept control of her fortune.

It may not be a compromising letter or a trove of damning documents, but it was proof of their former connection. Proof he'd accepted a costly gift from Miss Corvus in exchange for his promise to marry her. At minimum, that must at least be breach of contract, mustn't it?

Effie had to send a sampler to the Academy without delay. In the meanwhile . . .

"Pray don't attempt to have the writing expunged, my lord," she said. "It would only ruin the book and decrease the collection's value."

Lord Compton's mouth pursed with displeasure at the prospect. "It would be a risk," he conceded.

"One far too great to take. Ill-advised as well. That inscription is part of your history now. And one's history can never truly be erased, can it? No matter how much we might wish it to be." Carefully closing the book, Effie rose from her seat. There was no more point in remaining, not when she'd found such a seemingly valuable piece of information. "Forgive me, I must return to Brook Street."

He stood. "So soon?"

"I fear I have already lingered too long."

"Nonsense. Lady Belwood can surely spare you for a few moments more." He moved toward her, coming as close as the hem of her crinoline would allow. "There are nine books remaining in my collection, and I am presently at liberty to show them to you. I can't promise when I will be so again."

Effie backed away from him. "You are too generous, sir. But it's not my hostess I'm thinking of. It is my own obligations." Inclining her head to him in curt farewell, she turned in a swish of violet-sprigged organdy and swiftly exited the library.

She had a great deal of sewing to do.

23

When Effie returned to Brook Street, a note awaited her from Gabriel. Lady Belwood handed it to Effie as Effie entered the drawing room with her embroidery bag. Franc pranced alongside her on his thin velvet lead.

"It was delivered a quarter of an hour ago," Lady Belwood said, resuming her seat on the velvet settee. She didn't attempt to disguise her curiosity. "Who is it from, pray?"

Effie sat down on the sofa opposite, placing her bag next to her. Franc remained at her feet, gazing about the drawing room with avid interest. He rarely ventured into the public rooms. Lady Belwood preferred it that way. But he'd already been alone long enough today, restricted to Effie's bedchamber while she paid her afternoon calls. She wouldn't permit him to be confined any longer.

As he settled himself on the soft Aubusson, Effie broke open the wax seal on the envelope. Her pulse quickened with anticipation.

But it was no love letter. No passionate declaration or heartfelt apology. To be sure, it was no more or less than exactly what she'd asked of him.

Mrs. Young resides at Yew Cottage, Trowley Green, Hertfordshire. Take the 9:30 train to Sawbridgeworth Station. She expects you Tuesday at eleven o'clock.

Effie read it twice, a knot forming in her stomach. Gabriel hadn't even signed it. He hadn't even used her name. It was what she'd wanted—distance. But now he was giving it to her, she felt only disappointment and a dull sort of muted anguish.

She folded the note away, tucking it into her sewing bag. "No one," she said. "Just an address I required."

Lady Belwood's lips compressed. "Your dealings are a mystery to me, I confess."

Effie was glad of that, given what she'd learned today. She withdrew a sampler from her embroidery bag. It was already completed, save for the necessary bit of code. She threaded her needle, preparing to sew the first number necessary to spell out her secret message, informing Nell that Lord Compton was in possession of Miss Corvus's medieval books.

"There is no mystery," she said. "Last night I attended the performance at Cremorne Gardens, and today I visited Carena Compton."

"A fine, accomplished young lady," Lady Belwood remarked. "I have no objection to the association."

Effie stabbed her needle through the coarse cloth. "You are well acquainted with her father?"

"There are few in polite society who are not."

"Yes, but his lordship surely doesn't visit them all."

"I expect not. However, Lord Compton and I have known each other since he first arrived in London. It was I who introduced him to his wife."

Effie ceased her stitching. *"You?"*

"She and I were friends as girls," Lady Belwood said dismissively. "She was formerly Miss Axton, an heiress of no small fortune. After my marriage to Sir Walter, I gave a dinner. She was in attendance. So, too, was Lord Compton. He'd newly arrived in London. A well-to-do second son of an elderly viscount. He wasn't in line to inherit,

but he had already made a fortune in his own right and was, there-
fore, a suitable prospect for my friend."

"What if he hadn't had a fortune?"

Lady Belwood sniffed. "Naturally, I wouldn't have put him next
to Miss Axton at dinner. She'd been dealing with fortune hunters
since she came of age. You cannot know the burden it brings to be
pursued by such disreputable creatures."

"But Lord Compton wasn't disreputable, you believed, because he
was rich."

Lady Belwood adjusted the braided cuff of her green silk afternoon dress. "He was a gentleman then, and remains so today. After
he inherited the title, his social capital only increased. It is my honor
to boast an acquaintance with him of such long standing."

"Does he often call on you here?"

"When he can spare the time."

"And questions you about your houseguests?"

Lady Belwood's gaze flew to Effie's.

"I learned this afternoon that you had been discussing my history
with him," Effie said.

"I never—"

"My fortune—or lack of it—and my prospects."

Lady Belwood blanched. "He did inquire . . ." She stumbled over
her words. "I could scarcely reply with a falsehood. But I would not
betray—"

"It's no matter." Effie resumed sewing. "There is nothing you
know about me that cannot be shared." Her needle flashed through
the cloth. "Miss Corvus, on the other hand, is another matter."

"You need not remind me of *that*."

"I hope I needn't. She wouldn't be as sanguine about her confi-
dences being shared as I have been."

Lady Belwood drew herself up with dignity. "You may believe,

Miss Flite, that I have never mentioned that woman's name." She abruptly stood. "I would thank you to do me the same courtesy."

Effie glanced after Lady Belwood as she stalked from the room.

Did Miss Corvus know of her ladyship's connection to Lord Compton? That it was she who had put him in the way of a wealthy heiress?

Effie riffled through her embroidery bag. She had several uncompleted samplers remaining. Given the variety of things she'd learned, perchance she'd have to send them all.

· · · · ·

Tuesday arrived with unusual rapidity. Effie departed that morning for Hertfordshire, clad in her black dress and veiled bonnet, as anonymous as a widow. It was but an hour by train. Plenty of time for apprehension to grow.

Despite what she'd told Gabriel, she wasn't happy to be making the journey alone. Just once, it would be nice to have someone at her side, especially now when she was so anxious and uncertain.

Mrs. Young might tell her anything.

Or next to nothing.

Either way, it would be one enormous step further than the ignorance Effie had endured all her life. Years and years spent dreaming, imagining a mother who had loved her. A mother who had only given her up because she'd believed Effie would have a better life in an orphanage somewhere, surrounded by strangers, than she'd have if she remained in the Rookery.

Her mother had been wrong.

There was no substitute for the connection one had to one's family. That innate sense of belonging to someone that Effie had always felt lacking. It was why she had rebelled against Miss Corvus. Why she had, for so long, desired to return to that elusive someplace of her childhood. A place beyond conscious memory.

Goodness, what if her mother was still alive? Or worse—what if she had died in reduced circumstances, never knowing Effie had wanted to find her?

By the time she arrived at Sawbridgeworth, Effie had fretted herself into a headache. The train slowed with a grinding scrape of metal and a blast of steam. The conductor shouted unintelligibly as it came to a jolting halt.

Outside the window, the timber-built station came into view. Effie waited for the other passengers in the second-class carriage to disembark before she collected her parasol and rose to exit herself.

The wind whipped at her skirts as she emerged onto the platform. She was assailed by the smell of coal dust and hot metal, and the cacophony of overlapping voices. The whistle blew, and the porters called out to the stragglers. There weren't many to speak of, only a handful of ladies in full-skirted dresses and large shawls, and a few gentlemen in coats and caps. They brushed by, as some boarded the train and others departed.

Effie looked about from behind the veil of her bonnet. She was just turning to join the line at the cabstand, when she spied a familiar gentleman standing near the ticket office. His hat was pulled down over his brow, his black wool overcoat stirring in the gritty wind.

A surge of joy flooded through her.

It was Gabriel.

She took a hasty step forward, thinking of nothing but her desire to see him again. He closed the remaining distance. They faced each other amid the smoke and the steam.

"What are you doing here?" she asked.

Gabriel removed his hat. He was quiet a moment, his pale blue gaze scanning her face through her veil. "I thought you might be in need of support."

Her throat tightened. "But I told you—"

"I know what you told me," he said. "That was in London. This is Hertfordshire."

In other circumstances, Effie might have laughed at the nonsensical distinction. After recent events, she felt more like weeping.

He couldn't be here. This part of her life was private. She dare not let him in. Not when she couldn't trust him.

But she wanted him so much in that moment.

"I've procured a carriage to take us to Trowley Green," he said. "Unless you renew your objection to my accompanying you there. In which case—"

Effie threw her arms around his neck.

His arm came around her waist in return, strong as a band of iron. He turned his face against the side of her bonnet. She felt him inhale a deep, uneven breath.

She understood then that he'd been uncertain of her. He, the untouchable, unemotional Gabriel Royce. He had come here in full anticipation of rejection. Yet, still he had come, because he cared about her.

God help her, she cared about him, too.

"I don't object," she said.

24

The small village of Trowley Green lay in a valley five miles from the railway station in Sawbridgeworth. Effie sat silently beside Gabriel in the hired carriage, an ever-increasing swell of anxiety constricting her breast.

It wasn't only because of the revelations that may await her at Mrs. Young's cottage. It was because of *him*.

The firm length of his body was pressed against her side, from the curve of her shoulder all the way to her knee. Beneath her layers of clothing, Effie was vibrating as keenly as a tuning fork.

This was what came of unrequited intimacies. They made one feel too much—*want* too much.

And she wasn't the only one.

Since leaving Sawbridgeworth Station, Effie had been acutely conscious of the new edge of gruffness in Gabriel's deep voice and the tender regard that lingered at the back of his eyes.

His every word and every look had worked on her heart as potently as a caress, reminding her of all they'd shared that night at Cremorne Gardens. Just the two of them, alone in the lamplit woods, in those scorching moments before things had fallen so terribly apart between them.

For heaven's sake, how was she to pretend that she hadn't kissed this man? That she hadn't been clinging to him in the moonlight and whispering ridiculous things in his ear?

"She's a widow," he said.

She jerked to attention. "I beg your pardon?"

"The old woman in Trowley Green." Gabriel's gaze swept Effie's veiled face. "A real one."

Effie had kept her veil lowered the whole of her journey. A necessary precaution to protect her reputation. And not only that. Along with her crinoline, it provided a layer of armor between her and the greater world around her. Today, she found, she needed her armor more than ever.

"You mentioned she lived with her sister," she said.

"That's what one of my men told me. The sister's a widow as well."

Effie's palms dampened beneath her gloves. She didn't know how she was going to manage to adequately interrogate Mrs. Young without Gabriel learning anything compromising. What if the woman should reveal something untoward? What if—

But the time for what-ifs had passed miles ago.

"I know this Grace woman is important to you," Gabriel said as their carriage entered the village high street. "But you've never mentioned why."

"I told you. She was someone my family knew long ago."

"A servant, I presumed. Your old nursemaid, or your childhood governess?"

Effie was in no frame of mind to spin him a yarn of half-truths. "I don't remember the particulars of her position, only that her fate has always troubled me."

"Your parents dismissed her?"

This time Effie didn't reply. She looked out the window at the rolling green hills that surrounded the village, her hands clasped tight in her lap.

Gabriel's frowning gaze lingered on her veiled face.

She moistened her lips. "When we arrive, you will allow me to ask the questions, I trust."

"Of course," he said.

It was some consolation.

By the time the carriage came to a halt at the end of the narrow lane in front of Mrs. Young's isolated cottage, Effie had her nerves under some semblance of control.

Gabriel disembarked from the carriage ahead of her. He turned to offer his hand.

Normally, Effie would have ignored the courtesy. She was perfectly capable of climbing in and out of carriages on her own. This time, however, she was glad of the assistance. She'd faced too many difficult moments on her own. It was a relief to know this didn't have to be one of them.

She silently set her hand in his.

His face remained impassive, but his fingers immediately closed around hers, both gentle and firm, as though he was cradling something infinitely precious in his grasp.

He stayed by the steps, holding her hand as she descended. He didn't release her, only waited until her booted feet were firmly on the ground before tucking her hand in his arm.

"I believe I saw the curtains twitch," he said dryly.

Effie mustered a faint smile. "They're expecting us."

The small cottage was respectable enough, with its thatched roof and low stone wall. A pebble path led to a slatted front door with ivy growing over the lintel.

Arriving on the front step, they had no need to apply the knocker. The door was opened before either of them could raise a hand. A large, gray-haired woman in a matron's cap filled the doorframe. She looked them up and down.

"Mr. Royce, is it?" she queried. "That man of yours said you'd be here today. My sister and I have been waiting since half past ten." She wiped her hands on her apron. "I am Mrs. Sturges."

"Ma'am," Gabriel said. "May I present Mrs. Flite."

Effie took her elevation from miss to Mrs. in stride. She was, after all, a widow, and one who—judging by her unrelieved black—was still in her first year of mourning.

Drawing back her veil, she inclined her head to the woman. "How do you do?"

Mrs. Sturges examined Effie's face with interest. "Mrs. Flite." She bobbed a curtsy. "I wasn't aware Mr. Royce was bringing a lady." She stepped back. "Come in, if you will. I've made tea."

Effie entered ahead of Gabriel. Mrs. Sturges led them from a cramped front hall through to a small parlor. An aged woman in a poorly fitting drab dress was seated inside on a faded chintz sofa. Her back was hunched, her calloused hands and careworn face indicating a life hard lived. She rose on creaking legs as they came in, fixing her rheumy eyes in their general direction. It wasn't immediately evident if she was blind or merely approaching that state.

"My older sister, Mrs. Young," Mrs. Sturges said. Raising her voice, she addressed the woman: "Vera? This is Mr. Royce and Mrs. Flite come to see you." She waved Effie and Gabriel in. "She can't see so well anymore, but her mind's still quick as a trap. Sit down, the pair of you. I'll fetch the tea tray."

"I never knew you in St. Giles, sir," Mrs. Young said, resuming her seat. Her accent was coarser than her sister's, and the wisps of hair escaping her plain cotton cap were white instead of gray. "But I knew *of* you well enough. And so I told your man, Mr. Walsh."

Effie sat down in one of the pair of threadbare armchairs facing Mrs. Young. Gabriel took the chair next to her. The printed curtains on the small window were open, letting the sun shine into the room.

"He claims you knew of someone else as well," Gabriel said. "A servant woman who used to work for Mrs. Flite's family some years ago."

Mrs. Young's wizened face took on an acquisitive air. "Mr. Walsh indicated as how there might be some small reward involved."

"There might be," Gabriel said, "if the information you provide is useful to Mrs. Flite."

Mrs. Young turned her bleary gaze toward Effie. "This servant of yours, she end up in the Rookery, did she?"

"I believe she did," Effie said. "It was a very long time ago. I'm anxious to learn what became of her."

"I don't recollect Mrs. Grace having been anyone's servant," Mrs. Young said. "She could never have stuck it."

Effie's brows elevated. "*Mrs.* Grace?" she repeated. "I thought . . . That is, wasn't Grace her given name?"

"Oh no. Called herself Amelie or Celine or summat. A lot of them girls had similar-like French names what came out of Madam Marie's. Though she weren't there long. Couldn't stick that, either. The madam threw her out, if I remember."

Effie felt Gabriel cast her a frowning look.

At the moment, his curiosity was the least of her problems.

She leaned forward in her seat. "You mean to say she was a—"

"Oh, she were, right enough. A pretty lass. Never knew her real name. None of us respectable folk did. Wouldn't want to know it. She were that unpleasant."

Effie flattened her palms in her lap.

She refused to quail at discovering that Mrs. Grace—a woman who might very well be Effie's mother—had been a prostitute. Many poor females had been similarly reduced to selling themselves. What choice had they? It was often either that or starvation and death. One couldn't attach a moral valuation to survival. Even so . . .

Effie was suddenly cold. "Yes, I see."

"That wouldn't have been the woman," Gabriel said.

"T'were the only woman named Grace I remember from that time," Mrs. Young replied.

"Did you tell them, Vera?" Mrs. Sturges entered with the tea tray. "I warned that man he hadn't got the right woman." She set the tray down with a clatter on a low walnut table by the sofa. "Tea, Mrs. Flite? Mr. Royce?"

Effie managed a thin thank-you as Mrs. Sturges poured out her tea. She took the cup, grateful for something to warm her.

"I don't encourage my sister to dwell on her former circumstances," Mrs. Sturges said, serving tea to the others. "She married unwisely as a girl, and that husband of hers put her in the way of bad company."

"God rest his soul," Mrs. Young murmured.

"But she retained her honor and dignity, even at the worst," Mrs. Sturges went on. "She never fell into vice like some I could mention."

Mrs. Young nodded in eager agreement. "I did only what I must. No one could accuse me of—"

"That's all behind you now," Mrs. Sturges interrupted firmly. "We live a quiet life in Trowley Green, Mr. Royce. I've given my sister a place of respect in this village." She sat down beside Mrs. Young. "There's no good raking up the past and sullying her good name at this stage of her life."

"We have no desire to rake up the past," Gabriel said. "Only to learn what happened to Mrs. Grace."

"Dead," Mrs. Young said bluntly.

Effie started. "Oh." She lowered her cup back to its saucer. She had known it was a possibility. She had prepared herself. The tersely delivered information nevertheless gave her a jolt. "When—?"

"She were always ill with summat or other. That brat of hers, too. Screaming the place down all hours of the night and day."

Effie's fingers tightened spasmodically on the handle of her teacup. Any doubts she had that Mrs. Grace was, indeed, her mother vanished in a puff of smoke.

"Folk knew the mite were hungry," Mrs. Young continued unaware. "Still . . . it weren't any more likable than its mother. A strange brown little thing with unnatural blue eyes. Mrs. Grace had no fondness for it."

No fondness for her own baby?

Effie didn't believe it. She couldn't. The harsh fact was too far removed from the dreams she'd been constructing all her life. Dreams built upon a gossamer-thin understanding of a mother's self-sacrificing love.

"How do you mean?" she managed to ask.

"Didn't want it, o'course. Couldn't hardly keep it or feed it." Mrs. Young took a noisy gulp of her tea. "Mrs. Grace rented a bed in the attic room of an old rag-and-bone shop at the time. Used to put the child on the roof when its cries became too troublesome."

Effie's breath stopped in her chest. Again, she felt Gabriel's gaze on her. This time it was no brief glance. It was a long, steady look. There was an oddly arrested expression in his pale eyes.

She scarcely noticed it.

Her attention was wholly fixed on Mrs. Young. "She . . . She put the child on the roof?"

"It were the only thing to stop her crying, Mrs. Grace claimed. Been doing it since the child could toddle. The mite used to get real quiet and still up there for fear of falling. Not even her hunger could inspire a peep out of her."

A sickening numbness spread through Effie's limbs. She no longer cared about the possibility of Gabriel learning her secrets. Her thoughts were consumed by that long-ago child. A strange brown little thing. A mere toddler, placed on the roof, her cries of hunger silenced by her terror of falling.

And Effie had been that child.

Her mind couldn't recall it, but something in her did. The memory was imprinted deep, in her blood and in her bones. A scar gouged upon her soul. Never fading. Never healing. Always there to torment her whenever she ventured too high.

"What became of her?" she asked softly. "Of the child?"

"Can't rightly say, ma'am," Mrs. Young replied, drinking her tea. "She disappeared not long afore Mrs. Grace died. Some said she were sent to the workhouse. Others, that the father come and took her away. A lascar, I heard."

Effie was vaguely familiar with the term. A lascar was a sailor from India. Which meant she must be half Indian.

People had remarked on her singular looks all her life. Had asked if she was part Spanish or Italian or any number of things. Effie had never known the answer.

"But t'were only a rumor," Mrs. Young continued. "I didn't see the man meself. I did ask Mrs. Grace where the child went, but she only laughed. Said she never wanted the tyke and good riddance. She were ill at the time, coughing blood and all sorts."

"Consumption," Mrs. Sturges supplied. "Isn't that what you said, Vera?"

"Aye." Mrs. Young nodded. "She had the consumption. Died a few months after the child disappeared."

"There, you see, Mrs. Flite?" Mrs. Sturges said. "This Mrs. Grace woman couldn't have been anyone's servant. Not unless she'd fallen far since leaving your family's employ."

"No indeed," Effie replied mechanically. "This isn't the woman I was looking for." Returning her teacup to the tray, she stood abruptly from her chair. "I'm sorry to have wasted your time."

Gabriel was at once on his feet beside her. Effie didn't wait for him to speak, or for the others to protest her departing so hastily. She turned and strode out the door, left with only the fleeting impression of the two old women rising from the sofa, and of Mrs. Young extending her gnarled hand for recompense.

Lowering the veil of her bonnet, Effie exited the cottage.

Miss Corvus had warned her not to look backward.

But Effie had insisted on doing so, on learning the truth, like Pandora or Lot's wife or any other of the countless examples of women who had coveted knowledge at the expense of self-preservation. And the result had been the same. Chaos. Misery. Obliteration.

There had been no kind, self-sacrificing mother. No place where Effie had ever belonged. She was the bastard child of a prostitute and a lascar sailor. Abused. Unwanted. Unloved.

Her dreams had been illusions. Her long-held anger misdirected.

Miss Corvus hadn't stolen her away from anything worth having all those years ago—if she'd stolen her away at all. Indeed, it transpired, she had very probably saved Effie's life.

25

The train departing Sawbridgeworth Station whistled a shrill final warning.

"All aboard!" the conductor shouted.

Gabriel set a gloved hand on the small of Effie's back, wordlessly steering her toward the first-class railway carriage. She offered no objection, allowing him to guide her steps, just as she'd allowed him to purchase the two first-class tickets for their return journey to London.

The cost had been exorbitant, but any price was preferable to being cramped in an open railway carriage, with no ability to engage in unguarded conversation.

He and Effie hadn't spoken since leaving the cottage in Trowley Green. Seated beside him in the hired carriage, she had remained mute behind her veil, her hands clasped hard in her lap and her body rigid. Gabriel hadn't attempted to engage her. He'd been too stunned himself. Rendered all but speechless by the implications of the dreadful tale he'd pieced together.

It had taken him the full five miles to the station to get his chaotic thoughts in order. Only then had he resolved on something like a plan.

A railway porter in a green straight-buttoned coat stood at the door of the first-class carriage. He directed them to their compartment. Situated near the front, it was paneled in gleaming polished mahogany with four blue cloth–upholstered seats disposed in facing pairs.

Effie sat down in a seat near the oval window.

Gabriel shut the compartment door before taking the seat across from her.

Within seconds, a back-and-forth jolt and the grinding sound of metal announced the train's departure from the station. The conductor shouted unintelligibly as it lurched into motion. Outside the window, the now empty platform slipped by with a gradual increase of speed.

Gabriel lowered the window shade. He removed his hat, placing it on the empty seat beside him. "You no longer need your veil."

Effie slowly pushed the black net back over her bonnet, revealing her beautiful face by degrees. She was unusually pale. The shadows under her dark blue eyes appeared deeper in comparison. He'd noticed them earlier at the cottage. She looked as though she hadn't slept since they'd parted in Cremorne Gardens.

His chest tightened with guilt.

It had been a calculated choice not to seek her out before today. One he'd made the night of Galezzo's fall. Then, Gabriel had believed he was giving Effie an opportunity to recover from the upset she'd suffered. That, in his absence, her temper would cool and, when next they met, she'd be able to face him with something like an open mind.

When she'd flung her arms around him on the platform at Sawbridgeworth Station, he'd dared to hope he had been right.

But he understood now that one impulsive embrace wasn't enough to offset the hurt he'd caused her. A hurt that paled in comparison to the devastation she had suffered at that cottage today.

He gazed at her solemnly as the train rattled down the track. "Effie—"

"She was my mother," she said.

"I gathered that much."

He'd understood it from the instant Mrs. Young had described Mrs. Grace putting her child on the roof. He had looked at Effie then, had seen the dull horror in her face, and he had known. *This* was why she was terrified of heights. Why the mere possibility of falling left her incapable of moving or adequately drawing breath.

"I didn't know," she said. "I couldn't remember."

"How old were you when you left the Rookery?" he asked.

"Five, I believe."

"Was it your father who took you away?"

"No." She numbly shook her head. "I never knew anything about him. Not that he was a lascar or . . . or anything."

Gabriel hadn't been entirely surprised by that bit of information. Indeed, it explained much about Effie's singular beauty.

As for the less savory aspects—the idea that she was somehow tarnished by being mixed race, Gabriel had never subscribed to those beliefs. Purity of pedigree was a rich man's game. An obsession clung to by those who couldn't distinguish themselves in a more substantive manner. But poverty didn't discriminate. The Rookery was rife with people of every color and caste. Gabriel had learned early on that it was character that was important, not the vagaries of one's birth.

"It was a woman who took me," Effie said. "I stole her reticule."

Gabriel received this news without batting an eye. So, Euphemia Flite had been a child pickpocket. Another revelation—and one that strangely didn't surprise him, either. Rather the reverse. The scandalous fact of Effie's unsavory origins settled in his heart, warm and deep, an affirmation of everything he'd been feeling since the first night they'd met.

Like recognized like.

He had sensed it then, without doubt. Had seen something in her that told him they were the same. At the time, the feeling had defied common sense. She was a well-bred young lady taking part in the London season. A lady residing in Mayfair, garbed in fine clothes, and possessed of impeccable manners.

But all that was merely window dressing, wasn't it?

Underneath, she was the same as he was. A child of the slum who had, by some method, managed to infiltrate the razor-thin layer of the upper crust, turning her talents to her advantage.

"She took me when I was small," Effie said. "I was raised in an orphanage."

"The Crinoline Academy," Gabriel murmured.

She gave him a sharp glance.

His mouth quirked wryly. "That's what the barman in the village told Ollie the orphanage was called. I presume that isn't its name?"

"Some people call it that. But no. It's Miss Corvus's Benevolent Academy for the Betterment of Young Ladies." She paused before adding, "It isn't your typical charitable institution."

"I should say not." Not if they were raising up their inmates to masquerade as elegant ladies rather than women who kept to the humble station to which they'd been born.

Effie stared down at her folded hands in her lap. A deep line of anguish etched her brow. "I wasn't supposed to return to the Rookery. Miss Corvus forbade it. But I have always imagined that, one day, I might find my mother. It's been the secret dream of my life." Her voice cracked and her eyes filled with tears. "I might have known it would prove to be a nightmare."

Gabriel was up from his seat in an instant. He took the empty seat beside her and, without preamble, hauled her onto his lap. He held her there until her arms circled his neck and her body relaxed with a trembling breath. He removed her bonnet and tossed it aside. His hand cradled her head against his shoulder.

He was fully aware of the impropriety of his actions. Not even husbands and wives engaged in this degree of intimacy in public. It was vulgar. Unseemly. But Gabriel cared nothing for social rules at the best of times. And now . . . Well.

He cared only for her.

"Parents," he said. "They're always a disappointment."

She struggled to contain her tears. "What does her behavior say about me?"

"Not a blasted thing. You're no different now than when we walked into that cottage. All that's changed is that you've discovered your mother was a heartless tart. There's no point crying over it."

She squeezed her eyes shut. "I'm not. I'm done with weeping."

"Good," he said. "She doesn't deserve it."

"How could she——?"

"Because people are mad. Most can't be trusted with a dog, let alone a child. Yet still they produce them, year after year. Legions of starving, miserable wretches left to roam the streets with no guidance." His hand moved over her silk-encased back in a reassuring caress. Her bodice was fashionably tight, the hard seams of her corset rigid beneath his palm. "I speak from experience, sweetheart."

Her breath gradually grew quiet and regular under his ministrations. "You remember your childhood."

"Regrettably."

"What do you recall?"

"Hunger," he said without hesitation.

"Yes," she agreed. "And not only for food."

He turned his face against her silken, sweet-smelling hair. Honey and black currants. The fragrance filled his lungs, stirring untold longings within his jaded soul.

"You have no other recollections?" he asked.

"Only impressions. I'd hoped . . . But I couldn't remember." Her voice grew husky with emotion. "I had imagined the feeling of despair came later, but it's been there all long, hasn't it?"

Gabriel's throat tightened. He didn't want to think of her hungry and despairing. She wasn't made to suffer. She was made to be adored.

"I don't know about despair," he said. "But I know about want. When you start life without, you never lose the emptiness of it. If you're lucky, you can use it. It keeps you sharp. Helps you survive."

"Survival isn't the same as living."

"No?" He huffed a cynical laugh. "I never had the luxury of the distinction."

Her arms remained around his neck, her body pliant and trusting against him if only for this fleeting, precious moment. The full skirts of her black silk dress spilled about his legs in a profusion of starched petticoats and wire crinoline.

Mine. The word reverberated through Gabriel's veins, even as he counseled himself not to hold her too tightly, not to be too precipitous. It was dangerous to reveal the innermost desires of one's heart. A surefire way to guarantee those desires were left unfulfilled. And he didn't want that. He didn't want to frighten her away.

"You don't understand," she said. "After all these years, I thought I'd finally find the place I belonged."

"You have," he assured her. "It's here. Right here, with me."

So much for not being precipitous.

Her arms loosed from his neck. She slowly pulled back to look at him, hands resting lightly on his shoulders. Her troubled eyes were glistening, but true to her resolve, no tears spilled. "Gabriel—"

"I mean it," he said. "Nothing else matters."

Her brows knit. "How can you say that? Aren't you at all dismayed to discover I'm not who I've pretended to be?"

"I know who you are."

Her lips trembled. She shook her head. "You don't."

"I've known since the beginning."

A startled look crossed her face. "But how—?"

"We're the same," he said. "I told you so the night we met."

Understanding registered in her dark blue gaze. Her expression softened. "We may well be so. It doesn't change the facts. I came to London for a purpose."

Gabriel didn't have to ask what that purpose was. She'd admitted it to him that afternoon in Hyde Park. It was Compton who had drawn her here, not the glamour of the season or the hope of finding a wealthy husband. What Gabriel didn't understand was why.

"All this effort," he said. "The fine clothes. The Mayfair address. The tales about your French finishing school and your wealthy former guardian. Have any of them been true?"

"A version of the truth."

His brow creased. "And for what? Merely to stop Compton from standing in the way of some bill in Parliament?" He scanned her face. "Who's subsidizing it all? Lady Belwood?"

"No," Effie said. "Not Lady Belwood. Someone else."

"Who?"

For a moment it appeared she wouldn't answer. And then: "A lady who champions the causes of women."

"What lady?"

"It doesn't matter who she is now. It's who she was before. A vulnerable lady like so many others—exploited by a powerful man, unprotected by a loathsome half brother. Her fortune taken from her, and her reputation destroyed."

Gabriel stared at Effie in dawning understanding. "Good God," he uttered. "Not Wingard's sister?"

26

E ffie had no intention of revealing Miss Corvus's secrets. How could she when she didn't know the half of them herself? But after what she had learned in Trowley Green, and after Gabriel had accepted her—truly accepted her—she couldn't lie to him any longer.

He was right. They were the same.

Perhaps they even belonged together. It certainly felt that way, on his lap and in his arms. Here, at last, she was safe, and known, and . . .

Beloved.

Gabriel hadn't said it in so many words, but the emotion was there all the same. It was in the way he held her and comforted her. In the tenderness that deepened his voice and softened the hard edges of his granite-hewn face. No longer cynical, he had looked into her eyes with raw sincerity.

"I know who you are," he'd said.

Effie's heart had thumped heavily in answer. This connection between them . . . It was a form of kinship she'd never encountered. An elemental recognition, all tangled up with vulnerability and desire. The temptation to give in to it was great indeed. But in the aftermath of learning about her mother, another feeling had emerged in Effie's aching heart. An iron-forged sense of what she owed to Miss Corvus.

Reluctantly, she withdrew from Gabriel's arms. He didn't attempt

290 · Mimi Matthews

to stop her, only looked at her steadily, his expression intent, as she collected her bonnet from the adjoining seat and moved to take its place.

"I don't know her by that name," she said, arranging her skirts. "But I believe she may well be her."

Gabriel sat up straighter as she settled beside him, leaning toward her in her seat, his pale blue eyes riveted to her face. "Wingard said his sister went abroad. He told me she'd died."

"A version of death. The lady who raised me wasn't a broken woman. She was a creature of singular strength. So much so that I spent all my life imagining her cold and heartless."

His brows notched. "You say she raised you—"

"As much as a child can be raised in an orphanage. There was no love or affection in that place." The old bitterness threatened as Effie uttered the words. She recognized it now for what it was: childhood ignorance; a misperception of the facts.

For the first time in her life, she ignored the acrid sensation. The wave of bitterness passed over her and through her, leaving her clear-eyed in its wake. She may not fully know Miss Corvus's secrets, but when it came to her motives, Effie was at last beginning to understand.

"She saw that we were well educated," she said. "Not only in the traditional subjects, but in the untraditional ones. She ensured we could think for ourselves, and defend ourselves. That we would never fall victim to any man."

Through it all, Miss Corvus's prevailing message had always been clear. Effie was alone—intrinsically, inherently alone. She could rely on no one but herself. A valuable lesson, given Miss Corvus's own history, but one that had left Effie feeling isolated and abandoned. A girl with no place in the world where she belonged.

Until now.

Gabriel had said she belonged with him.

Effie met his gaze. He was still frowning. Still no doubt appalled. It was difficult to tell anymore. The softness that had been in his face when he'd told her that nothing else mattered was gone, replaced by something grim and implacable.

It made it easier for Effie rather than harder. Love and acceptance were unfamiliar waters, but she'd been navigating the stormy seas of adversity from childhood. Conflict was second nature to her.

"When I began to get restless," she continued, "dwelling too much on my past, she sent me to Paris to act as companion to a wealthy widow. I was only summoned back last month."

"Why now?" he asked.

"Because of Lord Compton."

Gabriel's expression darkened at the mention of the viscount's name.

"His opposition to a married women's property bill is an obstacle that must be overcome," Effie said. "As I'm the oldest, and the best capable of moving in society, it was only logical Miss Corvus would—"

"Send you to infiltrate his inner circle?" A spark of fury blazed in Gabriel's eyes. "Heartless is right. This champion of women you describe may as well have thrown you to the bloody wolves. If Compton gets wind of what you're doing—"

"He has no idea," Effie said. "He thinks all I'm concealing are my own reduced circumstances. That I'm looking for a protector—you, possibly."

Gabriel's gaze turned dangerous. "He said this?"

"His butler observed us coming out of the library on the night of the ball."

"Did he," Gabriel said flatly. It wasn't a question.

"Lord Compton told me himself but three days ago. I called in Grosvenor Square. He showed me his antique book collection. He knows I have no money. No prospects. He assumes I'm weighing my options. Either you or . . ."

"Or him," Gabriel concluded.

A shiver traced down Effie's spine at the look in his eyes. She'd never seen him so angry. At his worst, he became cold and remote. But this . . .

This was something else.

"No more," he said in a voice of perilous calm.

Her pulse skipped. "Gabriel, really—"

"No more chasing him. No more visiting his house and searching his rooms. I don't want you within a mile of the man." He caught her chin in his hand, compelling her to face him. His eyes burned into hers. "Do you understand me?"

A blush heated her face. She'd never been the subject of such hazardous intensity. Not even when he'd kissed her so passionately at Cremorne Gardens.

"Of course I do," she said. "You're attempting to order me about according to your whims. But I'm not finished with—"

"You're finished," he said.

Anger rose within her. She would have pulled her face away in outrage if he wasn't holding her chin so firmly. "No," she returned fiercely. "I'm *not*. Not until I've done what I set out to do."

"And what am I meant to do?" he shot back. "If something were to happen to you—if Compton hurt you or that butler of his—"

"I can defend myself. No one is going to—"

"If either of them lay a hand on you, I'll kill them."

A thrill went through her. Good gracious, he meant it. He was prepared to dispatch anyone who dared touch her. It was overbearingly protective. Indeed, it bordered on primitive. She should be appalled by the notion. She was a strong, independent lady, fully capable of protecting herself. Even so . . .

"That's very flattering," she managed. "But you needn't contemplate such a course."

His thumb pressed her chin, still holding her fast. He looked into her eyes, more serious than she'd ever seen him. "I found you," he said gruffly. "I've no intention of losing you."

Her heart thumped heavily. "You won't."

"Then promise me that you'll give up."

Effie would have loved to set his mind at ease. To tell him she would cease pursuing Compton, and shun all risk of danger. But it wasn't true. It wasn't her.

"I can't promise," she said. "More depends on my success than the passage of a married women's property bill. There's Franc—our life together—our entire future. If I fail, I shall have no money for a home of our own."

His eyes searched hers with sudden calculation. "She's offered you money?"

Effie couldn't tell if he was shocked by the fact. Indeed, she couldn't tell what he was thinking any longer at all. His face had gone peculiarly blank.

"How much?" he asked.

She hesitated to answer. She didn't like revealing her less honorable motivations. It was one thing to risk her life and reputation for the greater good of women. It was quite another to do it for material gain.

"Enough to gain my independence," she admitted grudgingly. "I shall get to keep all my clothes as well. The entire wardrobe that was made for me in Paris. I could never in my life afford such a luxury on my own. Without it—"

"I can buy you a new wardrobe," he said.

She stared at him, startled into silence.

"Gowns, jewels, anything."

She shook her head. "Gabriel . . ."

His hand lifted to cradle her cheek. "If that's all you desire, then let me give it to you," he said recklessly. "Fine clothes. A comfortable house. A coach-and-four if you want it."

Her heartbeat quickened, even as her stomach sank at the implication. "In exchange for what?"

"For being mine," he said.

She exhaled an uneven breath. She hated that she was tempted. "I don't want to be kept by someone. Not even you."

"We'll keep each other. Help each other."

"How?"

"The Rookery. There are plenty of women there whose lives you can make better. We'll work to reform it. You have opinions, ideas. I'll listen to you. Take your advice. We can reside in Sloane Street. You said you thought the house fine. It can be yours. Ours."

"And I'll be your . . . what?" She didn't dare say the word *mistress*; the prospect brought nothing but pain.

He brushed his thumb over the slope of her cheek. His voice deepened. "You'll be my love."

Her heart ached with longing. "Your love."

"That surprises you?"

"No."

"It offends you?"

"No."

His brows sank. "If you don't feel the same—"

"I do," she said softly. "You must know that I do."

The barest flicker of relief crossed his face. He smiled briefly. "I didn't know. I hoped, but—"

"Gabriel . . ."

His mouth quirked with sudden humor. He looked different. Younger. "If you want pretty speeches, you'll have to look elsewhere, sweet. I'm no fancy lord, just a rogue from Birmingham. All I can tell you is that you're magnificent. Doubtless you've heard it before."

"No," she said. "I haven't." Gentlemen had complimented her frequently enough on her eyes, her face, her figure. They had called her beautiful often, magnificent never.

"Bloody idiots," Gabriel said. Bending his head to hers, he pressed a kiss to her lips.

Effie's eyes fell closed and her mouth softened under his. A part of her had feared that his feelings toward her would change. That after learning the truth about her origins, he would respect her less. But it appeared the opposite was true. He was gentler, sweeter. As though it was the first time their lips had touched.

And perhaps it was.

On every other occasion there had been something between them. Panic, tears, lies, and artifice. But not now. Now, they were both fully vulnerable. Fully themselves.

She curved a hand around his neck, bringing him closer.

He obliged her, deepening their kiss. He was less cautious now, his desire for her evident in the way he cradled her cheek and the strength with which his arm came about her waist. He held her fast against his chest, so close she could feel the heavy beat of his heart.

Effie's own heart thumped hard in answer as she sank into the fierceness of his embrace. She kissed him back with warm, half-parted lips, sighing, yielding, her fingers twining in his hair. Her blood sang out—yes, yes, yes. This was exactly where she belonged. Where she'd always belonged.

It would have been so easy to succumb to the sensation.

Goodness, he'd all but said that he loved her! He'd offered her a house, fine dresses, a coach-and-four. More than that, he'd proposed something like a partnership. A mutual endeavor to reform the Rookery. The place both of them had, at one time, called home.

But Effie had another home. One she hadn't recognized for what it was until today. The remote, iron-gated stone house where she'd learned, grown, transformed into a woman to be reckoned with.

The train rattled down the track. London was still a distance away. There were other stops in between. The next was one with which she was intimately familiar.

"I can't," she murmured against his mouth.

"Can't what?"

"Be with you," she said. "Not on those terms."

Gabriel's hand froze on the curve of her waist. A moment passed in absolute stillness, his unsteady breath mingling with hers, before he drew back to look at her. He stared into her eyes. "On any terms?"

"I still have a job to do."

He released her from his arms, leaving her cold. "A job," he repeated. The sardonic edge in his voice left no doubt as to what he thought of it.

She mustered an air of offended dignity—not an easy feat when her face was flushed and her lips still swollen from his kisses. "I see how it is. The only way we can be together is if I sacrifice what's important to me. The notion of you sacrificing anything is ludicrous, I suppose."

"I haven't sacrificed?" His gaze hardened. "I'm here with you, aren't I? Tomorrow is Epsom. I have two horses running, a shop that's packed to the gills, a passel of gentlemen reformers waiting to meet with me, and I'm in bloody Hertfordshire."

"I didn't ask you to come."

"You didn't have to ask. I'd have been with you every moment if I could. I'd never have let you go with Mannering in the first place. I'd have taken you home with me that night where you belong. You'd have been mine and I'd have been yours." His eyes smoldered. "The only thing keeping us apart is you."

Effie steeled herself against another swell of yearning. "And yet, I'm the one who must bend."

"No. All you must do is cease pursuing Compton, for your own good, Effie, *and* for mine. God knows I've offered you enough in exchange for it. A fine home, handsome clothes, a carriage. And myself—which would be sufficient on its own if you felt anything for me even approaching what I feel for you."

"You forgot the thirty pieces of silver," she replied quietly.

He stilled. A derisive huff emerged from his lips. "My offer makes you a Judas, does it?"

"I would be if I accepted it. I'd be betraying my sisters."

"Your sisters," he scoffed.

"I'd be betraying myself. What security is there in being dependent on you for the smallest thing? You're not, after all, offering me marriage."

He looked at her steadily, his face taut with anger and some other emotion she couldn't fully grasp. "Why offer what you won't accept?"

"No. You're right. There's no need at all."

The train slowed on the track, approaching the station.

Know your surroundings. Know your opponent. Know yourself.

The three rules reverberated in Effie's muddled brain in time with the rattle of the wheels on the track. She had always believed that, whatever else happened, she knew herself. Her goals, her desires. But not any longer. She'd had everything backward and inside out. What she needed was clarity, and there was only one person who could give it to her.

Coming to an abrupt decision, Effie stood from her seat.

Gabriel rose at once beside her, his hat in his hand.

She backed to the door of the compartment, the floor of the train shuddering beneath her feet. "I'm disembarking. Pray don't follow me."

A flash of emotion crossed Gabriel's face. "Effie, wait—"

"I have something I must do alone."

"Next stop, Waltham Station!" the brakeman shouted down the corridor as the train rolled to a halt. "Waltham Abbey, Loughton, and the Epping Forest!"

Understanding registered in Gabriel's eyes. "You're going to the orphanage."

"I must," she said.

298 · Mimi Matthews

He moved to follow her.

She set her hand flat on his chest. "No."

His fist clenched on the brim of his hat. His jaw clenched as well. Every fiber in him seemed to be at war.

"Please," she said. "I know what I'm about."

"We're not finished," he informed her stonily.

"I know."

"When I return from Epsom, we're going to settle this thing between us once and for all."

Effie opened the door as the train came to a halt. Her gaze held his, raw and unflinching. She comprehended, then, exactly what it was she felt for him. This wild, aching madness that complicated her plans and defied common sense, while at the same time feeling so wonderful, so right. It could only be one thing.

Recognizing it now was hardly convenient. But Effie could deny it no longer. Not to herself—and not to him.

"I love you," she said.

Gabriel's cold expression fractured. He looked astonished. Shaken. His lips parted to speak.

She didn't wait to hear what he might have said. There was no time.

"Come and find me after the Derby," she told him.

With that, she slipped out of the compartment and off of the train.

27

A short hackney cab drive later, Effie arrived at the tall black iron gates of the Academy. This time, she didn't remain there, waiting impatiently for one of the junior teachers to let her in. Effie was no guest. No former inmate visiting her onetime place of confinement. She was a young lady returning home. She did what she'd been trained to do. She picked the lock.

It was slightly more difficult than the mechanism of an interior door or a simple desk drawer, but no match for her determination. Stabbing her dragonfly hairpins back into her rolled coiffure, Effie entered the grounds, shutting the gates behind her.

She strode up the pebbled path with uncommon purpose. She'd almost reached the door when Nell emerged. She wore a plain stuff dress, covered in a neatly starched apron.

Her eyes went wide. "Effie! What in the world—"

"I've come to see her," Effie said. "I know you advised me not to return, but it can't be helped. Circumstances demand it."

Nell frowned, but she didn't question her. She stepped back, admitting Effie into the empty hall. There were no students about at this time of day. The hour was yet early. They would still be in their classes.

"I just received your latest samplers this morning," Nell said. "I gave them to Miss Corvus. It's she who determines my replies."

"She can reply to me herself." Effie removed her bonnet and gloves. "Is she doing any better?"

"A great deal better, in fact. She still keeps to her rooms, but she's growing stronger by the day. A period of enforced rest has worked miracles on her constitution."

The weight of worry Effie had been carrying these many weeks began to ease. She had been afraid for her former teacher. Frightened she would die. It had made no sense at the time, given Effie's bitterness toward Miss Corvus. But it made sense to her now.

"I'm relieved to hear it," she said. "Will you take me to her?"

"Of course." Nell escorted Effie through the hall. The painting of *Judith Slaying Holofernes* loomed large ahead of them. So, too, the portrait of Miss Corvus standing in the doorway. Effie glanced at them as they passed, taking comfort from their familiarity.

Arriving at the iron-banded wooden doors that marked Miss Corvus's private chambers, Nell knocked once.

"Come!" Miss Corvus called out.

Nell opened the door. The faint, sickly sweet fragrance of decay emerged, tickling Effie's nose just as it had when she'd opened the medieval books in Compton's library.

"Miss Flite has come to see you, ma'am," Nell said. "Shall I—"

"Send her in," Miss Corvus replied tersely.

This time, Effie didn't quail at the sound of her old schoolmistress's voice. On the contrary, she was rather impatient to face her. Squaring her shoulders, she entered the cool, black-shrouded darkness of Miss Corvus's rooms.

Nell moved to close the door after her. "I shall give you privacy."

"There's no need," Effie said. "Indeed, I had rather you joined us."

• • • • •

Seated in the armchair across from Miss Corvus, Effie related what she'd learned about her mother, leaving out only the parts that overtly involved Gabriel Royce. She owed Nell and Miss Corvus honesty, but some things were lately too private to share. Gabriel was one of them.

It had been but a short time since Effie had left him on the train. Less than an hour altogether, yet her heart was still aching with love for him. It wasn't a burdensome ache. Quite the reverse. Knowing he cared for her and that she cared for him in return was a powerful elixir. It bolstered Effie's courage, giving her the strength to face Miss Corvus and to recount the awful details of what Mrs. Young had shared in Trowley Green.

Nell remained standing by the black-curtained window as Effie finished her tale, her arms folded and her face gone pale with sympathetic anguish.

Miss Corvus was similarly solemn, though it was irritation that etched her hardened countenance, not fellow feeling. She hadn't expected visitors today. Rather than her usual black silk, she was dressed in a gray flannel dressing gown. A linen handkerchief was crumpled in her hand.

"How much did you know of all this?" Effie asked her.

Miss Corvus remained silent. The malachite table was arrayed beside her, just as it had been on Effie's last visit. The same tray sat upon it, holding a glass of water, a silver pitcher, and a brown bottle of patent medicine. Despite the evidence of the sickroom, Miss Corvus did appear to be improving in health. She sat taller in her green damask chair, her eyes alert and her face no longer waxen with illness.

"Surely, there's no point in keeping secrets anymore," Effie said. "I already know the worst of it."

"You should never have known any of it at all," Miss Corvus snapped back at last. "What good has it done you to learn these dreadful things?"

"It is undeniably painful," Effie admitted. "But—"

"From the first, you've been determined to disobey me," Miss Corvus interrupted. "Every chance I've given you to spread your wings, you have used the opportunity to fly backward rather than forward."

"Learning about my past was the only way I *could* go forward," Effie told her. "You of all people should understand. The past may not decide our future but it certainly informs it. If you knew about the life I had before—"

"I knew nothing," Miss Corvus said tightly. "Only that you were emaciated and filthy, and moved as silently as a cat. Had I not turned around at the flower stall in that precise moment, I'd never have known you'd stolen my reticule. I'd never have known you at all." She adjusted the neck of her dressing gown with uncharacteristically restless fingers. "As for that creature . . . the woman you insist on calling *mother* . . . had I any knowledge of what she'd done to you, I'd never have criticized your fear of heights. Perhaps I was wrong to do so in any case. I might have guessed—"

"No one could have guessed at such cruelty," Nell declared from her place by the window. "That a mother should treat her child so! Any child. My heart breaks for you, Effie."

"Your heart needn't trouble itself on my account," Effie said. "I wanted understanding, and now I have it." It hurt her, yes. But she couldn't regret the knowledge of it. There were only a few finer points on which she still needed clarification. She turned to Miss Corvus. "Did you pay her for me?"

Miss Corvus's hand stilled at her throat. "I took you to her that day, intending to give her a piece of my mind. She had a rented bed in a communal room in the slum. The state of it. Of *her.*" Her lip curled with disdain. "I'd already founded the orphanage. The trustees and I anticipated choosing girls from the workhouse. But when I saw the conditions in which you'd been living, and when that woman offered you to me—"

Effie's brows shot up. "She *offered* me to you?"

"For a sum," Miss Corvus said. "There have always been those who would buy little girls for unsavory purposes. Brothel keepers and the like. The woman plainly suspected I was one of them, and sought to make a few coins for herself in the bargain."

Effie's stomach revolted at the thought. She pressed a hand to her midsection, willing herself to remain calm and unemotional. But to think—her own mother would have sold her into such circumstances. It was sickening. Devastating. "How much did she ask of you?"

"Four pounds," Miss Corvus said.

Effie exhaled a trembling breath.

Across the room, Nell angrily brushed a tear from her cheek.

"I paid it, naturally," Miss Corvus said. "You were half-feral, but you were quick and fearless and undoubtedly bright. I was confident I could make something of you. I flatter myself I succeeded, despite your constant attempts to thwart me."

"I always believed you'd taken me from someone who loved me," Effie said.

"I'm well aware what you believed," Miss Corvus replied. "It was better than you knowing the truth."

"How could it have been?"

Miss Corvus gave a dismissive sniff, as though the answer were obvious. "You were too young," she said simply. "The truth would have destroyed you. You were ill-equipped to hear it. It's the very reason you couldn't remember the details of the years before you came to me. The experience was too painful for you to recollect. I count it a mercy."

Effie stared at her former teacher, a powerful emotion holding her in its grip. It shouldn't have been a surprise to hear that Miss Corvus had acted out of kindness rather than cruelty. Effie had already learned so much of late that cast her former teacher's actions in a more flattering light. And yet, she was surprised anew, finally comprehending that someone had acted to protect her fragile young heart and mind from additional pain. Not her mother, it was true, but another woman. A stronger woman.

Miss Corvus had been that person, always.

"I daresay you were right," Effie said. "But it has been a long while since I was a child. You might have told me anytime since I came of age. I'm a grown woman. So is Nell. We deserve your candor if nothing else. There should be no more secrets between us."

"To what purpose?" Miss Corvus asked. "Your pedigrees don't define you. Nor do the actions of those who would abuse or victimize you. We forge our own identities here. The two of you have done so, not by my will, but through your own. It's that which marks your character. Your integrity and achievements, not any accident of birth."

"*Do* we forge our identities?" Effie asked. "Or are they manufactured for us?"

Miss Corvus's lips compressed at the suggestion, but she didn't deny it. She'd given them their names. Their knowledge. Their singular purpose.

"You taught us to be independent. To defend ourselves and think for ourselves." Effie paused. "So long as our thoughts don't diverge from yours."

Miss Corvus flinched. "Don't be absurd."

"Your disapproval weighs heavily. That, and the promise of a stipend. I'd have done anything to earn them."

"You never disagreed with my philosophy."

"Not on principle," Effie said. "But empowering women means allowing them to make their own decisions, for good or ill. Even if they wish to accept things as they are. To be part of society rather than battle against it."

"Is *that* what you want?" Miss Corvus couldn't hide her dismay. She looked from Effie to Nell and back again. "To be ordinary?"

"No," Nell said. "It's never been what I wanted."

"Nor I," Effie admitted. "But I'd rather it had been my choice. One made with full knowledge of my past." She hesitated but a moment before asking, "What was I called before I came here?"

"Effie Grace," Miss Corvus replied stiffly. "Not so very different from the name I bestowed on you."

Effie nodded slowly. She felt no particular connection to her former name. Miss Corvus was right. Effie's identity had been forged here at the Academy. She was Euphemia Flite now. Had been for more years than she'd ever been anyone else. "And what were you called?" she asked quietly.

Miss Corvus was silent for a long moment before answering. "Elizabeth Wingard."

At last. Effie had often wondered. She exchanged a glance with Nell.

"Artemisia Gentileschi painted the original of the framed reproduction in the entry hall," Miss Corvus said. "*Judith Slaying Holofernes.* The epitome of a woman taking matters into her own hands. When I returned to England, I adopted her Christian name as my own. It seemed appropriate."

"But not your surname," Nell said. "For that you preferred a raven."

Miss Corvus's slim shoulder lifted in an offhand shrug. "Birds have always been a fascination of mine. Unlike people, they can fly away from their troubles. Among them, the raven is unique. An intelligent and prophetic bird. Ravens don't abandon their young. They remain with them into early adulthood, flying beside them."

Effie's eyes prickled. She leaned forward in her seat in an earnest desire for understanding. "Why did you start the school? Was it because of what Lord Compton did to you?"

A spasm of pain crossed Miss Corvus's face. She drew back in her chair, reaching for her glass of water. "What do you know of it?"

"I know you believed he would marry you. That instead, he and your half brother conspired to steal your fortune. I know you went abroad afterward and that you returned with a different name. A different fortune."

"Not a fortune." Miss Corvus took a sip of water before returning the glass to the tray beside her. "A small sum, only. It was the remainder of my inheritance from my mother. That, Compton and my brother didn't manage to touch." She dabbed at her lips with her handkerchief. "It was my father's money they stole—in excess of fifty thousand pounds."

Nell gasped at the figure. It was more than most people would see in a lifetime. "Why did you not go to the authorities?"

"And say what, pray?" Miss Corvus asked. "I had no proof. The documents were taken away by my brother before I fully realized what had happened—the entirety of my correspondence with Compton, the little tokens of esteem he'd given me, the copies of the papers he'd bid me sign. All that remained was my own accounting of the events. Had I come forward, it would have been reduced to my word against his."

"You surely would have prevailed," Nell said. "If he was found to be in possession of your money and property—"

Miss Corvus gave a derisive snort. "Do you have any idea of the scandal it would have caused? What it would have done to what remained of my reputation? At the time, that was all I had left to sustain me. But to go public . . . Me, a jilted young lady, claiming such things against a man who no longer wanted me? A spinster scorned? I was already considered odd. Isolated. Friendless. While Compton—he had gone to London. He had allies. Connections."

"He went to London on *your* money," Effie said angrily. "It's how he was able to marry an heiress, making himself even richer and more powerful."

"Do you imagine I don't know it?" Miss Corvus's face darkened with remembered fury. "I was obliged to flee, as if I were the one who had done wrong. To relinquish my home. To change my name. For a time, I thought only of avenging myself on him. Even when I returned from the continent, even when I started the school." She looked at Effie with mingled bitterness and regret. "Even when I met you. I thought to forge you into a weapon. Not only against Compton, but against all men. You, Miss Trewlove, and Miss Sparrow—the three oldest of my girls. My formidable, intelligent army of women. No man could ever take advantage of any of you. You were too bright. Too dangerous. *I* gave you that."

"You did," Nell murmured. "Yet still you permit Compton to take advantage of you."

"We are not the same," Miss Corvus said.

"The devil we aren't," Effie retorted. "You made us in your image."

"No," Miss Corvus said. "I made you into what I wished I could be myself." She lowered her handkerchief from her lips. "I was raised as are most respectable British girls. Kept in ignorance of politics and the law. Brought up so the world—and even my own body—was a mystery to me. Only after having been exploited did I recognize what I was lacking. It was other women who illuminated me. They guided me during my time on the continent. Strong, extraordinary females. They already knew then what I was only coming to comprehend, that absent knowledge, absent rights, ladies are obliged to seek guidance from men. Our fathers, brothers, and husbands. It's how they defeat us. It's how they win."

"But they can't win," Nell said. "Not if we fight. Not if *you* fight."

Miss Corvus shook her head. "My battle is long past. You're the fighters now. That's what I've given you. The skill to affect conformity and the grace to move in society, when all the while you're focused on the future. Not just for yourselves, but for all women."

"A woman looking through a doorway, not behind her," Effie murmured, thinking of Miss Corvus's portrait. "Her true face hidden from the world."

"In time, perhaps, society will be different," Miss Corvus said. "When that day comes, we can show them who we truly are. For now, we must adhere to our roles. To change the world, we must seem to be of the world. And the world at the moment is no respecter of women's strength."

"Perhaps that's the problem," Nell suggested. "Perhaps we should show them our strength."

"And terrify the men in power?" Miss Corvus scoffed.

"Perhaps they should be terrified," Effie replied.

Miss Corvus again shook her head, sternly dismissing the idea. "They would be even less likely to enact change for our benefit. No. You must do no more and no less than exactly as I've told you to do. Find evidence of Compton's wrongdoing so we might expose him."

"There's nothing yet to connect him to any wrongdoing except that which he did to you," Effie said. "*That* must be how we destroy him."

"I agree," Nell said. "It will be unpleasant for you to relive it, but—"

"He can't harm me now," Miss Corvus said. "I left Elizabeth Wingard on the road somewhere between Paris and Marseille. The world believes her dead. I intend her to remain so."

"Then let her stay dead," Effie said. "It can only worsen the narrative of Compton's crimes against her."

"There's no proof of those crimes," Miss Corvus said.

"There is," Effie replied. "Not the documents your brother stole, I grant you, but the translation of Aristotle's *Historia Animalium*. I told you in my latest sampler, it has your note in it. It proves a connection—a contract of engagement. And the fact that he's now in possession of your entire collection . . . Surely, that must count for something?"

"A revelation, admittedly," Miss Corvus acknowledged. "I'd have thought he would have sold it by now."

"It belonged to your family?" Nell asked.

"My mother's branch. One of our treasured possessions. Generations upon generations had safeguarded it for centuries." A rare trace of self-loathing infiltrated Miss Corvus's voice. "All for me to give it to a man for whom I was deluded enough to cherish an affection. If I never see it again, it will be no less than I deserve."

"I shall get it back for you," Effie said.

Miss Corvus blinked. "Impossible."

"Not the whole collection," Effie amended. "Even I have my limits. But I can certainly retrieve the book that holds your message to Compton. It's proof, if you're willing to use it."

Miss Corvus stared down at her hands for a moment, appearing to wrestle with her thoughts. Longing and regret warred in her face. "Very well," she said at last, lifting her gaze. "Bring it to me if you can. I shall know how to act."

"And if that fails?" Nell crossed toward them from the window, arms still folded at her waist. "If you're unsuccessful in retrieving the book. Or worse—if it's not enough to undo the man. What then, Effie? What is your contingency plan?"

Effie's mouth hitched at one corner. "Chaos," she replied. "What else?"

28

Gabriel was in the habit of attending the Derby at Epsom Downs every May, both in his role as bookmaker and as horse owner. He had two young colts running today. The favorite was a striking bay named Sparkler who had shown great promise at Northampton races.

"A fine specimen," Lord Haverford said, joining Gabriel outside the young horse's loose box in the stables. "As good as any I've seen."

Gabriel leaned against the stall door. He was absent his coat, his shirtsleeves rolled up to his forearms. He'd spent the better part of the morning in the barn with the horses rather than at the track. It hadn't mattered that Lord Haverford and his influential friends had been present in one of the racing boxes. Gabriel had been in no frame of mind to engage them. He knew what he'd say if he did. It wasn't a conversation he contemplated with any degree of eagerness.

"Better." Gabriel gave the colt a distracted scratch on its gleaming neck. He wasn't a rider himself, but he was a fair judge of horseflesh. "He'll be worth a fortune after this afternoon's race."

"You're confident he'll win?" Haverford asked.

"He'll place today. He'll win in future. A horse who can run well at Epsom can run well at any track in the country."

"You're half owner?"

"Full owner," Gabriel said. "I don't go halves on something I care about."

Lord Haverford laughed. "An admirable philosophy if one can afford it."

"There's the rub," Gabriel acknowledged grimly.

But he wasn't thinking about his two promising young race-horses. He was thinking about Effie. Indeed, he'd been thinking of nothing *but* Effie since she'd left him standing in their first-class railway compartment yesterday.

"I love you," she'd said.

I love you.

No. Gabriel didn't go halves on something he cared about.

"I have a question to put to you," he said to Haverford.

They were alone except for a handful of stable lads mucking out the loose boxes. The third race was running. Most everyone else was at the track to watch it. The noise filtered from the stands in a distant hum, punctuated by the sound of stamping hooves and horses contentedly munching their hay.

"I'm listening," Haverford said.

"What would become of our plans to reform the slum if Lord Compton were no longer a component of them?" Gabriel asked.

"How do you mean? Is he unwilling to pen that editorial we discussed?"

"More than that. What if he withdrew his support completely?"

Lord Haverford's smile vanished. A somber expression came to take its place. "Is that likely?"

"If it was?"

"Then I fear the other support you've managed to amass would swiftly follow suit."

Gabriel had expected no less.

A soft breeze down the aisle of the stables stirred flurries of dust and hay. The fragrance was familiar—sun, turf, and sweetness. The perfume of a rich man's sport. Men like Gabriel existed on the fringes of it. Trainers, grooms, jockeys, and bookmakers. Necessary appendages. But not equals.

It took money to compete against the gentry. Even more if one was to win. Gabriel had enough put by to sustain him. But without his betting shop, he would never grow any richer. He would be, like the Rookery, a dwindling concern. Rapidly decreasing in power until . . .

"If I may speak plainly," Haverford said.

Gabriel saw little point in it at this stage. He'd already made up his mind. "By all means."

"When we met at my club last week . . . After you left, concerns were raised about your background. Your betting enterprise, specifically. Several of the gentlemen confessed to having heard things about you. They mentioned your past associations, and the rumors of violence and intimidation attached to your name."

"You knew I was a bookmaker."

"Quite. But there are degrees of acceptability, even among those as liberal-minded as we are." Haverford looked at him, frowning. "Tell me, just how egregious has your conduct been?"

Gabriel was quiet a moment before answering, reflecting on his past, on all the cruelties, insults, and indignities that had brought him to this point. A man of no birth, with nothing much to recommend him, except that he'd somehow managed to earn the love of a woman like Euphemia Flite.

It had changed him. It had changed everything.

"I have been brutal, it's true," he admitted. "I've also been a businessman. An unthinking brute wouldn't get far running a betting shop that traffics with the aristocracy, nor would he have much success inspiring loyalty among his men. I've done both, and well. The unsavory aspects have less of a place in my world of late. You've seen for yourself. The people of the Rookery look to me for leadership. Once the slum is reformed, my position will be solidified."

"The sons of the gentry still place wagers with you. Some of them are in debt to you for considerable sums."

"Your associates would rather I call in those debts?"

"They'd rather your business weren't so murky. It gives them pause."

Gabriel gave a short, humorless chuckle. "But not enough to terminate our plans. Not so long as Compton is still lending them countenance."

"I'm giving you the courtesy of candor," Haverford said. "It isn't I who is objecting to your character, after all. Not outright."

"No," Gabriel said with bitter humor. "Reform-minded people of your class enjoy a heartening tale of an impoverished street urchin who pulls himself up to a position of authority. It strengthens their arguments for charitable measures."

Haverford didn't dispute the fact. "So long as that street urchin hasn't done anything too disagreeable."

"What street urchin hasn't? More to the point, what politician hasn't? Disagreeable acts aren't limited to the poor."

"No. They're not. Regrettably, the poor aren't judged by the same standards as gentlemen in government."

"They should be." Gabriel straightened from the door of the loose box. "Though if we removed every villain from Parliament, I'm not entirely sure who would be left to run the country."

Haverford smiled briefly. "I fear there would be infinitely more villains waiting to take their place. Such is the way of politics."

Gabriel gave him a hard look. It was a jest, obviously. And yet . . .

A lunatic thought occurred to him.

Perhaps, just perhaps, he'd been viewing the problem from the wrong angle. It surely made no difference in terms of the outcome. Nevertheless, a glimmer of possibility beckoned.

That was all Gabriel required.

"You can tell your concerned friends that Compton is out," he said.

Haverford's face fell. "You've lost his support?"

"I no longer want it. Indeed, I have it on good authority the man is heading for a fall." Gabriel gave Haverford a hard thump on the shoulder as he turned to leave. "If I were you, I'd advise any well-meaning souls to abandon ship."

· · · · ·

Effie arrived at Lady Bartlett's house in Kensington at ten o'clock promptly. It was a neat brick residence near Holland Park, rather benign in appearance. Ascending the front steps to the door, Effie didn't know quite what to expect.

She had offered chaos as a contingency plan to Nell and Miss Corvus. However, in Effie's experience, chaos often took time to bear fruit. As a plan, it was best deployed concurrently. She hoped the notes she'd sent yesterday had been sufficient to set it in motion. There had been two of them—the first written on Lady Belwood's stationery and the second on the anonymous stationery Effie had purchased last week.

She had paid a street lad to pop the second note through the intended recipient's letter box. Whether that recipient would respond in the way Effie intended remained to be seen.

"Good morning, miss," the butler said, admitting her into the black-and-white-tiled hall. "Your name, if you please?"

"Miss Euphemia Flite," Effie replied.

"Very good, miss. Right this way."

Effie followed him up the curving staircase, her twine-filled reticule dangling from her wrist. She had come alone in a hackney. It was better Lady Belwood's carriage wasn't involved. Effie had already embroiled her hostess enough in her plans. Today must go seamlessly, and there must be no unnecessary casualties.

Upstairs, Lady Bartlett's drawing room was buzzing with activity. Upholstered sofas and chairs were arranged about the Turkish-carpeted floor, already half-filled with ladies of varying ages, and even a few gentlemen. Others milled about by a tea table set up at the back, talking companionably.

Unlike a society gathering, the people in attendance didn't appear to be limited to the fashionable elite. Some of them were plainly dressed, and others were downright eccentric in bright colors, garish hats, and feather-and-fur-trimmed boas.

The butler announced her: "Miss Flite."

An ample-figured lady in an elegant dove-gray silk dress approached. Several long strands of beads were draped about her neck. "Miss Flite. Welcome to my home." Rather than bowing, she extended her hand in a brazenly forthright manner.

Effie shook it as matter-of-factly as if they were two gentleman acquaintances. "My lady. We have a mutual friend, I believe, in Miss Ruth Mannering. It was she who invited me."

"No invitations necessary. We are all comrades-in-arms here." Lady Bartlett gestured to the few chairs remaining. "Have a seat, and do help yourself to refreshments."

"Thank you," Effie said.

Lady Bartlett moved on, seeing to her other guests.

Effie's gaze drifted over the drawing room, searching for familiar faces. The particular one she sought had only been glimpsed once before. Perhaps she wouldn't recognize it?

She'd nearly given up when her eyes lit on a porcelain-skinned woman with striking ebony hair sitting on a velvet sofa near the tea urn. Clad in an apricot silk morning dress with a box-pleated hem, she was looking about the room, as though not wholly certain how she found herself to be there.

Effie made straight for her. "I beg your pardon."

The woman looked up with wide, unblinking brown eyes. "Yes?"

316 · Mimi Matthews

"Forgive me," Effie said, "but I had the notion you might be a newcomer like myself."

"It is indeed my first time. Though at what manner of event, I cannot tell."

Effie smiled warmly. "Miss Euphemia Flite," she said, extending her hand.

The woman took it, clasping it briefly before releasing it. "Mrs. Dora Naismith."

Up close, her face illuminated by the sunlight streaming through the drawing room windows, Mrs. Naismith's beauty was revealed in all its glory. She was a striking woman in her middle thirties, long lashed and lush figured, with an air of childlike innocence.

"May I sit with you?" Effie asked her. "One so dislikes to be on one's own, even at a lecture."

"If you wish," Mrs. Naismith said. "I would be glad of the company."

Effie took a seat beside her on the sofa. She smoothed her skirts. She'd dressed sensibly this morning in her cherry red caraco jacket, black poplin, and jet-trimmed velvet hat. It wouldn't do to have ruffles and trimmings getting in her way when she stole the book from Compton's library. She needed to be sleek, quick, and relatively unencumbered.

Mrs. Naismith regarded her with a frown. "Did you receive an invitation?"

"Not formally. I was told about the lecture by a friend." Effie retained her smile. "And you?"

"I was informed it was a diversion not to be missed. That there would be society, refreshment, and music, perhaps."

Effie had indeed written that in the anonymous invitation she'd sent. She'd been confident it would be sufficient to tempt Mrs. Naismith. Unlike the mistresses of fashionable gentlemen, shamelessly paraded about town at the opera or the theater, Effie had surmised that the mistresses of outwardly moral men had little society. Tucked away in private houses, the guilty secrets of their protectors, their days must be dull indeed. Mrs. Naismith would surely jump at the chance to relieve her boredom. Or so Effie had hoped.

"There is certainly society and refreshment," she said. "The very best of both."

Mrs. Naismith looked around the drawing room. "Yes, but I see no musical instruments."

"No, indeed," Effie allowed. "Still . . . we are sure to be diverted."

The butler again appeared at the door. "Miss Compton," he intoned.

Mrs. Naismith's thin black brows flew up to her hairline.

Carena Compton entered the room. She wore a rose-pink dress and matching velvet paletot.

Effie raised her hand, signaling her presence.

"Do you know that girl?" Mrs. Naismith asked.

"I do," Effie said. "And soon, so shall you."

Mrs. Naismith flashed Effie a fascinated look. For an instant it appeared she might rise from her seat, but she made no move to do so, only sat there, observing Miss Compton's approach with an expression of ill-disguised curiosity.

"Miss Flite," Miss Compton said, dropping a brief curtsy.

"Miss Compton," Effie said. "May I present Mrs. Naismith? She is a newcomer to Lady Bartlett's gatherings, just as we are."

"Mrs. Naismith," Miss Compton said.

A bubbling giggle escaped Mrs. Naismith's lips.

Miss Compton glared at her.

"I'm sorry," Mrs. Naismith said quickly, covering her mouth with her hand. "But this is just too absurd."

Somewhat mollified, Miss Compton joined them on the sofa, seating herself on Effie's opposite side. "I'm glad to hear I'm not the only one to find it so."

"Nonsense," Effie said. "The lecture promises to be edifying in the extreme. By the end of it, the three of us will be fast friends."

"What is the lecture about?" Mrs. Naismith asked.

A woman in a chair nearby turned to answer. Her curling gray hair was contained by a felt turban trimmed with cerise feathers. "It is on the subject of girls' education," she said. "We shall be hearing the latest progress on the committee's findings as well."

"What committee?" Effie asked.

"The one Lady Bartlett has assembled to reform the married women's property law," the woman answered. "There was a similar committee several years ago, but its work came to nothing. We're determined to take up the charge."

Effie's interest piqued. Miss Corvus had mentioned that there was serious discussion about a bill being brought before Parliament. Could this committee be the source of it? "How have you proceeded?" she asked.

"We collect signatures on various petitions," the woman said. "We also collect testimonials from affected women. Their personal stories are powerful evidence. It only remains to find a sponsor for our bill—and to successfully combat any opposition to it. I have every reason to hope that, this time, our attempts will be successful."

"It's a splendid ideal," Effie said. "I endorse it wholeheartedly."

The woman offered her hand to Effie. "Mrs. Jefferies," she said, introducing herself.

"Euphemia Flite," Effie replied, shaking her hand.

"You are welcome to join us," Mrs. Jefferies said. "Young people are the lifeblood of our fight."

Before Effie could reply, Lady Bartlett moved to the front of the room, raising her hands to bring everyone to attention. "My dear friends, old and new, welcome, welcome. We have much to get through today, so if you've all taken your seats . . ."

Miss Compton whispered to Effie as Lady Bartlett continued speaking. "I don't think we should remain."

Mrs. Naismith heard her. She leaned across Effie to reply to Miss Compton. "Why ever not?" she whispered back.

"It's revolutionary talk," Miss Compton said. "We're not meant to hear it."

"Why shouldn't we?" Mrs. Naismith asked. "It sounds positively titillating."

"Exactly," Miss Compton replied ominously. "My father says that lectures of this sort are a poison to women. He warns most strenuously against them."

"Naturally, he does," Effie said. "That is how gentlemen remain in power, by making us fear the very thing that will set us free."

Miss Compton drew back with a dubious blink. "Lectures by radical bluestockings?"

"Knowledge," Effie said. "It's ignorance that's the poison, Miss Compton. This . . . well. I very much hope this will be the cure."

29

Some ninety minutes later, Effie emerged from Lady Bartlett's house alongside Miss Compton and Mrs. Naismith. Together, they descended the front steps to the busy street below.

Miss Compton's fair brow was furrowed deeply. Despite her initial protestations, she had listened intently as Lady Bartlett related the damning testimonials her committee had compiled from ladies who had suffered under the current property laws. Women of every class whose fortunes, both large and small, had been squandered or stolen by the men they had married. The same men whom the law believed were better custodians of a wife's earnings and inheritances than the wife herself.

And that hadn't been the worst of it.

After Lady Bartlett had finished her sobering report, she'd introduced Miss Wolstenholme, a prominent teacher from Manchester, who spoke on the evils of the current system of educating girls. She'd laid out in plain terms how girls were purposely kept in ignorance, dissuaded from engaging in politics or public affairs, and discouraged from having strong opinions else they be labeled unfeminine. Like the current laws, it was all predicated on the flawed idea that the more serious aspects of a female's life—finances, property, even intimate relations—were better left to be managed by men.

"Well," Effie said frankly, "I found that very enlightening."

"Oh, but it was!" Mrs. Naismith agreed. Like Miss Compton, she had been riveted by the lecture, seeming to be as fascinated by the topics discussed as she was at being newly acquainted with the daughter of her protector. "Do you think it all true?"

"Of course it's true," Miss Compton said. "And monstrous besides."

Mrs. Naismith nodded. "The injustice of it—men purposefully keeping us in the dark, and then chastising us for not being their intellectual equals? My—" she stopped, catching herself. "That is, a *friend* of mine, did recently say my concerns about money were unattractive. Unattractive, I tell you! But really . . . one must think of the years ahead. One isn't young forever."

Effie gave Mrs. Naismith a thoughtful look. Had she been pressing Compton about her future? And rather than reassure her, he had criticized her practical concerns as being unbecoming?

The unfeeling devil.

Though, Effie couldn't say she was surprised. Not when Compton had already made something of an overture toward her. Perhaps it was his habit to change his mistresses out every few years? She wondered how many had preceded Mrs. Naismith.

Cabs and carriages vied for positions in front of Lady Bartlett's house as the rest of the ladies who had attended the lecture departed. Miss Compton's elegant lacquered coach, with its gold crest on the door, was slowly approaching. A lighter sporting coach pulled by two matched grays preceded it. The vehicle was small but sleek, with a glossy black body and sky-blue painted wheels.

Mrs. Naismith brightened. "Ah! There is my carriage."

Effie admired the dashing vehicle along with Miss Compton. It had doubtless been provided by Lord Compton, along with Mrs. Naismith's fine clothes and her house in Ellis Street.

It occurred to Effie that, yesterday, Gabriel had offered her something strikingly similar. Clothes, a house, a carriage. A comfortable life as mistress, rather than a wife.

But no.

It wasn't at all the same. Gabriel hadn't proposed that Effie be his guilty secret, tucked away somewhere in a house of her own, to be visited at his leisure. He had asked her to be his love. To make her home—and her life—with him.

Effie's heart had yearned to accept his offer. Never mind that it wasn't an offer of marriage. Her heart didn't care about legalities. All it had wanted—all *she* had wanted—was to be with the man she loved.

But it wasn't her heart that was in charge today. It was her head. She had important business to attend to. She couldn't afford to be distracted.

Mrs. Naismith turned to Effie and Miss Compton with a smile. "Goodbye to you! Perchance I will see you again at the next meeting?"

"Perchance you will," Miss Compton said, exchanging curtsies with her.

"Until then," Effie said.

Mrs. Naismith waved at them as she boarded her carriage. The instant her coach set off, Miss Compton's carriage pulled up to take its place. The liveried footman jumped down from his perch to open the door for his young mistress.

Here, at last, was the moment Effie had been waiting for.

"May I beg a lift from you?" she asked Miss Compton.

"If you like," Miss Compton said, "but I must go straight home. My music lesson is at one. And after that, I depart immediately for the balloon ascension at Cremorne Gardens."

"You mean to attend?"

"Naturally. Lord Mannering will be there with his sister, will he not? I'm eager to tell her I attended the lecture."

"Yes, of course," Effie said. "It's sure to bring you closer to her."

"And then to him," Miss Compton said, allowing the footman to hand her into the carriage.

Effie climbed in after her. The interior of the coach was upholstered in blue velvet with gold edging. It appeared to be new. "An excellent plan," she said. "I shan't anything to impede it. Indeed, you need only take me as far as Grosvenor Square."

The footman closed the door behind them and the carriage started off, rolling smoothly toward Mayfair. It was but three miles away. A negligible distance in such a well-sprung vehicle. They arrived in front of the Comptons' mansion not twenty minutes later.

Miss Compton gathered her skirts to disembark. "You needn't walk," she said to Effie. "John Coachman can convey you to Brook Street quickly enough after I get out."

"No, no," Effie objected. "Truly. I had rather stretch my legs. But first . . ." She sunk her voice. "May I trouble you to use the necessary?"

Miss Compton's face turned a dull red. Ladies were discouraged from mentioning their bodily functions, even amongst each other. "If you must," she said with stiff dignity.

The footman opened the carriage door and assisted Miss Compton down. Effie followed, making sure her reticule was still with her. She had packed enough twine in it this morning to fulfill her plan. Without it, she'd have no way to spirit the book out of the house.

Before they had finished ascending the front steps, the Compton's butler, Parker, materialized at the door. He held it open for them as they entered the hall. "Mr. Lampert has arrived, miss," he informed Miss Compton. "He awaits you in the music room."

Miss Compton hurried to the stairs. "I must change," she said. "Tell him I'll be down in five minutes. And Parker? Do show Miss Flite to the washroom."

Effie waited at the foot of the stairs, her eyes lowered in what she hoped was a fair impression of feminine modesty. The house boasted an indoor privy on each floor. She didn't know where the ground floor one was located, but she suspected it was somewhere along the long corridor that led to the library.

Her suspicions were confirmed when Parker gestured in that direction. "This way, miss."

Effie followed him. She sensed he was looking at her again, still trying to puzzle out why she seemed so familiar. "Is Lady Compton at home?" she asked.

"Her ladyship is presently attending to callers in the drawing room," he said.

"Yes, of course. These must be her receiving hours." Effie hesitated. "And Lord Compton? Is he at liberty?"

"His lordship is in Westminster. He is expected back any moment."

Effie's pulse quickened. If that was true, there was little time to spare. "Pity I'll miss him."

"Indeed." Parker led Effie down the corridor to the door of a small coatroom that had been converted for the purpose. "You will find all you require inside, miss."

Effie stopped beside him, still refraining from making eye contact. "You needn't wait on me," she said. "I shall show myself out when I'm finished."

Parker didn't question her. Any servant worth his salt was aware that it was as indelicate for a lady to be seen entering a water closet as it was for her to be seen leaving one.

"Very good, miss." Parker quickly departed, presumably off to inform the music teacher that his pupil would be joining him shortly.

Effie exhaled the breath she'd been holding. She waited, hand on the door of the washroom for a full twenty seconds, wary of one of the servants seeing her. But there appeared to be none about. Lord

Compton was away, Lady Compton was engaged in the drawing room, Miss Compton would be occupied in the music room, and the servants would be kept busy ushering up any callers.

This was Effie's moment.

Slipping down the hall, she made for the library. She quietly opened one of the double doors. An excuse for her presence hovered on the tip of her tongue should she find anyone inside. But there was no one. No servants, no shadows, and no ravening wolves waiting to pounce. The large book-lined room was bright and empty, smelling of pipe smoke and lemon polish.

Silently closing the door behind her, Effie went to the shelf where Miss Corvus's books were displayed. She extracted the first one, turning to the page where she'd seen Miss Corvus's message.

It was still there.

Relief coursed through her. She had feared Compton might have made good on his threat to expunge it. But no. As ever, his attachment to valuable things superseded all other concerns.

Effie prayed it would be his undoing.

Acting swiftly, she opened her reticule and removed the wad of twine. She'd never secured an item as large as a book to her crinoline before, but given the circumference of her poplin skirts, she was confident it was possible.

Raising her petticoats and crinoline, she tucked the book beneath and used the twine to tie it to the underside of the wire cage frame. It wasn't a heavy tome, but heavy enough to exert an unfortunate pull. Not ideal, admittedly; however, it would do until Effie could get to Brook Street.

She dropped her skirts back into place, giving them a shake to test whether the book wobbled.

It didn't.

Effie was heartened by the discovery. She adjusted the remaining books on the shelf to better disguise the first book's absence. With luck, Compton wouldn't immediately discover it was gone. By that time, the book would be safe in Miss Corvus's hands.

All that remained was for Effie to slip out of the library and exit the house without drawing any attention to herself. Snapping the drawstring closure of her reticule shut, she turned to leave.

Parker stood at the door. "Can I help you, miss?"

Effie froze where she stood. Her stomach dropped. Good heavens. How long had he been there? Had he observed her taking the book?

It was bad enough that he'd seen her at all. She'd wanted no link between herself and the library today. No chance of anyone connecting her with the room when the book was later discovered missing.

Looking at the cruel set to Parker's mouth and the sinister intent darkening his brow, she briefly considered abandoning her plan. But it was too late. The book was already in her possession. She had no choice but to proceed.

"Not at all, sir." Pasting on a smile, she crossed the library. "I was merely admiring his lordship's collection."

Parker remained where he stood, all but barring the door.

Effie didn't wait for him to move. She pressed toward him, her enormous skirts going before her, forcing him to back out of her way. "I have a great fondness for books, as Miss Compton can attest."

Parker glanced at the shelf by the fireplace as Effie brushed by him.

Her heart plummeted. She hadn't accounted for being found out so soon. It meant an end to the fiction she'd been perpetrating. She would have to return to the Academy. Perhaps even go abroad. But first—

She had to get away.

Pulse racing, she strode down the carpeted corridor.

"Wait a moment, miss," Parker said.

Effie quickened her pace. She made for the marble entry hall. It was empty. The ringing chords of a concerto drifted down from the first floor, Miss Compton's flawless soprano voice accompanying the piano music in perfect harmony.

"Stop," Parker said, this time more forcefully.

Ignoring the command, Effie opened the front door. She dashed out, bounding down the front steps as quickly as she could without losing her footing. She had traveled lightly this morning, leaving her parasol behind. She had no convenient tools with which to defend herself. If Parker caught up with her—

"I said stop, miss!" Parker bellowed, pounding down the steps after her.

Effie's chest constricted with panic. She raced down the street, past the carriages and strolling pedestrians. The entrance to the mews was on the left. She ducked down it without thinking. The sound of Parker's footfalls was unrelenting. Good God—he was chasing her!

Another narrow alley was on the right. Effie darted down it at a full run, the book under her skirts slapping against her legs. Her hat fell off. She didn't stop to collect it. Parker was right behind her. She got no more than a few yards before his brawny fingers closed around her arm in a punishing grip, nearly wrenching her off her feet.

He dragged her around to face him. His bald head was gleaming with perspiration, his brows lowered in a fearsome scowl. "Stop *thief*, I should have said."

Effie attempted to pull away from him to no avail. He was far too strong. She glared up at him, summoning her best effort at ladylike outrage. "How *dare* you accuse me of theft?"

"You took one of his lordship's books. I saw you."

"You most certainly did not." She made another equally unsuccessful effort to free her arm. "I'll thank you to release me."

His grip on her only tightened. Effie gave an involuntary cry of pain. "It was you I saw last week in Ellis Street, wasn't it? That nosy woman with the veil?"

"I don't know what you're talking about."

"You have a way of walking. I knew I'd seen it before. When the master finds out—"

Effie pulled at him with all her might. "Unhand me!"

"Oh no," he said. "I'm taking you back to the house. His lordship will deal with you. Or I can call the constable. It's your choice."

Effie dug in her heels. "Let me go, you great oaf!"

Parker dragged her several steps. "The book's under your dress, isn't it? Devious slut. I'll retrieve it myself when I get you back to the house."

"I'm warning you," she said.

"Or how 'bout I retrieve it now?" He made a grab for the fabric of her skirts.

Effie's mind stilled at the physical threat. Her senses sharpened to a knife's edge, even as her pulse slowed and her respiration grew steady. Years of Academy training ignited in her as instinctively as breathing.

She *had* warned the man.

Rather than pull away from him, she came closer, gripping him by the front of his coat. As he lunged forward to grasp her skirts, she bent her knees, shifted her weight on her hip, and using his own great bulk against him, tossed him straight over her shoulder.

Parker landed on the ground with a resounding thud. Dust from the alleyway puffed up around him.

Effie lingered only long enough to see if he would remain down. He didn't.

He was back up with surprising speed for such a large man, coming at her again, too furious to employ strategy.

She deftly sidestepped him, delivering a sharp elbow to his spine as he passed.

Parker staggered forward, uttering an inarticulate roar of rage. Regaining his balance, he turned on her, his face contorted in a ferocious mask. He made another clumsy lunge.

Effie avoided him again. As he moved by her, she hooked his ankle with her foot, bringing him to one knee.

Panting heavily, the butler regained his footing. "What manner of female—"

"One whose business is no business of yours," she said. "I'd advise you to—"

He barreled straight for her before she could finish, knocking the breath out of her lungs. His arms came around her midsection in a crushing bear hug, lifting her straight off the ground. "Demented doxy," he growled. "I'll carry you back if I have to."

Effie struggled against him, pummeling him with her fists and kicking him in the legs with her booted feet. She couldn't get to his eyes. His head was bent against her shoulder, protecting his face, and he had no hair she could pull to force him to raise it again.

She attempted to knee him in the nether regions, but her skirts were in the way, and he was holding her too close for her to do any appreciable damage. She vaguely registered that the book was still attached to the inside of her crinoline. Perhaps he could even feel it there, pressed as they were front to front. If he could, he gave no sign of it. He was too focused on subduing her and returning her to Grosvenor Square.

Scrunching his face against her repeated blows, he conveyed her down the alleyway. It would be the work of a moment to carry her back to Compton's house. Once inside, Effie would be a prisoner, left at the mercy of the constable or of Lord Compton himself. There would be no escape.

She must free herself now or never.

With leverage no longer in her favor, she had but one option left. Reaching back, she tore one of her dragonfly pins from her plaited coiffure. She hesitated but an instant. She didn't like to be brutal, but . . .

She *had* given the man multiple chances to desist.

Raising the hairpin, she stabbed it straight into his ear.

Parker emitted an animallike howl of pain. He immediately released her. Effie fell to the ground in a bruising heap as the butler staggered past. His cries were interspersed with foul words, calling her every vile name under the sun, as his hand reached uselessly for the protruding pin.

She scrambled up, breathless. The full import of what she'd just done struck her with a sickening clarity. Catching her skirts in her hands, Effie ran.

30

E ffie held Franc tightly in her arms, her face buried in the soft black curls of his coat. She hadn't stopped trembling since she'd returned to Brook Street ten minutes ago, hatless and disheveled, missing one of her dragonfly hairpins.

It hadn't prevented her from doing what must be done.

Before withdrawing to her room, she'd first taken pains to hide the book. She'd put it in the Belwoods' library, wedged behind a high shelf of leather-bound tomes on the history of the Roman Empire. It would have to be wrapped in brown paper and posted to the Academy. Effie must do it herself. She couldn't trust the errand to one of the Belwoods' footmen.

In the meanwhile, she didn't dare keep the book on her person. Not when she expected Parker to appear at any moment, either alone or with the constable. They would almost certainly demand to search her, and very likely insist on searching her room.

Seated in an armchair by her chamber window, Effie cradled Franc, willing herself to remain calm. The little poodle pawed at her cheek in canine concern.

"If only Gabriel wasn't at the dratted Derby," she told him. "I've no doubt he would manage this situation impeccably."

But Gabriel wasn't in London. Effie was on her own. And she had no time to spare.

"We must away from here," she said to Franc. "As soon as I catch my breath, we'll pack a bag. I'll post the book, and then we shall board the next steamer for Calais. Madame Dalhousie will give us shelter until Miss Corvus can determine what I'm to do next."

Franc blinked up at her.

"What *we're* to do next," she amended.

Franc's tail quivered. He licked her cheek.

"Don't worry," she said. "I'll keep you safe."

Ten minutes later, her carpetbag packed, Effie was just heading for the bedroom door to see about wrapping the book when a knock arrested her step.

"Miss Flite?" Mary poked her head in. "Sorry to disturb you, miss, but Lady Belwood requests your presence in the drawing room."

"Now?" Effie asked, incredulous.

Mary cast an interested look at Effie's carpetbag. "At once, miss."

"Very well." Effie settled Franc back on the bed. Giving him one final pet of reassurance, she exited the bedroom. She followed Mary down a flight of stairs to the drawing room.

Lady Belwood awaited her there on the brocade sofa. She wasn't alone.

"Miss Flite." Lord Compton rose as Effie entered, a cold smile curving his thin lips. "The very person I've come to see."

Effie stared at the man for a full five seconds. Her every instinct told her to flee. She ignored the impulse. She wasn't going to run only to be caught in some ignominious fashion. Compton was the one in the wrong, not her. Despite the anxiety pulsing in her veins, she had no intention of showing even a scintilla of fear.

She summoned a smile. "Lord Compton. How delightful."

Lady Belwood looked between the two of them with a frown. She fluttered her pastel painted fan, appearing much vexed. "His lordship has a matter he most earnestly wishes to discuss with you," she said to Effie. "If you would be so obliging?"

"Of course." Effie came to join them.

"There is no need for you to stay, my lady," Lord Compton said to Lady Belwood. "The matter is between me and your ward."

"As you mentioned." Lady Belwood stood. "Though I must say it is most irregular. Were it anyone but you, sir, I would insist on remaining to chaperone Miss Flite."

Effie's gaze held Compton's. "I require no chaperone," she replied to her hostess. "But I thank you for your consideration."

Lady Belwood reluctantly departed the room. Lord Compton followed her to the door, closing it behind her. He turned to face Effie. He didn't mince words.

"You have something of mine," he said.

"I don't," she replied.

Compton walked back to her. He motioned to the sofa. "Do sit down. This needn't become unpleasant."

Effie preferred to remain standing. She folded her arms.

His lips flattened. "Very well. If this is how you wish to proceed . . ." He stopped in front of her. "There are severe punishments for theft, young lady. Just as there are severe punishments for assault. You may believe that you—and your pretty neck—will find neither of them to your liking."

"I've stolen nothing," Effie said. "And I've assaulted no one."

"My butler would beg to differ."

"Your butler? That hulking brute better suited to a bare-knuckle brawl?"

"Parker does what I require of him. He looks after my person, and he protects my valuables. Not half an hour ago, he was grievously injured in the pursuit of his duties. I'm informed it was you who injured him."

"You believe that a woman of my stature could harm a man as large and forbidding as he?"

"Yes, it is extraordinary," Compton allowed. "But the evidence—"

"It was *he* who assaulted *me*. I merely defended myself."

"You stabbed the man with one of your hairpins, Miss Flite, in the course of robbing my library. I presume this has something to do with Royce. He's ensnared you—ruined you, I don't doubt—in an effort to ruin me."

"Mr. Royce has nothing to do with this."

"Is it greed, then? You think to sell my book and make yourself a tidy profit?"

"It isn't your book," Effie said.

Compton's gaze narrowed.

"The proof is there for anyone to see," she said. "Do you dispute the fact?"

"I don't know what you're referring to."

"My gift to you on the eve of our marriage," Effie quoted. "But you didn't marry Elizabeth Wingard, did you?"

Something dangerous glimmered in Compton's eyes.

"You had a contract with her and you breached it. You kept her books. You took her fortune. You defrauded her, and presumed that shame would keep her silent. But you have been the author of your own downfall. Your greed and lust for riches have done you in."

Compton moved closer to her. "Where have you heard this nonsense? From Royce? From someone else?"

"From Miss Wingard, naturally."

His face betrayed a flare of uncertainty. "Miss Wingard is dead."

Effie would have loved to tell him the truth, that Elizabeth Wingard was alive and thriving. But Miss Corvus desired her past self to remain dead. Effie must respect her wishes.

"Yes," she acknowledged. "And her voice cries out from the grave. Too long you've evaded justice. Consider this your reckoning."

He stared at her, all traces of doubt gone. His face went hard with calculation. "What do you want of me? Money?"

"No, not money."

"What, then?"

"Resign from Parliament," she said. "Write a public letter of apology, acknowledging your crimes against women."

Compton gave a sudden laugh. It was a chilling sound, short and contemptuous. "Like all females, you overreach yourself." He took a step toward Effie, lowering his voice. "Do you imagine your threats can harm me? You're no one. You have no family or connections. No money. You might have made an interesting diversion in the bedchamber, but let us be frank, my dear. You are in no ways my equal."

"On that we can agree," Effie said.

"A word from me and you'll be hauled to prison. No one will save you, nor will they wish to do so. Society has no love for violent, conniving females. When they hang you, the crowds will cheer as your neck snaps."

Effie's heart beat heavily. This time it was anger that surged in her blood, not fear. "A diverting picture. I trust you'll enjoy the spectacle from your cell at Newgate."

Compton loomed over her, gritting his teeth. "Who do you think you're speaking to? Do you imagine you know me? That I'm a man to be trifled with?"

"Oh, but I do know you, my lord. I know you well, indeed. Ask your mistress. Ask your daughter. You have no idea of what I've set in motion. You, sir, are on the brink of being besieged on every front."

Compton reached for her.

Effie stepped back, avoiding his grasp by inches. "Have a care, sir. Do recall that violence is the last resort of a desperate man."

His expression hardened. "Enough of these games. Return the book, and we shall end this amicably. I'll allow you to leave London under your own power."

"A generous offer. I fear I must decline it."

"Don't be hasty, Miss Flite. Think on it. I will await your answer. I give you until two o'clock today."

"You will wait in vain, my lord," she said.

His lips curled into a smile that had more in common with a sneer. "We shall see." Turning on his heel, he exited the room.

Effie pressed a trembling hand to her midriff. Her stomach was roiling and her pulse was pounding in her ears. She remained in the drawing room until she heard the fading tread of footsteps descending to the hall. Venturing out on the landing, she peered down in time to see the front door shut.

The instant it did, Effie dashed upstairs to collect her things. She found her bedchamber door standing open.

A dull sense of horror overtook her.

She had shut it after leaving. She *always* shut it. One of the servants must have opened it in the course of their duties. Franc would have immediately availed himself of the opportunity. He couldn't resist wandering.

Effie rushed inside. She cast about the room with increasing desperation. Just as she'd feared, Franc was gone. She told herself not to panic. He must be somewhere in the house. It wouldn't be difficult to find him, providing no one had inadvertently let him outside.

She was turning to exit her room, intent on starting her search, when a scrap of white on her coverlet caught her eye. Something twinkled atop it—a glitter of glass sparkling in the sun from the window.

It was the dragonfly hairpin she'd left in Parker's ear.

Someone had used it to stab a note to Effie's bed. She tore the paper free. The blood drained from her face as she read it.

If you want to see your dog alive again, bring the book to the balloon ascension at Cremorne Gardens. You have until two o'clock.

• • • • •

Gabriel's carriage stopped in front of the Belwoods' house in Brook Street. He straightened his freshly starched black cravat. Effie wasn't expecting him today. He'd told her they would talk after the Derby—tomorrow, at the earliest. But once he'd made up his mind, Gabriel had seen no reason to delay. Not even the business of the track had been sufficient to keep him at Epsom. Not when his whole future was hanging in the balance.

He'd traveled home this morning, shortly after speaking to Lord Haverford at the stables. On returning to London, Gabriel had first gone to Sloane Street, and then to Fleet Street to speak with Miles. After that . . .

Gabriel had made for a jeweler's shop in Oxford Street.

Climbing out of the carriage, he patted the small, flat box in the pocket of his waistcoat, assuring himself his purchase was still there. Anxiety simmered in his chest. He was nervous, by God. A baffling sensation. He wasn't a lad. He didn't get *nervous*. But there was no mistaking the feeling.

He ascended the stone front steps of the house. He'd nearly reached the top when the door flew open and Effie charged out, hatless and disheveled, clutching a book. She ran straight into Gabriel's arms.

"Oh!" she gasped. She looked up at him wildly as he steadied her with his hands. Her eyes were damp with the threat of tears. "Gabriel!"

His heart lurched. "What is it? What's happened?"

"Is that your carriage?"

"Yes, but—"

"We must go." She pulled free of him, bounding down the steps.

He followed her. "Go where?"

"The balloon ascent at Cremorne Gardens. I haven't a moment to spare."

Gabriel opened the carriage door for her, assisting her in without question. "Cremorne Gardens," he called to his coachman. "Quick as you can."

Effie looked at Gabriel gratefully as he climbed into the cab beside her. He shut the door. The carriage jolted forward, the driver spring-ing the horses into an extended trot.

"What the devil is going on?" Gabriel asked her.

"Compton has taken Franc," she said.

"What?"

"Or one of his servants did it. I'm not perfectly sure. Lady Bel-wood said he came with a footman. He must have sent the man to search my room while he was interrogating me. When he didn't find the book there, he took Franc instead. Compton would have told him to do so. He knows what Franc means to me."

Gabriel's attention briefly fell to the aged, cord-bound book Effie was clutching to her bosom. He gave her a questioning look.

"I took it from Compton's library," she said. "Parker caught me red-handed. He chased me. We fought in an alleyway. I-I stabbed him with a hairpin."

Gabriel's blood went cold. His voice took on a dangerous edge. "Parker put his hands on you?"

"He tried to. I'd hid the book under my crinoline and he was attempting to take it back." Effie's fingers tightened on the book, her knuckles going white. "If he's hurt Franc—"

"He's a dead man," Gabriel said.

"Yes," she agreed. "If he's harmed a curl on his coat—"

"I'll rip his bleeding head from his shoulders."

"Not if I get to him first," Effie said.

The carriage bounced hard as Gabriel's driver raced the horses toward Chelsea, weaving in and out of the traffic on the Brompton Road. A clatter of hooves sounded over the street, punctuated by the noise of other drivers shouting, horses whinnying, and wheels rat-tling like thunder.

Gabriel made an effort to master his temper. He would be no help to Effie if he was in a blind rage. "What did you mean about Compton interrogating you?"

"I confronted him with what he'd done to Elizabeth Wingard."

Gabriel absorbed the information without a flinch. "And he did nothing to you in return?"

"Aside from abducting Franc?" She gave a dismissive huff. "He threatened me with prison. And he related a rather graphic fantasy of my being hanged. But other than that . . ."

The words *prison* and *hanged* echoed in Gabriel's head. Unlike her, he didn't treat them lightly. His composure fractured. "Bloody hell, Effie. What if I hadn't come back today?"

"Why did you?" she asked. "I didn't expect you until tomorrow."

"Because I haven't been able to think straight since you left me on the train at Waltham Cross."

Her mouth ticked up briefly in a rueful smile. "Oh. That."

"Yes, that." He searched her face. "Did you mean it?"

Her expression softened. "With all my heart."

His own heart swelled in reply. "Effie—"

"But I can't think of it now," she said. "Not when Franc might be hurt or frightened. Compton could do anything—"

"He won't. Not if wants his book back. It's in his interest to keep Franc safe."

The reassurance seemed to calm her fears, even if only a little. Some of the tension left her brow. She nodded her head. "Yes. Yes, you're right, of course. He won't harm him."

Gabriel took her ungloved hand, holding it safe in both of his. "I'll get him back for you," he swore. "I promise you that."

Her fingers curled around his. She gave him another faint smile. "You're very chivalrous, given the circumstances."

"What circumstances are those?"

"Objectively bad ones. I stole a book. I stabbed a man." Her smile faded. "I'm not the fine lady you originally thought me, only an orphan from the Rookery. You'd be within your rights to think less of me."

"I think more of you than ever." He brought her hand to his lips, brushing a kiss to the curve of her knuckles. "You're the whole world to me, Effie Flite. You do know that, don't you?"

Her eyes met his. A hint of color bloomed in her cheeks. "I didn't know," she said. "But I'd hoped."

He recalled his words to her on the train, recognizing them in her answer. It prompted a fleeting, foolish grin. "There," he replied. "See how well matched we are?"

"And yet still unaccountably at odds," she said. "Even more after today. I've made an enemy of Compton. There will be no going back. Not for me."

Gabriel grew serious. "As to that . . ."

The carriage rattled to a jolting halt before he could finish.

Effie's head jerked to the window. "Are we there already? Thank heavens!"

He glanced outside. They'd reached the entrance to Cremorne Gardens with uncommon speed. His speech would have to wait.

He opened the door for them and he and Effie jumped out. Passing through the black iron gates together, they made straight for the expansive grounds near Cremorne House. It was a temperate day, the skies blue and the white clouds billowing, with only a slight wind.

Ahead, the orchestra was playing a rousing tune, and clowns and acrobats capered past, dancing and juggling. Balloon ascensions were still a novel enough sight, but—despite the fine weather—today's event hadn't drawn a sizable crowd. It was likely owing to last week's tragedy with Galezzo. In the aftermath, people had temporarily cooled on the pleasure gardens' more dangerous feats.

There was only a smattering of ladies and gentlemen in attendance. They milled about the fringes of the rolling tree-edged lawn. At its center, a midsize red-striped silk-and-canvas balloon attached to a small gold-painted wicker gondola was anchored with the aid of sandbags and heavy ropes. A familiar figure stood beside it—a large, hulking bald man in a cloth coat, with a conspicuous plaster covering his left ear.

"It's Parker," Effie said grimly. "He doesn't look best pleased. His ear must be paining him awfully."

Gabriel regarded the butler with cold menace. The man had better get used to pain. By the time Gabriel finished with him, he'd need more than a blasted sticking plaster. He'd need a pine box.

Effie clutched Gabriel's sleeve as she scanned the clusters of people. "There's Lord Mannering and his sister. And there's Miss Compton, with Lady Lavinia and Miss Whitbread. But where is Lord Compton? He must surely be nearby."

Gabriel temporarily set aside his bloodlust for Parker and joined her in looking. He spotted the viscount standing on the opposite side of the balloon. He was talking with two ladies and an older gentleman. "There he is."

Effie followed Gabriel's gaze. Seeing Compton, her face paled with anger. "He's spotted us."

The viscount had indeed seen them. He smiled thinly from across the distance, touching his gleaming ebony walking stick to the brim of his gray silk hat in a brief salute. He moved away from his friends to a place of privacy by the trees.

Effie marched toward him. Gabriel kept pace at her side.

"Miss Flite," Compton said. "I anticipated you would be here promptly." He withdrew his pocket watch to check the time. "And not a minute too late."

Effie's countenance was hard as marble. "Where is he?" she demanded. "If you've hurt him—"

"And Mr. Royce." Compton fixed Gabriel with a flinty stare. "Why am I not surprised?"

"She asked you a question," Gabriel said. "Where's the dog?"

"First things first." Compton extended his hand. "My book, if you please?"

Effie thrust it at him. "Take it and be damned," she said. "What have you done with my poodle?"

"Parker has taken charge of him," Compton said. "He's guarding Mr. Chapin's balloon while Chapin takes tea in the refreshment tent. Parker has a great fondness for aeronautics. Never misses an ascent." His lips curled. "I believe he's put your little beast in the basket for safekeeping."

Effie's eyes widened in horror. "The basket of the *balloon*?"

"Safe enough, as I said. So long as you arrived in time."

"You're a monster," Effie said. Turning away from him, she bolted toward Parker, her skirts clutched in her hands.

Gabriel moved to follow her.

"A moment, Royce," Compton said, catching his arm.

Gabriel stopped. He faced the viscount, hard-pressed not to do the man violence. Indeed, were they not in full public view, he *would* do him violence, and hang the consequences.

"She's told you what has transpired, I presume?" Compton asked.

"Every cursed detail," Gabriel replied. He glanced after Effie. Parker was standing back from the balloon with a mutinous scowl, permitting her access to the wicker gondola. She climbed inside of it to retrieve Franc.

"It needn't affect our business together," Compton said. "So long as I have your word that Wingard's papers are safe, and that you had nothing to do with Miss Flite's regrettable actions, I am prepared for our arrangement to continue on the same terms."

Gabriel's gaze returned to his. "Our arrangement is finished," he said. "*You're* finished."

Compton blanched. "Now see here, Royce—"

A shout drowned out the remainder of the viscount's words. "What in blazes are you doing?" a fellow exclaimed. "Don't touch those ropes!"

Gabriel turned sharply in time to see the balloon floating swiftly upward. The ropes that had secured it dangled from beneath. Some-one had untied them from their moorings.

Parker.

The hulking brute stood back, admiring his handiwork with a leer of triumph.

Above him, Effie peered over the edge of the gondola in pale-faced horror. She held Franc tightly in her arms. *"Gabriel!"*

Gabriel's heart leapt into his throat. Good God! She was still in-side the basket! He sprinted toward the escaping balloon at a full run.

Parker moved to block Gabriel's path on the grass. "You're too late. That thieving she-cat is getting exactly what she—"

Gabriel didn't hesitate. Drawing back his fist, he delivered two pun-ishing blows in quick succession, one to Parker's jaw and one to his in-jured left ear. Parker staggered back, stunned. Before he could recover his senses, Gabriel slammed his forehead straight down on the bridge of the butler's nose. There was an audible crunch as the bone shattered.

Parker fell to his knees with a shrill cry, clutching his bleeding face.

Gabriel would have liked to continue the well-deserved beating, but there was no time. Catching the dangling rope in both hands, he pulled it with all his might.

"Gabriel!" Effie's voice carried from the gondola, high-pitched with fright. "Don't let me fly away!"

"You're not going anywhere," Gabriel shouted back to her.

A man in a shabby coat and cap ran to assist him. Another work-man joined them, and then another. Together they heaved on the ropes to no avail. The balloon had caught a northeasterly wind. The ropes were already unfurled to their full length. The men's arms stretched above them, struggling to hang on. If they persisted, they would be lifted off the ground right along with the balloon.

"It's too late," the first man gasped. "The scoundrel has thrown off some of the sandbags."

"We'll have to wait for it to land," the second declared, panting. "She'll be safe enough 'til then."

The third workman agreed. "You must let go."

"Like hell I will," Gabriel muttered.

The woman he loved was inside that blasted basket. He may not be able to rescue her outright, but he would be damned if he left her to face her greatest fear alone.

Gripping fast to the rope, Gabriel did the only thing he could think of. He allowed it to pull him into the sky.

31

Effie hunkered down in the bottom of the gondola, holding Franc. Terror threatened at the edges of her consciousness. She refused to let it rob her of her self-control. Gabriel was here. He'd said he wouldn't let her fly away, and she believed him.

The basket rocked back and forth as the men pulled on the ropes. Despite their efforts, she didn't appear to be returning to earth. The balloon continued to float upward, wind buffeting the silk and canvas. It seemed to be rising at a steady clip.

Fear constricted her chest. "Gabriel!" she cried out.

The basket swayed sharply on another tug of the rope.

"Almost there," Gabriel called back. His voice no longer sounded as though it was coming from a distance below. It was close. *Exceedingly* close.

Effie looked up in alarm as his hand appeared over the edge of the gondola.

"What in the—?" She got up in a flash, leaving Franc on the floor of the basket. Dizziness assailed her. She ignored it. So long as she didn't look down, she would be all right. The alternative was letting Gabriel fall.

She grabbed him by the shoulders as he heaved himself up. Clouds billowed ahead, a stark reminder of how high up they were.

Higher even than Mr. Galezzo had been when he'd fallen from his wire. If Gabriel lost his grip—

If Effie lost hers—

But she didn't think. She only acted.

Wind whipping at her face, she grasped Gabriel by the waist, helping him swing over the side and into the gondola. The basket tilted wildly as he landed beside her, his hair disheveled and his chest heaving from exertion.

Together, they sank down to the floor, wrapped in each other's arms. Franc frisked about them, his pom-pom tail quivering with joy.

The crowds below set up an enormous cheer.

Gabriel struggled to catch his breath. "I should have said, 'You're not going anywhere alone.'"

Effie didn't know whether to kiss him or strangle him. "You daft man. What on earth were you thinking? You might have fallen—"

"No chance."

"But to climb that rope—"

"Had to. It was the only way to get to you."

She shook her head in wonderment. "You're mad."

"Clearly." He smiled at her. His pale blue eyes gleamed with un-varnished affection. "I'll say one thing for you, sweetheart. You're never dull."

Franc climbed into Effie's lap. She wrapped an arm around him as the balloon was carried along on a soft blowing breeze. The gondola swayed to the left. Effie's trembling stomach swayed with it. She briefly closed her eyes, leaning into Gabriel's embrace. "I wish life *were* dull at present. Anything rather than this."

Gabriel held her as protectively as she held Franc. He looked around the interior of the gondola. It contained folded blankets, a hamper of food, a writing box, several maps, and a leather compass case. There was even a red silk–padded seat for those who weren't disposed to sit on the floor.

"This isn't so bad," he said. "You and me in absolute privacy, and no way either of us can storm off?"

"I've never stormed off," she replied, on her dignity.

He cocked a brow at her. "In Hyde Park?"

"I was furious with you."

"And on the train at Waltham Station?"

"I wasn't furious then, but . . ." She wrinkled her nose. "The timing was less than ideal."

"Timing," he said. "Another thing in our favor today."

"Yes. We're stuck up here, aren't we?" Effie suppressed another tremor of terror. She couldn't dwell on how high up they were. It would only lead to gibbering panic. "When do you suppose we'll land?"

"Soon," he said. "But not before I've had a chance to tell you what I came to say in Brook Street."

She gave him an uncertain glance. She'd been too distraught when he arrived at the Belwoods' house to fully consider what had brought him there. All she knew was that, for bookmakers, the Derby was the most important event of the year. And instead of being there, Gabriel was here.

The significance of it wasn't lost on her.

He gazed down at her steadily. His expression grew serious. "I tried to tell you in the carriage, but you were too distracted. Understandably so, with Franc missing."

Effie hugged the little poodle close. "I have him back now, thank heaven. He's in excellent spirits, and doesn't appear to have been harmed. My only regret is that I had to give up the book to earn his freedom."

"The book, yes," Gabriel murmured.

"It was the sole proof I had against Compton. Without it . . ." She was loath to admit she'd been outmaneuvered. But one must face facts. "I suppose I've failed."

"You haven't failed," Gabriel said. "Book or no book, Compton's reign as Lord Solomon is over."

Effie lifted her head from Franc. A hopeful thought occurred to her. "You're not saying you'll give me Wingard's papers?"

"I can't give them to you," he said. "I don't have them anymore."

She stared at him in alarm. "What do you mean you don't have them?"

"This morning, when I returned from Epsom, I collected Wingard's papers from my safe and I took them to Miles Quincey. As of this moment, they're in the possession of the *London Courant*."

Effie's mouth nearly fell open. The implications were extraordinary. "Are you saying that Mr. Quincey is going to publish a story about what Compton did to Elizabeth Wingard?"

Gabriel nodded. "He's a hardheaded, cynical bastard at the best of times, but Miles is fearless when it comes to a good story. This is just the kind of piece he lives for. He says he'll publish the whole of it."

"Goodness," Effie breathed. "It will be explosive. Possibly libelous. Is Mr. Quincey prepared?"

"Not only prepared, but eager. He presumes Compton will sue, but it doesn't trouble him. Apparently, truth is an absolute defense—whatever that means. At any rate, it's done. And there will be no connection to you. You'll be safe from blame. You can even remain in society if you choose."

Emotion rose in Effie's throat. "Why did you do it?"

Gabriel shrugged one broad shoulder. "For you. For love. Why have I done any of the crackbrained things I've done recently?"

She swallowed hard. For love, he'd said. *Love.*

As ever, he seemed to read her mind. His mouth hitched at one corner. It was the same wry half smile he'd given her on countless occasions, but this time it wasn't accompanied by a coolly detached stare. There was nothing distant or remote in the way he was looking at her. He was here with her body and soul.

"I love you, Effie Flite," he said. "*That's* what brought me back from Epsom. It's what brought me here. What's been driving me since the moment you threatened to knock me down. Before you walked into that library, I didn't have a future. Only endless, empty days and every one of them with more of the same. But not anymore. I dream of building a life with you, if you'll have me. If you'll let me love you—"

She framed his face with her hands and kissed him.

His arm tightened around her waist as her lips shaped to his. His brow creased. "Effie—"

"I love you, too, Gabriel," she said.

It wasn't the first time she'd uttered the words. They nevertheless sent a visible jolt through him. He made a gruff sound in his throat as he kissed her back, fiercely, deeply.

And she forgot they were sailing far above the ground. There was no such thing as heights or fear or gravity. Nothing else existed except them and their love for each other.

"But what about the Rookery?" she asked when they finally paused for breath.

Gabriel held her fast. Franc was no longer between them. He'd abandoned Effie's lap in favor of the stack of blankets on the floor of the gondola. "I'm still going to reform it, but not with the help of some feckless politician. I'll do it myself. I'm going to run for a seat on the St. Giles District Board of Works. After that, who knows? Perhaps I'll stand for Parliament. There are already villains aplenty in politics. One more won't do any harm."

Her fingers threaded in his hair. This time, no gloves impeded her. She could pet him as much as she liked. Indeed, he appeared to relish her proprietary touches. He held still for every caress, his breath fracturing in the most delicious way.

"Oh, Gabriel," she said. "What a splendid plan."

His lips brushed over her cheek. "Then, you approve?"

"Entirely. If you're in Parliament, you can assist the passage of a married women's property bill. With Compton out of the way, there's every chance it will come to a vote."

He gave a husky chuckle. The sound tickled her ear as sensually as a purr.

"You *would* support it, wouldn't you?" she asked him.

"Darling," he said, "I'm yours to command."

She smiled. "I shall try not to let it go to my head."

His hand moved over her back. His expression sobered. "I should tell you, this likely means an end to my betting shop. I'll have no great riches. No particular power. If you join your lot to mine, minx, you must take me as I am."

Effie recalled his offer to her on their return from Trowley Green. "What are you proposing this time?"

He slowly drew back to meet her gaze. His face was as serious as she'd ever seen it. Only his eyes betrayed the truth of his vulnerability. The deepest desires of his heart were written there, laid bare for her to see. "Marriage," he said.

A gust of wind whistled over them, snapping against the silk of the balloon.

Effie scarcely noticed. The whole of her attention was focused on Gabriel's face. His answer wasn't the one she'd been expecting. "On the train, you said—"

"I know what I said then. I was playing the odds. Offering you what I thought you'd accept, instead of what I truly wanted—you as my wife. I want no more question in your mind about where you belong. Which reminds me—" Releasing her, he reached into the pocket of his waistcoat. "I have something for you."

Effie watched, pulse quickening, as he withdrew a flat velvet box from his pocket. It wasn't shaped like a ring box. It was something else. She couldn't imagine what.

He handed it to her.

She felt the weight of his regard as she lifted the lid. The sun caught the contents, making them sparkle and flash like wildfire.

Her heart stopped.

It was a dragonfly brooch. And not one made of cut glass. This was comprised of real jewels, with wings of rose-cut diamonds, a body of square-cut emeralds, and a face of glittering cabochon rubies.

She lifted her gaze, stunned.

Gabriel's color was high. "I went to buy a ring," he said. "The jeweler had this in the display cabinet. It's not a hairpin. You can't pick a lock with it. Still . . . It was too great a temptation to pass up."

She looked at him in amazement. "I thought you believed dragonflies were bad luck?"

"You and I make our own luck," he said. Removing the brooch from the box, he helped her secure it to her cherry red jacket, pinning it right above her heart. His fingers lingered there, his head bent to hers. "Marry me, Effie. Say you'll be mine. I'm already yours. I have been since the night we met."

Effie brought her forehead to rest gently against his brow. She had never seriously contemplated joining her fate to another. Her life up to now had been spent on the outside of things. Never belonging. Never quite fitting in. The future, for her, had seemed a lonely road, meant to be traveled with only Franc as her companion.

But no longer.

She knew who she was now. She knew what it was she truly wanted. Perhaps what she'd always wanted. And it wasn't fine dresses, or wealth and position. It was this. It was him.

It was love.

For that, she'd risk anything. Even marriage.

"I am yours," she whispered. "And yes, I will marry you."

Gabriel exhaled an uneven breath. "You said yes."

Her eyes glistened, her mouth curving in a tremulous smile. "I said yes."

His arms circled her waist and his mouth captured hers. He kissed her again, and then again, smiling himself now, telling her he loved and adored her, that they would wed without delay.

Somewhere below them, beneath the clouds, Big Ben chimed the quarter hour as they floated over Westminster. The future beckoned, filled with revolutionary possibility. Effie no longer feared it. Whatever it held, she knew that she and Gabriel—and Franc—would face it together.

EPILOGUE

Two months later . . .

"Mr. Quincey has published another article about Lord Compton," Effie said to Gabriel. Still in her ruffled lawn nightgown, she sat among the tangled coverlets of their carved four-poster bed, the early edition of the *London Courant* spread open before her. A tray was on the mattress beside her, the remains of their breakfast providing an unholy temptation to Franc.

The little poodle was staring at it fixedly, silently transmitting his desire. Effie absently tossed him a piece of bread crust. Franc caught it in a flash, hopping down from the bed to eat his prize in privacy.

Across the bedchamber, Gabriel stood in front of the washstand, clad in a pair of trousers and nothing else. The muscles of his bare chest flexed as he mixed up the lather for his morning shave.

He met Effie's eyes in his shaving mirror. His pale blue gaze was warm, taking in her unbound hair and her naked shoulder, exposed by the drooping cap sleeve of her nightdress.

They had wed at the registrar's office not two months ago, almost immediately after the balloon had brought them gently down on the green near Victoria Park. Life since then had been something of a perpetual honeymoon. They lingered in bed most mornings, reluctant to quit each other's company. It had made them unreliable companions to their friends and business associates.

Gabriel didn't mind. Quite the opposite. He frequently professed that there was no place he'd rather be than in Effie's arms.

Effie readily admitted to feeling the same. Theirs was a passionate marriage—both of them possessed of strong tempers, decided views, and healthy appetites. It wasn't unexpected that they should take such enormous enjoyment in each other. Indeed, the only surprising fact of their marriage was how exceedingly sweet it was.

Gabriel was an attentive husband, as tender as he was fierce. He never lost an opportunity to kiss her or to clasp her hand in passing. And when they were intimate together, in those scorching, honeyed moments when he took her and loved her, he left her in no doubt that she possessed him body and soul.

It was a heady feeling, to know someone cared for her this much. Effie was still not entirely accustomed to it. Neither was Gabriel, she suspected. He seemed to relish the intimacy of their new life together as much as she did. The brick house in Sloane Street with its black-painted door and its unconventional staff had become a home to them. A place of safety and sanctuary, where they had, at last, found themselves truly happy.

"Another one?" Gabriel asked as he lathered his face. "I'd have thought Quincey would be finished by now. Compton certainly is."

The viscount's public downfall had been as swift as it was decisive. Shortly after Mr. Quincey had published his story, exposing Compton's fraud against Elizabeth Wingard, Compton had departed London in favor of his country estate. He'd spent the first month attempting to ride out the storm in Hampshire. But the storm hadn't subsided. Calls for Compton to withdraw from politics had only grown in fervor.

Compton's private life had been equally devastated by the revelations about his past. Rather than joining him in Hampshire in a show of solidarity, his wife and daughter had remained in London, where Miss Compton had lent her voice to the burgeoning women's movement. Along with Mrs. Naismith, she had quickly become a fixture at Lady Bartlett's salons in Kensington. Many in fashionable society interpreted her presence there as an unspoken condemnation of her father's actions.

"Mr. Quincey says that Compton is abandoning his seat," Effie said. "That he'll no longer involve himself in affairs of Parliament."

Gabriel lifted his razor. "It's about time."

"Yes, it is," Effie agreed. "Now we need only deal with the remaining opposition to a married women's property bill. With Compton gone, it shouldn't be insurmountable."

"I expect the revelations about his conduct have only strengthened the case."

"I should say so." Effie cast aside the paper. "Thank goodness for Mr. Quincey."

Gabriel began shaving. "Speaking of Quincey . . ."

She raised her arms over her head in a languorous stretch. "What about him?"

"He's been asking about the Academy."

She gave him a sharp look. "Whatever for?"

"He may have found a connection between it and Elizabeth Wingard."

"What?"

Gabriel once again met her eyes in his shaving mirror. "I told you, the man's part bloodhound."

"He doesn't propose to print something about it, does he?"

"No," Gabriel assured her. "I've told him, it's off the table."

"Then what?"

"He wants to talk to Miss Corvus."

Effie gave a scornful huff. "That's never going to happen."

"Someone else, then," Gabriel said. "What about your friend, Miss Trewlove?"

"Nell?" Effie had mentioned her to Gabriel several times, but the two of them had yet to meet. They were set to dine with her next week at an inn in the neighboring village to the Academy. Nell had invited them both particularly. "She would never submit to an interview."

"Ask her," Gabriel said. "Miles doesn't bite."

Effie thought on it as her husband finished shaving. It *would* be nice if Nell came to town. She deserved a bit of fun before taking up her permanent teaching position. Perhaps she might visit the theater as Effie had once suggested? Perhaps, she might even find a handsome gentleman to kiss?

Speaking of which . . .

Gabriel returned to the bed after rinsing and drying his face. He sank down beside her.

Effie reached up to caress his clean-shaven jaw. Her wedding ring—a large rose-cut diamond set on a band of gold—twinkled in the morning light. "Mmm," she murmured her approval. "Pity you must go out."

He turned his head, pressing a kiss to her palm. "Who says I must?"

"You have the Board of Works meeting to get to," she reminded him.

Gabriel had been elected to one of the open seats at the end of May. He was already making a name for himself, zealously advocating for improved conditions for those in the Rookery.

"Not until ten," he said, gathering her in his arms.

"It isn't much time," she remarked as she encircled his neck. "But I shan't be greedy. We have our whole lives together, after all."

"Forever," he said huskily.

"Forever," she whispered back.

He bent his head to kiss her. "I suggest we make the most of it."

AUTHOR'S NOTE

Rules for Ruin was inspired by many facets of Victorian history, from fashion and feminism to literature, law, and tragedy. For more about these inspirations, see my notes below.

GREAT EXPECTATIONS

I first read Charles Dickens's 1861 novel, *Great Expectations*, when I was a girl. The character of Miss Havisham made an enormous impression on me. Jilted by her fiancé on her wedding day, she withdraws inside her dark, dismal manor house, where she stops all the clocks to the hour of her abandonment. There she remains in her bridal gown, her wedding cake growing moldy and her mind sinking into madness.

The underlying facts of Miss Havisham's sad tale played a large part in inspiring the origin story for Miss Corvus and her Academy. Like Miss Havisham, Miss Corvus was jilted by a disreputable gentleman working in concert with her dissolute half brother. Also similarly to Miss Havisham, Miss Corvus takes on orphan girls with the goal of transforming them into weapons. However, unlike her Dickensian counterpart, Miss Corvus is forging her Academy girls not into weapons against men but into tools for combatting the patriarchy, with the ultimate goal of advancing the rights of women.

THE MARRIED WOMEN'S PROPERTY ACT

Prior to 1870, a married woman in Victorian England had no right to her own earnings or property. Her very existence was subsumed by her husband. It was he who controlled her money and property, for good or ill. In order for married women to gain some measure of independence, the married women's property law would have to be reformed.

Rules for Ruin takes place in 1864, exactly seven years after the last piece of legislation to reform the married women's property law had failed. It wasn't until 1868 that reformers would make another attempt at a bill.

Victorian women weren't idle in the years preceding that attempt. In her book *Wives & Property: Reform of the Married Women's Property Law in Nineteenth-Century England*, historian Lee Holcombe states that "The year 1865 marked the dawn of a new day in the history of English women." Victorian ladies were beginning to organize and to discuss all manner of reforms, not only in law but in education and "all subjects relating to the position of women." These organizations included the Kensington Society and figures such as Elizabeth Clarke Wolstenholme-Elmy, a champion of commonsense education for girls.

The members of the Crinoline Academy are critical to ushering in this new day, clearing the path of obstacles like Lord Compton, and paving the way for the reformers who would ultimately achieve passage of the Married Women's Property Act. To me, this prelude period felt more interesting to research and write about. It's a stage of political action where those toiling know they may not see the fruits of their labors, but they toil on just the same, laying the groundwork for the generations of women to come. It's truly heroic work, I feel, and perfectly suited for the dauntless heroines of Miss Corvus's Academy.

WOMEN AND SELF-DEFENSE IN 1860S ENGLAND

In *Rules for Ruin*, the students at Miss Corvus's Academy receive a thorough education in self-defense. To modern readers, this may not seem like anything very revolutionary. To denizens of mid-Victorian London, however, it was exactly that.

In the first half of the century and entering the early 1860s, it was widely believed that the job of physically defending a woman fell to a man. Women, by contrast, were viewed as the gentler sex: hothouse flowers whose role was to be protected and admired, rather than resourceful individuals capable of defending themselves in their own right.

During the time when *Rules for Ruin* is set, these kinds of beliefs were just beginning to be challenged. In her 1858 book, *A Woman's Thoughts About Women*, Victorian author Dinah Maria Mulock Craik declares:

> The age of chivalry, with all its benefits and harmfulness, is gone by, for us women. We cannot now have men for our knights errant, expending blood and life for our sake while we have nothing to do but sit idle on balconies, and drop flowers on half-dead victors at tilt and tourney. Nor, on the other hand, are we dressed up dolls, pretty playthings, to be fought and scrambled for—petted, caressed or flung out of the window, as our several lords and masters may please.

Instead, according to Craik, women had to learn to depend on themselves. For women moving through overcrowded Victorian cities like London, this meant learning to deal with all sorts of assaults and encroachments. Popular publications of the day, including etiquette manuals, would have women believe that simply dressing modestly and adhering to social rules—like refusing to acknowledge impertinent men—would be enough to protect them. But rational Victorian women realized that etiquette and drab dresses weren't enough. They required a familiarity with self-defense.

Miss Corvus's students learn boxing, fencing, and jujitsu. These skills are historically accurate for the period, but for the latter, I had to massage the time line a bit to make it work for my story. Though Japan opened trade with the West in the 1850s, it wasn't until the close of the century that martial arts began to become widely known to the British public. In her excellent book *Femininity, Crime and Self-Defence in Victorian Literature and Society* (2012), historian Emelyne Godfrey expands on the rise of Japanese martial arts for Victorian women and "the phenomenon of the 'ju-jutsuffragettes.'" Her book was an invaluable resource when crafting the self-defense curriculum for the Crinoline Academy. I highly recommend it to any readers who want to learn more about women's self-defense in Victorian England.

ST. GILES AND THE VICTORIAN SLUM CLEARANCES

The location of the St. Giles Rookery made it unique among Victorian slums. Instead of being on the outskirts of the city, it was in London's West End, bordered by the wealthiest communities. At the time of *Rules for Ruin*, the acreage of the Rookery had already been reduced during the slum clearances of the previous decades and was on the verge of being further diminished by the clearances still to come.

Reform of the slum was never the goal, at least initially. The object was to clear the old neighborhoods away to make room for new development. Unfortunately, amid all these improvements, there was no plan for rehousing the displaced poor. Some Rookery residents relocated to other London slums. The rest remained in the Rookery, crammed into a progressively smaller space, where crime, filth, and vice still ran rampant.

This period was a pivotal time for residents of London's slums, and a perfect encapsulation of the greater changes taking place in the Victorian era. Even as industrialization and invention were revolutionizing every aspect of the age, the poorest of the poor were being left behind, pushed into increasingly overcrowded slums or relegated to workhouses—out of sight and out of mind.

For a character like Gabriel Royce, reforming the slum is an uphill battle. It's also an ultimately unsuccessful one. Public housing for the poor wouldn't begin to be implemented until the 1890s, more than thirty years after Gabriel first proposes his model lodging house scheme. Today, the corporate offices of Google stand on the ground where the Rookery once stood. The slum itself is no more.

THE TRAGEDY AT CREMORNE GARDENS

In *Rules for Ruin*, the character and ultimate fate of wire walker Mr. Galezzo were based on the tragedy of real-life acrobat Carlo Valerio. The twenty-five-year-old Valerio was killed at Cremorne Gardens in the summer of 1863 when his rope gave way and he plummeted forty feet to the ground.

A huge crowd had gathered to watch Valerio's display that evening. When he fell, the result was pure pandemonium. Newspaper reports of the day claim that several people fainted, and that one lady had to be conveyed to St. George's Hospital. Valerio himself was carried away to his residence in Stanley Villas, Chelsea, where he died of his injuries in the early hours of the morning.

The depiction of Galezzo's death in *Rules for Ruin* is an exact account of what happened when Valerio died except for two instances: to work with the time line of my story, I needed his performance to happen one year later, and one hour later in the evening. Other than that, the account of the events of that night is exactly as described in contemporaneous reports.

LASCARS, DIVERSITY, AND IDENTITY

At the close of *Rules for Ruin*, Euphemia Flite discovers that she's the product of a liaison between a white British prostitute and a lascar sailor. In *Culture and Empire*, the fifth volume of *Religion in Victorian Britain*, edited by John Wolffe and published by Manchester University Press, a lascar is defined as "a native of the territories administered by the East India Company." These Indian sailors were mainly Muslim, hailing from "Bengal, Gujarat and Punjab."

Liaisons between foreign-born sailors and British prostitutes weren't uncommon. Neither is the fact that Effie's mixed heritage is largely accepted by Gabriel and her peers. Unlike the neighborhoods of the upper classes, the slums were diverse places, both in terms of race and religion.

That doesn't mean that racism didn't exist there. Far from it. However, in this story, Effie's heritage is more central to her own identity than it is an obstacle to her happily ever after. She's relieved to discover her origins, rather than shocked by any potential problems they might cause in Victorian high society. As someone who is half-Indian myself, I felt this distinction was important—the significance of who you are, the way it impacts your own sense of self, irrespective of the opinions or biases of the rest of the world.

NEWSPAPERS, VILLAGES, AND BOOKSHOPS

While most of the names and locations I use in *Rules for Ruin* are based on historical fact, there are several instances where I rely on fictional names, such as Farrer and Devonport's bookshop in the Strand and the village of Trowley Green. Also fictional is the *London Courant* newspaper, which some of you will recognize as the newspaper that publishes the groundbreaking exposé on private asylums in my Parish Orphans of Devon series.

ACKNOWLEDGMENTS

No book is written in isolation, this one least of all. From its inception, I've been blessed to have the support and encouragement of so many amazing people, both personally and professionally. To them, I extend my heartfelt gratitude.

To my devoted mom, thank you, as always, for reading early drafts, pet care, tea making, and barn shuttle services—and most of all, for putting your own life on hold so I could give this novel my uninterrupted attention. You are my ballast.

Thanks are also due to my wonderful agent, Kevan Lyon, who was a crucial sounding board when I first conjured up the idea of the Crinoline Academy. To my endlessly patient editor, Sarah Blumenstock, whose enthusiasm inspires me so much. And to Liz Sellers, Yazmine Hassan, Anika Bates, Lynsey Griswold, Christine Legon, Marianne Grace, Lisa Davis, Sierra Machado, Rita Frangie Batour, Kelly Wagner, and the rest of the stellar team at Berkley / Penguin Random House who work tirelessly to get my books in front of readers.

A huge thank-you to my critique partner and friend, Isabel Ibañez , whose feedback was invaluable in getting Effie and Gabriel exactly where I needed them to be. Thank you, as well, to Alissa, Sandy, and Flora, who read early parts of this novel and offered such heartening words.

Additional thanks to Rel Mollet for her friendship and grace, and for taking charge of things so I can write. To historian and friend Jacqueline Bannerjee for research help on the St. Giles District Board of Works (and for all her kind words and encouragement). To the amazing and always supportive Lyonesses—I'm so honored to be one of you. To my little brother, Joe, for putting his black belt in jujitsu to good use by helping me choreograph a fight scene. And to my spectacular readers for sticking with me and my stories all these years, even that one time I threw in a Victorian vampire.

Last but never least, much love to my animal family—Stella, Tavi, Bijou, and Asteria. And to my own little black poodle, Jet, who served as the inspiration for Franc, all the way down to his occasional fearsomeness and the joyful quiver of his pom-pom tail. I never believed life could truly be better with a poodle, but it is—it is!

RULES
for
RUIN

Mimi Matthews

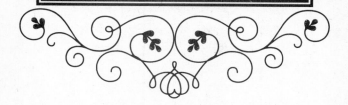

READERS GUIDE

QUESTIONS FOR DISCUSSION

1. At the beginning of the novel, Euphemia "Effie" Flite returns to the Academy in hopes of obtaining a stipend that will fund her independence. Given her complicated history with Miss Corvus, would it have been better for Effie to have cut ties with the school altogether? What roles do the concepts of family, loyalty, and sisterhood play in her decision to accept Miss Corvus's bargain?

2. Effie spent the first five years of her life in the Rookery. How do her early experiences in the slum inform her actions throughout the novel? Why might Effie have initially believed she'd been taken by Miss Corvus rather than saved?

3. Gabriel Royce subscribes to the belief that like recognizes like. In what ways does he see himself in Effie? In what ways do the two of them differ?

4. Effie and her Academy sisters are proponents of the controversial wire cage crinoline. How did the constraints of Victorian fashion hinder women of the 1860s? How does Effie turn fashion to her advantage?

5. Effie's purchase of her poodle, Franc, was her sole act of rebellion during her time in Paris. What does Franc mean to Effie in the story? How is he like her? What might he symbolize?

6. Gabriel is determined to provide model lodging houses for the poor of the Rookery. How would adequate housing change the

character of the slum and the lives of the people who live there? What reasons might Victorians have had for preferring to raze slums rather than reform them?

7. Effie often dresses as a widow so she can travel through the city unescorted without causing remark. How else does Effie subvert Victorian restrictions on unmarried young ladies?

8. Effie sends secret messages through her sewing samplers. In what ways did real-life Victorian women express themselves through their handicrafts? How do those compare with the outlets modern women have for self-expression?

9. At the time that Lord Compton jilted and defrauded Miss Corvus, she didn't report his crimes. Why might an unmarried Victorian lady have been discouraged from speaking up about a man who had wronged her? What reputational repercussions might she have experienced as a result of coming forward? How does this compare with the response women receive today when they speak out against bad men?

10. Effie is well aware that she will lose some of her legal rights if she marries. Knowing this, why does she accept Gabriel's proposal? What benefits will she derive from being a married woman in Victorian England? What might be the consequences?

Don't miss Nell's story in

THE MARRIAGE METHOD

the next installment of the Crinoline Academy

August 1864

Penelope Trewlove followed the harried young clerk down the hall of the Fleet Street offices of the *London Courant*. Similarly harried-looking newspapermen bustled in and out of the small offices they passed, shuffling papers and addressing each other in urgent tones. At the sight of her, some of them faltered, their attention caught between the fluttering black veil that shrouded her face and the pronounced limp that marred her gait.

Nell's gloved fingers tightened reflexively on the raven's-head handle of her ebony cane. It was her first visit to London, and not a willing one by any means. She had been putting off the paper's editor, Mr. Quincey, for weeks, each of her exceedingly formal replies to his letters penned with an effort to discourage his relentless curiosity. But she could put him off no longer. His last letter had made that abundantly plain. Either Nell travel to London to answer his questions about Miss Corvus's Academy for the Betterment of Young Ladies, or Mr. Quincey would come to the isolated stone manor house at the edge of the Epping Forest and put his questions to Miss Corvus herself.

As if Miss Corvus would ever risk allowing a journalist inside the charity school's iron gates! She had, instead, sent Nell to deal with the situation. To come here today, in her role as deputy headmistress, and put an end to Mr. Quincey's problematic inquiries once and for all.

A painted door at the end of the hall bore the vexing man's name in stenciled letters. The clerk opened it without knocking. He ushered Nell into a moderately sized office distinguished by a wall of overstuffed bookcases; a small, threadbare sofa with a fringed skirt; and a massive desk covered with chaotic piles of papers and three open bottles of ink. The great leather chair behind the desk stood conspicuously empty.

"Mr. Quincey is engaged at present," the clerk said. He gestured to one of the two slat-back wooden chairs that were arrayed in front of the desk. "If you would care to wait?"

"Not at all." Nell gratefully availed herself of a seat, propping her cane beside her. After two hackney cab rides and a railway journey of nearly twenty miles, her left hip and thigh were aching like the dickens. She did her level best not to betray the fact. Her spine remained ramrod straight, her veil still firmly in place as she arranged the full skirts of her black bombazine carriage gown over the imposing frame of her wire crinoline.

Miss Corvus wasn't a woman given to fashionable indulgences, and she had no patience for excess frills or frippery, but she had made an exception for the controversial cagelike undergarment. All of her teachers donned them like armor, as did many of the older orphans.

It was no mystery as to why.

The sheer circumference of a crinoline kept its wearer separate and apart, protected from all but the most determined encroachments. Not only that. She took up space for herself—demanded space—on the pavement, in a crowded conveyance, and in every sphere through which she traveled. The greater world must step aside and let her pass. They dare not stop her.

The clerk bowed and withdrew, shutting the door after him.

Nell took the opportunity to cast an eye over the room. *Know your surroundings. Know your opponent. Know yourself.* They were the three most important rules she had learned at the Academy. Rules meant to keep young ladies safe. To ensure they were prepared for anything, never overmatched or left unable to defend themselves.

It was the first rule that occupied her now. Unlike men, women didn't have the luxury of entering a situation blindly. A female must know the four corners of where she stood—the entrances, the exits, the problematic terrain. She must, at all times, think both defensively and offensively.

Fortunately, Mr. Quincey wasn't a complete unknown. Nell's recently married Academy sister, Effie Royce, had a passing acquaintance with him *and* his premises. Among other things, she had warned Nell to anticipate cats.

There appeared to be none in residence today. The room was seemingly empty. Although . . . Was that a faint rustle of movement beneath the sofa?

The door jerked open before she could investigate the matter. A deep male voice sounded behind her. "Miss Trewlove?"

Nell's head turned sharply. Never mind that she'd been expecting him, the sight of the tall, raven-haired newspaper editor still served to send a jolt through her. She stared up at him from behind her veil. "Mr. Quincey?"

He was in his shirtsleeves, his cravat askew and his black waistcoat rumpled. It did nothing to lessen his air of command. Self-assurance radiated from every inch of him. "Apologies for the delay. One of my reporters has gone missing and my staff is up in arms." He entered, closing the door behind him. "I trust you don't mind my not leaving it open? I've no wish to let the cat out."

"The cat?" She flicked another glance to the sofa as she moved to rise. "I didn't see any—"

"Pray don't get up. We're not much for formalities here. We've precious little time for them." Rather than bow, he reached to shake her hand. "I am, however, very pleased to meet you."

Nell's mouth went dry as his fingers engulfed hers. His hand was easily twice the size of her own, surely better suited to holding a broadsword than a pen. His shoulders were quite broad, too, lending an unmistakable power to the leanness of his long-limbed frame.

Alarm bells jangled in her head, inspired as much by his physical presence as by the peculiar intensity that gleamed at the back of his dark brown eyes.

This was the gentleman who had penned the explosive series of articles that had lately brought down a powerful politician. A dogged and indefatigable reporter, possessed of an unassailable firmness of character, unafraid of retaliation or threats.

For the first time, Nell considered the possibility that she might be out of her depth.

"As to the cat," Mr. Quincey continued, releasing her hand, "she's barely civilized. She'll be hiding here somewhere." He crossed to his desk, taking a seat behind it in the large leather chair. "Did Higgins offer you tea? I can have some brought in for you."

"I thank you, no," Nell said. She made an effort to regain her composure. To be sure, she was rather astonished she'd lost it—even if it *was* only for the space of a heartbeat.

She wasn't accustomed to dealing with men, that was the trouble. She'd spent the majority of her life at the Academy, first as an orphan, then as a teacher. Nearly the whole of her three-and-twenty years, surrounded by girls and women. The only gentlemen to ever set foot through the gates were the antiquated members of the Parish Council, and then but rarely. Miss Corvus saw to that.

Nell couldn't recall when she'd last been obliged to deal with any gentleman under the age of fifty. Unless one counted the stripling lads from the village who sometimes attempted communication with the orphan girls. And Mr. Quincey was no stripling. He must be thirty, at least.

He regarded her from across his desk's cluttered surface. He wasn't a handsome man. Not in the classical manner. His face was too angular and severe—his brows too stern, his clean-shaven jaw too hard, and his bold aquiline nose a fraction too large. But his features hung together in such a striking way that one could easily forget their asymmetry.

"Your journey wasn't too taxing?" he asked.

"Not terribly," she said.

"Yet still a lengthy business. I'd have preferred coming to you. It would have saved you the trouble."

"I have multiple reasons for coming to London," Nell said. "My trip will not have been wasted."

She was to visit Effie when she and her husband returned to town in two days' time. Until they did, Nell had other Academy business to attend to. *Important* business. It was that which should rightly be occupying her thoughts, not the solemn countenance and unusually broad shoulders of a prying newspaperman she would likely never see again after this morning.

"I'm pleased to hear it," he said. "I won't keep you overlong. There are just a few matters about the charity school that I'd hoped you might clarify." Small talk dispensed with, he picked up his pen, giving every indication that he intended to take notes of their conversation.

Nell would have expected nothing less. "By all means," she said. "Miss Corvus's Academy has nothing to hide."

It was a falsehood, to be sure. And one Nell didn't blush to utter. The Academy was her vocation. Her life. Her home. She wouldn't quail at defending it, even if it meant occasionally speaking something less than the truth to those who threatened its well-being.

Gloved hands folded neatly in her lap, she waited for Mr. Quincey's questions. But he didn't give voice to them. Not immediately. He only looked at her with a pensive frown, as though something about her person prevented him from pursuing his logical course.

"Forgive me," he said at length. "Mrs. Royce failed to mention that you were lately bereaved. Had I known of your loss, I would never have pressed you to—"

"I am not bereaved," Nell said.

"No?" He swept a glance from her black-veiled hat to her lusterless black mourning dress with its tight-fitting bodice and wide, untrimmed skirts. "You can doubtless understand my confusion."

Nell would have thought it plain enough. "I traveled alone from the Academy. I preferred to do so unmolested." She paused, adding, "Widows are generally accorded a degree of respect not offered to unaccompanied young ladies."

Mr. Quincey didn't bat an eye at her explanation. She suspected he was a man who wasn't easily surprised. "In other words, it's a disguise."

Nell's expression tightened. Leave it to a man to reduce a woman's desire to protect herself to a childish pantomime. "It's a practical necessity," she said.

"I see. And do all teachers at Miss Corvus's Academy for the Betterment of Young Ladies employ such arts? Or is it only you who . . ." His words died away as she pushed back her veil.

Ah. Perhaps he was capable of being surprised after all.

Nell met his gaze, a hint of a challenge in her own. She wasn't vain. Neither was she guilty of false modesty. She knew herself, both her weaknesses *and* her strengths. "Feminine ingenuity isn't limited to the staff room at the Academy," she informed him. "Though, I assure you, it's in no short supply there."

Mr. Quincey collected himself in a blink—so quickly Nell wondered if she'd imagined the look of masculine alertness that had flared in his eyes on first seeing her face. Clearing his throat, he very slowly and very methodically returned his pen to the brass holder on his desk. "Something else Mrs. Royce failed to mention."

"What might that be?"

"How young you are."

Nell stiffened at his frank tone of disappointment. She wasn't used to anyone implying she was lacking in wisdom or experience. On the contrary. In times of crisis, people generally looked to her for guidance. During Miss Corvus's recent illness, Nell had all but been running the school. "Is my age of importance to your inquiries?"

"Only as it pertains to your tenure," he said. "You can't have been in your position long."

"I have been employed as a teacher for five years, sir."

He sat back in his chair, frowning at her again with an attitude of impatience. One would think she had wasted his precious time. "Mrs. Royce led me to believe you had been present at the Academy's founding, nearly twenty years ago. It's why I consented to meet with you instead of pursuing an interview with Miss Corvus herself. I had anticipated your providing certain information about the institution's origins."

Nell at once grasped the cause of his irritation. He'd wrongly presumed she would be a much older woman. One who had spent the whole of the past eighteen years teaching at the charity school. "Mrs. Royce did not mislead you."

"Not only Mrs. Royce," he replied. "You, as well, Miss Trewlove. Your letters gave me to understand that you had decades of experience at Miss Corvus's Academy."

"I do," she said. "Or nearly that long. I was one of its earliest students."

Understanding registered on his face. He stared at her with renewed attention. "You were an orphan?"

Nell's chin ticked up a notch. "That's correct."

378 · Mimi Matthews

There was no shame in it. Not as far as she was concerned. It was just as she often told her girls. One wasn't accountable for the circumstances of one's birth, only for the choices they made and the actions they took. It was that which defined a person, not pedigree.

"As are all the students at the Academy?" Mr. Quincey asked.

"To a one," she said. "They come to us from all over the country. I flatter myself that we do our best for them."

"Your best being . . . ?"

She lifted one shoulder in a deceptively casual shrug. "We feed them, house them, and provide them with an education that will best help them meet their potential."

Mr. Quincey narrowed in on the word with single-minded precision. "Their potential for what, exactly?"

Nell's mouth curved in a slow smile. She comprehended the unspoken crux of his question. He believed the Academy was a home for dangerous revolutionaries. Budding feminists and crusaders for equality, willing to go to any ends to achieve their goals, even if that meant destroying the occasional man who got in their way.

He wasn't wrong.

· · · · ·

Miles was *not* amused.

He might have known Miss Trewlove would turn out to be some manner of goddess. It was, after all, Gabriel Royce's wife who had pointed Miles in her direction. And the newly minted Mrs. Royce was nothing if not trouble personified.

Miles was in no mood for it. Not this morning. Lawrence Cowgill had been gone for three days straight , leaving nothing behind in his desk but a notebook marked with a series of meaningless dates. In his absence, Miles had been forced to assign the paper's famous gossip column to another of his reporters. A poor salve on a potentially fatal wound, but it was either that or go to press without it. The latter hadn't been an option. Like it or not, the majority of the *Courant*'s dwindling circulation was owing to that cursed column.

They couldn't afford to lose any more subscribers. They'd already lost too many as it was. In the aftermath of Miles's series of articles exposing the treachery of once-revered politician Viscount Compton, many in society had closed ranks against the paper, no doubt frightened that they'd be targeted next—exposed and ruined by one of the *Courant*'s notoriously ruthless exposés.

It was only the gossip column that kept the fashionable public coming back. Without Cowgill to write it, the paper stood to lose a fortune. No one else was in possession of the secret sources that enabled him to deliver such unusually incisive tittle-tattle.

And now this.

Another disappointment, albeit one disguised in a rather beguiling package.

Miles ran a hand over the side of his face, wishing like the devil he'd followed his instincts and gone to Miss Corvus's Academy himself. Instead, he'd wasted months engaged in correspondence with a woman he had foolishly assumed was an antiquated spinster.

But she wasn't.

Antiquated, that is.

With her flaxen blond hair, heart-shaped face, and graceful figure, Miss Trewlove had more in common with an angel than she did with his admittedly narrow preconception of a schoolteacher.

A sultry angel, at that.

Her hooded, long-lashed gray eyes had a deceptively sleepy quality to them. Like a tigress drowsing in the sun, as languorous as she was lethal. The effect was intensified by the elegant curve of her high cheekbones, and the voluptuous fullness of her lush, Cupid's-bow lips.

"It's a personal calculation," she replied to him. "Every girl has a different set of strengths. A head for mathematics, for example. Or an aptitude for writing, or a skill for sport."

"Sport," Miles repeated. "Such as hunting down corrupt lords like Viscount Compton?"

Miss Trewlove lifted her winged brows. They were thick and arched, a shade darker than her hair. "You presume the Academy is connected to his downfall?"

"I more than presume it. Miss Corvus's name came up often during my investigations. Or rather, the name she went by at the time she was connected to Lord Compton, some two decades ago."

Miss Trewlove noticeably did not refute that connection. "A man has done wrong and has finally been punished for it. What benefit can there be in violating his victim's privacy—whomever that victim might be?"

"I don't mean to publish her story," Miles said. He'd promised Gabriel he wouldn't. He hadn't, however, promised to forego further inquiry. The mystery of Miss Corvus and her charity school was the single loose thread in his investigation into Lord Compton's crimes. And Miles couldn't abide a loose thread.

"Then what does it matter?" Miss Trewlove asked.

"Call it professional curiosity," he said.

Disapproval darkened her gaze. "At a lady's expense? That isn't very gentlemanly."

Across the office, the fringe on the bottom of the sofa twitched. Shadow poked her gray striped head out to listen to their conversation.

Miles cast an absent glance in the little tabby's direction. He had found her only last week here in Fleet Street. Small and thin, with a battered ear and weeping eye, she had summoned up the bravery to eat from one of the dishes he regularly put out for the other street cats. He'd really had no choice but to rescue her.

She'd been living in his office ever since, spending most of her time hiding while she healed from her wounds. Miles intended to remove her to his house in Chelsea as soon as she was stronger. He had six strays already in residence. Cats were his weakness.

His *only* weakness.

"Not just any lady," he said. "The lady who Compton jilted and defrauded. His crimes against her are what ultimately led to his downfall."

"Elizabeth Wingard," Miss Trewlove mused. She adjusted her voluminous skirts. "Yes, I read your articles. She was treated abominably, as far as I can tell."

"She was," Miles acknowledged. "Rumor has it that she died abroad. Instead, as I discovered, she returned to England, armed with a new identity and a new purpose."

"This is all quite fascinating—"

"She founded a charity school for girls. One of those girls—now Mrs. Royce—played a role in bringing about Compton's political demise. Do you dispute that there was a relationship between her actions and the mission of Miss Corvus's Academy?"

"I'm sorry, are you implying that Miss Corvus founded a school solely to raise up a generation of girls to settle a score with her former fiancé?" Miss Trewlove smiled, revealing a startling glimpse of a crooked front tooth. The unexpected flaw lent a roguish quality to her expression. "I am not a worldly woman, Mr. Quincey, but that does seem excessive."

"Not only Compton," Miles said. "All men who have wronged women."

"*All* men? How very ambitious of her."

"You don't deny it?"

"On the contrary, it sounds an admirable goal." Her face reverted to somber lines. "Truly, sir, in all seriousness, if that is what you believe, your imagination has run away with you."

Miles repressed a flare of aggravation. He had long learned not to judge people too quickly, and Miss Trewlove provided ample evidence as to why. She sat across from him, ladylike and subdued in her faux widow's weeds, and yet she was sparring with him as effectively as one of the bruisers he often faced in the ring at the boxing saloon.

"I have no imagination," he said. "I concern myself with facts and only facts. It's what makes me so good at my job."

"Facts, then," she said. "It's just as I told you in my letters—"

"Your very brief letters." None of them had been over a few sentences in length.

She ignored the criticism. "Our charity school is wholly reputable, and the character of both our students *and* our teachers is beyond reproach. Any member of the local parish council can verify that fact, and that body is uniformly male and hardly what one would label progressive."

That much Miles *did* know. He had an appointment with one of its members later this morning. A Reverend Pettiman. Miles had arranged the meeting last month in a last-ditch effort to get information about the Academy after Miss Trewlove had repeatedly rebuffed his requests for an interview.

"As to the role of our girls once they enter society," she went on, "I can give you the current locations of as many as ten of them who have, after leaving our care, found genteel employment. They are governesses. Schoolteachers. And one is private secretary to a gentlewoman of some stature. None of them can be classed as avenging furies."

"What about the rest of your graduates?"

"You already know Mrs. Royce." Miss Trewlove's impossibly provocative mouth tipped slowly at one corner. The expression was uncannily feline. "And now you know me."

Miles held her gaze, ignoring the pulse of heat that threatened to dull his senses. He could see what was happening here. Miss Corvus and Mrs. Royce had clearly believed that Miss Trewlove's astonishing beauty would be sufficient to distract him from his questions. And it *was* distracting. But he'd faced worse obstacles in getting a story, and overcome them, too.

"Not yet, ma'am," he said. "But I intend to." Again, he picked up his pen.

Miss Trewlove might not be the proprietor of the charity school, but she had been one of its orphans and was now one of its teachers. If there were secrets to be had, she must be in possession of a few of them. All that remained was to wrest them from her.

"At what age did you come to the orphanage?" he asked briskly. "And under what circumstances?"

"I doubt my humble history can be of interest to your investigation."

"On the contrary. You interest me exceedingly. If Miss Corvus has deployed you to the front lines—"

"A troubling metaphor."

"But an apt one, I discern. You're the heavy artillery."

She didn't smile this time, but a dimple formed to the right of her mouth. *"Me?"*

"You," he said.

As they spoke, Shadow emerged from her hiding place, step by cautious step. Encouraged by Miss Trewlove's stillness, she slowly crossed the carpet to inspect the edge of her skirts.

"If it's a case study you're after," Miss Trewlove said, "I must surely be the least interesting subject of all our graduates. Unlike the other girls, I chose to remain."

"You had no desire to strike out on your own as a governess or secretary?"

"None at all."

"Teaching is your prevailing passion?"

"It is, though I wouldn't describe it in such lofty terms. I—" She broke off, her attention caught by the sight of the little tabby bestowing a delicate sniff to her hem. Her face lit with pleasure. "Why, hello, little one. I was beginning to doubt your existence." She looked at Miles. "Does she have a name?"

Miles required a full three seconds to recollect it. The look Miss Trewlove had given the cat had knocked him off his axis. It was so frank. So authentic. The whole of her countenance was transformed by it. A strange sort of alchemy, but in that moment, she changed from an untouchable goddess into an infinitely more desirable human girl.

He swallowed hard. "I've, uh, been calling her Shadow."

"How appropriate." Miss Trewlove stretched her gloved hand down as if to administer a pet.

Shadow's eyes widened to the size of twin saucers. The sofa being too far away, she darted for cover under the only shelter available—the billowing expanse of Miss Trewlove's skirts.

A rosy blush seeped into Miss Trewlove's cheeks as the cat disappeared beneath her hem. "Goodness," she said. "This is rather alarming."

"She means no offense," Miles said. "She's attempting to hide, that's all. She's still quite wild. You'll have to shake your—"

Before he could finish advising her, Miss Trewlove discreetly reached under her skirts to remove the cat herself. She jerked back her fingers with a cry of pain.

Miles was up from behind his desk in a flash. He strode around it. "If you would permit me—"

"Heavens!" Miss Trewlove leapt from her chair before he could reach her. She staggered backward. Shadow's small form was visible beneath the swell of her skirts, thrashing wildly. "I think she's caught!"

He closed the distance between them. "Caught it in what?"

Miss Trewlove's face flamed. "In my *crinoline*." She took another stumbling step back, losing her balance.

Miles extended a hand to steady her, but he was a split second too late. Miss Trewlove's left leg inexplicably gave way. He caught her an instant before she dropped to the floor, breaking her fall with his body as the two of them landed with a thud on the office carpet.

She struggled up on her elbows. Her veiled hat had been knocked askew, and a stray lock of blond hair had come loose from its pins to curl around her face. "She's still tangled up in it!" she gasped. "And her claws are quite sharp!"

Miles grasped a handful of Miss Trewlove's skirts, hesitating only long enough to ask permission to inflict what would, in other circumstances, be a reputation-ruining indignity. "May I—"

"Yes, yes," she said breathlessly. "Anything. Only remove her!"

Miles hoisted up the layers of black silk and starched petticoats, revealing the enormous cage crinoline Miss Trewlove wore underneath (and a pair of shapely, stocking-clad legs he pretended not to notice). Shadow had woven herself through the wire and fabric tapes of the undergarment's frame. The little cat looked at him, panicked, her chest vibrating on a low, continuous growl.

"Easy," Miles said to her. "I won't hurt you." He covered the cat's body with his hand. She responded by sinking her teeth into his finger. He sucked in a breath. "*Bloody hell.*"

"Did she—"

"She's fine."

"I didn't mean the cat," Miss Trewlove said in a strained voice. "I meant *you*."

"I'll live." He slowly untangled Shadow's legs from the wires, ignoring her continued hissing and spitting. Extracting her from the crinoline, he set her down on the carpet. The little cat tore free of his grasp the instant she was able. Streaking across the office, she plunged under the sofa.

Miles exhaled. "There," he said, sitting back on his haunches. "No damage done."

No sooner had he uttered the fateful words than the door was thrust open and Higgins burst in, carrying a small box in his hand.

"Mr. Quincey? This was just delivered at the front desk. Bob said as how you'd want to be notified directly . . ." The newspaper clerk's words trailed away as he beheld the scene before him—Miss Trewlove on the floor with her skirts above her knees and Miles looming over her like some vile seducer.

Higgins wasn't alone. An older, distinguished-looking gentleman stood a short distance behind him in the hall. The esteemed member of the parish council, presumably, come early for his appointment.

Seeing him, the color drained from Miss Trewlove's face. She scrambled to a sitting position, hastily pulling her skirts into some semblance of order. "Reverend Pettiman!"

Pettiman's florid countenance went crimson with outrage.

Miles didn't flinch. Neither did he hesitate. "I'll be with you in a moment, Higgins," he said in the same brisk, businesslike tones he employed when dealing with any other workplace catastrophe. "If you wouldn't mind closing the door?"

"Yes, sir. Apologies, sir. Completely my fault." Higgins backed out of the office, shutting the door after him with a power that rattled the doorframe.

To Miles, the sound was as significant as the crash of the gallows' trapdoor. His fate was plain. He accepted it with a grim sense of resignation.

Miss Trewlove's eyes found his. "Mr. Quincey—"

"Given our current predicament," he said, "I believe you had better accustom yourself to calling me Miles."

Photo by Vickie Hahn

USA Today bestselling author **Mimi Matthews** writes both historical nonfiction and award-winning Victorian romances. Her novels have received starred reviews in *Publishers Weekly*, *Library Journal*, *Booklist*, *Kirkus Reviews*, and Shelf Awareness, and her articles have been featured on the Victorian Web, in the *Journal of Victorian Culture*, and in syndication at *BUST* magazine. In her other life, Mimi is an attorney. She resides in California with her family, which includes an Andalusian dressage horse, a sheltie, a miniature poodle, and two Siamese cats.

VISIT MIMI MATTHEWS ONLINE

MimiMatthews.com
 MimiMatthewsAuthor
 MimiMatthewsEsq
 𝕏 MimiMatthewsEsq

Ready to find
your next great read?

Let us help.

Visit prh.com/nextread

Penguin
Random
House